Upon a Time

To Jolene Carol,
May all your stories
have happy endings!
Elliot Frankel

Upon a Time

The Darkness behind the Tales

Elliot Francke

ISBN: 978-0-9831839-9-0

Library of Congress Catalog Number: 2016938927

Printed in the United States of America

First Printing: 2016

Edited by Angela Wiechmann
Book Design by Christopher Fayers
Cover Art by Alexandra Burniece

Publisher's Cataloging-in-Publication data
Names: Francke, Elliot, author.
Title: Upon a Time : the darkness behind the tales / by Elliot Francke.
Description: Eagan [Minnesota]: Amber Skye Publishing LLC, 2016.
Identifiers: ISBN 9780983183990 | LCCN 2016938927.
Subjects: LCSH Fantasy--Fiction. | Fairy tales. | Characters in literature--Fiction. | BISAC FICTION / Fairy Tales, Folk Tales, Legends & Mythology | FICTION / Fantasy / General.
Classification: LCC PS3606.R373 U66 2016| DDC 813.6—dc23

AMBER SKYE PUBLISHING

1935 BERKSHIRE DRIVE
EAGAN, MINNESOTA 55122
651-452-0463
AMBER SKYE PUBLISHING LLC
IS NOW ON FACEBOOK

This book is dedicated to my wife, Cheryl; my children, Tara, Jordan, and Devon, and Tara's husband, Russell Nadel; and our grandson, Ari Nadel.

• • •

It is also dedicated to lovers of fairy tales and history and to those who enjoy a mystery.

• • •

Finally, it is especially dedicated to all those who have suffered and survived physical and sexual abuse. Though you often suffer in silence, you do not do so alone.

~ Prologue ~

Autumn 1450, central Germany

There is darkness in Besse's vision. She is comforted, enveloped by it. It is her blanket, and under it the world cannot intrude. No monsters of the night hiding under the bed for her. No, her nightmares are in the broad light of day.

Besse huddles in the deepest recess of her chamber, clutching her rag doll, her one true companion, sewn by the servant Fee. The young maiden tries to shrink into herself as she folds her body over.

She sighs. "Dolly, you are my one true friend and confidante. We are alike, you and I. You are ugly and, best of all, silent. We do not want to be noticed. Gray and black are the best colors for us. Fee wants to find you to clean you up—clean us both up and put us in bright colors. She says the change will do us good. But she does not know us at all."

Besse hesitates a moment, in deep thought. "Fee cares for me, but she wants me to be like Mama. But that would be impossible. Mama is beautiful. She sits up in her chamber in the tower, brushing and brushing her long flaxen hair all day. Sometimes I visit. She teaches me sewing and needlepoint. That, she says, will make a *lady* of me, so that someday, I can find a husband. Husbands, she says, are necessary in a man's world, as no lady can survive alone. That frightens me. I have no desire for a husband. And anyway, I am only thirteen."

Besse pulls the doll close and whispers, "But there's more to share with you, Dolly. Today during my sewing lesson, I heard soft singing outside Mama's window. It was a man. He sang of her long, beautiful hair."

Besse's voice gets a bit louder with a tone of mockery. "He sang that he would *cli-i-imb* it endlessly to be at her side in her private little tower. Then he would steal her away from the ogre who has imprisoned her there. When Mama heard the singing, she hurried me through my sewing and pushed me out of the chamber! I stayed outside the door, and soon I heard a man's voice inside. Then I ran here to find you."

Besse hugs her rag doll. "But I don't want that singing man to take her away. Not because I really love her—I just need her to take care of me." Besse pauses again, having surprised herself with the revelation that she feels the need to be loved by her mother. "But Mama doesn't take care of me—not really. She rarely leaves her bedchamber. She hides up there." She winces and whispers, "I know why."

Besse's mood darkens, and she frowns. "We hide too, Dolly, in the comforting shadows. But it will not last. Soon enough, *he* will come. He will rant and rave and demand the servants tell him where I am. He is doing naught more than exerting his authority. They are afraid of him. Except Fee, of course. She will have none of him. He can threaten to throw her out, but Mama will allow no other personal servant in the household.

"The *household*!" she repeats with more mockery. "A decent home is the province of a lady. But Mama leaves the household duties all to Fee, and *he* knows it. So he will not send Fee out even if she tries to keep me hidden. Mama will not hide me. No, she will not! Why not?" Besse is unable to answer, so she sighs again.

"No matter—he can find me easily. There is no excess of places to hide. He *will* find me, and he will do unspeakable things. I will not describe them, Dolly. I cannot. I do not want to think of them. This I will endure alone, but not forever." She shudders but with some resolve does not allow herself to pout. "Until then, I will suffer his attentions. He is my father."

~ Chapter 1 ~

A solitary figure makes her way through the streets of Quellestadt, cloaked in the morning fog, which offers her some security of anonymity. Nevertheless, Fee still does not feel completely protected. She stops at various shops to acquire the necessary staples for the Hammer household. She shivers in the cold, damp air, pulling her cloak more closely about her, but not only to provide some additional warmth. Her mind is full, as always, with the tribulations of her charges in the household: Beata, the wife of Master Dunkel, and his daughter, Besse, as well as with the general needs and welfare of her brothers and sister. For most of the thirty-one years of her life, she has served her family, her peers, and the Hammer household. No, not just served—protected.

The stench in the tanners' quarter evokes the memory of her master's abuse, which she would prefer to forget, but she shakes it off. She continues on her rounds, ending at the tent of her sister, Flor, where she need not haggle over the price of salt and herbs.

Flor senses her sister's inner turmoil and offers her a small spray of local wildflowers, a weak attempt at consolation. "I fear you will worry yourself into an early grave, sister dear. Focus your mind instead upon this small bounty of God, and be at peace."

"Thank you, dear Flor, but you know I cannot. I am inadequately successful at the protection of my mistress—worse of the young Besse. And what has become of our vagrant brother, Peter, who roams the woods surviving I know not how?"

"You must not think, Fee, that I do not frequently ponder their fates. I am well aware of our family's abrupt change in situation, and I do lose some sleep over it. But Jurg, you, and I are better situated now, and there is always hope the same will happen for our wayward brother. For the which, I have complete faith in you, as you have ever been our guardian, even our savior, since the loss of our dear parents. You will always sacrifice yourself to that end. It is you I worry about the most. Now, pray accept this little gift, and be off to your duties."

Fee sighs, takes the flowers, and hoists the sack of necessities over her shoulder, giving herself somewhat the appearance of a vagabond, but folded inwardly. She finds she cannot smile, but she offers her sister a brief hug and turns to walk her accustomed path back to the home she must serve, in a corner tower of the wall of the city.

~ Chapter 2 ~

Dappled sunlight casts camouflaged images along the edges of the glade. The glade is conveniently located in the wooded mountainside just outside the walls of the city. Great oaks, birch, and alder offer cover for those who would hide in ambush, or shade for those who would dally for a little discrete romance. The glade itself is covered with but little of the tall grasses of the low mountainside and more of the mosses that offer a cool, welcome relief to sore feet. A cold stream passes through the edge, and many rocks, fallen from the cliffs above, are strewn randomly.

Prince Henrik surveys the scene with satisfaction. His armsmaster considers this the ideal location for training knights and soldiery. It affords the advantage of multiple types of terrain: rocky, exposed, shady (ideal for training against ambushes), hilly, and flat (ideal for archery and weaponry practice). The armsmaster has well earned his reputation with the prince and the principality's surrounding nobility. He pushes his trainees to the limit in all conditions of weather, day and night.

Moreover, he does not spare the prince's two favorite trainees: the dauphin and his friend, Hans, the son of merchant Artur Handler. The boys, at age fifteen, have reached the end of childhood. They are best friends and often return to the glade on their own to play and practice. Artur is pleased with their progress. He knows his son, like himself, will soon lead small caravans as far as the northern cities, Russia, and even England for trade. The safety of these forays is paramount. Traders can hire the best protection in Quellestadt, but are even better off if able to defend themselves.

As for the prince, he has the wisdom and custom to know the tithes his merchants willingly surrender to him will be well supplemented if he offers his soldiers for hire to all the European nobility. To that end, it is necessary to maintain the reputation of training the smartest and strongest men. He spares no expense, and therefore he affords the finest armsmaster and weaponry—which in turn attracts the finest Hanseatic traders, tithing more than enough to supply the necessary treasury.

Prince Henrik smiles, which actually seems to enhance his regal bearing. He is an unusually tall man, betraying his Nordic ancestry. His hair is the color of the bright sunshine and falls long to his broad shoulders. He is easily recognizable, not only for his size and royal comportment but also for his proud carriage and demeanor. This is not to say he is condescending to his subjects or guests, but it is clear he would brook no challenge to his authority. Nonetheless, he is not given to overt display of his wealth and position when it would serve no other purpose than arrogance. He is an evenhanded man. His subjects trust him to mete out justice with both wisdom and compassion and to ask no more of them than is his due.

Normally, therefore, he would just arrive at the glade in a simple wool tunic and leggings, but not this day. Today, he hosts several noblemen from France and the Italian city-states loyal to the pope and Holy Roman emperor, among them a certain duke with a well-educated, marriageable daughter of an age appropriate for his own son.

The Duke of Burgundy is a more flamboyant man than the prince and has not hesitated to accoutre himself in a doublet liberally embroidered in gold on a rich black background of silk. It is clear he intends to make an impression upon the prince—who inwardly smiles at the thought, as it betrays the purpose of the duke's visit all the more apparently. The duke makes occasional favorable comments about the various training exercises, but he has other matters on his mind.

Henrik himself has therefore chosen to dress himself in his finest riding clothes: silk undergarments, black-dyed linen shirt, ornamented doublet, and high breeches. He gestures broadly across the practice field and intones, "Note, my lords, how my men are trained in all manner of combat, from one-on-one swordplay, to ambush, to full battalion tactics in and out of armor. Moreover, they are schooled in the techniques of historical warfare, from Roman to Ottoman. They must exercise and eat well and are not permitted too much beer or wine. They are also required to practice under all manner of conditions adverse, including rain, snow, and darkness. For this, they are to be paid and fed well, especially if they are to be of service far away from home and family."

As he speaks, his eyes wander only briefly over the varied venues of mock combat, alighting upon two youths practicing with staffs at one end of the glade. They leap over rocks and logs, laughing but not bantering as they concentrate on their actions and positions. They clearly enjoy themselves. But one has taken a position allowing escape, while the other must press his advantage, if any, with his back to a large boulder. Nevertheless, he ducks under the staff of his erstwhile foe, rolling across the ground and coming up to position behind him. But Charles, the dauphin, is too slow in getting to his feet. His staff is knocked from his hand as he arises. An advantage win is awarded to the lad clever enough to have forced this position. Yet the two boys leave the field with arms clasped, best of friends.

The prince allows himself a smile, which does not go unnoticed by the Duke of Burgundy.

"Perhaps, sire, you know those two young boys. They do seem a bit young to be on the field of combat training."

The prince responds, "The victor is Hans Handler, son of Artur, one of the finest Hanseatic traders of the city. The other—not to be underestimated by the lack of success in this encounter—is Hans's closest friend and ally. And, incidentally, he is my son, Charles, first in line to my own throne."

"You would allow your son to place himself in such a dangerous position?" The duke smiles. "I am sure you have very special reasoning. It clearly keeps him strong and sharp of reflex, even if it does expose him to a minor degree of danger to his person."

The prince takes this as a slight challenge, but is not offended. "I will send for the boy at once. You may inquire of him yourself, Monsieur le Duc, as I have no doubt you are eager to do, as well as make his acquaintance."

He smiles at the duke and nods to him, revealing his understanding of the true purpose of the duke's visit and implicitly offering his approval.

"Thank you, sire," answers the duke with a slight, formal bow.

~ Chapter 3 ~

Charles and Hans pick up their staffs, arrange their clothing, adjust the sheathed daggers at their sides, and set out along the path to the main road leading to the city above.

"I think we should stop at the waterfall and wash off this grime," says Hans.

The dauphin is quick to agree. "I am sure the ladies of the town, not to mention our mothers, would appreciate a cleaner countenance."

They are discretely followed, of course, by two well-trained soldiers who had also been practicing on the field, assigned to them as bodyguards. The prince may be proud of his son's accomplishments and prowess, but he is not about to trust him entirely to his own fate. Nevertheless, he is inclined to allow his son at least some privacy in conversation, and the bodyguards are not to intervene unless they deem his actions too rash or dangerous.

The trees abutting the creek are somewhat younger than those more distant, having been planted to replace trees the peasants and townspeople removed for fuel. The creek itself sparkles with clean water, unsullied by the local inhabitants' refuse, by order of the prince so it may be used as potable or for production of beer. The area below the small waterfall may be used for bathing and laundry. Nevertheless, the ladies of the city rarely venture off the main road into the woods for this or any other purpose, as the area is not guarded and a few brigands are inevitably about. Any outlaw familiar with the city inhabitants, however, would know better than to attack the dauphin and his companion.

The boys, therefore, have the lower creek to themselves and are not averse to splashing about as they allow the accumulated dirt to wash downstream. The water is very cold, and they do not remain in it for long. After a few minutes, they dress and head for the main road.

The sound of hooves and wheels temporarily distracts them. "If I do not miss my guess, sire, there are wagons and horses ahead," notes Hans.

"Which means we must be on the alert for brigands," interrupts Charles, turning his head to look for the guards he knows are nearby.

Suddenly, the dauphin hears a whoosh past his left ear, then feels a slight sting. He puts his hand to his neck, hoping to trap the insect responsible, then removes his hand and sees . . . blood! Before he can even react, a hand grabs his arm, pulling him down behind a tree. It is Hans, who covers Charles's mouth before he can speak. He motions to the guards, rushing to the boys as the threat becomes apparent, then shows Charles the arrow on the ground that thankfully missed its mark.

The boys look up to see four figures hiding among the trees. Their keen eyes also detect two heading toward the road, focused no doubt on the caravan and unaware of the commotion behind them.

The guards see the men too. They circle around the men rapidly, all the while keeping their eyes on the two figures nearing the road.

Even four brigands are no match for two of the prince's finest guards. The four men are certainly outarmed by the two soldiers, whose ability and training is of no little fame to all in these parts. The men are smart enough to realize this fact. They drop their bows and chance running into the forest in separate directions, with no plans to return in counterattack. They count on the guards' need to address their fellow brigands approaching the caravan. And indeed, they are not pursued.

Their two comrades heading to the road are far enough away to miss the entire exchange. They only hear frantic rustling in the woods. They believe their friends are positioning themselves, as planned for the ambush, and they are more than a little annoyed at the noise they are making.

- Chapter 3 -

The caravan consists of several wagons—trade goods concealed by canvas tarps—drawn by sturdy horses. On each sit two men in hooded garments of linen so their faces are hidden. But curiously, no guards ride alongside, ahead, or in the rear. The approaching miscreants surmise the merchants have lost their protection.

But not so Charles. He whispers to Hans, "I would not believe such a caravan to be unguarded. I think the guards are among the hooded drivers or perhaps under the tarps. Do you not think it would be best to raise a shout to alert them against these two?"

"If we draw their attention, my lord, how do you think they would judge *us*? We are certainly not known to them, and we have the appearance of ruffians armed, as we are with staffs and dressed for combat practice."

"Thus shall we do," responds the young dauphin.

He motions for his bodyguards to place themselves visibly in the center of the road ahead of the caravan. His hope is to deter the would-be robbers with the mere sight of the protection offered by the prince. The soldiers, dressed as they are in mail and with shields adorned with the arms of the prince, understand immediately and hasten to place themselves in the path of the caravan.

At the same time, unaware of the abandonment of his companions in the woods, one of the outlaws reaches the lead wagon and swiftly climbs onto the seat. The intent is to secure a hostage to assure their safe passage—and perhaps even later, a ransom. He pulls back the rider's hood to reveal a maiden! And not just a lady, but a most strikingly beautiful visage. She glares without even a dint of fear. As she shakes out long tresses of auburn hair, a look of defiance elevates her natural beauty to even greater heights.

Both robbers are momentarily startled, and this is enough of a moment for Charles and Hans to arrive. Yet the outlaws are not without reflexes. One turns, grabbing ahold of the dauphin's staff to prevent its use against him.

The other pulls out a long knife, and Hans struggles to grab the brigand's wrist just before he can position for a stab. Hans twists the arm without releasing his own staff, then balances on one leg, swinging the other into the miscreant's knee. The robber's lack of balance allows Hans to grab the knife. As the robber falls, Hans delivers a blow with his staff, rendering the boy unconscious.

The riders of the other wagons push back their hoods to reveal they are indeed hired, armed guards, as the dauphin and his friend suspected. Also as suspected, they make haste to restrain Charles and Hans. But the soldiers suddenly appear in the road ahead and gesture for them to withdraw—and the maiden does the same.

Charles faces an adversary with a long knife in hand. He grabs the robber's arm, and the two tumble off the wagon, managing to regain their feet simultaneously. The brigand lunges. Charles pulls in his stomach and throws his rear backward, allowing enough time to grab the boy's arm again. He twists, and the knife falls. The brigand then wraps Charles in a bear hug, thinking to butt heads. But Charles is too quick. He brings his knee up to the boy's groin.

The caravan's guards grab both boys and pull them apart.

"You may release that one," says the maiden, pointing to Charles. She speaks in French-accented German, so the boys as well as the guards can understand. "These men may look young and rough," she continues, "but they have not hesitated to place their lives in danger to save ours. I would guess the guards ahead are not here to vouchsafe our safety, but that of one or both of these brave souls. There is no need to mistrust their intentions. I would make my acquaintance of them, so that we may all thank them properly."

She turns with a flourish, nearly taking Hans's breath away. She smiles radiantly and with a slight curtsy says, "Know, sirs, I am Ebouisante, the daughter of Serge Kaufmann, who sits here beside me and is equally grateful for your assistance. Might I be so bold as to inquire your names?"

"A fair name that hardly begins to do justice to the most fair mademoiselle!" replies Hans. "*Je suis le plus enchanté de faire une telle connaissance.*" Continuing in French, he adds, "We are Charles, son of Henrik"—pointing out his friend—"and Hans, son of Artur Handler."

The dauphin begins to protest the familiar introduction as inappropriate, but Hans waves him off.

"We are longtime friends and very familiar with these woods, as well as longtime admirers of such beauty and intelligence. Our guards are at your service and will accompany us all into the principality you will shortly see upon this hillside—which must be your destination. Further, sir and mademoiselle, as a son of a merchant loyal to the prince, I appreciate the need and would be honored to provide you safe passage and the hospitality of my father's home. He is always honored and eager to meet fellow traders—not to miss the opportunity to increase his trade as well as yours. May we have the honor of accompanying you to your destination?"

"So," says Herr Kaufmann, "you are not the poor ruffians your dress and use of the peasants' preferred weapon would suggest. I warrant these bodyguards are provided by your fathers for your protection. With profound gratitude, I accept your kind offer of accompaniment, the better to ultimately make the acquaintance of your family, as you offer. Perhaps you would be so kind to enlighten us as to how you come by such a base appearance, while you clearly betray your own well-breeding and education in your speech."

"Our fathers deem it important to learn the art of self-defense in all its forms," answers Charles, still not quite understanding why these good people are being deluded about his station in life.

"Indeed, young sir," says Herr Kaufmann. "It is my intention to offer goods for sale with tithing to the prince. He has proffered me the kindness of an invitation to establish myself here in the city of my birth. I have spent these last many years developing trade relationships with the Moors, the Castilians, the Aragonese, the Medicis of Florence, and the doge of Venice. Thus I carry much news of the politics of this continent. I admit to some nostalgia for Quellestadt. And I appreciate the opportunity to extend my trade to the northern reaches, which have connections with England and the Slavic lands, so I may therefore have better access to the goods and spices of the Orient than the Ottomans are likely to allow.

"My good wife, in fact, is not with this company but has preceded us in order to establish a household. We would strongly favor the advantage of the opportunity to make the acquaintance of both your families, to make an offer of gratitude for your actions of today. Please be so kind as to join us on the wagon, poor offer of carriage as it is, and we will proceed into the city."

Charles takes note of the fact that during the merchant's entire speech, Hans has not removed his glance from the man's beautiful daughter. It now occurs to the dauphin that Hans restrained from introducing him as true royalty so as not to distract her attention from himself. He smiles at Hans as they clamber onto the wagon. Hans relaxes his composure, relieved the dauphin has surmised his intentions.

Now Hans fixes his gaze again upon Ebouisante. How aptly named, for she is even more beautiful from close vantage. Her blue eyes and auburn hair shine brightly in the light of the setting sun. And even though she is hidden beneath the bland hooded linen garment, he can see she is of attractive proportion. Nor does she blush under his scrutiny. She is all the more beautiful without a hint of powder expected of a lady of the middle class or nobility. Her voice seems highly melodic, as if the nightingale would respond to it naturally. In short, he is enraptured.

She smiles, almost enigmatically. "You should not judge by first impression," she says, seeming to read his mind. "Perhaps I will turn into a frightful old hag after the sun sets." This with a giggle.

"You do not impress me as the reverse of the Wife of Bath, nor am I aware that Monsieur Chaucer has written of you. But as he has a tendency to fantasize, I believe he could do no better than to include you amongst his finest characters. No, actually, I believe you would better fit the work of Chrétien de Troyes."

"The stuff of Arthurian legend?" She laughs disapprovingly, frowns, and places her hands on her hips. "I hardly think I would qualify, as I have no pretension of nobility. Nor would I, in fact, have myself considered as a totally helpless damsel, repeatedly in need of your bravado to be saved from the crueler men of the world!"

"No offense intended, mademoiselle." It is Hans who blushes.

Ebouisante decides to demur. "We are grateful for the chivalry you and your friend demonstrated. It is comforting to know that the citizens of the principality have a high sense of honor. I look forward to making the acquaintance of your family. It is clear they consider the importance of literacy and education beyond the study of the Gospels."

"One would think you consider yourself a humanist, mademoiselle."

"Would that offend you? My father has no son and is in need of someone he can trust to help keep his accounts. Accordingly, I have willingly submitted myself to the study of several languages as well as the sciences and algebra freely taught by the Moors of Iberia. They are of the Islamic faith and are far more tolerant than Christians of those who hold other beliefs. Yet they are at least equally moral in their relationships with men—*and* women. I dare say we all have lessons to learn from them. But to be above tolerance of them—indeed, to consider their faith as equal to ours—would be entirely blasphemous."

"Unless one is a true humanist and accepts that the nature of man is to follow the faith taught by one's parents, without disparaging that of others."

"Precisely! So let me put to you the question: Do you believe, sir, that all men who respect the Commandments are worthy of equal deliverance, regardless of their professed faith?"

"Mademoiselle, the question is rhetorical. Therefore I will only answer that it is dangerous to promote tolerance in the presence of the clergy, but not in the presence of the citizenry and nobility of this principality." Hans pauses, uncomfortable with the challenging direction of this conversation. "But now you can see the city ahead as we round this curve. If you wish, we may stop at the inn at the base of the walls for refreshment before entering."

Herr Kaufmann has heard this entire exchange, laughs, and takes this as an opportunity to intervene before his headstrong daughter can lead the conversation into more embarrassing territory.

"You can see, Ebouisante, that Hans is wise enough to dodge your provocation. And, sirs, we would prefer to be safely ensconced within the city before the sun has set entirely, as we have had enough attacks upon our safety for this day. Therefore will we continue anon and not stop at the inn. I, for one, am eager to embrace Ebouisante's mother, of whom Ebouisante is also very fond and has not seen these many months."

"As you wish, sir," answers Charles. "Our own families are expecting us as well and would be distraught at a delay in our return. We thank you for the opportunity to pass this time in making your acquaintance, and we hope to meet with you under more pleasant circumstances."

"Thank you, Your Highness," Ebouisante says with a smile, startling everyone on the wagon with her deduction.

"How did you know?" asks Hans.

"Charles, son of Henrik? Bodyguards bearing the herald of the prince? Also, to be modestly observant, it is clear the guards' gaze is fixed on him more than it is on you!"

Hans smiles broadly. Here is a maiden of wit, education, intelligence, and beauty. It would indeed be worthwhile to continue her acquaintance. He realizes he must introduce this family to his father and beg him to consider the advantage of linking trade. In these turbulent times, there is great opportunity with the rising city-states of southern Europe, which have fleets capable of bypassing the traditional road to the Orient in reaching the Spice Islands and civilizations of the East. Indeed, the Ottomans have laid siege to Constantinople and will most likely close off that trade route entirely. Of course, all of this is an opportunity to spend more time with Ebouisante, which is no small advantage!

~ Chapter 4 ~

"Ye'll do it again, until ye get it right! Such work as this'll not bear the name of Dunkel Hammer!" bellows the armorer. "Nothing'll leave this forge 'less it's fit for the prince!" Unfortunately, the apprentice can see nothing wrong with the links of steel mail, on which he had spent three tedious days of repetitive labor. These were to be carefully combined into a hooded hauberk designed to allow flexibility while protecting exposed parts of the head and neck. Tomorrow he will start again, until he satisfies the master. He knows better than to try the man's patience and to release his foul temper by protesting the complaint against the quality of his work.

Once Dunkel leaves to see to the storage of an order of coal, Rudi, the journeyman, approaches the apprentice with a word of solace.

"You understand that he does not really disapprove of your work," he says. "If he did, he would fire you on the spot!"

"Then why is he so uncompromising?"

"He is waiting for *you* to be satisfied with it. Are you?"

"Now that you mention it, not really. I must consider whether I would be happy wearing this into battle, but I think it will not form a flexible enough protection." He sighs, then adds, "I will rework this metal tomorrow, until I have the correct feel of malleability."

Rudi smiles. He remembers being in the same position as the apprentice only a few years earlier.

He looks at the sky and notes the sun well past zenith. His thoughts turn to the possibility of another rendezvous with Beata, the armorer's wife. She is quite beautiful and much younger than her husband, whom she cannot abide. Rudi thinks he is clever to win her over. He does not approve of the master's bellowing, carousing, and ill treatment of his household, but he knows it will probably not be long before he will be gone. The master drinks too much mead and beer, and his appearance and demeanor are already showing signs of a foreshortened future.

Rudi quietly laughs to himself as he ponders how Dunkel exhorts them too much. The master was once a very fine armorer, though he must now rely upon Rudi for most of his work. For this reason, Rudi has mastered all of Dunkel's skills, and now he bides his time until he can claim the master's wife as his own and thereby become a master himself.

Once the master is gone, Beata will have six months, by guild law, as master herself until she can wed anew. And that shall be Rudi's personal honor—nay, his pleasure! He is almost ready to assume the full responsibility of the forge, and he is ambitious enough to have begun his masterwork preparations. He will not fail to impress the guild with his work, as he has learned well from the master.

Tonight, the master will undoubtedly stop at the inn yet again before returning to the city. Rudi will take advantage of this time and pay another visit to his beloved Beata, with her long, flowing hair and soft, milky skin . . . Enough! Return to work!

The forge sits just within the woods on a gentle hillside very close to the river, downstream from the city. Dunkel has diverted some of the flow for cooling the forge and for running the bellows. He uses coal as fuel and as a source of carbon that is added to iron to create steel of the best strength and lightness for plate and mail. He has only of late shared the secret of the precise combination with his journeyman, whom he trusts—seeing as Rudi is unable to test for mastership within the guild without his permission.

Dunkel shakes his head. The journeyman does work hard and well and will make a good armorer. Perhaps his Besse will take an interest in him. Dunkel laughs. Rudi will not, however, take an interest in her! Dunkel has his own plans for her! Later. For now, he will see to this shipment, then dismiss the boys for the day and head to the inn before dark.

- Chapter 4 -

Dunkel Hammer has the reputation of being one of the best craftsmen of his art, creating nearly perfect lightweight steel of excellent strength. He pushes his trainees to their greatest effort and is particularly glad that they themselves are never completely satisfied with the quality of their work. That is why *he* is the master.

The coal is secured, and Dunkel reenters the forge. "Boys, ye've tried me patience enough for one day." He frowns. "Be off with ye. Beata'd not forgive me if ye return too late after dark. Eat well, sleep well, and think only upon how t' improve your work enough t' make it passable t'morrow! I'll make decent armorers of ye both yet! There'll be no laziness here! We must needs finish this order of plate, so that I can afford t' pay ye more than ye deserve!"

Rudi and the apprentice finish their immediate tasks, wash their hands and brows in the trough of diverted river water, don their hooded jerkins, bow to the master, and take their leave.

"Will you walk with me back to the village tonight?" asks the apprentice. "I notice of late that you do so less often. Perhaps you have a little distraction?" He laughs.

Rudi frowns at him, then thinks better of it and laughs. "It will not be too many years before you will have distractions of your own. It is only my own business. Now run on ahead. I want to sit here, out of sight for a moment, and ponder my choices."

Dismissed, the apprentice steps lightly on ahead, pleased he has discovered a great secret of the journeyman.

How shocked the apprentice would be if he really knew the truth! Rudi will certainly not enlighten him nor offer any inkling of suspicion to the master, for he knows full well his life and future depend on discretion. He waits in the shadows for Dunkel, then follows him carefully to ensure he diverts his path to the inn at the base of the road. Then Rudi hurries ahead to another assignation with his beloved.

Dunkel is distracted by his thoughts. He and the boys have nearly completed an order for a nearby count, whom Dunkel expects will pay generously. Some of the bounty will go for a few barrels of beer; some will be given to Beata to run the household. He is glad and appreciative of her frugality. His is not a household lavishly decorated, nor does he expect to be served the finest meats. A stew is as good to him as a venison steak. Lately, his taste for food has diminished. But not his taste for beer or women!

He decides to veer off the road into the inn, with thoughts of a certain young maiden in mind. He checks his purse to be sure he has enough for the distraction, and he smiles as he makes his way. Beata will be glad for his absence. Of course he knows why but feels no guilt of his treatment of her. She is his, and she is beautiful, and she lives and runs his household by *his* grace. No woman should disobey her husband nor express her own wishes!

Dunkel is almost too distracted to notice a young emaciated waif in his path. The boy makes no attempt to step out of his way. Rather, he bows at the armorer's approach, smirks, and bars his passage.

Dunkel has little patience for this intrusion on his thoughts. He glowers at him, gruffly ordering him out of the way. "Young man, do not disturb me, as I've little time for the likes of you!"

The boy, Jacques, is nonplussed. Having planted himself at this spot precisely to accost Dunkel, he whines, attempting to sound obsequious. "Sir, forgive me. I must take but a moment of your time t' 'splain me problem. Seems there's a smith, makes armor for the prince, he does. And then there's me. Ye see, I'm his son, I am. Just not by his wife. And me mama and me, we're too poor to buy anything. But me papa, he can. Ye understand?"

"Why, ye young whelp! Ye think t' get something out of me?"

Dunkel's face reddens, and the boy steps back a pace, seeing he is in danger of a beating from this raging bull of a man.

Dunkel continues, "Ye'll ne'er get a pfennig! Ye're nothing t' me, nor is your mama! Get out of me way!"

Thinking it a good time for a strategic retreat, Jacques bows again. "I'll go for now, sir, but ye'll hear from me again!"

Before he angers the armorer further, he turns and runs off faster than the man with the limp could follow. But he thinks, *he'll pay somehow, he will!*

- Chapter 4 -

The inn is relatively modest, belying its prominent location. The site affords its owner a fairly rich clientele of merchants and noblemen heading for the city. These men almost always comment on its simplicity of furnishings and largely rough-hewn wood, but also its contrasting cleanliness and excellent cuisine. This is due to the careful and skillful attention of the owner's wife.

She is also, of necessity, very discrete, as many of the patrons—unaccompanied by their spouses—require an entirely different form of satisfaction than a full stomach. Some of the servants are only too happy to comply, either to augment their rather meager income or in hopes of a more lasting liaison with someone of higher social or financial status. Thus, the large central room serves as a dining hall and entertainment venue, with minstrels playing, boisterous singing, and loud patrons eating and drinking.

Dunkel notes the passage of a trade caravan, surprised to see the dauphin seated atop one of the wagons. He discerns this is the reason the caravan bypasses the comfort and services of the inn. He shrugs, then enters.

He has not noticed the gaze of two would-be robbers who have followed the caravan at a safe distance. These men now set their plotting upon the inn patrons, presuming full purses and lesser reflexes, as the patrons have been plied with beer or mead. They wait patiently outside for any likely prey. They are also willing to wait until the caravan guards have passed safely within the city walls.

Once inside, Dunkel seeks out his favorite serving girl, catches her eye, and seats himself heavily at a nearby table. She is buxom, if not entirely attractive, and cleanly dressed in a blue surcotte. She wears only a trace of makeup, enough to enhance what attractiveness she offers. Her best feature is her disarming smile, which she now offers to Dunkel, as she knows him and sees no better prospects for this evening. She draws a flagon of beer and leans over his shoulder to serve it. Dunkel takes her hand and squeezes it lightly as a signal.

"Keep 'em coming, my dear. Tonight I have the means t' afford it—and 'haps a little something extra."

"A gen'leman'd kiss a lady's hand and not be so presumptuous!"

"'Haps I am no gentleman, then. But I know what I like!"

"I see ye do, and I'll certainly provide all the beer ye like."

"And something extra?"

"A little later. I've other patrons t' serve."

"Indeed! As long as ye serve the others within the confines of this hall, I'll be most gracious. Save the dessert for me!"

"That I will, and it'll cost ye dearly!"

"I 'spect it'll be worth every pfennig!"

Rudi smiles as he watches Dunkel enter the inn, then proceeds to walk up the road leading into the city. Rudi thinks him a fool. But a necessary fool. He cannot imagine what Beata sees in him. Although it was not her choice. Dunkel is large, burly, and uncouth, and an occasional bath would not hurt.

Yet he is a very determined man and superb at his craft. Rudi imagines the master was mercilessly teased for his limp during his childhood, and he imagines that led Dunkel to excel in his artisanry as a means to achieve recognition beyond his deformities.

But what Rudi does not imagine is that the teasing also led the man to become as strong as possible, so he could threaten off any would-be taunters or thugs. Instead, Rudi focuses on how he must learn all he can from Dunkel before his drinking habit overcomes him.

At that, his thoughts turn again to the radiant Beata. Although Rudi lives in the same household—as it is custom for journeymen and apprentices to become part of a master guildsman's family—he thinks nothing of usurping the hospitality of Herr Hammer. He smiles inwardly at the thought. She is truly beautiful. Rudi finds himself exceedingly lucky to have a virtually unblemished face, so that she may find him attractive as well. He considers developing a song to attract her attention this night. Perhaps a sonnet to impress her.

"Let's see. Hmm," he says. He composes aloud:

Eyes pools of blue and countenance fair
Eternal youth and lustrous hair . . .

"Yes, her long, silky hair may be her best feature. I could climb it forever."

As he muses, he is almost distracted from the sight of two shadowy figures dashing across the road to hide in the shrubbery adjacent the entrance to the inn. He hums softly to himself in order to give the impression of having missed them. He listens intently.

"That certainly was a near miss. The caravan'd surely have held some useful treasure for us. And Peter'll now be the subject of the prince's justice. We'll have t' lay low for a while, we will."

"Unfortunately, that'll take some immediate money, I think. What do ye think'd be the prospects with that young lad out there, mooning over some unacquired love? He certainly looks ripe for the picking, he does."

"He's clearly, at best, only a journeyman or 'prentice and not likely t' be endowed with any significant purse. More, he's strong of muscle from whate'er craft he studies and may be a bit formidable if we lose the element of surprise. I would prefer t' seek out better prey, such as the noblemen being entertained within."

"I cede t' your judgment, but I think we should take the first opportunity that presents itself."

"Agreed. Now let's be silent and invisible!"

Rudi thinks this is good advice for himself as well. He saunters around a curve, and then, as silently as possible, redoubles his steps off the road to a vantage point of the inn entrance. He is concerned Dunkel himself may be the target of these two outlaws. He may prefer to woo Beata, but he is not so head over heels in love that he is ready to lose his master tonight. Moreover, he would not enter a fray if Dunkel could handle it himself, but if he did enter, perhaps there would be some reward or advantage for him.

He stations himself out of sight of the two ruffians, yet behind them, so that the element of surprise will be his.

~ Chapter 5 ~

"You may come out of there now, fraülein. There is no one here but Fee."

Besse sighs, props Dolly against the corner of the wardrobe she is hiding behind, and steps out.

Fee leans over her lovingly, a frown of concern on her face, and continues, "Look at you. What a sight! It is time for you to learn to be a lady of the house, and that disheveled appearance will not do. Come here, and I will brush out your hair and change your surcotte. We must go together to shop for dinner, and the hour is late."

"You have never asked me to the market with you before. I do not like to be out in the bright sun. Must I go?" Besse pouts.

Fee straightens, hands on hips, and responds, "Your mother is not likely to help with this part of your schooling. Every hausfrau needs to know the secrets of the market. Some day you will have a husband who will rely upon your judgment, if not your skills as a cook. It is time to learn." Now she taps her toes, brooking no disobedience.

Besse is flustered. "I would rather rely on the servants, as Mama does with you. The crowds frighten me, and I cannot bear the taunts of the children. I am too ugly to be seen in public."

Fee throws up her arms in despair. "That is not so at all, Besse. You have the beauty of your mother, albeit darkened by the skin tone of your father—and the layers of dirt you continually insist on carrying around. I will clean you up, and you will see you are the equal of any maiden at the market!"

"Do not touch me! I am happiest as I am! I do not want to be attractive to anyone!"

Fee is shocked by Besse's response. Besse starts to run away, but Fee is quicker, grabs her arm, and sits her down heavily.

~ Chapter 5 ~

"I may not be much older than you, but I have been given the charge by your mother. I am stronger for my labors, and I mean to obey it! Now sit, and I *will* brush your hair and clean your face and hands."

Besse knows she cannot win this battle. She relents but continues to pout.

Fee is aware of the real reason Besse needs to remain unattractive, but she also knows it is futile for the poor girl. She might as well learn to put forward her best countenance in public, so that someday she can marry out of the household, safely away from her menacing father. Fee is actually doing her a favor!

She hums as she carefully brushes out the tangles, then dips into a washbasin with a clean rag and washes the grime from Besse's face and hands.

"There! That is much better. Now hurry into this gray surcotte. We have little time left of daylight to shop, and almost all of the meats, fish, and vegetables will have been completely picked over. I warrant we can bargain a very good price for what remains. Good! Let us depart. Now, do I have adequate coinage in my purse?"

The two head down the spiral stairs—Fee bounding, Besse dragging herself reluctantly.

As they leave, Besse contemplates her best hiding place for the evening. The corner behind the wardrobe in her room will not do, as it is too open and obvious. Perhaps the root cellar beneath the tower?

The pair enter the solar, a large, drafty room on the ground level that serves as a family gathering room, dining room, and entertainment room for guests—as if there would ever be guests in this house! The solar is almost unadorned. There is only a too-small trestle table, and only thin linens cover the walls—not enough to hold the heat of the large hearth that opens on the other side to the kitchen behind the wall. The only ornate features in the room are the intricate ironwork sconces upon the walls, the pride of the blacksmith who is her father.

The solar has no windows, a concession to the need for the tower to stand in protection of the city. Wind enters the chamber through the hearth and from the more-open rooms above, which have, at least, long, narrow openings facing the city. In actuality, Besse approves of the lack of light and cheer, but there is no place to hide in this room. She sighs as they tread through. Pots are already heating over the blaze set in the hearth, a reminder that the servants are awaiting the upcoming purchases of the two departing marketers.

Entering the city, Fee leads Besse through a maze of narrow streets with houses often leaning precariously overhead. She decides to walk through the Jewish quarter, though Besse disdains the jewelry and fine leather goods displayed just inside the open upper doorways. By this route, however, they avoid the tanners' street with its foul odors.

They arrive directly into the central market, a series of small streets barely wider than alleys and quite ancient. Here, the ground levels of houses open into the still-bustling streets. Each house is fronted by a double door, the top half of which opens and is fastened upward, allowing a display of goods and a view of the working masters and apprentices within. The chatter of the small crowd is punctuated by criers singing out offers to fix clothing or furniture.

Fee stops first at a bakery and purchases bread, both fresh and day old—the latter to be used as serving platters on the trestle table. Next the meats: a small capon, a hare, and a small quantity of ham.

"You must learn to inspect the meats, wine, and cheeses, Besse. Meats can be blown out, fish can be stained with the blood of pigs to look fresher, and cheese can be soaked in broth to look richer. We will need leeks, onions, salt, eggs—and if there is any coinage remaining, perhaps figs and spiced wine for dessert! I will have to bargain well, and you would do well to note the method."

For her part, Besse is somewhat overwhelmed by the cries of the men and women from their houses, mingled with the street criers, young children underfoot, the odors, and the need to watch carefully where she steps! But Fee negotiates all such hazards with the guidance of long practice. Fee takes little, if any, notice of the blood and offal left at the feet of the meat butchers who perform their slaughtering on the spot, while Besse thinks she will possibly never eat meat again. Nevertheless, she knows Fee is correct and only trying to help her. She pays close attention as Fee bargains the price of the hare to three silver pieces.

Finally, they arrive at the stall of a young lady selling spices. Here the air fills with a much happier aroma, one of sage, coriander, mint, and others. As the Hammer household has no garden, Fee must purchase these here. Curiously, she does not bargain with the proprietor, who is only a few years younger than she. Besse realizes this is Fee's sister, Flor, and an appropriate price will be charged without argument.

Flor brightens visibly at the arrival of her sister and the young maiden. She smiles and says, "Well, what can I provide for you today, Fee—and whom have we here? Is this to be the new lady of the Hammer household? I do believe you are quite the attractive young fraülein, and the young, aspiring burghers will soon take notice! Perhaps you would wish to purchase some of my finer herbs to sweeten the complexion? Or some of my most special ones to create a tea to stir the passions of a suitor? Or—"

"That is quite enough, sister mine. I would not have you enticing the fraülein with wares she should have no need or knowledge to acquire!"

Fee turns stern eyes toward her sister, then shakes her head. Flor does well at market and pays a more-than-modest tithe to the prince. Fee is very happy for her, though she questions some of the items for sale within the tent. She has taken Flor to task on several occasions, but only because Fee fears for her sister's safety, as she does for all her siblings. If Flor were ever to make an enemy who disapproved of her more secret trade, Fee does not know what she would do. Yet Flor does provide balm to all the citizens and will not deny those in need who are unable to pay. She has a good heart.

"Here, Besse," Fee says, "take these back to the cook and be so kind as to allow me an opportunity to visit with my family. I will follow presently. Be sure to follow the exact route we used to arrive here, as you are indeed vulnerable to those who would accost you unnecessarily, and I would not have you suffer the air of the tanneries.

I will take you with me daily, until you feel comfortable bargaining your own purchases."

"Please accompany me, Fee. I do not feel safe in these streets, and I do not like the excessively bright light of day. I am accustomed to remaining at home. And I do not see why I should learn what you yourself have been willing to do in the stead of Mama."

"Your mother has expressly required me to teach you the way of the city, and marketing is a skill you will need to master. You are of age to understand it. You will someday do the marketing for the household on your own, making selections according to your own tastes. Your mother and father, not to mention the young journeyman and apprentice, will have little cause to complain. Now be off with you, as I do not want you roaming these streets after the sun sets, and cook will require adequate time to prepare the dinner!"

Besse takes her leave, burdened with a basket of goods. Flor gives her a sly look and a wink as she departs.

◆ ◆ ◆

Besse begins to realize marketing is indeed a way to be out of the house when *he* might be in. She will scout the streets another time for a less exposed route, unconcerned by Fee's warnings about tanners and accosters. Odors do not bother her. And she would not make an attractive appearance of herself, at any rate. Such flattery is false; she knows she is not likely to win the gaze of the young men, nor would she seek to gain it.

Now, which street did we use, she asks herself. *Oh, yes. There is the Jewish quarter.* Such frivolous, immodest baubles and clothing! Of these, she would ever want none.

The sun is falling behind the higher mountains as she walks. The shadows lengthen behind her, seeming to follow her and ultimately engulf her. Loss of light drains the cheer from the overhanging houses, giving them a brooding appearance. In contradiction, Besse's mood improves as the surrounding cityscape darkens, and people withdraw within their homes.

~ Chapter 5 ~

Besse is too distracted by her thoughts to watch her way carefully. An emaciated youth passes her unseen. It is Jacques, having just accosted his father, Dunkel Hammer. He has no realization that the man is also this young maiden's father.

This day, Jacques has sold his mother's last cow for next to nothing, barely enough to buy some beans for a meager dinner. He then secreted his way into the quarter and into the home of one of the jewelers, not quite deftly lifting a prize and placing it in his pouch unnoticed.

Now Jacques entertains the sudden thought that the contents of the maiden's basket would serve a better meal than mere beans—and come to think of it, the maiden herself could serve better.

Unexpectedly, a rough hand reaches out to grab Besse's surcotte. She lets out a startled cry, then decides to shout. "Unhand me, foul knave, or I will surely demand the wrath of my father, Dunkel Hammer, upon you!"

Jacques is momentarily startled. Dunkel is *her* father? Suddenly revolted with his own prior intention, he rapidly releases his grip and grimaces.

The commotion attracts the Jewish women's attention. They call for their husbands, who chase the young man out of their quarter.

"A thousand pardons, fraülein," one of the jewelers tells Besse. "Please understand that that ruffian is not of this part of the city!"

The Jews fear that any accusation would arouse the hatred and retribution of the townspeople, who are always suspicious of them. Besse only reinforces her image of the crudity of all men. She bears no specific grudge against the Jews, yet she will not deign to thank them.

She continues on her way, amazed at her own assertiveness in warding off her aggressor. She picks up her pace. As she arrives at the ground floor of the house, she realizes she has forgotten to breathe. Letting out a great sigh, she steps within.

♦ ♦ ♦

Fee is not happy with her sister. "It is not for Besse to know the nature of your more clandestine goods for sale, sister. I am sure she will learn the true ways of the world in her own due time."

"If you bring her out to study them, then it is time she does learn. The world is not a playground for children, nor is life the stuff of some child's tale! I will seize my opportunities for a sale where I may find them. You, of all people, should understand the difficulties of creating a life. One has only to think upon the fortunes of our brother Peter, forced to live as an outlaw in the absence of any decent available land or apprenticeship! And both you and our brother Jurg—having to live as servants. At least you and I can hope to find good husbands someday . . ."

At that, Fee blushes, and Flor realizes Fee may already have found a liaison.

"My dear," says Flor, raising the pitch of her voice in excitement, "does that countenance betray a secret love? You must tell me!"

Fee frowns, then sighs. "I can hide little from you, dear sister. This you shall know in good time."

Flor has ever been the attractive one of the family and not averse to enhance with powders and berries. When they were younger, Mama drew the line at Flor's attire, demanding she dress modestly. None of those flouncy dresses for her! Nor for Fee, for that matter. The elder sister has always been content to be herself, feeling there was naught she could do to make herself attractive to the opposite sex. Which is why she puzzles over her lover Dien's attraction to her.

But Fee must brush aside such thoughts with Peter's current situation being so dire. "I will say, though, it is, in fact, a boon that Jurg serves the prince himself, as I may need to ask of him a favor. Perhaps the good Lord guides us in our positions and pursuits in life, and I bear Him no rancor on Peter's behalf. As for me, I ask and expect very little, other than that which is my due and that I might protect our own interests. I fear that someday even Peter will have need of our concern and assistance, if he is not very careful. Although His Majesty does not abide the hunting of outlaws within his domain, he also does not suffer the deeds of anyone who would accost his good citizens and guests unlawfully."

Fee sighs in resignation. "It is my place to look after the fortunes of Besse and the mistress, Beata—whose fortunes are none too happy in the hands of the master, Herr Hammer himself. I may have to look for the rewards of my efforts in the next life! Yet I see the shadows are growing longer, and I will have to return soon."

A caravan nears the market stall bordering the main road, where the sisters converse. Fee says, "Is that not a rather poor-looking caravan winding its way? My Lord! It is preceded by the prince's guards, and there sits the young dauphin himself with Hans Handler! And who is that draped across the guard's horse? I cannot tell, but this bodes ill, I think!"

Despite the late hour, Fee feels she should not yet leave the scene. She waits with Flor as the shadows that followed Besse now engulf the market stalls and the approaching caravan. It is becoming very chilly. Fee shivers.

Suddenly, Flor exclaims, "Over the horse—that draped bandit! It is Peter! Oh, what has he done? What will we do, sister? We must speak to Jurg at once!"

Fee is startled a moment and her eyes go wide, but her judgment, as always, gets the better of her. She turns to Flor and replies with yet another sigh of resignation.

"The prince will not allow harm to come to Peter without a judgment, as he is a fair and just man. I will speak to Jurg on the morrow, so he can first acquire knowledge of Peter's behavior and possible fate. But I must hie to the house of Master Hammer and see to my own duties first. Fear not, sister. I will do what I can on Peter's behalf!"

She adds to herself, *Though that may be very little. This day does bode ill for us all.*

Flor catches Fee before she turns to leave. "Wait! You must take some herbs to Jurg to ease Peter's pain. I will give you some bark of willow and some meadowsweet, and you must have Jurg arrange to make infusions." Flor ducks briefly behind a back curtain, then soon emerges with a cloth containing the promised ingredients. "You see, Fee, the goods I offer are of many worthwhile uses. Do not be so quick to criticize. Now, off with you."

Fee hurries through the darkening streets, paying close attention to the smaller alleys she passes, always careful to see to her own safety—or how else could she be of help to anyone else? It does not occur to her to bemoan her lot, consigned to the needs of her master's wife and daughter and now to her poor brother. Not to mention her sister, if she is not more careful in announcing her wares!

~ Chapter 6 ~

The road winds its way uphill, gradually revealing the walls and towers of the city, with its palace atop the mountain. Ebouisante can make out a line of light shining upon the city as well as a river arriving from the same heights. She realizes the line is an aqueduct, bringing pure mountain water into the city. Yet she does not see any water exiting the town, and she frowns momentarily.

Hans takes notice. "You are disappointed, mademoiselle, in the appearance of our city?" he asks, both bemused and a bit hurt, as he takes pride in his allegiance.

"I have it!" she exclaims. "It all exits underground, far enough downstream to provide no danger to the citizens. How clever!" Her gaze turns back to Hans, and she demurs. "Oh, I am sorry!"

"You must forgive my daughter, sirs," Herr Kaufman says with a stern look to Ebouisante. "Her mind never stops working. But you will find she is quite capable of appreciating the beauty of nature around her."

"I have apologized, Papa, but I cannot restrain the process of thought. My father, sirs, would have me just intelligent enough to assist with the business, and just feminine enough for his future plans for me. I am sure it would not be possible to live up to such a perfect combination of virtues."

The caravan arrives at the gate to the city. The guards at the fore of the group hail those on the ramparts above, speaking the daily password that grants entry without a search. Serge is grateful to forego the tedious process of presenting his credentials and allowing review of his inventory. Ebouisante, on the other hand, is grateful to forego the usual bribes and their challenging bookkeeping. She is also glad to forego the perusal of her own person, occasionally open, but often surreptitious, by the same guards. The journey and events of the day have left her with a mixture of fatigue, shakiness, gratitude, and happy anticipation of seeing her mother again, separated from her these last several fortnights.

"Perhaps, Papa, we should allow these gentlemen and their bodyguards to take their leave." She turns to the young men with a gentle smile. "We cannot thank you enough, sirs, and will remain in your debt. I shall entreat upon both Papa and Maman to devise a suitable mode of demonstration of our eternal gratitude."

Ebouisante watches the retreat of the guards and boys with interest and a wry smile. She thinks she will not allow herself the luxury of emotional attachment, as she knows her father will eventually have the honor of arranging a match for her. Yet she could perhaps have some influence, if she is careful enough.

She has to admit, Hans is both attractive and intelligent, but a little more maturity is wanted. This will come only with a little experience in a less protected environment. It is one thing to view the world as a playground for adventure, another to realize there are adventures to be avoided, if possible. She would like him best with an added touch of pragmatism. But she does believe she likes him more than any other she has met. This little drama will yet play itself out over time.

Ebouisante and Serge reach their new home, uncover the wagons, remove false floors, and reveal a wealth of fabrics, tapestries, and spices. Plus there is a large trunk containing jewels and items the Venetians rescued from Byzantium before the Ottoman Muslims' siege of Constantinople. There are also gifts for Serge's wife, Blanche; the prince and princess; and others.

Herr Kaufmann will indeed do well in this city, more so with the possibility of new trade routes and goods not generally or easily available to the burghers and nobility of Northern Europe. For the moment, he is happy and eager to establish himself in his own original home city.

~ Chapter 6 ~

Hans and Charles, having lived here all their lives, take little note of the singularity of their principality, distinguished as it is by its cleanliness and prosperity. The guards ride ahead, comfortable in the knowledge that the boys are safe within the confines of these walls—for who would dare harm them and face the wrath of the sovereign? The boys are quite pleased with themselves and are both eager to impart the events of the day to their respective families.

"Do you not think this has been an adventurous and fruitful day, Hans?" asks Charles as they begin their ascent through the narrow, winding streets.

"I think you understate the case, sire. I cannot decide which was the most exciting: the combat practice, the rescue of the caravan, or the opportunity to acquaint myself with Ebouisante. Do you not think she is the most beautiful maiden you have ever seen?"

"Perhaps, but I must be careful of my opinions. It is not for me to choose a mate, alas, and I think my father is well on the path to making a selection for me. I only hope she has half the appearance and wit of the young Fraülein Kaufmann. Yet I would refrain further from opinion, as I can see that my closest friend and ally is smitten and virtually captured himself!"

Hans laughs, leaning toward the prince as if to offer a punch to the shoulder, but he knows he must restrain himself. "Smitten? I am not ready for that trap, sire. I have not yet lived to have the adventures I crave. Moreover, I must be careful myself. My own parents have not seen fit to divulge their plans for me, and I am ill prepared to thwart them. I have much to learn of the merchant trade. Adventures or not, I certainly desire to follow my father in the guild. There are adventures enough—hazards enough—in the caravan, as we have just seen."

Now Charles laughs, sitting tall in the saddle. He winks, then states, "But it would not be beyond your capability to exert some influence upon your parents, I warrant. We will see what transpires, Hans. And I shall, of course, endeavor to be at your side, if that offers some assistance—or some solace, as the case may be."

Hans harrumphs. "Always a true friend! But who is this shadow racing out of the Jewish quarter? I do not think I recognize him!"

Charles recedes into the shadow of an alley, awaits the passage of the young man, then reaches out an arm to grab his tunic, pulling him up short.

Caught breathless, the youth is unable to resist. Ironic, he finds it, to be caught in the same manner as he had intended to entrap the young maiden! Then his eyes widen as he recognizes his assailant.

He acclaims, "Sire! Forgive me! I was merely in a hurry t' return home before darkness with a purchase for me mother! She's sent me on this errand and pleads me return before the sun sets on penalty of lack of dinner!" He bows deeply, his face flushed with exertion and embarrassment.

Hans surveys this scene with some amusement. "You may arise, but I would have a view of your 'purchase.' Be so kind as to empty your pouch. Unless, perhaps, you want to let him go, sire," he quips with a wink. "He has done us no harm."

"I think not," Charles responds. "There is plenty of time before dark, and no need to be in such a hurry as this one." To the boy, "Empty it."

The boy fumbles with his purse, ultimately spilling the contents onto the cobblestones. A few pfennigs clang onto the street, followed by a large red stone. "Me purchase, sire."

"Have you a receipt for this ruby?"

"I must have it here, somewhere." He makes a show of attempting to find it upon his person.

"Enough!" Charles bellows. "Let us enter the Jewish quarter, and you will direct me to the place of purchase!"

Hans follows, still amused, as the boys turn into the quarter and approach a house. The man of the house, a gem merchant, quickly recognizes the young prince, bows, and invites the boys inside. Charles displays the ruby in his hand, and the merchant's eyes widen.

"Is this a test, sire?" he asks. "That gem disappeared from my display not an hour ago! How comes it into your possession?"

"Did you not sell this to this boy?"

"No, sire, I did not!"

"He's a lyin' Jew, interested in taking me money, then recovering the merchandise!" claims the boy, almost screaming. "Would ye believe a Jew before a God-fearing Christian citizen of your own principality, sire?"

"Irrelevant," says the dauphin with a wave of his hand. "This is easily settled. Sir, you will please do me the honor of displaying your accounts for the day to my young merchant friend, Hans, over here. We shall know immediately what transpired!"

"Gladly, sir," the merchant says as he retrieves his ledger.

Hans reviews the ledger and announces, "There is no transaction concerning the stone in question, sire." There is a touch of affectation in his voice. Here is another little adventure of the day. But now Hans will have to accompany them both to the castle, to help assure the boy does not get away.

As they turn to take their leave, the woman of the house arrives to see what is causing the delay in serving dinner upstairs. Suddenly, she gasps and presses her hand to her face as she stares at the youth.

"Do you know this boy, madame?" asks the dauphin, somewhat taken aback.

"I swear, sire, I do not personally. But many of us on this very street accosted him this evening, preventing his unkind attentions to a young maiden who passed this way! Forgive me this revelation, as I fear he will speak evil of us to the townspeople—who would seek unwarranted retribution. And forgive my rudeness." She curtsies deeply.

"Such will not happen in Quellestadt while my father or I rule. Your people are always welcome here, especially as you show great fealty and share your successes in your tithing to our family. Moreover, this is a thief, and I am utterly inclined to believe you. I am returning your merchandise in good faith and will bring this wraith to my father for more appropriate justice. In regards to the maiden, further judgment will require that she herself pursue justice. Good day, sir and madame, and may you continue in good health and success."

Charles and Hans take their leave. It is to the relief of the merchant and his wife, who yet remain fearful of the city inhabitants' reaction, but have no choice but to rely upon the dauphin's honesty and kindness.

The boys continue to restrain the young thief, conveying him to the guard of the castle.

"It seems, my friend, you will not have to wander far for the adventure you seek in life. Here we have apprehended criminals not once but twice in one day! I am happy to think of nothing more than a hot meal with Their Highnesses, but I warrant I shall have to relive our experiences in recount and explanation before retiring," offers Charles, his voice lighthearted but with an edge of fatigue.

Hans bows. "Then I shall take my leave, sire, in anticipation of the same at home. No doubt I shall face some scolding, if not from Mama, then from my sister, Greta, who worries over me like a mother hen."

~ Chapter 7 ~

Besse runs up the spiral stairs that hug the inner wall of the tower and without a word drops the burden of her purchases into the arms of the waiting servant, leaving her speechless and dumbfounded. Besse is exceedingly restless, feeling safe neither in the streets nor in her own home.

In her room, she throws off the gray surcotte and dons her old, familiar, dingy one. Instinctively, she feels better in the dirt. She retreats with Dolly into a dark corner of her room, selected for the lack of light reaching from the high, narrow window. Herein lies her only comfort and consolation. Such an atmosphere would weigh heavily upon the soul of anyone. But for Besse, this is the closest she comes to complete anonymity, near nonexistence.

"Shall I tell you of the recent events, Dolly?

You see, Fee wants me to learn the basic care of the household. Mama never does that, does she? She sits in her chamber all day, fussing with her hair and her dresses and her . . . Oh well, I suppose you are well aware of that. I have told you so many a time, haven't I?"

As usual, the doll does not answer nor pass judgement.

"There is not much else for Mama to do in there, is there? She knows little of the world around her, but then she takes great pains to hide from it, doesn't she? One would think she were bewitched, locked in her chamber."

Besse considers this for a moment. "Then again, I myself do not care to go out into the city, Dolly. It is so bright and cheerful, and you and I, we are not at all like that, are we? No. So I guess I am a lot like her. Am I bewitched too?"

Besse sighs, frowns, and shudders, as if against an unseen blast of cold air from the netherworld. After a moment, she squares her shoulders.

"Perhaps, Dolly, I am not bewitched after all. For today I went out in the city and did the marketing, didn't I? Fee was proud—I could tell. But I will have to learn a lot more to plan the meals and run a household. And this I must do, Dolly. I must!"

Her voice rises in emotion, though not volume. "I cannot bear to live here one day more than necessary, Dolly. Not with him! Men are such beasts! They are composed all of hands, greed, and evil desires. The very streets are unsafe! Who will help a poor girl, cast adrift in such a broiling, loathsome sea without a rudder to steer by? And no safe harbor!"

She pulls her confidant closer. "You see, Dolly, there was this boy. An ugly and mean boy. He meant ill things, I am sure, and he accosted me in the Jewish quarter. But I stood up to this wretched boy and escaped! I have no doubt that young lout will go unpunished, though. It is a very sad world indeed. It is truly a man's world. Is there not at least *one* out there to take pity, perchance even to love? No. Men love only superficial beauty, and I care not for that!"

Besse continues, as if these revelations would give respite to her soul. "So you see, Dolly, even God is not to be entirely trusted to protect us. It is, I am told, on account of the original sin—when Eve, fooled by the serpent, disobeyed God's order and betrayed Adam. Everyone is taught that women are not to be trusted, are to toil in the home and in childbirth, and are to serve the whims of men. How can any woman worship such an unforgiving God? And who will protect *us*?"

She shivers, then sighs. "Who will protect *me*, Dolly? I must seek until I find someone. There is certainly *someone*, Dolly. Fee tries, but she is only a servant and ultimately subservient to the will of the master. Oh, there must be some man out there who is wise, handsome, and will protect me! The journeyman and apprentice must surely have some idea of the ill, terrible behavior of their master, though their interest in their own futures requires at least discretion, if not outright rejection of the knowledge. So who else? I will—I *must*—begin searching. And so I *will* follow Fee into the markets, learn what I must to survive, and make discrete acquaintances. Yes, I must take measures to influence my own fate, my own future."

Her discourse is interrupted by Fee's call from the stairs below that it is time for supper, breaking her darkest thoughts. Suddenly realizing she has been shaking the doll vigorously, she unclenches her grip, sighs, and hugs it.

"And now, I must leave you for a short time. I hear Fee calling us, and I must finish before *he* comes home."

~ Chapter 8 ~

Across the dining hall of the inn, a group of noblemen and their retinues observe the activity of the serving girls with a less-than-objective eye. One of the Duke's guards notes, "I am not entirely impressed with the selection, my lord, but I suppose we are in no position to be highly selective. The food, I must say, is well prepared and flavorful, and the atmosphere quite convivial."

"I would agree, sir," responds the duke.

The party had declined the hospitality of the castle, having an eye toward a potentially more entertaining evening, though they did not wish to travel too far from the city at night. Although the duke loves and remains devoted to his wife and daughter, he sees no contradiction in his inconstant pleasure-seeking behavior away from home, as is the custom of the times. The inn presents a convenient opportunity for good, if not exquisite, cookery, as well as convivial company.

As he surveys the activity and inwardly measures the potential of the waitstaff, the duke inhales the heady odors of roasted meats, herbs, unwashed citizenry, and wood smoke, combined with the occasional wafting of forest air from the entry and windows. He feels the atmosphere a bit tawdry and ignoble, but such is the price one pays for his intended sort of evening entertainment.

He continues, "I would, however, have an eye toward some selection of my own creature comforts. I note, particularly, that rather buxom young maid serving that sooty, old, yellow gentleman with the limp. Do you not think it would be possible to entice her with a more chivalrous approach?"

The guard replies, "To be honest, my lord, I would rather expect she would show greater interest in a larger recompense for her services than in a more flattering appearance or address. It is at least certain she is familiar with that particular denizen and would have to consider the potential loss of future income were she to divert her attention to travelers. One would have to offer her far more than her modest beauty warrants. Perhaps you should allow your gaze to wander to one of the other maidens. There are a few with more surpassing countenance than that one, I am convinced."

Duke Philip is unconvinced. He waves his hand in dismissal of the suggestion. "I thank you for your insight, sir, but I believe it would be something of a lesson to the citizen to know he must yield his inclinations to those of the nobility. I will do the young maiden the courtesy, however, of allowing her to serve him within the confines of this dining hall before I accost her personally. She may not be of surpassing beauty, but she is attractive enough and clever enough to improve the accommodations available here considerably, such as they are."

Dunkel Hammer does not fail to notice the wandering gaze of the noblemen seated closer to the large fireplace, where they are assured of greater warmth against the chilling autumn air. He is approached by the serving maiden Rose, carrying a small pot of stew, which she ladles into his bread bowl. She leans over him suggestively, winking and smiling.

"I do believe, Rose, that foppish gentleman has fixated 'pon ye! Ye'll have a difficult choice to make, but I see he does nothin' to in'errupt your service at *this* table. I'm of a mind t' keep ye for meself this evenin', though I could ne'er hope t' offer a price t' match *his* purse."

"That foppish gentleman, as ye call him," Rose replies, "is a duke leavin' th' city, having concluded some business with the prince, I warrant. It'd not be t' either your benefit or mine t' counter his proposals, it wouldn't. Yet me inclination'll always be toward me most regular admirers."

She throws a smile the way of the duke as surreptitiously as she can, and receives a slight nod in return.

"What'd ye have me do?" she asks, turning back to Dunkel.

"A difficult decision, t' be sure. I'd be most seriously disappointed if ye were t' prefer such a man as *that* to a strong, more practiced one such as I! Yet I am not so drunk as not t' be mindful of the potential loss of business that would ensue from curryin' the ill favor of the nobility, both local and otherwise.

"I propose ye continue t' serve me some of your wonderful stew, ply me wi' a few pints of your best mead at a reduced price, then pretend t' throw me over and allow the gentleman t' come t' your rescue. I'm quite capable of seekin' me pleasures elsewhere, and I know he'll be gone in the mornin', leavin' ye behind for future attention from me! Now, let's make a grand show for the noble party!"

Rose laughs. "How generous of ye! Not like ye at all! Ye mustn't be plied enough with the ale. I'll do better than that." Rose glances back at the duke. "See, he beckons me t' his party e'en as we speak. By your leave, I do have other customers t' serve. Let's see what he has in mind, and I'll make a proposition t' the advantage of ye both."

"Ye've aroused me curiosity—among other things, Rose," answers Dunkel conspiratorially with a wry smile. "Let's see what *ye* have in mind, as I can certainly guess what the gentleman has in both mind and pouch!"

Dunkel muses to himself as Rose makes a show as she approaches the duke. She is quite the beauty, he notes as he admires her ample bottom swishing her skirt and surcotte—more attractive than the sway of tall rushes in the breeze to a lovesick romantic. He decides he would rather have the duke believe he is making a gift of Rose for the nonce, rather than a concession.

Dunkel inhales the heady aromas surrounding him—stew, mead, and beer, all of which give him cheer. He knows the duke will have need of the best armor available, and he is certainly prepared to provide it. He decides to have at least a word with him before he retires. Yet not to seem too hasty in conducting business, he must only propose a future show of the value of his art. For it is, indeed, an art, and no one can create better armor than his!

- Chapter 8 -

Dunkel smiles with the inward understanding of a co-conspirator as Rose approaches the duke and bends suggestively to his ear. He realizes she's displaying like a French hen not just for duke, but also for him.

"My Lord, I'm at your service," Rose offers the duke with a slight curtsy. "What is it ye'd have me serve?" lightly said with a coquettish grin.

"Now—or later?" he answers slyly.

"For now," she replies, ignoring the inference on purpose, "we have excellent meats, veg'tables, and stew. An' the mead is partic'larly good this evenin'. For later, the servin' maids may all be preoccupied."

This time she throws a smile the way of Dunkel, assured that the duke will not miss it. Dunkel smiles back, and she winks.

The duke, for his part, feels the air of electricity across the room and is more determined than ever to appropriate the attentions of this young maiden for himself. It is all the more exciting to achieve one's goals as the result of a challenge, however unspoken. But how to elicit the compliance of this one?

Surprisingly, Rose herself offers a solution.

"It would be difficult for me," she whispers into his ear, "t' desert the 'tentions of a regular customer, 'specially as ye'll soon be departin' our company and unlikely t' return with any frequency, me lord. Howe'er, I might suggest that ye offer t' pay for the gentleman's dinner and a pint of our finest mead. I'd be happy t' convey your regards and the offer of recompense for me services and t' remind him that I must remain here at his future disposal. That should work, I think. He's in no position t' refuse any offer, 'specially such a generous one from an important nobleman such as yeself."

The duke considers for a moment, then gives out a hearty laugh. "You are hardly in a position to bargain, my dear. But then, I have had a successful day and am in a generous mood. Offer the *gentleman* my regards and a pint of mead, then bid him good night!"

In truth, the duke would like to finish his own dinner with

some dispatch so he can sooner enjoy the company of the girl. He finds her to be a smart one and thinks she will make a challenging entertainment. Still, he believes she is no match for his own charms. No matter, he thinks. She will be his for the one evening, then he will be off to more important matters at home.

Dunkel has observed the exchange across the inn with inward amusement. He thinks how easy it is for his *lordship* to command what he desires! Dunkel thinks the duke has not the slightest idea of true hardship. He does not know how easy it is to be hurt by the bullying of one's supposed friends, to have your own wit and determination sharpened as if whittled by a painful paring knife into the most useful tool. Yes, determination to be the strongest, the most creative, the smartest! The need to develop *skill* to earn one's way with genius and frugality.

So tonight he will allow the duke to enjoy Rose, though he may not have truly earned the right. In exchange for the fruits of his own labor, Dunkel will eventually assist the duke in some small separation from his unearned wealth, while Dunkel partakes of the women and wine he has achieved entirely on his own!

He downs a few pints of the inn's own brew, admittedly not the nectar of the gods, but as good as such to Dunkel's taste. He betrays no emotion whatsoever as he watches Rose serve a fine venison and wood-roasted vegetables to the duke's party, who then inhales the food without the slightest show of appreciation to the cooks or serving maids. Yes, they do take it all for granted!

Rose brings a jug to Dunkel, stating boldly, "With his lordship's compliments, sir. But I must now leave you t' attend t' his own service!" She winks at Dunkel, who chuckles inwardly.

"Ye do have a way with gentlemen, Rose. Go about your business. I'll find mine elsewhere t'night."

He nods toward the duke, then drains the jug. He rises, hefts the jug as if to offer a toast to the duke, and approaches him with a deep bow.

"I would be remish, m' lord, if I did not offer my gratitude before I withdraw." His speech is a little slurred under the influence of the mead, but he appears to still have his wits about him. "I am Dunkel Hammer, armorer t' the prince, and alwaysh at your servish, sir."

"Indeed! Are you the creator of the magnificent plate armor displayed by the prince's soldiers on the field? If so, you have my compliments, sir, and I shall desire to do more business with you directly upon my return to this amiable realm. Would you care to join my company, or must you be off so soon?"

"Thank ye, m' lord, but the sun is almosht shet, and I musht find my way home while I shtill have the witsh about me t' do it!"

Dunkel bows again and turns to leave. He is not so besotted, however, as to miss giving Rose one little swat in passing. She deftly avoids him and continues on to serve another fine venison steak to the duke. Dunkel laughs and exits the inn.

Outside, the air is as crisp and fresh as a fine new day, but Dunkel takes little notice. He contemplates completing his dinner at home—followed by some time with Besse afterward. Stepping a little carelessly, he allows the coins in his purse to jingle.

To the ruffians in hiding, this is a ready signal. They leap from behind the nearest trees, two dark panthers ready to pounce upon their unwitting prey, silently and efficiently.

But only one reaches the armorer. The other is taken by complete surprise from behind and knocked breathless to the ground with a long stick against his neck.

"Make not one sound, or you are dead," whispers Rudi.

This rapid exchange is so deft that the other outlaw fails to notice the loss of his comrade. He continues onward, the jangling purse fixed in his sight. This only is his goal, having no real intention of harming its owner. He would be most grateful and satisfied to achieve its acquisition and depart swiftly, its current owner none the wiser. But he is not skilled in the art of the pickpocketing, and his attempt is ill fated, indeed.

Under the effects of mead, Dunkel is aware of neither the encroaching danger nor even the clear, starry night brisk with autumn air and alight with the full moon casting long shadows. Nearly besotted, his vision is, in fact, fogged. And his thoughts are clouded with the memory of his childhood tormentors. Now he imagines himself finally well enough situated to have the better of them.

"Yesh," he mutters, "let 'em try shomethin' now! I'm shtronger and shmarter than any of 'em. I will show 'em now!'

Suddenly, he feels a pull on his belt. In his confusion, he wheels around, imagining he sees a tall, slim child aiming to play a trick upon him, as happened so many times in the past. He grabs an arm and twists, hard, throwing the wraith to the ground. He sits hard upon the youth to take the air out of him, and he begins to pound away at his head repeatedly.

"Ye think ye can have the better of *me*?" he shouts. "Enough! I'll take yer hounding no more! I am Dunkel Hammer, and I'll be an important man!"

In short order, the man is unconscious. But Dunkel does not stop. All of his pent-up anger is focused on the outlaw, released as rage against the unfairness of his youth, against the indifference of his family and community, against a world based in cruelty. He hardly hears the pleading of his journeyman, who has released the second ruffian with an admonishment to keep these events to himself and never show his face in the city.

"Master, you must stop! He is unconscious and can do you no further harm! Let us leave here and return to the warmth and safety of your own hearth and home!"

"Rudi, ish that ye?"

Dunkel is brought back to the current reality, suddenly thinking much more clearly. He takes a deep breath of the cold air, snapping back to himself. Even his speech rights itself.

"Why're ye here, and not home? Why, ye must've seen these ruffians and thought t' hide here t' protect me—or even any other potential victim! I must thank you. But I must tell ye that I'm not hindered by a few draughts of beer or mead! Ye had naught t' fear for me!"

He looks down upon the man he has badly beaten. In fact, his face is crushed, though not bleeding.

- Chapter 8 -

"I believe he has learned his lesson, and we can be off!"

Rudi is not so sure. He bends down and with a slight gasp notes that the man is not breathing at all. His hands are turning blue, judging by the light of the bright moon.

"Master, you have killed him! We must hide him in the woods. The prince would not look lightly upon murder, even in self-defense!" Rudi trembles as he speaks. "Will you help me lift and carry him?"

A cloud drifts over the moon, offering the men the welcome cover of darkness.

"Nonsense, he cannot be dead!" But even as he speaks, Dunkel knows his journeyman is correct in his assessment. "No, by God, ye're right! We must move him out of the way of discovery."

As he helps Rudi with the body, Dunkel realizes he is not totally recovered from the effects of the mead. The men lift the body onto Dunkel's broad shoulders, rather clumsily. They then proceed behind the inn, past the stables, and into the wood.

As they walk, they look only ahead to their path, failing to notice that the cloud has departed from the moon. They also miss the figure of a young maiden in the window of the inn, who sees their progress in the newly available light. It is Rose, opening the window to the night air as an opportunity once again to display her attractive bottom to the duke awaiting her in bed, busily removing his clothes under the cover of the heated linens.

"You look startled, my dear," he says as she straightens suddenly and peers out the window more intently. "Come to me now, and I will keep you warm."

Rose is indeed nonplused. She recognizes Dunkel, with his distinctive limp, carrying the clearly inert body of a man into the woods. She will have to investigate in the morning. This could be useful to her, although she has no thought whatsoever as to the potential plight of the victim. In her position, she must take advantages where they lie—which reminds her of the advantage currently calling to her from the bed.

She sighs and retreats to her destiny.

- Chapter 9 -

As the setting sun casts a rose light to the west of the palace grounds, the weary guards enter through the arched granite entry, bearing their burden of the still-unconscious would-be bandit. They call out the password to the guards, who would recognize their comrades anyway.

The guards were previously a disinterested lot, but seeing the prisoner, they become somewhat more animated. They turn their thoughts away from the relative boredom of their duties and the lack of ability to spend time with their families—or with a good pint of beer and a damsel or two.

"Now there's an interesting gift. Is it for the princess or part of the tithing?"

"Not your business, Grundig. This one's for the jailer, at least till the next Council of the Prince. Attacked a merchant and his daughter as they approached the city. Actually made a hero of the young sire and his friend, who wouldn't let us ward off the bandits and come to their aid. I warrant ye'll hear the detail of it soon enough."

"Is the dauphin with you? I've not seen him enter this portal."

"He's no doubt off in the town with his friend Hans. I'd expect him shortly, but I deemed it safe, within the walls, t' let him have his freedom of movement. He knows that much later arrival'll cause sufficient anxiety in his parents t' consider some punishment. In the nonce, I'll deliver this baggage t' the jailer, then report perso'nally t' our lord."

He rides off to the east entrance of the palace, next to the servants' entry. There a stone staircase, polished from centuries of use, spirals up the interior wall, leading to the foreboding heights of the dungeon. Like most castle dungeons, this one is above ground. It is built of heavy granite quarried from the surrounding mountains. Narrow slit openings serve a double purpose: providing light and sheltering archers who protect the grounds.

With word having passed swiftly from the soldiers to the servants, the jailer himself appears quickly at the entrance, somewhat flushed, to receive his charge. He shoulders him with deceptively relative ease and enters the dungeon tower.

A cold draft of autumn air accompanies the pair as they ascend, partially arousing Peter but not fully awakening him. He moans in his state of semiconsciousness, then falls deeper into obtundation again.

"Ye'll have ample opportunity t' groan 'fore I'm done with ye, bandit. Perhaps the prince'll allow me a little, shall we say, *largesse* t' teach ye a few things—though I admit I'm out of practice. His majesty's a bit soft, I think, when it comes t' corporal punishment, and the chamber upstairs is much too often empty. I should be grateful t' ye, for I much prefer this duty t' those more mundane. Ye'd do best t' be good company. Well, ye cannot hear me in your current state. I'll have t' apprise ye of the rules of behavior later!"

The jailer unceremoniously drops Peter on a palette of straw in the top chamber, which is furnished with a small table and chair, a chamber pot, and sets of chains built into the masonry. The rushes on the floor are stale and clearly have not been swept out or changed for a long time. The jailer fastens a shackle onto Peter's leg, sets the chamber pot nearby after blowing a thick layer of dust out of it, locks the shackle with a key tucked into his belt, replaces the key, and bends over the boy for a closer look.

"Not bad, that bruise—at least not yet. It could be we'll have ourselves quite a bit of 'musement. I'm t' me supper now, boy, I am. Be sure I'll see ye come the morn," he says before heading back down the stairs.

A beam of dying light enters a narrow wall slit and alights upon Peter's face. The sudden warmth wakens him a bit. He is sure he heard someone just a moment ago, something about amusement, but he is not fully aware of himself or his surroundings just yet. Nor does he feel amused. His head is throbbing with pain. Did he fall or sustain some kind of blow? Where? And where is he now?

This place seems dark. He falls into a dreamlike state, the pain forcing him into a relative stupor. Then suddenly a blinding light enters his unconscious mind, as if the lightning and hammer of Thor were reaching for him personally, meaning to punish him for deeds unknown. Has he truly angered the gods?

Flashes of memory swim through his mind, unhindered by the surrounding reality. Playing "Knights of the Round Table" with his oldest brother, Dolph. Wooden swords clash, clanging only in the imagination. Chasing his brother through the squash fields, never quite catching up, until he drops with exhaustion. Now his brother is upon him—not pummeling him, but tickling him mercilessly until Peter begs him to stop.

Fortunately, Mama calls all the children in to supper as the sun sets, though not allowing the boys into her thatched-roof home until they scrub off all the dirt of the field. A bountiful supper with an overabundance of bread, fruit of the harvest, and goat's milk and cheeses.

Another scene—Papa is dying. Fee does all she can to comfort Mama. She cooks the main dinner, gathers herbs from the garden, cleans the house, prepares poultices for her brothers' cuts and bruises, sews clothing for the boys and her sister—all without ever thinking of her own needs. Mama cannot cope without her. Neither can her siblings. Fee wipes away their tears, reminds them of the good times and the bountiful yield of their farm. She comforts them all, but she cannot save Papa.

The farm will go to Dolph. He is Papa's greatest joy, an excellent farmer. But at business, he is hopeless. The others may stay and help or may seek other employment. But none of them can read or write, so options are limited. Yet Mama has taught them how to speak properly, like the bourgeoisie or the nobility, thinking it might help them find apprenticeships later in life.

- Chapter 9 -

Another, later scene: Dolph is avoiding the work on the farm. He has been taken by the curse of wagering. He drinks too much and gambles away all recompense for the produce—even the extra beans and squash. He cannot pay the tithing, so the prince plans to confiscate the land.

Dolph cannot tolerate what his weakness has done to them all. It is Peter who finds their brother in his chamber, poisoned by his own hand. How could he leave his family so utterly destitute?

Middle brother, Jurg, secures a position in the palace of the prince himself. A compassionate man, the prince cannot leave the entire family insolvent after the confiscation of the land. As a kindness to the family, he takes Jurg into his own service, thinking him a potentially good valet and confidant. Both Jurg and Fee have inherited the practicality and kindness of their parents.

Fee enters the household of the local armorer. She knows well how to care for a home, having cared for her own family. And after tending a small garden of herbs and flowers for years, Flor uses her connections to set up a small table in the village marketplace. Ultimately, the business blossoms, and she manages a tent with the finest blooms and herbs available in the principality. She is content in her element.

But what about Peter? His only skill is farming. He is certainly skilled in the growing of squash as well as the tending of goats. None of the surrounding farmers is in need of him, however. Ultimately, he is forced to consider becoming an outlaw. Fee is both outraged and petrified at once. There must be some work for Peter, if not in this principality, then in the next, or the next. But apprenticeship is not to be. Peter gathers his few belongings and heads into the woods. Fee fears he will not survive long, but what can she do?

He sees a few successes in the woods. He joins a band of outlaws, like himself, with some capable of hunting to keep them all alive. Peter's expertise proves to be in strategy, allowing the occasional raid on trading caravans. But didn't one go wrong?

As Peter feels hands upon him, his memory slips back to mock combat with Dolph. Isn't he dead? But this time, his brother does not tickle. He pounds at him and is shouting.

"Wake up, ye mis'rable filth, or ye'll have no supper at all!"

Peter awakens groggily, suffering from the worst headache of his life. Gradually, he realizes the jailer is shaking him bodily.

"I've brought ye some supper, some herbs t' soothe your ills—or at least make ye forget 'em—and a few surprises."

~ Chapter 10 ~

Fee arrives at the Hammer household totally despondent, shoulders drooping, hunched over like an old woman with a cane. *What shall I do?* she asks herself.

She must first see to the evening meal and the needs of the lady, then attempt to leave before the arrival of the master himself. Flor wants these herbs delivered to ease Peter's suffering. And Jurg must know what is happening to poor Peter. She can only hope that Jurg can influence His Majesty to some leniency.

Feeling so helpless is a thought nearly foreign to her. Only twice in the past had she felt this impotent: once with the loss of the farm due to the debt Dolph incurred, and once at a more unthinkable time. No, she will *not* think of it, even now.

At that, she is determined. She has always devoted herself to finding the solution to everyone else's problems in an entirely selfless manner. Her name, Fee, means she is everyone's godmother. Indeed, their mother gave her the name in late childhood, when she observed how her eldest daughter was always the one she could depend upon. Fee will not let her mother down. She promised to watch over the boys, and she will find a way to help Peter.

Poor Peter. Fee knows he would have been an excellent farmer. It was his one joy to watch the squash develop on the vine, especially the gourds. The family would scoop out the flesh, then carve funny, wonderful faces into the shells. But there was no money to buy back their farm or new land, and no other farmer would have Peter. He is not suited for apprenticeship at anything else. Being an outlaw was a desperate move, and even that eludes him! *Yes, I will help him,* she thinks. *I must!*

In this reverie, Fee arrives at the kitchen of the solar still very distraught. She smells the large pot of stew and notes with satisfaction that Besse has made her delivery. She then distracts her own morose thoughts by busying herself in the solar arranging the trestle table. At each setting, she places a knife beside a loaf of day-old bread intended to serve as a bowl. She adds tankards for water or ale. For the master, there is his one favorite wood bowl, as he will not have his stew in a bowl that sops up the gravy. At sight of the bowl, she frowns, hating all reminders of the man, even in his own household.

As she works, she remembers to feed herself with one loaf of bread, then helps herself to a taste of the stew before trudging up the spiral stone staircase to the tower chamber of her lady, Beata. She knocks on the door.

"Enter, Fee. I presume that is you."

Beata is alone, and, as always, is assuaging her boredom by humming to herself and brushing her long golden hair. She seems nervous, evident to Fee in the rapid brush strokes. She is expecting something, but Fee is too preoccupied to care about her lady's thoughts. Before she can depart for the castle, Fee merely wants to ensure both Beata and Besse have an opportunity to eat, preferably before the arrival of the master. She looks about the room, pleased to find nothing in disarray. Thus, her services may not be required long.

She has brought a covered pan of fire embers to serve as a bed warmer, and carefully she places it under the mattress of straw. Taking a broom from the corner of the room, she commences to sweep the old rushes from the floor. Fresh candles are already set in the wall sconces, ready to light after sunset. The chamber pot will need to be emptied, rinsed, and reset, and the servant will need to be sent for fresh rushes. This Fee will do as she leaves.

The lady, of course, does almost nothing for herself. But at least she attends to some of Besse's domestic training, teaching her to weave, sew, and embroider. Yet she does not allow Besse to hire a tutor to learn to read. Does she do this out of love—or pity? More likely, she cares little for Besse's fate, but she knows Fee *does* care and will leave the household if Besse's needs are not met.

Soon Fee will need to broach the subject of Besse's future, perhaps her finding a suitable husband. How about the apprentice? He is likely to be much kinder toward the young girl than is her father.

This is not the time to raise the subject, however. Fee finishes sweeping, raising the collected rushes to the window slit and dropping them to the ground below, outside the city wall in which the home is situated.

"Supper is served, my lady," Fee says deferentially.

Throughout Fee's ministrations, Beata has not stopped brushing her long burnished locks, seeming to ignore Fee's very existence. Now she sighs, starts to arise, then reseats herself. She gestures for Fee to approach more closely.

"What is it, my lady? How may I assist you? You look particularly beautiful this evening, but I must attend to Besse."

Beata, in turn, notes that Fee seems impatient. Beata has the thought that Fee may have other business to attend to, perhaps more personal.

"You seem in such a hurry this evening, Fee. Do not think it escapes my notice how quickly and perfunctorily you perform your chores here. Yet the result is adequate, and I am satisfied. Tell me—how did Besse perform in the market? She is generally an obedient child, but her thoughts seem never to be where they should."

"She did well enough," Fee replies, "though she will require a few more trials with bargaining. I will be sure she accompanies me each day as I—"

"See that you do," Beata interrupts brusquely. "Soon, it will be time to seek a husband for her. It would be in her interest to show some appreciation for the skills taught to her. I fear for her ability to attract the attention of a potential husband. I would feign have her begin paying more attention to her own personal appearance and hygiene. It would otherwise quickly be noticed that she carries more of your ragged, unkempt look than my more refined one. Would that she only had some special, attractive feature."

"Like your hair, madame?"

Fee is blushing. She knows Beata is reminding her of her place. She would argue, but she knows it is a favor of the Hammers to provide her with a position and sustenance. She shudders to think where she would be if she were left in the same position as her brother Peter.

"You have been most generous toward her, madame. I am, of course, grateful for the opportunities you afford us both. Now, may I take my leave? I would have both you and Besse enjoy your supper while it is hot, and, if possible, before the arrival of the master."

Fee shudders as her wandering mind suddenly returns to the thought of Peter.

Beata, unaware of the plight of Fee's brother, mistakes the source of Fee's reaction. "Be careful what you say about my husband, Fee. I am well aware of his nature. Yet he is the sole provider for this household, including its servants, and any malign word is sure to reach his ears. In fact, it is not of Besse that I wish to speak to you."

Beata frowns, darkening her appearance even further than can do the shadows. "The servants are not very good at keeping secrets, Fee. There is always one or more who feel that information—yes, even gossip—is worth a little extra bonus, a few pfennigs. They are not averse to following someone about the city surreptitiously in hopes of a little recompense."

Fee is somewhat taken aback. Beata could not possibly know . . . but she does.

"I know why you are in such a hurry to complete your duties here this evening. I am aware of your little rendezvous with the valet to the Handlers," Beata continues. "But I have continued need of your services, and I am not of the inclination to allow you to leave our employ once Besse is settled. Do not get any foolish ideas, my dear. You know I can prevent their execution. Perhaps you should rethink your plans this evening. Or, if not, remember your place. That is all. You may leave now."

Relief! Fee does not care if anyone knows about her love for the servant Dien. She sighs deeply, turning to leave the chamber. She remembers to remove the chamber pot, taking it with her down the spiral stairway and handing it over to another servant.

"See that you empty it properly, then wash it thoroughly and return it to milady's chamber unobtrusively. She is in a dark mood, and it would do well not to disturb her."

At that, Fee spies Besse hastily downing her stew, looking rather agitated. Her gray surcotte is disheveled, and, as always, she has receded into the darkest corner of the solar. Fee has a fleeting thought of fear for Besse's future, then she sighs again. She has much on her mind this evening, and her need to reach the castle cannot move far from her thoughts.

Yet she must always keep the plight of the young maiden in mind. She manages a weak smile as she addresses Besse. "Oh, my dear, what has happened to you? Did you follow my instruction precisely to return home straightaway? We will have to launder your clothing first thing in the morn! Oh, dear. Your mother would certainly prefer that you exercise the manners of a lady. Soon, she will begin to search you out a suitable husband, and we cannot have you frightening all prospects away! And slow down, please. The master is not in the house, nor has he been spotted anywhere nearby."

Besse exhibits a fleeting look of indignance, then drops her shoulders and pouts. "Oh, Fee. You are the only person in this household truly concerned with my welfare. What is to become of me? I know the importance of what you and Mama teach me, and I am certainly grateful. Yet there is no solace for the likes of me in the world of men! Even today, I was approached in a vile manner as I traveled home. I held off the ill-mannered young brute on my own, and the ladies of the nearby houses scared him off.

"If I am attractive at all, it is merely to the most abusive of men.

I shall be resolved to disdain their company altogether, but I know well that no lady can survive alone without means of support. Should I enter the nunnery or resign myself to becoming a servant in another's household? I would feign not!"

At that, Besse bursts into tears, throws her now-emptied bread bowl onto the trestle table, and runs to Fee. Fee enfolds her with a tear in her own eye. How is she to protect the girl? Once again, she feels utterly inadequate. When will she be relieved of so many burdens? Fee will have to settle for mere consolation tonight, as more pressing matters await her. The shadows lengthen yet again, as if to hide Fee and Besse from the cruelty of the world—or its reality.

"I will do what I can for you, my dear. Have no fear," Fee says. "For now, there is nothing more. I will certainly make inquiry of the young hooligan so that he may bother neither you nor any other maiden again, at least not within the walls of this city. Now dry your tears, sweet. I must be off. Attend upon your mother, and retire to bed. Perhaps the master will be content with another evening away from the house and will leave us all in peace."

Fee gently pushes her charge away and turns with a smile she does not feel internally. She takes a bread, a plum, and her bundle, then takes her leave with yet another sigh.

Fee walks up the streets without a thought toward her surroundings. A few children take advantage of the setting sun, creating new places to conceal themselves in hide-and-seek or pirates-and-soldiers. She ignores them all, although she shivers in the rapidly cooling air and feels a bit of menace from the overhanging houses, now closed and bolted for the night. The air is scented with the smoke of numerous cook fires and bedchamber fires, but little light emerges from the houses. She draws her cloak tighter and hastens to the castle entry.

There she is recognized by the sentries, who let her pass and send word to Jurg of her arrival. In short order, Jurg greets her in the entry courtyard. She clings to him in a hug.

"What is it, Fee?" His voice betrays his anxiety. He is quick to realize the prisoner, recently arrived and brought to the dungeon, must be the reason for her visit.

"It is Peter. He was brought in the custody of the guards right past Flor's tent. He was unconscious, strung across a horse. There can be no mistake. He is in danger, Jurg, though I know not what he has done.

Jurg knows the corporal habits of the jailer, and he represses a shudder of his own.

"He will awaken in pain and confusion," Fee continues as she passes him the bundle Flor provided. "These herbs will soothe him, once made into an infusion. But you must ascertain the nature of his transgression—you must intercede on his behalf, if possible. There is little else I myself can do. Please, Jurg. He does not have the mettle or the cunning of an outlaw, and I fear greatly for his future and his safety."

Fee's voice is shaking. Once, she could do anything to keep the family together, to solve any problem. Now what can she do? She is inadequate to the task set for her in life, but she will not give up.

"Please tell the prince Peter is really a good boy, Jurg. He begs only the opportunity to do what he knows best. He can be a good farmer and enrich the stores of the city, if allowed. Does he really need his own land? Tell them, Jurg, if they helped meet the needs of such men, there would be no outlaws! Tell them. *Tell them*!" Fee bursts into tears.

Jurg enfolds her. "Oh, my sister, my sister. These are indeed dark times for our little family. I do have the ear of the dauphin. I will try. I will try. And I will get word to you as quickly as I can of his condition."

Jurg guides Fee by the shoulders, turning her to leave. "But please, do not wait here in the meantime. This is not the safest place for a woman alone. Go home. I will approach the dungeon at once and see to the fair treatment of our wayward brother. That much I can do. Thank Flor for the herbs. She understands we must always stand ready to help each other. I will not fail you, Fee. Nor Flor. Now take your leave."

Fee controls her sobbing, pulls her cloak even tighter, then turns back to Jurg. "I almost forgot! There is also a young miscreant who assaulted Besse this day. He must be caught. You will have the appreciation of the lady Beata, as well as mine."

With that, she departs the compound, remembering to thank the sentry for allowing her entry. She turns not toward home but to the house of Artur Handler. She will need some consoling this evening and will not find it in the Hammer household.

Jurg approaches the entry to the dungeon. Behind him he hears the arrival of the dauphin with his friend Hans. They have escorted another prisoner, whom they loudly turn over to the sentries, then Hans takes his leave. Jurg wonders if it is the young miscreant, but he has no time to satisfy curiosity. He hurries up the stairs to the dungeon, fearing what he will find there.

~ Chapter 11 ~

Peter slowly brings himself to focus upon the bearded face of the jailer. He sees a giant of a man, clearly quite strong. His breath betrays his strong attraction to beer. He is dressed very plainly in a tunic of rough wool and a rope belt with a pouch and keys suspended from it. A large sardonic smile reveals a lack of more than a few teeth.

A sudden realization of his position dawns upon Peter's throbbing head. He already begins to feel fear and loathing for the man while he attempts to calculate how to outsmart him and obtain those keys. Before him the jailer has set a large tray, upon which are a loaf of bread, a wooden bowl with a small quantity of some kind of stew, a few herbs—but also a leather lash and a small device with a screw of curious but indeterminate use.

"Allow me t' acquaint ye with these various items, boy. As ye've undoubtedly surmised, ye're now subject t' the hospitality of the jailer of the palace." He bows with a smirk, then laughs. "This is a duty served humbly t' the prince by meself. I have the good fortune t' advise His Majesty regardin' the behavior and quality of his unwillin' guests."

Here, he chuckles a bit. "So, it'd be best for ye t' consider how t' fall into me own good graces. Pleasin' us bothed certainly help t' mitigate any punishment he may deem t' mete. Ye see before ye the means t' that end, as well as the fruits of me generosity. Let it not be said that the jailer'd deprive ye of sustenance or healin'. No, he won't. The supper's for ye and is from the kitchen of the prince himself, it is. The herbs are t' help ye heal from the blows ye've earlier sustained. There's meadowsweet, which'll ease the pain of a headache or bruised bones, and opium t' help ye forget. These're yours in exchange for your coop'ration, they are. Failin' that," he said, pointing at the lash and strange device, "these other items are equally useful in obtainin' it. So, ye'll first eat and quench your thirst, then we'll have a little discussion. I'm eager t' hear your story, I am."

"Thank you, sir."

Peter chooses not to think about his quandary for the moment and eagerly devours the stew and bread under the watchful eye of the jailer, who nods contentedly.

"May I request some water to slake my thirst? It would help me remember the events leading up to my arrival here."

He reaches for the meadowsweet, unsure whether to trust this man. And he is right. The jailer lifts the lash and brings it down firmly upon his hand.

"That ye'll have t' earn, boy. Besides, we'll have t' make an infusion of it. Tell me of your plight." The jailer leans toward Peter threateningly, reminding him of a bear about to pounce upon its prey.

Peter cringes, sighing. "I am but a poor farmer's son, sir. My father died, leaving the farm to my brother, who managed to gamble it away. We were expert at raising gourds, the like not available from any other farm—"

"Enough!" bellowed the jailer. "I'm not int'rested in your childhood! It's clear ye had t' leave the farm. What crime could ye have committed t' end up an outlaw? I've ne'er seen ye in this dungeon 'fore, and I've been here these many years. Ye'll tell me now!"

"No crime, sir, other than to be poor and illiterate and unable to apprentice myself or hire out to another peasant. So, I come to an ill fate for which I am even more ill-suited, else I would not be here." Peter is almost whimpering at this point. "Thus, I find myself at the mercy of you and our good lord."

"I presume ye mean the prince. He'll have his turn in due time, he will. But now it's mine. Let me look ye over. Ye could use a bath. I'll send me own 'prentice out for some hot water and a linen. There's a price t' pay for 'ssaultin' our good citizens, and it's time for me t' begin t' extract it. Lean against the table, here."

- Chapter 11 -

The jailer, somewhat drunk, raises his lash, and Peter's eyes go wide. He prays to himself silently, but he has little energy to resist. As he extends his hand in a futile effort to hold the man off, his head pounds with pain, and he nearly faints. But then he is sure he hears the noise of someone climbing the stairway below. Yes, he hears footsteps getting closer. The door bursts open.

"Jailer! Stop!"

It is Jurg, his eyes suddenly widening and his face suddenly pale.

"Peter! Leave him alone, jailer, or I shall surely go directly to my master, and he will not take kindly to the news I bear." Jurg is nearly breathless.

"What's he t' ye, Jurg? He's just a common criminal, he is! He's my charge, not yours!"

Jurg stomps his foot indignantly, his face reddening with anger. He shouts, "He is my brother! You will treat him with respect, or I will see to it that your circumstances are no better than his!"

His shoulders now drooping with concern, he turns to face his brother. "Peter, are you all right? I have brought you some Achillea and the bark of a willow to chew to ease your pain. Fortunately for you, Fee and Flor saw you in passing. Flor provided these, and Fee brought them to me. As always, we remain indebted to the good graces of our sisters."

Peter is relieved, but still too groggy to show it. "Oh, Jurg! Thank the good Lord you are here!"

Jurg shakes his head. "Is it true—you attempted to kidnap the daughter of a merchant outside the city? What have you come to, my wayward brother? Could you find no better means to employ yourself?"

"I beg you to recommend me to the mercy of the prince," Peter says, "for I am a victim of my own circumstance. I cannot find any other employ, and what am I to do for sustenance? I would be willing to do any work, however menial, rather than this! What is to become of me?"

"Fortunately for you, the prince is not inclined to capital punishment. But I shudder to think what he will decide. Oh, Peter. I will try to intercede for you any way I can. But you must inform me of the exact circumstances. And do not be afraid to relay to me the behavior of our *good* jailer here. I do have *some* influence."

"Thank you, Jurg, and bless Fee and Flor for me. I am too much in pain and too muddled to think how to repay you at the moment. But I would not have you put yourself at risk merely to mitigate my own punishment."

"Fear not, brother. There must be some accommodation possible. Here, chew this bark, and try to be at least somewhat comforted."

Jurg does not feel at all comforted himself. He knows he has to convince the prince that it would be of little use to punish Peter. He must be convinced that the boy is capable of *something* useful to the principality. But what? What about Fee's idea of Peter farming?

His thoughts are interrupted by the arrival of the guards with the young miscreant Jacques, remanded to the jailer by Hans and the dauphin.

~ Chapter 12 ~

Hans takes his leave of the dauphin, takes a deep breath of the crisp autumn air, and steps outside the castle grounds. He has always wanted some adventure in his young life, and now he has quite the story to tell!

He holds his head high and hums an old, familiar tune as he passes the shuttered houses of the burghers' quarter, still appealingly cheerful despite the afterglow of the now-set sun. Although the houses lean over the street, this cobbled road is wider than the usually narrow streets of the city. The wider road allows passage for wagons of goods as well as horsemen and pedestrians. Houses here are in excellent repair, with wood and stucco fronts and stone masonry built to last centuries. This is the wealthiest part of town, save perhaps the Jewish quarter. No one knows the hidden wealth of that area, whose citizens prefer not to proffer displays of arrogance for fear of incurring the wrath of their neighbors, most of whom are unafraid to express their prejudices.

But Hans takes no notice of any of this. Like all young denizens of the city, he takes his surroundings for granted. At the moment, his mind is full of the events of the day. He misses the approving glances of the burghers, not to mention the longing in the faces of the young maidens, as they gaze through open windows and note his passage. If he had stopped to think, he would have been somewhat surprised to find these good people on the ground level of their abodes, generally reserved for the storage and display of their wares. Normally, they would be gathered in the solars upstairs or in their chambers going about the evening's chores or discussions.

At home, he is greeted by his parents, Gute and Artur, and his sister, Greta. The elder Handlers are beaming with pride, and Hans knows they have heard of his earlier events. Greta's countenance betrays only concern. She has inherited not only her mother's rosy complexion but also her compassion and sense of practicality. She worries about her brother's tendency to insert himself into dangerous situations, and she is not afraid to offer her own remonstrance.

"Heroes die young, my Hansl," she rebukes, using the affectionate diminutive of his name as she wags a finger at him. "Papa counts on you to continue the family name and tradition, and he needs you to be intelligent and levelheaded. I would be prouder of you alive and well."

"*Tsh*, Gretl," he retorts, also with affection and a wink of the eye. "I have but little time for frivolities, as I know my duty well. I take only calculated risks. Charles—I mean, the dauphin—and I are well trained and were in no danger from the likes of those young lads, especially with the element of surprise. We did not seek out the opportunity. It merely presented itself, and there we were!"

Unimpressed, Greta responds with a frown. "You and the dauphin's guards, who should have known better than to allow you to put yourselves in such danger. I imagine the soldiers will be headed for an upbraiding of their own! And that is not also to mention the young thief you two apprehended and brought to the palace—"

"You were following me again!" Hans interrupts excitedly. "You must stop that, Gretl. I am quite capable of handling myself. If it makes you happier, I shall not seek out my fortune like Sir Lancelot, though I be the son of Artur himself!"

Now indignant, Greta stomps her foot and wags her finger yet again. "You would not make a good martyr, Hansl. And if you must know, I only shadowed you inside the gate of the city." She sighs, then shrugs and smiles, relenting. "Now come enjoy a bite of supper. You can recount your adventures to us all. I promise to be a rapt listener, if only you forego the exaggeration. But you cannot stop me from watching over your safety nor admonishing you when appropriate, as Papa seems unlikely to do so."

- Chapter 12 -

"Enough, Gretl," says Artur. "Now it is you who are in need of some discipline. It is time Hans joins me as an apprentice in the trade; I am decided. He has been well schooled, and his training in the glade will serve him well if ever threatened in the caravan." He softens his stern countenance with a laugh. "What think you, Gute? Is it time for our boy to grow into a man?"

"You have already missed that, Artur, if you need to ask," she replies. "But I do agree. Let's to the hall for a bite and a story, then we shall make our plans . . . for all of us. Life passes all too quickly and requires some planning and anticipation. I fear our Hansl will be the center of attention of the town, and we will be besieged with the entreaties of the parents of every eligible maiden in the city. I also fear the children in the streets will exaggerate the adventures of our son, who needs no boost to his self-image!"

Hans blushes at that, and Greta cannot suppress a smile. Yes, she is indeed the image of her mother.

The family retreats through the display room to the stairs leading up to the hall. Furs, salt, gems, and fabrics, plus forged tools and other implements have been secured in heavy chests, bolted and locked, along the walls. The floor has been swept clean of straw and rushes, then scrubbed to a sheen.

Hans still takes no note, as his thoughts are now upon Ebouisante and the events to come. He will, of course, attend the prince's council, as he may be called as a witness. That will not be for a few days, however. He will spend this time helping his parents with the trade, perhaps planning a caravan of his own under the protection of the Hanse.

It is good to have membership in the Hanse, a loose collection of northern cities that have newly defeated the king of Sweden. It offers protection to its merchants. However, the rising tide of nationalism in Russia, England, and other lands may overshadow the loose association. The Hanse has never been able to consolidate governance to the point where it can force these much stronger countries to allow footholds for trade. The future will indeed require some new alliances and planning. Here is yet another opportunity for adventure!

Hans turns his attention back to the dinner conversation just in time for his mother to address him.

"Yes, your father and I think it is time, Hans, for you to join the trade. You may wish to continue your training with Prince Charles, but the days of general schooling are past. The days of apprenticeship have arrived." She eyes him sternly. "Moreover, it is time more formally to meet the eligible young maidens of the city. Most of them have cast an eye upon you, though I have no doubt your head is so full of future adventures that you have failed to notice."

Greta chimes in, "You must know, Hans, that Mama is not exaggerating. The girls do talk, and you have become the center of conversation more often than not. Continually, I must politely rebuff all entreaties to influence our good parents on maidens' behalf. It is getting more and more difficult and more tiresome. Now, with the events of today, it will be wholly impossible!" She crosses her arms. "Please be considerate of our needs. Bring your head out of the clouds, out of the world of dragons and knights and damsels in distress, so you can begin to learn how to take up more mundane responsibilities."

"Well, Gretl, I wonder if your thoughts do not wander toward some potential beau of your own. Would you not want to have some influence upon Mama and Papa?" Hans teases in hopes of a change of attention away from himself.

"Enough!" bellows Artur. "Your mother is right. Hans, you will join us in the showroom tomorrow, and I will begin to show you how to keep the accounts. We must soon plan a caravan, and I will have you fit and ready."

Hans suppresses his smile at this remonstrance, lowering his eyes as Artur turns to his wife. "To that end, are we prepared, Gute, for our annual feast? We can invite families with eligible maidens as well as take orders for our suppliers."

"Precisely my thoughts, Artur. I think I will seek the services of a storyteller to entertain the guests. What do you think? Or better yet, we can do a complete traditional Michaelmas celebration, in the English manner, with mummers to perform the tale of Saint George!"

Hans, suddenly more animated, seizes the opportunity. "Mama, I have an idea. Perhaps we could have the merchants discuss the future of the Hanse at the celebration, with the goal of creating alliances for better business. Those with daughters can bring them, and we could meet them all. Oh! Perhaps we should invite the Kaufmanns as well and introduce them to the community of burghers! They could bring Ebouisante. I would like you to meet her—I mean, *them*."

Artur laughs. "You are entirely too transparent, Hans. But your idea is certainly not without merit." His smile turns serious though still kind. "And please keep in mind that the decision for the proper matches for both you and Gretl lies with Mother and myself. We will always have your best interests in mind. Fear not."

He claps, and the smile returns. "There. It is done. We need only determine the necessary supplies and set a date. Michaelmas, if I am not mistaken, is the celebration of the harvest. We should plan for the first colors on the trees, do you not agree?" he muses aloud.

Gute nods enthusiastically.

Artur then turns to his son. "Now, tell us of your exploits of the day. We will promise to be attentive, doting upon you thoroughly and heaping lots of praise upon your head so it may swell too large for your pillow tonight."

It is now Gute's turn to laugh. "That is quite enough, Artur. Hans, tell us of your day's encounters. We are as eager as the rest of the town to hear them."

~ Chapter 13 ~

Having delivered his charge to the jailer, Charles heads through the bailey to the main castle entry. Chickens, goats, and pigs create a cacophony around him as their stewards round them up for the evening. The castle is home to over three hundred servants, garrison soldiers, farmers, herders, blacksmiths, coopers, and other skilled workers—many of whom bow before Charles as he passes, begging his pardon for their clumsiness in allowing such animals in the way of his path.

He takes no notice, other than a little surprise that, having heard of his exploits of the day, they do not regard him with any more pride or deference than is their wont. His own head is full of himself, to be honest. But under the circumstances, he does not consider it arrogance, as long as he is not boastful about it. Come to think of it, does this not merely prove the usefulness of his training with the soldiers?

There is much to think on this eventful day, and he will want time to sort it out with his parents. Charles sighs. There will not be enough time this evening. At least supper awaits, and he finds himself quite famished after a day of great activity.

As Charles enters the castle, still distracted, he nearly trips over the valet Jurg. Jurg seems somewhat distracted as well and a bit distraught. Why would he be here, at the portcullis, when his duties would likely call him elsewhere?

"A thousand pardons, my lord," he says with a deep bow. "We are all quite excited to hear of your great exploits. All the servants are proud to hail you as our own nobleman, and we are sure you have made His Majesty proud this day."

"One would think quite the opposite, Jurg, as you are the first to grant me such a reception," Charles replies. "Yet I thank you for your felicitation. I am sure I am expected at supper as quickly as I can wash and exchange these rags for more appropriate accouterments. Perhaps you can oblige me by offering some assistance in that regard."

"With pleasure, sire. I have, in fact, this day been assigned by His Majesty to your own service. I will not dissemble to say I shall miss the opportunity to continue in his own service, yet it gladdens my heart to be of use to you. I am at your command."

Charles is taken aback a moment, then realizes Jurg's reassignment is intended as a message from the prince. It is meant to instill the dauphin with a sense of maturity and responsibility, while affirming parental love. He grins, knowing a particular response is required.

"That explains well your immediate attendance upon me as I arrive home. You may report to His Majesty that I understand and am appreciative."

Jurg says nothing about how the dauphin realizes his father will expect regular reports of his actions and speech. It troubles Jurg to be expected to spy on his young charge, but such is burden of serving royalty. It is all he can do to shrug.

Charles eyes him. "Yet I sense there is something more, as you are not your usual, jovial self. Speak to me as you accompany me to my chamber, as I would know what is in your heart. Even a young dauphin is the servant of his people, and one must start with one's closest subjects. I am sure there is something I can do to gladden your heart in my service. Speak always freely with me."

Jurg carefully chooses his words. "It does not escape me, sire, that you are offering a hand of kindness to this poor, wretched soul. I promise to serve you well. I can certainly keep you informed of the temper of the community, as my family is well positioned in its midst, though I would never be so arrogant as to offer advice. Yet I like your temperament to serve in the interest to lead. Happy is the lord whose subjects are kept most content. Your father has always followed this path, and the citizens adore him, as you well can surmise. Kindness begets kindness, as favors beget favors. Perhaps, moreover, wisdom is the ability to turn an adverse situation to one's favor."

Charles laughs. "Here you offer me both homilies and advice, Jurg, before you have even begun to serve. What favor can I grant you? Be forthright. You need not be so formal with me in private. I would sooner have you as a friend, even a confidant, as long as what is said between us remains absolutely private."

Jurg wonders if he means to ask for loyalty above that to his father, an impossible request. Setting the thought aside, he sighs. "My lord," he says, "I will state it flat outright. The would-be thief you hold in the tower is my wayward brother, Peter. A most incompetent thief—forced into the role by the lack of available land or employment. He is too proud to beg, yet I am not too proud to beg on his behalf. He will face the judgment of your father and will be found wanting, through the fault of ill circumstance. Mostly, I must blame my older brother, who gambled away the family farm before taking his own life and casting us all out to find our way in the world. What am I to do? My sister, Fee, has always seen to the welfare of the family, but she finds herself incapable in this situation. But none of us can support Peter. If only he could farm again—he is the best squash farmer in northern Europe! What is to become of him?"

Charles takes on a stern look, unconsciously imitating one he has seen many times upon the prince when addressing the dauphin's own behavior, but he decides to answer in a less imperious voice, indicating some compassion.

"It is not the practice of His Highness to invoke capital punishment, as it does not seem to act as any sort of deterrent. But you must know the acts of highwaymen cannot be left unpunished. I will think upon it. Now if you will please accompany me to my chamber through the kitchens, I would be most obliged. I would not present myself to our lord and his guests in my current condition."

"With pleasure, my lord."

Jurg hopes he has planted the seed of a solution in the young prince's mind. He must not seem too forward, however, and the solution must ultimately come directly from Charles to the prince, as it would not be accepted directly from a valet. Has he said just enough? Time will tell.

The two make an interesting sight as they pass the boiling kettle in the large fireplace, stopping only briefly to inhale the aroma of the fish stew. Fresh trout have been brought in from the river below the castle, mixed with fresh vegetables from the royal garden within the bailey of the castle.

Charles finds the aroma quite savory, in sharp contrast to his own at the moment. The scullery maids bow in deference but giggle—it is nearly impossible to tell the nobleman from the servant.

Charles decides he will wash again before dressing. Jurg can lay out appropriate clothing as Charles freshens himself. And yes, perhaps a small quantity of cologne. It will all have to be done quickly, so as not to test the patience of his parents.

As he walks briskly, he thinks it would do well to provide a favor for his new valet, as Jurg has been of excellent service to the prince. A favor would draw Jurg closer in loyalty, which could be very useful. Yet the boy, Peter, must be punished, and that is the more important. *We shall see*, Charles thinks to himself.

The royal family's chambers are behind the great hall. Fortunately, there is access from the private council room behind the hall, with a connection to the kitchen, so servants can deliver meals to the prince as he works. Charles takes no notice of the central table, but warms his hands at the fireplace before entering his own chamber.

Jurg follows closely behind, quietly but deeply in thoughts of his own. He goes immediately to the washbasin, fills it from the pitcher, and lays out a linen towel for Charles.

Charles laughs. "You read my thoughts. I would prefer to appear as pleasurable company rather than an animal in the woods."

Although his heart is heavy with the plight of his younger brother, Jurg puts on a lighthearted countenance for Charles's benefit. Jurg has been in the household since Charles was a small boy, and he feels free to tease the dauphin a bit.

"Well, sire, given the choice of a clean tunic or antlers, I feel it does not take much to divine which would appeal to His Highness and his guests more. But if you wish, the antlers are on the wall, still attached to the head of their original owner. Perhaps you desire that I request an opportunity to borrow them briefly?"

In the darkening light of the room, the oil torches cast flickering shadows upon the deer head, which almost could be described as threatening.

"The buck, however," Jurg adds, "seems to be looking upon us with some disapproval."

Charles laughs again as he removes his clothing, totally unabashed in Jurg's presence. He has become muscular, but his youth prevents any comparison to the appearance of the captain of the guard, whom he admires. Jurg hands him his tights, a silk shirt without cuffs, a vest, and a blue tunic. Charles dons them all, as well as a belt for his short sword, after thoroughly drying himself.

Jurg gathers Charles's sweat-drenched training garments. "I will have this all cleaned for the morrow, sire, and will have your bed warmed with coals upon your return. Now off with you to the company of Their Majesties."

Jurg tries to keep a positive tone but cannot avoid an undertone of sadness. The dauphin understands but will not allow this mood to affect his own buoyant one.

Charles enters the hall, noting the open seat reserved for him next to his father. The maids are bringing in bowls of fruit and stew along with steins of ale for the guests. They serve the prince and princess first, then Charles.

"There you are, son! Welcome home! I dare say you have had quite the day!"

The prince gives his son a look of warm approval, and an idea occurs to the dauphin.

"Thank you, my lord. I must say, I first thought my events went unnoticed in the household, as I have yet to be accosted in their regard. But word spreads too quickly for that. Now, rather, I realize you have given instructions of behavior to the servants as a lesson in humility for me. Fear not that I will swell with too much pride. What I have done is merely duty, utilizing the skills you instilled in me via my tutors in the martial arts."

"He is too astute, my lord," interrupts Princess Amalia.

Henrik gives his wife a nod and an affectionate smile.

He claps his hands, and musicians enter the hall, softly offering folk tunes on the lyre and clarinet. The atmosphere of the hall—alight with torches, warm with tapestries on the walls and rushes on the floor, filled with savory odors and soothing music—was as congenial as one could ask.

He laughs. "And now, son, it is time to hear the story of your adventures, no doubt worthy of a retelling by Chrétien de Troyes himself!"

~ Chapter 14 ~

A despondent figure wends her way through the shadowed streets of the old city. With her hunched, dark, and diminutive stature, she is nearly folded upon herself, as if to hide from the world or at least to shrink from it. She withdraws into her own morosity, lost in her own thoughts.

Having delivered her burden to her brother at the castle, she delves into the depth of her spirit, centering upon the spark of love that is her center, warming her body and soul despite the chill of the evening. She sighs, lifts her head, and redevelops purpose as she traverses the burgher's quarter.

How fortunate is she to have the love of her family. She feels she is not worthy of them. She cannot be of enough help to them, yet they shower her with their trust. And Dien—her godsend and her rock. He forgives her anything and everything and refuses to see the plainness in her visage. She believes there is little he could possibly desire in her, yet there he is, constant and interested in no other. *The Lord is truly kind to me, and I am grateful,* she thinks. *There. I feel so much better.* But the deep stoop in her shoulders says otherwise.

Her reverie has brought her to the doorstep of the Handlers, where she taps tentatively upon the door, signaling her arrival to Dien. He opens the portal presently, takes one look at his beloved, and envelops her with open arms, planting a gentle kiss upon her forehead.

Dien shakes his head. "You're disturbed, me beloved," he says softly. "Ye must allow me t' calm ye, t' cheer ye, for I have good news. I would have ye always content in me arms, and I ask for nothin' more in this life. Grant me a kiss, and we shall brighten each other's presence."

~ Chapter 14 ~

Fee is loath to forbear and, truthfully, has come for just such assuaging. She returns the kiss with eager passion, finally collapsing into Dien's welcome embrace. Only then does she allow herself to take a deep, staccato breath—prelude to a wail.

Dien leads her through the display hall, fleetingly noting how the covered furs and other valuable goods reflect the true nature of his beloved—herself a treasure cloaked in humble garb. He is truly in love.

"Come, me love, and ye'll share with me the nature of your sorrows. Then I'll cheer ye with the best of tidin's, and ye'll feel released from all sorrow and concern."

They climb the stairway to the relatively bare chambers of the servants. The torches are alight in his own room, signaling his expectation of Fee's arrival. She wonders always how he knows to anticipate her, as she is not wont to come every evening, nor is she able.

Her thoughts too alight upon the possibility that Hans has told his story, and Dien has surmised the prisoner's identity. Could Dien's good tidings be of benefit to Peter? It is too much to hope. She is too tired to hope for anything more than the solace of Dien's embrace, his understanding, his love.

The torches reveal Dien to be a plain man of average stature but muscular build, dressed in a plain gray tunic and loose leggings. No matter. To Fee, he is the handsomest figure of a man she has ever encountered. Love enhances all images.

"Sit, liebchen, and relieve yourself of your burden. I'd hear what it is that troubles ye so, so that I may lift it and disperse it into the wind. I shall raise your spirit t' the highest level, as ye never fail t' lift mine."

"You wax poetic, love," she replies tentatively. "But I desire only a kiss and a little solace before I return to the needs of my mistress and my Besse. Bear with me but for a short time, and I will be on my way."

"That I will not do. It's time for ye t' share all with me, after which I'll in turn share with ye the best of news, and ye'll go home in light spirit."

Fee can tell Dien is serious about his news and will not back down. She is eager to hear these tidings, if only they would bear upon the welfare of her brother. But first, she must tell him her own tidings, which are not so glad.

"This you know, love: we were once the happiest of families, farmers under the grace of His Majesty. But now . . ." She hesitates, shaking her head.

"Go on—tell me more, liebchen." He wants to keep her talking, perhaps to ease her disquiet—or perhaps to create a more appropriate mood for his own revelation later. Besides, he enjoys the opportunity to hold her and comfort her; he won't deny it.

"But, dearest," she says, "my family is *my* burden, *my* joy. You have no need to worry about them." She pulls her cloak tighter.

"Ye have no need of that here. Let me take it." He helps her remove her cloak, then hugs her closer, wanting to share her personal space, wanting to prevent her from withdrawing further into herself. "Take your warmth from the fire. Take it from me."

To her surprise, Fee does feel some comfort—even some security—in his embrace.

She thinks, *Could it be I truly love this man?* Only he brings her solace when she most needs it. She begins to realize that to share one's woes and joys is to make life all the more bearable.

Feeling free to let go, she cries out, startling Dien. "It is Peter!"

Dien wraps her in his arms more tightly. "There, ye mustn't cry so. Let me know what disturbs ye, and I'll endeavor t' banish it entirely. I cannot bear t' see ye in such a state!"

"It is not fortune but misfortune that Peter has found!" Fee breaks down again, this time virtually inconsolably.

"What is it, Fee? What has become of him? How can I help ye? How can I help him? Tell me, tell me. I cannot bear t' see ye in such a state, I cannot!"

Dien is frantic. This is not how he wants this evening to go. The fire seems to cast nothing but dark shadows across the chamber. Dien knows he must get Fee to speak again, to relieve herself of what she cannot bear.

"Where were ye this evenin', liebchen? Tell me. I'm here for ye, now and always."

With the searching look in Dien's eyes, Fee realizes her lover's good news cannot relate to Peter. He does not know of her brother's woes. Now she doubts any news would bring her cheer this evening. She gathers her wits, sighs, and folds herself even deeper into Dien's willing arms.

"I have just departed from the castle, having delivered some herbs and solace to Jurg. Lord be willing, may Jurg have some influence upon the mercy of His Majesty on behalf of our brother."

Realization suddenly comes upon Dien. "Oh, no! Do not tell me Peter was the bandit Hans and the dauphin subdued this afternoon. That means he's in the clutches of that ill-mannered jailer, he is!"

Dien knows the man's reputation and shudders momentarily to think of Peter's fate in his hands. This disturbs Fee, who begins to sob again.

"No, dearest," Dien continues, rubbing his lover's back gently. "Do not fret. The prince is a man of fair judgment and compassion, and I'm sure he'll take pity on such a hapless soul. I'll talk t' Hans meself, I will. He shall appear as witness. I'll beg him t' ask for mercy for your brother." He draws her nearer still. "Here, here. Let me console ye."

Fee's emotional energy is spent, yet she warms to the touch of her lover. The two hug, then kiss, then kiss again. Finally, they let the embrace lead to other actions, indulged without guilt, much to Fee's surprise. Satisfied by the fire of their own devotion and warmed by the fire in the hearth, they ultimately rest in each other's arms.

Dien feels he can now reveal his news to Fee. "Me love, me one and only," he whispers into her ear. "I cannot exist without ye. I must tell ye, I must: I've entreated me master Artur t' insist in havin' ye join this household, which'll be only in your best interest. Ye're more deservin' of a happier life than ye'll allow, ye are—a life ye'll not achieve in the Hammer household. He's frugal t' the point of becomin' a miser. He pays ye ill, he does, and treats ye and his charges e'en more ill. Master Artur is pleased t' be of like mind t' me own, and would welcome ye here t' serve the mistress. Please say ye'll consent."

Fee sits bolt upright in alarm. This is not the reaction Dien expected.

"No!" she exclaims. "I do love you, dearest, but I cannot leave my mistress alone! She does naught for herself. And to leave her and Besse at the mercy of that . . . that drunkard! You know not what he is capable of doing, and there is no one but myself to intervene, no matter how poorly. I will come to you at will, Dien, but I cannot leave that household."

She places a hand on Dien's crestfallen face. "I am loath to contradict you, as nothing could make me happier than to spend a lifetime in your arms. But it cannot be done, love."

"But know that it *is* done, it is," he says. "Hans accomp'nied me t' the priest and has posted the banns for us 'pon the church door." He smiles at her lovingly. "I'm askin' for your hand in marriage, I am. I've no gift of betrothal, other than t' promise t' influence young Hans on the behest of your brother, liebchen. "

"Oh, Dien! What have you done?" Fee is now the frantic one, gathering her clothing. "Word will get to my mistress, and she will be furious. Then the master himself will be even more furious. May God save us all! I must be off." She looks back at him before rushing out the door. "Oh, what have you done?"

"Fee, wait! It's done, and I *will* protect ye! I'll love ye! We'll have a long and happy life together!" Dien calls out into the empty air.

This was to be a joyful occasion. How could Fee not see the need to leave that household and enter a happier one—one with her one true love in legal bonds of matrimony? He does not understand, but he will prevail upon the Handlers to influence the prince's council. Anything to help his love, even if it may be inadequate to convince her. Somehow, Fee will have to see her own need.

This is not a selfish impulse. Dien firmly believes their match is made in heaven, and he hopes Fee will see it herself in time. He does not, cannot, know Fee has deeper reasons not to leave the Hammer household. But he will not allow Master Dunkel to interfere with the one chance of happiness in Fee's life.

No, Dien will not ask the priest to take down the banns.

~ Chapter 15 ~

A moment of peace is a welcome relief. The jailer is gone, and Peter begins to feel relief from the Achillea and willow bark.

The shadows are lengthening, but he can make out the limbs of pine and spruce trees allowed to grow close to the windows. They fill him with ideas of freedom. Little good it does him and his cellmate, at any rate. They are chained to the wall, and it would be easy enough for the guard to catch them if they even tried to escape.

Ravenously hungry, Peter almost shovels the stew into his mouth, feeling little remorse for not sharing his meager fare with his mate.

Jacques, the young thief, just smiles as he looks at their surroundings.

"I fail to see the humor in our situation, sir," Peter says. "We are certain to face but little mercy from His Highness—and even worse from the jailer."

"I've faced worse in me life," Jacques replies. "Me major concern is for the welfare of me poor mum. She must rely on me, and I've failed her, I have. I care not for the concerns of the jailer. I warrant I'll handle that problem when it presents itself."

Peter relents a bit. This one is an arrogant sort. "Pray tell the motive behind your smile. I wonder if you have a plan in mind."

"Actually, no, not yet. However, I'm smilin' at the proxim'ty of those trees. I must remember that, I must." Jacques now gives a cunning smirk of some hidden knowledge. "Yet I'll be 'bliged t' share with ye me story in exchange for your kindness in sharin' your meal. I note the jailer made no 'rangement of similar kind for meself!"

~ Chapter 15 ~

Peter shrugs and agrees to share his stew, despite his own hunger. He hopes this lad will offer a good story—a distraction that might alleviate Peter's anxiety.

"Perhaps our good host has some other means of coercion in mind for you," Peter says. "I doubt this generous meal was provided for me out of any sense of compassion."

Jacques nods. "That's for sure! But I'll give ye enough of a tale of woe t' make your own tale seem petty. See if I don' earn me meal withal, for me Mum and I've seen naught but the hardest side of life in these so-called chiv'rous times, we have."

Peter moves closer so Jacques can reach the stew as well. The two must dig the morsels out of the bread bowl with their fingers.

"Ye must know we're not of these parts," Jacques begins. He lights up a bit with the telling, almost as if he were a dandy with an affected swagger. His manner can captivate an audience, and Peter is no exception, captive as he already is.

"Actually, we lived in Burgundy, we did, workin' the fields of some vassal of the great duke just now takin' his leave of this principality. He's a mean one, that duke." There is not even a trace of deference in Jacques's voice as he impugns the aristocrat. "I wot that ye know little of him yeself, not havin' the *opportunity*"—with a grand gesture—" t' make his lordship's *'quaintance.* Well, I have. That is, I and me mum."

He stops to scoop another bite, staring at Peter and searching for interest in his eyes. Peter says nothing. Instead, he continues to eat, preventing Jacques from taking the entire meal for himself. Somehow, Peter is sure the boy would, given half the chance.

Jacques continues, oblivious to any judgment Peter may impose upon his character, silently or otherwise, but eager to prove his the greater suffering. "Now me mum, she was a very pretty maid in her day. The boys always looked for her, they did. But even when I was little, they knew better than t' have t' deal with *me.* And deal with me they would if they bothered her too much. Not that I could do them any *physical* harm, but little boys do know how t' make a great nuisance of themselves, if ye un'erstand me. So's it weren't worth the bother t' pursue her. And no one did, for a few years. Yet there was one man who did, and it was one I could dare do nothin' about. I'm speaking of the self-same duke himself. Yes, I mean his *lordship* has an eye for the ladies, that one has. And who's t' deny him? He's the law, itself, he is.

"So, he takes an *interest* in me mum, no doubt seein' her bent o'er her labor in the fields. I'm nowhere near, still bein' too young for that sort of work at the time. And he accosts her, and she blushes, but she can hardly say no t' *him*. I don' like t' think of it, but she comes home all in tears and disheveled. A mess. I ask her who did it, and she won't say, she won't. But I know none of the peasants would do it, not without me findin' out. So I knew it had t' be some knight or squire. And that's not the only time she come home in that state. So I beg her t' tell me after a time, as I mean t' make it stop. She won' say, and she won' say. But finally I catch him after her, I did. The duke himself!"

Peter does feel some pity for the boy's mother, but he finds it difficult to know how much of this story to believe. Jacques pauses, expecting Peter to encourage him to continue, but Peter only continues to eat silently.

Eventually, Jacques shrugs.

"Seeing him with her, I forget meself. I'm really angry. I run up, kick dirt at him, and tell him t' get off me mum or marry her. I knew, of course, that there was already a duchess in the palace. So I say, 'What would Her Highness think if she finds out?'"

Jacques puffs out his chest. "'You impudent whelp!' says the duke, all red as a beet. 'I'll do as I please, and ye'll abide your place. Run off, and be sure I ne'er come across your path again, or I'll have ye properly whipped for your insolence!' But I says, 'Leave me mum alone, and I'll be out of your path fore'er, sire. Be sure of it,' says I."

There is a fire in Jacques's eyes now. He is deep into himself, allowing his anger to color his speech. Peter realizes this part of his story is certainly the truth.

"No doubt he's now down at the inn, enjoyin' his fav'rite pursuit with one of the servin' wenches," Jacques says.

Peter chews thoughtfully for a while, waiting for Jacques to continue. Surely there is more to the tale. When the boy turns more of his focus to the stew, Peter decides to push his newfound companion to finish his story.

"I am certainly sorry for you," he says. "I cannot say I have suffered such a plight, though you find me in these tenuous circumstances. I will be the first to admit I have true reason to beg the mercy of His Highness. Caught in the act, as it were. But undoubtedly, no less desperate than you. So tell me, then, what brought you to this most *benign* of principalities."

Jacques takes on a somewhat darker countenance, leaning a bit closer to Peter. Peter recoils a bit, suddenly uncomfortable in his presence. He now feels this lad is untrustworthy, even if a victim of a difficult life. Should Peter believe everything he hears? No matter. It is merely a history worth half a meal and half an evening, and it certainly helps distract from melancholy.

With shadowed eyes, Jacques says, "Ye must know that eventually a young boy can make too much of a nuisance of himself, he can. At length, the others workin' the fields revealed t' me mum that the duke was lookin' for 'that young whelp.' Me mum took fright of what His Liege would do to me, and decided it was time t' flee. So we came to settle in this realm."

Peter's eyes go a bit wide with disbelief. He counters, "You must have done something more than kick dirt to cause the duke to come after you personally. I doubt he would care to point his attention at a mere nuisance of a serf!" Peter glances toward the remaining stew. "Tell me what you really did, and I will forego any more of this bounty and allow you to finish it at will."

Jacques accepts the offer. "I waited for the duke t' send for me mum t' his castle. Hid meself in the cart, I did," he whispers—no, hisses. "Ye know, he'd never send for her with a proper *carriage*.

Too good for her. A mere playthin', was she. Never give it a second thought if she died." There is now a clear tone of malice in his voice.

"So I let him do what he would anyway while I quietly went about the palace—shall we say, examinin' the contents. I found an irresistible bauble in the duchess's chamber, I did. And"—hesitatingly and more softly now—"I *appropriated* it."

"You *what*? You stole from the duchess? Did you get caught? Were you out of your mind? You could be killed for that!"

Peter is astonished. Not so much at the act, as he definitely believes this miscreant quite capable of such folly, but at the possibility that he could get away with it. Or maybe the boy is exaggerating his self-importance again, and none of this is truth.

"Me mum felt the same way as ye when I showed it t' her." His voice slides to a higher pitch. "'Now we'll be 'bliged t' leave for sure,' says she. 'But ye'll first find a way t' return that thing. Ye cannot sell it, surely, for it'll be recognized, and ye'll be seized. Ye're all I have, Jacques, and I'll not be parted from ye for such foolishness, I won't. So ye'll return it, ye will, as if ye found it outside the tower window of Her Highness, then hurry home t' me.'"

Now his voice goes back and forth as he describes the dialogue. "'But, Mum, where shall we go?' says I. 'Ye're of an age where ye must learn some trade or work yeself in the fields,' she says. 'But we'll need some sustenance, we will. I'll take ye t' your natural father, I will, and we'll beg a boon.'"

Peter is as surprised now as Jacques was then, according to his little drama.

"'Me father lives?' I says. 'But ye've ne'er spoken of him before! Where is he? What's he do for his own sustenance?' Mum says, 'He lives in the principality t' which we'll travel. I'll speak no more of him before then, I won't.' She shivered at that, and I knew better than to press for more."

Jacques shrugs. "So here we are. We'd only one old cow left after years of tryin' t' build somethin' for ourselves. So me mum sends me into town today t' sell her—the cow, I mean. Then she says she'll swallow her pride and take me t' me papa. So there I was, hardly gettin' enough for the old thing t' buy a handful of beans, when along comes his young majesty and his friend. And they accuse me of stealin'! I did espy the duke himself in the city just today, so I thought they mean the old bauble of the duchess, which I had returned years ago. But no! His majesty says these *Jews* told him I stole some gem, they did! He takes their word against mine—a good Christian, I am!"

Peter doubts this is the whole story. But it is a good tale. Suddenly, though, it is interrupted by the sound of heavy footsteps on the long climb up the tower.

Peter is rather surprised to see who enters the chamber. If this is a vision, it is a hideous one. It is a woman—or at least so he thinks, as her cloak does little to reveal her gender. She is large. Very large indeed. But that is not what draws the boys' attention. Her hands, her face are covered in ugly growths, and she has done nothing to hide them. These give her an appearance worse than old, dried fruit.

Jacques recoils momentarily, but Peter feels a sudden, deep pity. Such growths do not seem to diminish her energy. They must be a curse not of her own choosing. He certainly understands what it means to be a victim of circumstance.

And then there issues from this apparition the sweetest of sounds, music of the Sirens. "Hello, lads," she croons.

Peter notices for the first time that she carries a tray of the most desirable kuchen, with an aroma to match the sweetness of her voice.

"I know that Jurg's made arrangements of some sustenance, but I thought I'd grant ye a boon, ye poor things. Why, look at ye! Young and bedraggled, but good enough t' eat!"

It is clear from her speech that she was not genteelly raised, likely the daughter of a peasant, which makes Peter feel even more compassionate. Clearly her affliction has consigned her to her role in life, or so he surmises.

"Me husband, alas, will make short work of ye, he will," she adds.

"You are married to the jailer?"

Peter is incredulous. The jailer himself is an ogre, and then he is married to a woman like this? Her appearance far outweighs her kind disposition—and Peter has firsthand experience with the jailer's disposition.

"Don't judge by 'pearances," she scolds. "I'm aware of his sadistic tastes, I am, and I'm aware of me own shortcomin's. But we must use our wits in this world, and I was determined t' have a husband. That one had no one else t' marry. And though he may take more pleasure from the whip than from me, he offers the opportunity t' meet the likes of ye. So, I offer some treats . . . but only if ye'll oblige by an offerin' in return."

Peter is repulsed at the thought of obliging whatever favor she seeks. But then he remembers his consolation for this woman.

"I thank you kindly, madam, but I am inclined to refuse your generous offer."

Now Peter is even more grateful his brother can exert some influence to help him—it means he does not need to accept help from others, such as this woman. Jacques, on the other hand, has no such option.

"Woman, I'll definitely accept your offer, I will," he replies. To wit, he greedily grabs a kuchen off the plate and nearly swallows it whole. Then he winks at her and gives a little raise to his eyebrows.

She clucks her tongue. "Ye will call me Frau Katrina, ye will. And ye mistake me, young man. The favor I seek is not so base."

Katrina opens her surcotte only the slightest amount, revealing a large bruise just below the neckline. She covers it quickly, but both boys understand how—or rather, from *whom*—she received it.

"Ye see, I need t' leave this place. I'll require assistance in that regard, as I mustn't be . . . *reacquired* by him."

At that, the woman retrieves her tray and descends the stairwell.

Peter looks back at Jacques, whose grin reveals a calculating nature.

The thief frowns back at Peter, warning, "Ye're in no position t' judge, ye're not. Ye know well what she's askin', an' I'm not above it when the opportunity arises. More, it'll only get worse with the jailer. Ye see, I've little choice. And I certainly understand what it means t' have little choice, as I've told ye."

Peter now knows the boy is undoubtedly a true thief, untrustworthy, a liar. He is capable of vengeance.

Again comes the sound of footsteps on the stairwell, clearly those of the oversized jailer himself this time. The jailer enters, retrieves his flogging whip, and holds it up high, as if to strike. Peter winces and ducks, holding his arm in front of him, but Jacques faces the whip defiantly. The jailer smirks, then turns and departs with a shrug.

"I'll wait for the council, then I'll have me turn anyway," they hear him say as he begins down the stairs.

~ Chapter 16 ~

"Whar is she, the little whelp?" booms Dunkel as he throws open the heavy wood door to the tower house.

As thunder causes an avalanche, his voice carries to the kitchen, where the maidservant is preparing the next day's meal. She nearly drops her work on the straw floor. She contemplates leaving her station. If the master finds her, he will force her to reveal Besse's location, even though he knows well enough exactly where she likes to hide.

The maidservant shudders. Poor Besse, with little defense against Master Hammer while Fee is away. Fee seems to have such power over the brutish master. He must instinctively know his household would not function at all without her.

But the maid thinks too long. She is startled by the sudden appearance of the burly man before her.

"Tell me whar she is, or ye know what I'll do!" He raises his hand. He is clearly both drunk and distraught.

She whimpers and shrinks away from him, though he has never hit her. "I s'pose, master, that she's in her room, where she always is at this hour."

Dunkel can see she is cowering. It is good, he thinks. It pays to put the fear of God into all the servants, so they will do their jobs properly.

Deprived of satisfaction at the inn, he means to take up with his daughter. He leaves the kitchen, to the relief of the servant, and staggers up the stairs.

◆ ◆ ◆

- Chapter 16 -

"Oh, Dolly," sighs Besse as she cowers beside the wardrobe in her chamber.

She is almost as disheveled as the object of her attention as she huddles, fully shadowed from the torchlight emanating from the wall sconce opposite the bed. She tries to make herself as small and unnoticeable as possible, although there is no one else in the room to see her at all.

"What a day it has been with that horrible boy accosting me. I was very lucky to get away unharmed, was I not? I should be more careful, and do what Fee says. I think she really does care for me, do you know? But now, Dolly, I am getting drowsy, and I think I shall rest."

"Sometimes I wish Mama would come read me a tale before bed," she murmurs as she closes her eyes. "I do like the stories about King Arthur, but not the Bible stories so much."

The doll drops out of her hand as she begins to doze. Images of her day swirl through her head, and she begins to imagine herself as a character in her favorite stories.

She is a fair maiden attending a great feast at the castle in Camelot. Now she must leave under cover of darkness, which she favors. The air is redolent with the aromas of the feast, wafting on the wind blowing in and out of the castle. She pulls her fur tighter about her slender, attractive body, then sighs and begins her descent toward her carriage and four.

But where is the footman? Where is the driver? They are nowhere to be seen. She is suddenly angry, then concerned, then frightened.

She turns to reenter the castle, but her way is blocked by a large, ungainly, ugly man, somehow vaguely familiar. He is clearly besotted, slurring his speech. And he reeks of ale, totally blotting out the more pleasant, heady aromas she has just experienced.

She yells into the wind, "Stand aside, sir, for I will pass. It is a cold night, and I shall reenter the castle. As you can see, my carriage is not yet prepared for me."

"Ye'll not pass. I'll have me way with ye!" he exclaims. He strikes her across the cheek.

She feels herself drifting downward, downward. The twilight sky is gray, but she squints to gaze upward. Now she sees a bird circling lower and lower. Is it a hawk, seeking its prey? It seems to be fixated upon her.

"No, no!" she calls out. "I am no mouse or rabbit to be carried off by the likes of you! Begone!"

Yet the raptor refuses to hear. Closer and closer it comes. She cannot shrink away from it. There is no place to hide. Where is she, anyway? Her surroundings are blurred, dark, contracted about her.

The bird lands upon her belly—but wait. It is no bird at all, but rather a dragon, hot and heavy, with very foul breath. Is it wheezing? It sinks claws into her, but, oddly, they do not hurt, at least not much. Somehow she knows she will not be entirely devoured.

She turns her head away from it, willing it to depart and leave her alone. She hates the dragon. This dragon, she recalls, has attacked her before, leaving her alive but somehow diminished, ashamed.

Is there anyone to help? Is there no champion to defend her? No Lancelot, no Arthur? Why should they care? She is no Guinevere.

But she does hear a voice, a familiar one, louder, now shouting. Who can that be?

◆ ◆ ◆

"Get off! Get off of her, you big oaf!" Fee shouts and pulls at her master.

He groans and rolls to the side.

Fee takes her charge into her arms. She is barely able to carry the girl, disheveled and lethargic, to the servant's chamber up the winding stairs. She finally deposits her upon her own straw bed with a great sigh.

"Besse, my poor Besse, you will sleep in my bed tonight, and I will stay with you. No more harm shall come to you tonight. No more!"

Only then does she allow herself a great cry, collapsing into tears for the second time that night.

"How shall I protect you, little one, when I can hardly do for myself?" she cries as she gently smooths the girl's hair. "Beata is of no use to you, is she? And of how much use am I to you—to Peter, to Flor, to Dien, to anyone?"

Fee wipes her burning tears from her eyes. "I must think. I *must*. Yes. First, you must learn to care for a household of your own, to fend for yourself. Then we must find a mate for you, and he must be suitable."

Ultimately, Fee crumbles on the floor by the bedside, drifting off to sleep.

Next to Fee, Besse is adrift, neither awake nor quite asleep. But she feels safe again, for the moment. She vaguely hears the words of the devoted servant. In her tightly clutched hand, Besse discovers Dolly.

She tells the doll, "Yes. Fee will help me find a champion. A knight in armor of my own. And I will learn to make him do as I need. I can do this. Did I not fend off that ruffian on my own today? A dragon is more difficult, but not if I find the right Lancelot! He must be out there. He must! For the dragon must be slain. Yes, that is it."

Finally, she allows herself to fall into a deep sleep, though a vaguely discontented one. Tomorrow she will begin to think how to find her man—and slay her dragon.

~ Chapter 17 ~

Rudi is relieved to reach the entry to the tower house. He bounds up the stairway two steps at a time and hones in on the cook servant. He is almost overcome by the sweet aroma of the stew. He kisses the servant lightly on the cheek, causing her to blush involuntarily.

"That'll be quite enough!" she says. "I have no hopes for the likes of ye, journeyman! I haven't. Off with ye."

"So be it, love. But will you do me the small honor of setting a bowl of that most delicious stew aside into the hot ashes, so that I may partake later? I have had little sustenance this day. If you will so indulge me, I will later repay you with a story you will be most anxious to hear." He stops and bows his head with a smile. "And you will note that I do not demand such service, as is my due in this house, but merely offer a polite request with humble gratitude."

"Ye're a charmer, young man, and without excuse for arrival beyond the mealtime. Yet I'm inclined t' oblige out of kindness—not t' mention what Fee'd say if I didn't do me duty t' the household. But she's the heart of kindness herself, she is, though out and about late herself this eve."

The maidservant bends over the kettle to the task, and Rudi is almost too distracted by the aroma of the stew to appreciate the sudden view of her most positive attribute. He shakes all such thought from his mind, however, when the maidservant turns back around with a look of foreboding.

"Be warned—the master's in a surly mood, he is. Best t' finish here quickly or make yeself scarce. Hurry now—go t' it!"

~ Chapter 17 ~

Rudi nods in understanding before racing out the door, retracing his earlier steps to the city gate. He knows this will not be a good night for poor Besse nor most in the household. But he can take no responsibility nor risk his position any more than he does. Such is the way of the world and none of his making. Plus, he has other plans in mind.

Rudi moves on, absorbed in his own thoughts. He stays close to the wall of the city, finding reassurance in the sturdy gray-granite structure as it keeps him in its protective shadow, more so as the sky darkens. His is not a mission wanting discovery, at least not yet.

Moreover, the darkness prevents further distraction, as he needs to think through the events of the day—and about the sweeter events of the evening, toward which he is heading. As he ponders, a flock of geese in strict V formation sails overhead, pointing the direction to his love's destination. This is surely a good sign, were he to be superstitious. He waves off the thought.

What a day! he thinks. The master is surely in trouble for killing that young thief, but he always forgets his carousals. How shall Rudi remind him? He must put this all to good use.

He steps over stones absentmindedly yet does not trip or stumble, as this is a path he has virtually created with his own footsteps, repeatedly and easily. Accessing Beata's tower chamber is best done from the outside, avoiding discovery indoors by the servants, or worse, the master himself.

He stoops to pick wild violets in late bloom, a gift for his paramour. Thus his thoughts turn to Beata. Will she be cross with him for his tardiness? Does she long for him as he does for her? Surely she does, as she cannot help but prefer his suit to the manner of her husband. How shall he woo her tonight? He must celebrate her finest features and flatter her undying beauty.

He tries out several rhymes in his head as he saunters, now oblivious to his surroundings. Rudi's quiet movement will not catch the attention of the guards, as close as he is to the stones themselves. Yet he does not go entirely unnoticed.

The brigand Bo has been watching the city gate. He hopes again to come across some client of the inn, returning to the city in a sufficiently inebriated state to be accosted and deprived of his purse. This will be more difficult now that he is acting alone, of course. The lad has been deprived of the companionship of his partners—one during the unsuccessful raid on the caravan and another during the unsuccessful robbery.

He curses the men who, he believes, assaulted him and his accomplice outside the inn. It does not occur to him that such misfortune is entirely of their own making. Intsead, he cannot recover from the scare and embarrassment, not to mention the grief of seeing his companion—who in fact was his brother—beaten unconscious, likely even killed.

Thus, wiping tears and sweat off his tunic, Bo is surprised to see the younger man who restrained him while the older, larger man brutually attacked his brother. Bo still fears to accost this man. He has already experienced his great strength, and it is clear this one has touched neither mead nor ale this evening.

Perhaps if Bo can follow silently, in the shadow of the trees, he will see what the young man is about. It must be of some interest if he is outside the safety of the city wall at this hour yet again. Perhaps an illicit assignation?

Rudi is oblivious to his new shadow. He thinks only of his Beata, and finally he arrives beneath the tower window. He picks up a stone, aims carefully, and throws. He knows Beata is listening for the clatter against the wall.

She leans out the opening. In the glow of the fire-lit chamber, he can see she is wearing only a loose bodice. She knows her appearance will excite the young lad. But she feigns a look of disdain, as if her evening has been rudely and unnecessarily interrupted.

She sighs. "Is there anyone below? I wonder who would disturb my beauty rest at this hour? Could that be you, Rudi? I should think not. Rudi would not disturb my need to relax away my wrinkles of concern—worrying, as I have been, about his whereabouts as he did not arrive when promised this evening." She smirks. "Though, I admit, I would not be averse to your company, if it is you, Rudi. If not, be off, and do not disturb the purity of my thoughts and prayers!"

Rudi chuckles. Pure thoughts, indeed. What games she does play! She chastises, so he must beseech her pardon and play up to her good graces.

"Though I do not wish to disturb your thoughts, my love, I certainly hope to beseech you to share in my desires. As to your need for rest, I can see no capability to improve upon that which is already perfection. Listen, and I will sing of your great beauty for all the woodland creatures to hear and be envious that only I may share in its appreciation:

Oh, beauteous maid of visage fair
Trapped high above, in tower's lair
Couldst lower to me thy wondrous hair
That I may climb to height so rare
Wherein thy beauty lies, nor tear
Mine eyes from yours, the perfect pair.
The skies were n'er so blue—beware
The love of one so lost in their
Perfection. Thou didst thus ensnare
My love for thee alone fore'er.

"Maiden, is it?" she asks. "You are indeed blinded to see me in this light. Or perhaps it is because there is a lack of light. But you shall have your chance to make amends for the late hour and win my love anew. Such a pretty song must have taxed your thoughts a prettier length of time, as I know your inclination is not that of the poet.

Hmph, thinks Rudi, *I waste my artistry upon this woman.* But at least he must admit to himself that he does love her and her beauty alone makes it worth the effort.

"In lieu of lowering my hair, as your ode has requested, I will lower to you a rope," she calls. "This even, I have spent my time in worry of your safety, and I accompanied my forlorn thoughts with the process of brushing the very locks you so kindly praise. So I would not have them pulled or entangled by the likes of you."

Beata lowers the rope of tied linens she keeps hidden in a shadowy nook for just this purpose. Rudi fashioned it himself for Beata to tie to her bedpost.

So does Rudi long to spend the precious remaining hours of the night in her company. He notes how the soft light of the torches glisten off her long blonde locks, enhancing their radiance and the shadow of her silhouette. He is lost in it and likely doomed, yet he will climb.

As Rudi scales the tower, he sees she has embellished the rope with ribbons of silk infused with perfume Rudi himself brought for her. He laughs, realizing she uses it because he purchased it at an unbearable price and because it pleased his own senses to daydream of her wearing it. *There should be a guild of enchantresses,* he thinks. *She would the master of masters! Or of mistresses!* This thought makes him chuckle again.

He reaches the top and climbs over the steep, deep sill of the tower opening. There is no glass here. Beata has forbidden it, despite the cold of winters. She tells the servants and Besse that the cold is necessary for the best complexion—it keeps one young and clears the mind. But Rudi knows better, of course. When one has need to bar the chamber door to inside entry, a potential escape route is useful.

And it certainly creates an advantage for Rudi.

~ Chapter 18 ~

The mists rise from the fields, revealing a tapestry of autumn color worthy of the finest artist of the day, conducive to an almost festive mood. Indeed, Duke Philip feels quite pleased with himself as he surveys the view from the vantage point of his favorite horse. He savors the scents of horse, fresh air, and a hint of burning wood from somewhat-distant chimneys. He is rather proud and complacent in the realization that he has spent his life expanding his realm to a size greater than that of Charles of France and that it owes fealty to neither France nor England.

For once, he has no desire to use the politics of marriage to expand his jurisdiction. The principality is clean, healthy, and well protected. That is the perfect situation for the safety and well-being of his daughter, Giselle. And the young dauphin is not ambitious beyond his means or ability, which will ensure a long life. As for his father, he is well aware of the advantages of marrying into the family of Duke Philip of Burgundy. A good match for both children—and their fathers!

He must commission his current favorite artist, Jan van Eyck, to paint the young couple once the necessary arrangements are sealed for betrothal. (He does not consider his patronage of the arts a luxury, but rather a solace, a necessity.) At last, Philip can contemplate an appropriate companion—handsome and highly intelligent yet considerate and chivalrous—for La Claire. Such a nickname! It is true. She is quite pale, but it only enhances her beauty. He finds himself looking forward to her company and that of her more darkly beautiful stepmother.

His thoughts wander back to the various enjoyments of this excursion,. This has been a most successful tour and caravan, with prosperity abounding. Even the hunting has been successful: in the woods, providing great repast, and at the inn, other satisfying quarry. He chuckles. All in all, a very good journey.

Perhaps it was marred a bit by the brief view of the lad in the city streets, reminding him of the young upstart who confronted him in the fields in a poor attempt to protect his mother. Philip had banished them entirely, then promptly forgotten about them.

He shakes the thoughts away. Better to enjoy the remaining ride to his loving wife and daughter. Nobility, he notes, offers far more than mere physical attraction. He will certainly appreciate them all the more. He realizes he misses the duchess more on each successive journey, as he misses his daughter. How much transformation, he wonders, will he see in his beautiful Giselle? Yes, Charles will be perfect for her and will treat her with the utmost respect and kindness. Philip could ask for nothing more.

"See, my knights?" he calls out to his retinue. "There, ahead, lies the castle of Brugge—my true love and my beloved daughter. I am eager to arrive. If we ride well, we shall be there well before dark. And so, onward!"

He gestures grandly with sword in hand toward the castle in the distance, the light glistening off the blade. It is a bit of theater, calculated to inspire awe and loyalty.

◆ ◆ ◆

The leaves are beginning to fly, offering a multicolor display. La Claire leans over the parapet of the castle turret, lost in her own thoughts. She appears brightened rather than pale in the waning sunlight, as if she could capture and hold it, then radiate at will. Her lustrous black hair and deep blue eyes contrast against her skin but actually enhance her beauty in the eye of the beholder. She is slight of build, compared to the more preferred rotundity of the day. Her maidservant constantly rebukes her to eat more. But she prefers herself just as she is.

She sighs and extends her hand as if to catch a leaf or provide a perch for a passing sparrow. She muses that her father will return soon with news of a potential suitor. She is weary of her lessons in the castle, supervised by her stepmother, the duchess. Etiquette, protocol, reading, history, religion—some intensely boring, but all necessary for a young woman in her position.

For her part, Duchess Enchanteresse remains exasperated with her charge. She climbs the stairs of the tower, having surmised the whereabouts of her stepdaughter without even having to ask the servants. With the duke returning soon, the duchess has little time for La Claire's frivolity.

Enchanteresse is glad she charged His Liege with the task of finding a suitable match for La Claire on this caravan. She is of age, and the duchess tires of the duties her stepdaughter forces upon her. There is hardly enough time to rule the household when she must chase the girl throughout the court several times a day.

Her huntsman, Gaillard, runs up the stairs behind her.

"A moment, your ladyship. I would desire to know if you have a special request for supper this even, as I am about to leave for the hunt."

This is spoken loudly, for anyone in earshot to hear. But it is really no secret to the court that the duchess favors this man with special privilege, allowing him to rule some of the daily necessities of service. It is also no secret—except to the duke, of course—that he provides other services to her, as she finds him irresistibly attractive.

Gaillard is tall, dark of complexion, not too young. His deep, booming voice carries easily throughout the court, and he carries himself with the self-assurance of a nobleman. Indeed, he is descended of counts and princes but carries the misfortune of not being a firstborn, therefore unable to inherit land and power on his own. This gives him sufficient charisma of nobility, yet his lack of noble prospects has instilled sensitivity to the needs of the peasantry and the skills to enjoy his time in nature.

He approaches the duchess with alacrity, bounding up two steps at a time without any evidence of loss of breath. He smiles when he reaches her.

"Perhaps more than just a moment?" Gaillard whispers. "I find your beauty impossible to depart, and you are particularly radiant today."

Actually, he believes not a word of this. Truly, she was once a great beauty—tall and thinner than the custom of the day, her hair well oiled to a shining blackness of interminable depth, and a perfectly symmetrical visage with pouting red lips. These days, however, she must use large quantities of powder to conceal the deepening ridges about the eyes and elsewhere. Enchanteresse never goes into the public domain without long black silk gloves to hide the spots appearing on her hands and the painful swelling of the joints. The light through the turret window slits still shines brilliantly off her hair, as if in mockery of the deterioration evident on her body. This pain has made the lady surlier than she was in her youth, because her ego, her *arrogance*, derives entirely from her vanity. She is a harsh mistress, an even harsher stepmother to La Claire.

The woodsman has assured the banishment of all reflective surfaces from all castles frequented by the duchess. Instead, he insists her beauty is best reflected in the eyes of her adoring subjects—in his eyes most of all. This, of course, is yet another prevarication, but one of necessity and fear of her power. Her husband, not to mention her loyal subjects, is oblivious to her vanity. And she, in turn, is oblivious to how fortunate that is. The woodsman protects her from such realities.

She still truly believes herself the most beautiful in all the land, and the woodsman prefers to keep it that way.

"You may attend me in my chamber when the sun reaches zenith, sir. I would like grouse and venison this evening, and that should give you the opportunity to provide it. I shall not dally with you here, though, for I am on a mission yet again to locate my errant young stepdaughter, once again totally neglectful in her studies and duties." She grimaces. "She is near hopeless. One can only hope she is attractive enough for some nobleman or burgher. It will be a wonder if her father can arrange any kind of satisfactory match for her. If only she had the beauty I carried in my own youth. Or even now!"

~ Chapter 18 ~

"Yes, my lady," the woodsman says. "Until the noon hour, then."

He must be off to secure her dinner, then to secure her desires. This is not the most contentious duty, after all!

The duchess reaches the parapet and rolls her eyes in exasperation as she approaches her stepdaughter in a huff.

"Giselle, my dear, I must rebuke you once again, child! You are due for your lesson in court etiquette, and the master awaits in the ballroom. Hie yourself there this instant!"

"How beautiful you look when you are angry, Mama!" the girl replies. "I only wish I could grow to be as attractive as you."

La Claire knows how to defuse the duchess's rages. Yet the young maiden really does believe what she says. Lacking mirrors, thanks to the efforts of the huntsman, she has no image of herself for comparison. She is absolutely heedless of the stares of the male citizens and nobility when she passes. She believes these are merely her due as the daughter of the duke.

"I shall be down directly," La Claire says. "I have not forgotten my lessons, but I could never resist the attraction of the fresh air and the colors of autumn. Even the birds seem to greet me here."

"A bit too heady a mood, my dear. These are luxuries not to be abused in exchange of your duties. How will we ever find you a suitable nobleman if you continue to place your head in the clouds you cannot reach! I have ever feared for your future, my dear. Now, let us straighten your appearance, then to your lesson."

She brushes her hand along Giselle's hair disapprovingly, frowns, then makes a motion of dismissal. La Claire sighs, takes one forlorn look toward the circling birds, turns, curtsies, and descends the spiral stairs.

Enchanteresse shakes her head reproachfully as she watches her stepdaughter descend. Then she turns and leans over the parapet. This gives her the startling appearance from afar of a black vulture. The birds no longer circle closely overhead, affording her a wide berth. She, of course, is unaware of such an impression.

She takes the opportunity to organize her plans for the day. First, she will see to the preparations for the dinner, then retire to her chamber to await the huntsman—handsome brute, that, and so dutiful and obedient. Then she will refresh herself, perhaps allow herself a scented bath, before planning for the return of her husband. She has just received a missive informing of his imminent return, perhaps as early as the next day. All must be in order.

Before long, the castle is abuzz with activity. Kitchen servants prepare a large feast of roasted pig, venison, seasonal vegetables, apples, soups, and breads. The savory aromas permeate the entire court, and not a few mouths are salivating.

Enchanteresse—after a private encounter with the huntsman—is bathed, perfumed, and dressed in her best finery, with silk blouse and skirts and a surcotte of the finest velvet. The black fabric contrasts and enhances the caked white makeup and piercing blue eyes. Her raven hair is allowed to fall, glistening with scented oils and blending invisibly with her surcotte. She dons her finest jewelry, all gifts from her husband: ruby brooch, emerald pendant on a thick gold chain, diamond tiara, and rings, rings, rings!

The duchess has instructed the maidservants to dress her stepdaughter in blue and white silk with a single strand of pearls about her neck. La Claire, for her part, refuses makeup, except for cherry lips minimally applied. Her appearance can melt the heart of the least noble courtier, though, as always, she fails to notice.

In the assembly hall, the thrones have been cleaned and fresh straw and flax lain upon the stone floor. The walls are adorned with tapestries bearing mythological themes rather than religious ones. The casual observer would be taken aback by the resemblance of the young maiden with a unicorn to the young La Claire, as ever one with nature around her.

As word arrives of the final approach of the duke, the members of the court take their places, most standing along the walls, leaving an open area for the entry of their ruler and his knights. Gaillard attends to the duchess, herself carefully arranged upon the lesser throne of wood and inlaid gems. The huntsman will remain somewhat out of view, behind her but close enough to be heard in a whisper.

~ Chapter 18 ~

La Claire, full of excitement, runs outside into the bailey, wanting to greet her father as he alights, before more formal behavior is required. Indeed, he is delighted to see his daughter and is once again taken aback by her natural beauty. The sun seems verily to shine upon her alone, yet he knows this is an illusion.

A broad grin crosses his face, and he jumps off his mount and hugs her. She holds her arms wide as he lifts her off her feet, giving the appearance of a graceful swan in flight. Then she leans down and wraps her arms around his neck.

"Oh, Papa! How I have missed you! Will you stay with us for a long time? Winter approaches, and I would have the warmth of your kind words and company."

He kisses her lightly on the cheek. "You are fresh as ever and more beautiful than nature itself! It is so good to see you. You must ask the count to remove that sack"—he points to his brother and riding companion, now entering the courtyard—"and then off with you. I must greet your stepmother, conduct some business, and freshen myself and these loyal men. Then shall we feast, if my nose catches this delicious air correctly, and I will be at leisure to describe to you my travels."

"And do you have news for me, Papa?" she asks eagerly.

"You have no subtlety, my dear." His eyes twinkle. "There will be news, of course, and I shall share it at supper."

"Thank you, Papa!"

She barely remembers to curtsy, then bounds along the caravan to the specified package. The count, with a bow, hands her a small box. She thanks him and curtsies. She marvels over the black lacquer and mother of pearl inlays enveloping the gift box. She has never seen its like; it is clearly from some far, exotic kingdom.

"It is from the Far East, mademoiselle," states the count on cue. "That is very far, indeed. The artisans do exquisite work, do they not?"

"How did you ever acquire it?"

"Ah! It cost his grace a pretty penny in trade, especially now that the fate of the route to the Orient is in question. Do open it, my dear niece."

"Thank you, uncle."

She opens the box gingerly, not wishing to tarnish the exquisite art, then her eyes go wide as she espies the large amber pendant enclosed. She takes it out, inspecting it more closely.

"Oh!" she exclaims. "It has a butterfly encased in it! How did that get in there? It is the most exquisite gift I have ever received! I shall place it on a gold chain immediately. Thank you! Thank you!"

"You must thank your father, not me, dear Giselle. Now off with you, and attend upon your family at the feast. I look forward to hearing all the court gossip and a demonstration of all you have learned in our absence!"

Watching the exchange, Philip takes satisfaction from the grateful exuberance of his daughter. He brushes the dust of the road off his tunic, then turns and enters the assembly chamber. He nods to all present, who bow or curtsy as he passes. He says a few kind or amusing words to most, then stops before the thrones and the vision of his wife.

"My breath is taken away, as always, my dearest! How ravishingly beautiful you are. None in all my travels were the like to it!" He stands straight and tall, smiles as he places one hand behind his back, and extends the other to Enchanteresse. "Come, descend to me and let me present to you a very small token of my love and devotion. Then shall I greet the assembled court, and we shall retire to make ready for this feast that assails my nostrils. I declare I am ravishingly hungry!"

Philip turns and calls out, "Guards! Please bring in the large gift, with care for its fragility. Then direct the servants in the stabling and care of our noble horses and the storage and distribution of the cargo."

He has no need to be so polite, but he judges such chivalry will please the duchess. To the contrary, she is never so deferential herself and rather disapproves. A ruler should always behave in regal fashion with its subjects, she believes.

She frowns, but her eyebrows rise upon the approach of two servants bearing a large silk-covered object. The fabric is deep blue and alone must be of great worth—certainly too great to be used as packaging.

"Even the cloth, as you can see, is of value and is yours to make what you will of it," says the duke, reading her thoughts. "Now," addressing the servants, "remove the cover!"

At once, all members of the court gasp as a large obsidian mirror is revealed. The huntsman's eyes go wide as he nearly loses his balance. All of his careful work to forfend the presence of such an object has suddenly come to naught.

"I have noted the absence of reflecting glass in this castle in the past," continues Philip. "I have thought this would be of exceeding value to you. Note how the frame is carefully gilded and adorned with all of your favorite woodland creatures. And, my dear," he adds, "it is the only way I can present great beauty to my greatest beauty of all!"

But the duchess is not at all pleased. She does not notice the gilding or carvings. She is fixated upon her image in the dark glass. And she is horrified. She raises her hand to her mouth, glares, then turns swiftly. Without even a word of thanks to her husband, she gestures to the huntsman.

"Come with me!" Enchanteresse bellows.

She marches out of the hall to the chamber behind the thrones, leaving an astonished court—and even more surprised duke—behind.

~ Chapter 19 ~

Even before the sun rises, the Hammer household begins to stir. The servants are dressed and about the business of preparing the fire in the hearth, obtaining water at the local well for cooking and laundry, sweeping and replacing the rushes on the floors of all the rooms.

There is a bit of a chill in the air, savored by Fee, leaning out the window opening in the tower. She notices some movement in the mist below, outside the city wall, and dismisses it as a foraging deer or other forest animal.

Her mind wanders as she imagines herself with the freedom of the creature. To roam and exist off the bounty of nature, unhindered by the exigencies of life as a household servant, trapped inside hard labor for a master who ill appreciates her talent but seems inescapable. There is nothing in the world she would want more than the opportunity to live with her beloved Dien, to leave all the problems of this household behind, and start a new life. Yet the fates are not so kind. She cannot leave the daughter to the wiles of her father, and the mistress is of no use. No, Fee must stay with her. She must stay with them both.

Fee exhales, resigned to what life has to bring. It is not in her nature to complain openly of her position. *At least the lady has the consolation of a young lover,* Fee muses, *and that will have to do for us both!*

She checks on her young charge, who is sleeping fitfully. Fee decides not to rouse her immediately, especially while the master is still in the house.

She sighs and turns to face her duties of the day. At least she has brought excellent quality meats and vegetables for the day's fare, complemented by an ample supply of fresh and dried herbs. She makes her rounds of the servants, sees that the cook and maids are all hard at work.

Then she knocks at Beata's chamber door. It slowly opens, revealing the lady herself, humming and brushing her long blond locks with one hand—an automatic gesture clearly much practiced over the years. She ushers Fee into the room quickly, then secures and locks the door.

◆ ◆ ◆

In early autumn, mists envelop the principality, a point of annoyance to many who start their day early, notably the purveyors of meats and vegetables and those with the responsibility to keep the cobblestone streets washed. To others, however, the fog allows inconspicuous activity. One can enter the gates undisturbed, right under the noses of the guards patrolling the walls.

Today there is one who spent the night outside the walls, nursing his grief at the loss of a brother outside the inn. Bo has had little sleep and much fear. He knows that, if he were seen by that great hulk of a man with a slight limp, he would be no match for him. More the man would not want to leave Bo alive to tell the tale.

Therefore, the ruffian's choices are few. He could leave this place entirely, but it is clear he does not have the skills to survive as much more than a beggar. He is Roma, far from his home, unable to learn the skills his parents taught him, unwelcome everywhere.

Bo could tell his tale to the guard in hopes of an audience with the prince, who is a rarity—a ruler benign and conscientious. But sharing his story would only bring into question Bo's true purpose of being outside the inn. If the prince is as wise as he is said to be, he would not take long to guess that purpose without any additional testimony from the limper.

A thought suddenly strikes the miscreant. It is a risk, but it could help his position. He must find the man's home and approach him directly, but only in plain sight of the citizens. He will offer his silence in exchange for a chance to earn some sustenance in the household. If this scheme works, he will be able to find other skills and perhaps even settle.

His mood lifts, and he cautiously waits for the proper moment to slip into the city unnoticed. As he wends his way around the wall, he notes only the shadow of a woman against the hearth light through a slit in a tower wall. He shrugs it off with the realization that because of the fog she cannot recognize him as even human.

However, Bo does not realize his appearance—ragged and unwashed—leads even those unhindered by fog to mistake him for a wild animal. He is repelled by the citizens he approaches. They withdraw from him without allowing an opportunity to inquire about the man with the limp. The citizens are sure he is a mere beggar and have no time for the likes of him. He slinks through the city, then decides to approach one of the guards, who can hardly ignore him.

"Please, sir. A boon, sir." It is better if he is thought to be a beggar.

"Be off with ye!" the guard replies. "Don't bother these good people who're about their business. As am I. I have no time and no money for ye this morn. Ye must know the location of the church. The priest's a most generous and most honorable man, he is, and will grant ye what charity he has."

"Sir, I seek no such charity. I'd only ask of ye the location of the home of the man with a limp. He's a large, strong man, he is, and I wish t' repay a favor, I do." Bo slouches in submission.

"Dunkel Hammer? The armorer?" The guard eyes Bo suspiciously. "That man's no one's friend, he's not, and does no favors for anyone—no less the likes of ye! What sort of favor is it possible he's done for ye? Tell me, and I may do ye the honor of accompanyin' ye t' his household, I will, for this I must see for meself."

The young man straightens up and harrumphs. "It's quite personal-like and private, sir. It involves a young maiden." This is a lie, of course, but Bo must think fast. "I can tell ye no more. If ye know this man, ye'll not want t' be present when I approach him, as I can assure you he'd appreciate it but very little."

The guard laughs. "Very well. If ye turn here and follow this street t' the end, ye'll come t' a tower in the wall. That tower's his own, it is, by the grace of His Majesty, whom we all serve. Now, off with ye, and don't let me catch ye botherin' the citizenry in these streets!"

He mocks a kick at the boy. He considers he has done his own charity for the day.

Bo realizes he is seeking the very tower he skirted earlier and decides to hurry to his destination, staying as unseen as possible. At the tower, he hides in a convenient corner of the wall outside the heavy oak door. He listens closely as he overhears the conversation of two passing guards.

"His majesty'll have t' rein that one in, says I," says the one. "It's a little too 'xciting t' have those two off savin' maidens in distress and rescuin' caravans, 'specially when our comrades are there t' assist and protect them."

"And now," says the other, "there's another pris'ner, caught robbin' the Jews and approachin' a young maiden in the street. These aren't hard times, they're not, but one must wonder what's becomin' of our youth. In our day, we were completely obedient t' our fathers, who'd never put up with such behavior."

Bo strains to listen as the garrulous guards pass. Good. They had not noticed him, nor had they made mention of any event outside the inn. This brings thoughts of his brother, and he winces but does not allow himself to cry. He must be resolute, not vengeful, and devote himself to the matter at hand. He crouches low, holding on to his knees, and waits. Nevertheless, he gives the impression more of a starved feral dog than a tiger about to pounce.

◆ ◆ ◆

Inside, the kettle is on to boil, the fire is stoked. The cook, hearing the journeyman and apprentice bound down the stairs, cuts thick slices of fresh bread, then wraps some wild strawberries and apples and slices of ham.

Rudi takes her hand, roughened by years of hard labor, and

kisses it. "As always, my dear cook, you are the best at what you do, and we are blessed to share the bounty of your work."

"You flatter me always, sir!" she replies, blushing at the treatment as some sort of found love or nobility. "Now here's your reward. Take it and have a good day."

"Thank you," says Rudi with a smile.

The young men take their meals, and Rudi grabs extra fruit for himself and the apprentice. Before the cook can disapprove, they rush out the door.

They must prepare the forge for the master's arrival. The apprentice expects him to be in a better mood today, with new orders from the just-departed Duke of Burgundy.

The journeyman knows better, however, though he wonders how much the master will remember the incident outside the inn. Perhaps that is the only positive advantage of the long-term effects of too much beer and mead. Rudi shrugs, then smiles with the thought of his own plans. Soon he can present his work to the guild masters. With the events of last night in mind, the master should not be able to stand against him.

As the two young men emerge from the heavy oak door, Bo sees his chance. The fog is beginning to lift, and concealment is not an option much longer. He gathers his courage with the thought that this is his best plan for survival.

"Sirs, a word."

The journeyman and the apprentice are a bit startled. In particular, Rudi's eyes go wide as he recognizes the young man, a fact that does not go unnoticed by Bo.

The apprentice, however, sees nothing more than a poor beggar before him. "Here—take half an apple, and bother us no more! We have much work to do, we do, and no time for idle conversation. Nor do we have any work to offer you, unfortunately."

Rudi turns to his companion. "Let me deal with this waif," he says. "Continue on ahead, and I shall join you shortly."

He waits for the apprentice to advance out of earshot. Then, turning with a scornful look to Bo, he says, "How dare you show your face here! Are you daft? Do you know what the master would do if he recognized you? Be off! He is sure to be about his business, following us shortly."

"Sir, I wish no harm t' ye or the master," Bo begins. "Nor am I here t' beg of ye, I'm not. But it should be clear from me appearance that I'm not capable of the violence set upon me unfortunate brother last evenin'. I grieve his loss. I beg your forgiveness for the circumstances, I do. But as ye can now understand, we were of little means and no ability t' find suitable work. It'd be reasonable t' ask your assistance with the master or the lady of the house t' permit the hirin' of one more servant or valet—"

Rudi interrupts. "So that you can pilfer precious personal goods and thereby cost the lady her own reputation? I speak nothing of the master, whose reputation is of no concern, but the lady is important and has done nothing to harm you. And who would hire one with your appearance and demeanor, *sir*?"

Rudi is aghast at the nerve of this boy. It is both daring and desperate. Rudi pities him but can do nothing to improve his situation.

Rudi takes on a stern appearance, strokes his chin, and says in a considerably softer tone, "I am truly sorry for the loss of your brother, sir. Yet have I little boon to grant and little money. I am a mere journeyman." He pauses. "But this will I do for you: if you are capable of a more honest existence, and if you can wait but a few months, I may be able to accommodate you. Promise you will abandon your current profession, then watch and wait. You will know when the time is opportune to seek me out."

There. He feels better, capable of charity to the very man who attacked his master.

"I thank ye, sir," Bo says, "but what shall I do in the interim? If ye could but share some small sustenance . . ." The miscreant trails off, giving his best appearance of a poor, wide-eyed beggar.

Rudi softens a second in response, then realizes Bo's intent and frowns. "I have said all that I will say—and it is more than you deserve! I am not the author of your situation. You are very fortunate I prevented you from facing the wrath of the inebriated master, who would have helped you join the fate of your brother last night!" Rudi glances around. "Now I must hurry to my duties. I would appreciate not seeing your face again before the opportunity I have mentioned becomes available. Be off before the master himself appears."

Bo is still afraid of this strong young man, yet he must state his case. "I fear the master not, for if he'd kill me, what life do I have that he'd prevent, sir? I can, however, approach the prince with the news of a murder most foul within the bounds of his 'sponsibility and serve as a witness."

Rudi turns red with this outrageous suggestion. He raises his arm, and the boy instinctively covers his face. Then, regathering his wits so as not to attract the attention of the guard, Rudi turns on his heel and storms out of the city without another word.

Let the boy call in the prince, he thinks. H*is majesty will deal with them both, and I can only benefit.* He laughs at that thought and calms down. He feels pleased with himself for leaving the boy perplexed. So much for charity. It is still a world of lions and prey, and Rudi would rather be the hunter than the hunted.

◆ ◆ ◆

Dunkel is unsteadily moving about his own bedchambers, nursing a severe headache and somewhat confused about the previous day's events. His condition leaves him more and more with blank memories, sometimes rushing in to fill the empty space like water through a broken dam. He gives the appearance of a lost child in the body of an old man—a very grumpy old man, at that. A permanent state of gloom seems to surround him, underlining the appropriateness of his name.

It takes some time to orient himself to his plans for the day, but he finally notes that his journeyman and apprentice have already departed. This is good, he surmises. They are well and about their business, and the forge will be well prepared. Dunkel is glad to have obtained a goodly supply of coal, as he is now ready to deal with the needs of the duke.

He smiles—more of a grimace, actually. This he does remember. It is a large order, and he will need the assistance of Rudi and the apprentice. It will allow Dunkel to pay them well, but not too well. Perhaps this will also be an opportunity for the younger boy to increase his responsibilities and prove he is ready to become another journeyman.

Then a thought suddenly strikes Dunkel, as they do more and more frequently in his current condition. He seems to remember a rather uncomfortable event last eve. Was there a fight? He cannot be sure. But Rudi was there. Did he assist? He must have, as the master does not recall how he came to be in his own chamber this morn.

For a moment, he ponders whether he is too harsh on his journeyman. Perhaps Rudi is more loyal than Dunkel grants him. But he quickly chases the notion away. No. Rudi is an ambitious one. Dunkel must control it. He is not fool enough to believe the journeyman's skills are much less than his own. Dunkel suspects Rudi will soon start working on his masterpiece. In actuality, Dunkel does not know the young man is nearly finished with his piece. But he does know he is not ready for the competition if Rudi were named a master in his own right. Perhaps the large order from the duke will thoroughly occupy Rudi's time and delay his presentation to the guild.

Well, I'm hungry, I am, Dunkel concludes. *Some fruit and a bit of ale are in order, then let's see what the day'll bring.*

He stumbles down the stairs, using the wall for support with one hand while he holds his forehead with the other. He is used to these headaches, all too frequent these days. He grabs an apple and pours himself some ale, unmindful of the dinner basket awaiting him to be brought to the forge, then moves out the door.

Suddenly he is greeted by Bo, the young outlaw.

"Sir, your pardon, sir."

The boy looks vaguely familiar, but Dunkel cannot quite place him. It is not the whelp who approached him last night with a tale of woe about his mother—and an unspoken accusation. Was this new boy involved in that supposed fight last night? Dunkel shakes his head as if trying to order his memories and thoughts, but it only exacerbates his headache. This boy is simply an unwelcome interruption, and he waves a dismissal.

"Don't disturb me this day, lad. I've naught for ye and much t' do. Be gone!"

"A word, sir. I seek only a honest job, sir. Perhaps as a servant in your household."

"Why come t' me? I've no such position t' offer, nor would I recommend ye t' others without the appropriate reference, I won't. Now 'scuse me, as I'll be on me way."

He frowns, signifying an end to the conversation, with ill consequences if the boy persists. He makes to continue into the street.

"Oh, no, sir!" Bo says, moving in front of Dunkel's large frame. "I *must* have some employment, and ye *can* provide it, ye can. Ye see, I know when t' keep silent, sir. I'd like t' assure His Majesty doesn't acquire any account of the events outside the inn, if ye get me drift. As a witness, I can 'roborate any story, sir."

Dunkel grabs Bo by the tunic, twisting his fists hard enough to make it difficult for the bandit to breathe. He is not sure what the miscreant could tell the prince, but he is sure he can deny anything and be believed.

"Leave this city, boy, and don't let me see your face again! If ye value your life, ye'll no longer present yeself here, ye won't. Do ye not think the prince'd sooner listen t' an honest citizen than t' the likes of ye? It's a dangerous game ye play."

"Oh, but there's more!" Bo manages to say, stretching his neck this way and that to relax the tight grip. "I happened to saunter past your tower, and I saw somethin' interestin'. Perhaps a young man climbin' into a certain chamber? Would it be worth ye knowin' who?"

The master's face ruddies even more than possible. "Ye'll tell me who, or—" Then he stops. It is no bother. Dunkel can guess for himself.

With that, he pushes the boy to the ground and trudges onward, muttering under his breath. His headache increasing by the minute, he heads out of the city without even a nod to the guard at the gate.

Watching the master walk away, Bo is perturbed. But he knows he must do whatever is necessary to survive.

I'll not betray ye, brother, he thinks. *Ye'll be avenged, and this man'll pay!*

~ Chapter 20 ~

Rose allows herself the luxury of arising late, after the autumn mists have largely dissipated. She stretches, yawns, and smiles as she remembers her evening with the duke. She smiles even wider as she notes the quantity of ducats set upon the small table against the wall. A portion of the bounty will be sequestered. Someday her attraction to clientele will wane. Perhaps she will be lucky enough to secure the support of a husband—even if not her own. She chuckles at the thought.

In short order, however, she recalls her vision out the window, and her smile changes into a more puzzled look with furrowed brow. That was, indeed, Dunkel dragging his *cargo* into the woods last eve, though she did not recognize his younger companion.

Perhaps there is a better future for Rose yet, or at least an opportunity for more remuneration.

First things first, she rises, splashes her face from the bowl of cold water, and dresses herself in gray tunic and surcotte, ignoring the shivers engendered by the cold air. The fire in the hearth has been allowed to diminish to mere embers, affording no real warmth or comfort. She gathers the payment, securing most of it in an inner pocket she has sewn into her dress. She smiles again and proceeds out the door, down the hall, and down the stairs.

The dining hall is empty of patrons at this hour, but serving maids are busy sweeping straw, wiping tables clean, and generally performing the necessary chores to prepare for the evening customers. The odor of stew wafts from the large kettle on the hearth, carried on a pleasurable breeze of warmed air.

~ Chapter 20 ~

The proprietor looks upon this activity with satisfaction as he reviews his books at a table next to the fire. His gaze does not fail to miss the appearance of his most productive serving maiden as she finally descends into the company.

"Well, princess, have ye deigned t' honor us with your presence this morn? Perhaps ye're a bit above the simple work of cleanin' and preparation, are ye, now that ye've secured a connection with nobility? Come, let me kiss your hand, I will," he offers, with a bit of a twinkle in his eye.

Rose sashays past his perch and makes a show of dropping a larger than usual share of coins from a great height. A smile from ear to ear spreads across the owner's face, giving him an almost demonic appearance.

"Thank ye, m' dear. Now, seein' that Duke Charmin' has failed t' sweep ye up t' ride t' the castle upon his great white horse, I'd appreciate a little hand with the housekeepin', I would."

Rose curtsies, turns with a flourish, appropriates a broom, and joins the other maidservants. She avoids the usual chatter until she is able to sit with her portion of bread and stew that serves as breakfast. In her buoyant mood, the fare is particularly delicious this morning.

Her colleagues gather around her, eager to hear details of the deportment of the duke, hoping to pry any secrets that may have been revealed to her.

"I wouldn't be likely t' share such confidences with the likes of ye, would I?" Rose offers coquettishly.

"Ye mean, what's it worth t' us, don't ye?"

"Ye're a sly lot, all of ye. Ye know very well his grace is too intelligent, he is, and not drunk enough t' share his state secrets with his one-night assignation!"

Nonplussed, one of the maidens continues, "Come, Rose, we all know ye're cleverer, ye are, than the great noblemen of Europe, the entire lot of 'em. Give us somethin' useful. Ye know, somethin' that might turn a coin or two."

"Really, girls, there's nothin'," Rose insists. "He's a wonderful lover, but he's gettin' on in years, he is, and he has a larger territory than France. All I could share with ye's the placement of an interestin' mole or two, which is of no use t' either ye or me. Unless, of course, ye plan to use such information t' acquire a small fortune from His Liege before approachin' his wife. I don't think ye'd value your pretty necks so little. Now, I must be off for the nonce, I must."

One of the servants squeaks, "Ah, a secret errand! Could it be for the duke? Do tell, dear."

Rose responds, "Not for His Liege at all, but for me own purposes, it is! Now be off, and leave me t' me own necessities. Curiosity's not becomin' t' the likes of ye, it's not, and it'll do ye little good, at any rate. I'm afraid me affairs are much more mundane, they are. See t' your own welfare!"

Rose rises from the table, dons a heavy wool tunic with a hood, and proceeds out the door. She allows herself a small grin as she exits, and she inhales the fresh scent of the fall breeze as she rounds the inn and heads into the wood. She must confirm what her eyes saw in the twilight.

This is no problem now, with bright daylight scattering the morning mist. Indeed, there is a slight trail made by dragging the outlaw's body, and she follows it carefully. It ends under a large oak, where it is evident the ground has been disturbed and a poor attempt made to restore it. Men are so clumsy when drunk and in a hurry, she notes. They should have been more careful. But then, they did not suspect they were being observed, did they?

She prods the ground with a fallen branch, revealing the briefest view of an arm. There is her proof. She is not blinded by age yet! Now she must hie to the forge—and indeed *forge* a plan on the way. This must certainly be done before others discover these poor remains.

But first, she must secure the path. Backing up to the inn, Rose carefully uses the branch to remove any obvious trace of the tracks, then looks carefully both ways to be sure she herself has not been observed. She pulls her tunic closer, suddenly chilled, and begins to make her way to Dunkel's forge.

◆ ◆ ◆

At the forge, the apprentice busies himself with the necessary preparations for the work day. He collects wood for the fire and kindles it. Satisfied with the developing flames, he sweeps, positions the master's tools, then goes outside. The mists have cleared in the bright light, and the view of the forest is glorious. But he has neither the time nor the inclination to take notice. He hurries down to the river, lowering the mechanisms for the water hammer and the bellows into the swift current. That completed, he returns to the forge to await the arrival of the journeyman and master.

Rudi arrives first, no longer displaying the buoyant mood of home. His face is more drawn, and the apprentice is loath to disturb his thoughts. Rudi takes no note, however, that the boy is even present. He digs under the scrap metal pile and pulls out his masterpiece—a suit of armor.

The apprentice has seen this armor only on occasion and was not aware of this hiding place. Rudi suddenly realizes the boy is standing there, watching him. Both of their faces flush for a moment, then Rudi shrugs and displays the armor to the young boy proudly.

"You know, with a certitude, that I cannot rely upon the master to grant me the time and materials to create my showpiece. I intend to present this to the guild in the near future, as I feel ready to apply for admission. The master, no doubt, will have other ideas, so I will not ask his advice. Yet I can ask yours."

The apprentice studies the armor, pretending a stern look of condescension, which causes Rudi to laugh. Notwithstanding, the boy looks carefully up and down the loosely bound pieces, glistening in the light of the forge fire, deliberately taking a moment too long. Then he shrugs.

"It will do, I suppose. I find it fit for an apprentice, if not for a duke." He returns Rudi's laugh. "However, I am glad to be of service in lightening your morose mood, sir."

"You are naught but a scalawag, and I am sure I should never count upon the opinion of one such as you! Can you not see the lightness and thinness of the well-hammered plate, or does its brilliance blind your eyes? Note that I have reduced the number of pieces needed for fitting, without loss of flexibility or coverage. Here, take the sallet, and you will see how light it is. And yet I have tested the strength of this steel, which will not permit perforation by even a closely released shaft from a longbow. All that remains is to etch the insignia, which I have not yet fully designed!"

"Sir, I mean no offense," the apprentice says sincerely. "This work is indeed more splendid than any I have seen of the master himself. It hefts lightly yet bears considerable strength. The cuisses and poleyns, even the sallet, are incomparable. And I note you have created not one, but two breastplates—I surmise one for dress and one for the joust. I am duly impressed."

Rudi proudly smiles as the apprentice continues. "Moreover, I would warrant this piece is intended for more than display before the guild masters. It must be for actual use. And who might be the intended recipient? I am not aware of any time you have had available to measure anyone in particular, and I can see it is not fitted to either yourself or to me."

Before Rudi can speak, an additional thought occurs to the boy. "Ah! The new forge that is slowly and magically developing upstream around the bend, about which we have bantered and speculated without answer as to who might be its master . . . that might not, perchance, be of your own hand?" He grins conspiratorially.

"Hush," Rudi says, looking over his shoulder, "but thank you for your kind words! Yes, indeed, the new forge is my own. But I am not yet ready to reveal the fact, at least not until I can declare myself a master. As to the patron of this work, I shall neither reveal that fact at this time. I must now place the insignia, then hide this, as I do not think it will please the master, who must be one to pass ultimate judgment. We shall see."

Although he has shared his plans for the new forge, Rudi does not tell the apprentice he is also repairing an old abandoned house in the wood—a safe house of sorts, as a contingency for himself and Beata in case events go badly while Dunkel still lives.

Rudi applies the etching on the interior of the breastplate, having finally decided to use a phoenix rising, surrounded by his own initials. Soon he is finished, and he hides the armor just before the apprentice signals the master's arrival.

Dunkel is in a surly mood indeed. He grumbles as he surveys the forge. The fire is hot, the tools and anvil have been laid out for him, fresh firewood has been carefully laid into a pile against the inner wall, and the bellows and water hammer are ready to engage.

"Good work t' ye, apprentice. Today we'll undertake the creation of several breastplates of various dimensions, we will. We'll be favored with an order from the Duke of Burgundy himself. Prepare yeselves, gentlemen, for some hard labor." He turns to Rudi. "But first I'd have a word with ye, journeyman. Outside!"

As Dunkel heads outside, Rudi smiles and shrugs toward the apprentice, then follows the master.

Dunkel places both hands, outstretched, on Rudi's shoulders, then looks deeply and sternly into his eyes. "I've trusted ye with me secrets, I have. I've trusted ye with me home. Me memory is not what it used t' be, but I believe ye were of great assistance t' me last night. Is this so?"

Rudi is touched, and he smiles while looking deeply into Dunkel's own eyes.

"I did what was necessary, master. You did what you needed to do, and I was there to help."

In his mind, Rudi has much more to say. *You were a big fool. The ale is killing you. Look at you—rotund and yellow as a squash! Your wife? She must lock herself away against your approach. So yes, I was there to help last eve. But not for long, sir. No, not for long. You are a fine—even a great—armorer. But I am ready to become my own master, and then we shall see. His Highness is by now well aware of the source of skill at this forge.*

As if in answer, Dunkel's look darkens. His grip on Rudi's shoulders tightens. "I've had a most peculiar experience this morn, I have. Did ye happen t' run across a most disagreeable young man, purportin' t' have information for sale?"

Rudi tries not to blink. "Yes, I did. And what did you do, sir, when he approached you?"

"Why, I dismissed him, I did, of course! I'll not be bothered by the beggars in the streets, I won't. Yet it strikes me that he carries an air of superiority, he does, and a most peculiar story, some of which he did share with me."

"You threatened him, sir, I am sure." Rudi is suddenly sweating, even trembling slightly.

Dunkel laughs. "Indeed, ye know me only too well, ye do. But I know *ye*, sir, I do." His grip tightens. "And just lookin' at ye now, I surmise e'en more. Know ye not how many eves I sought ye out in your chamber t' discuss work, only t' find ye gone? It was clear ye had other business than mine in mind, ye did. Dare I say even a tryst?" He pauses. "Yet I ne'er dreamed the source of your affection lay *within me own household*!" These last words are spoken loudly, as the great brutal man shakes Rudi's shoulders.

Rudi is now as white as the ghost of his ancestors. "What did that impertinent boy tell you, sir? I deny it all!"

Dunkel flushes in anger, which would have him red as a beet if it were not for his deep yellow jaundice. "He told me naught, but ye tell me all. Ye'll clear all your meager possessions out of me house this e'en, ye will. I'll not suffer your presence any longer near me house nor me forge. I'll see t' it that ye'll ne'er be a master in this guild! Begone!"

Rudi's blood-drained appearance dissipates as he first thinks to deny the accusation, then thinks better of it. Instead, he takes on a countenance of stern resolution.

"I do not fear you, sir. Remember I am a witness to your actions last night, not to mention your behavior in your own household! And I would be careful what you tell the guild, as I intend soon to present my petition for recognition. So I will take my leave, though I beg you to hold your foul tongue, if you would desire that I hold mine! There, that is the bargain I will offer, sir."

Rudi steps back carefully out of reach of Dunkel and within sight of the apprentice inside the forge. He will return later to remove his masterpiece. He will finish his work on his own forge.

For now, he must return directly to the tower house, for he cannot bear to leave his love in danger. She must leave with him.

◆ ◆ ◆

Rose makes her way to the forge, still not fully sure how approach to Dunkel. She knows this may be her one chance to escape the servant's life, and she is not getting any younger. She follows the path down the mountain to the riverbank, passing alternately between deep shadow and bright light.

Above, geese are making their way aerodynamically south. She envies their single-minded perseverance. Ultimately, she must adopt their resolve and just take an open and honest approach with Dunkel. If he rebuffs her, she loses nothing—and so much the worse for him.

She smiles and takes a deep breath, inhaling the aroma of newly fallen leaves only now tainted by the competing aroma of coal and wood burning at the forge ahead. Small creatures of the forest floor scamper across her path with increasing scarcity as she nears the rising smoke.

As she approaches, she hears the voices of the master and journeyman raised in anger. Soon enough, the younger man stomps right past her, taking no notice whatever of her presence, and is gone before she can even utter a simple good morrow.

Rose comes to a halt in the path. Perhaps this is not the best time to present her proposition to the armorer. But then she lifts her chin and continues forward. She has not yet entirely lost her charms, and Dunkel certainly has a singular preference for them. It is time to soothe the savage beast!

"Goo' day, Master Hammer!" she calls out. "I'd have a word with ye, sir!"

Dunkel, still reeling from his exchange with Rudi, is taken somewhat by surprise by his visitor. He frowns at first, then takes a deep breath and manages a grin, perhaps with a visible touch of guile. He raises his eyebrows, strokes his poorly shaven chin, and saunters up to Rose.

"So, ye're missin' me attention already, are ye? Though this is hardly the place for ye t' return me largesse of last evenin'. What'd ye have of me t'day? Let me guess. His grace so thoroughly enjoyed your company that he's summarily decided t' eliminate his wife and make ye his own. So ye're here t' tell me ye can't repay the kindness, as ye're movin' out of the city forthwith!"

Rose laughs, then blushes. "Ye mistake me, sir, ye do. I'm no lady of the court, I'm not, as well ye know. I'd prefer t' think meself a match for a more practical gentleman."

"A baker, perhaps? Certainly not an armorer," Dunkel says with a laugh. "This one's well attached and of no more inclination t' dispose of his spouse than the good duke, I'm not. Come, what'd ye have of me? Though I can promise me attentions better after the work of the day is well put t' bed—at which time I meself'd be inclined t' be well put t' bed!"

He laughs again, but Rose is not amused.

"Sir, ye mock me!" She blushes attractively but not demurely, a signature appearance since childhood and to which she owes her name. "But no matter. I'd say I'm indifferent t' your attentions, but it'd be a falsehood, it would, as ye know me too well already." She takes a breath. "I've come t' share with ye a story of some import t' your reputation, I have, which I hope ye'll allow me t' recount."

"Me reputation, ye say? Do I have one, aside from me work—which, I should think, is beyond the criticism of the likes of ye? Come, tell me what the gossips say of me. Should I be flattered?" He offers a great, deep laugh that gives him the countenance of nothing more than a carved gourd, so deep is the yellow tone of his skin.

"Master Dunkel, ye know well that me room at the inn has a view t' the back woods, it has. And so, I had the *misfortune* t' steal a view just prior t' darkness last e'en. And what do ye think I spied? Two gentlemen unceremoniously draggin' a third into the woods! I fear I wasn't the only person catchin' a glimpse of the scene, but this I can't confirm, I can't. Nevertheless, there was enough light t' see the men, though I only recognized the one."

She pauses and lets her words float between her and the armorer.

At this, it is Dunkel's turn to blush—not a pretty site. "What're ye tellin' me, girl?" he thunders. "Is this an accusation? I admit t' nothin'—certainly nothin' ye can verify!"

"Ah, sir, but I can!" she says with determination. "I took it upon meself t' take a walk into the woods this very morn. I stumbled across a most upsettin' discovery, I did. All that remains is for me t' find a corroborative witness."

Dunkel is enraged yet again. "Saucy wench! I doubt your ability t' connect me t' this event of yours!"

"We're obliged, sir, are we not, t' inform the prince's guard of all such shenanigans? Perhaps ye can help me with this dilemma. Certainly for your sake, I might be inclined t' risk sudden amnesia."

"What would *ye* ask o' *me*?" It is not a question but rather an insult.

Rose knows this is her chance. "Well, sir, ye've been inclined t' seek me favors in the past, and ye must admit me ability t' satisfy, ye must. Yet I'm not gettin' any younger, I'm not, and I can't rely entirely upon me only assets fore'er." She is too nervous to smile, but she makes a show of adjusting her clothing to lift her breasts. "I should think it's time t' settle down, t' find a husband, if not a benefactor."

"Ye'd *dare*!" Dunkel thunders. "I'd advise ye t' stay clear of me wrath, or ye might find your features of e'en less use t' ye, fräulein. I'll not be blackmailed, I'll not. Nor can ye prove a thing! Begone with ye!"

Dunkel raises a hand as if to strike, and Rose winces and ducks. She recovers some dignity, turns with a swish of her surcotte, and walks several steps before turning around briefly.

"Ye'll hear from me further, sir, ye will. I'll allow ye t' think upon it."

As she walks back to the inn, glancing back several times, she realizes she may have taken too great a chance. He has killed once, she realizes, suddenly afraid. She cannot trust him again. She must move the body. And she must be sure to have someone scribe a message to His Highness, in the event of ill activity.

Or perhaps there's another way . . .

~ Chapter 21 ~

As the morning light casts away the last of the mist, the woods and the city are revealed in greater detail. Entering the gate, Rudi ignores the ignominious salutations of the guards, who just laugh but make no effort to slow his progress. He heads straight for the tower, throws open the door, and bounds up the stairs to Beata's chamber, startling the servants along the way and nearly colliding with Fee and Besse, who are on their way out to market.

Fee catches her breath, then calls up to him, "What is it, sir? Has something happened to the master? Heaven forfend, to the apprentice?"

"Keep to your own business, Fee, and leave me to mine! They all fare well—more's the pity to me!" Rudi calls back briefly without stopping.

He knocks heavily on the rough wood of Beata's door. Throwing all caution to the wind, he cries, "Beata! You of silken golden hair, you of bright sunshine, allow me entrance! Beata!"

In due time, seeming to Rudi half an eternity, the door opens. Good. Beata is alone. This is the ideal opportunity for him. He sweeps the lady into his arms and kisses her passionately.

She is at first quite startled, then alarmed. Her eyes open widely. She pushes herself away, attempting to regain her composure. She considers this an intrusion. She is barely dressed and has applied only powder to her face and nothing yet to her lips—to say nothing of the inadequate opportunity to brush her long, flowing hair. This makes her angry, and a scowl intrudes upon her normally serene composure.

"And what, sir, is the meaning of this? You have disturbed my morning ablutions. To what do I owe this dishonor—oh!"

Suddenly she realizes she is thinking too much of herself and not at all of the portent of Rudi's unannounced and unabashed arrival.

"What has happened? Has my husband taken ill? Has there been an accident?"

"What? Oh, no! I have worse news than that, my dearest. We are discovered! You must away with me. I have prepared a dwelling for us outside the city. I have labored long and hard to prepare it, with just the right light to shine upon the brilliance of your hair and complement your complexion, most beauteous one. No one but I knows the location." Rudi's voice rises with urgency. "You are not safe here!"

Beata takes but a moment to think and regain her composure. "You must calm down, my precious. It is you who are not safe. You must leave, then get word to me of your whereabouts, so that I may stay in contact with you. But I shall remain here. I have managed to avoid my husband's presence all this time, and I shall continue to do so."

"I do not trust him, milady," Rudi says, shaking his head. "Come with me, my dearest. Do not live in this dungeon tower one moment longer, in shame under the eye of the master, who would do you great harm, given the opportunity. I am forlorn!" Rudi's concern is clearly evident in the furrowing of his brow.

"Fear not, my love," Beata soothes him, stroking his chin gently. "I shall ever be yours and yours alone. It is not shame before Dunkel that motivates me but shame before the citizens of the city, who will surely gossip if I leave with you now. For this same reason, Dunkel will agree to my staying—he will not be made a cuckold before the citizens. Though I will stay only upon the condition that he no longer disturbs my chamber." Beata looks into Rudi's eyes. "I must ask the same of you, as a boon. I will not risk his finding you here."

Exasperated, Rudi gives out a long sigh. How could she allow mere propriety to keep her in this—yes, this dungeon! And with that ogre! Has some witch stolen her away, only to hide her here, away from her one true love? He gives one more try to sway her from her decision.

~ Chapter 21 ~

"I am near to completing my masterpiece for submission to the guild," he says. "I will beg them to exclude the master in judgment. Even His Highness knows the real origin of his commissions these latter years, as the effects of mead and ale have taken hold of Dunkel's skill. I will soon build you a home within the walls—a castle to rival that of the prince, if you must have it. How shall I convince you to follow your own desires and come away with me for now?"

"Even if he manages to spoil your advancement, we both know he will not live long," Beata replies coolly, her hand on his lips in an attempt to calm him. "His position will become mine for six months, and you may marry me and claim it as yours."

Rudi drops his shoulders, smiling weakly as he demurs. Beata, relieved, returns the gesture.

"So take with you my undying love and watch over me from afar, till the day his illness overtakes him. It cannot be long, dearest. Be of firm mind and constant devotion, and we shall have it all! Now, gather your belongings and go, before I can no longer bear to be without you."

As she speaks, her face becomes more and more shadowed. Even white powder cannot hide the darkness of her thoughts, an appearance Rudi mistakes for grief.

"Fear not, love—*my* love," he says with resignation. "I will ever be watching over your safety. Grant me one kiss, and I will away."

Beata kisses him. He grabs her and holds her tight for an instant, then he is gone.

As he disappears, Beata thinks, *Truly, it will not be long, my love. My existence is intolerable. So I will be strong for us both and see to it that we are together in body as well as spirit.*

Rudi gathers his few possessions and gives one last, longing glance about the tower home he has shared with the apprentice and the family of Dunkel Hammer. At first wistful, then touched with a modicum of grief, his countenance changes from one of sadness to one of resolve.

Beata is his, and nothing the armorer can do will change that. He must cheer himself, as nothing is truly lost here. What he has earned, he will claim as his own. In time, he will gain entry into the guild, and Beata will be his entirely.

Sooner than later, if it were left to the journeyman.

~ Chapter 22 ~

The young dauphin awakens in his chamber as the morning mists stream through the opening in the thick granite wall that serves as a window. The fire in the great hearth has been stoked and resupplied with wood, lending a pleasant scent to the room and dispelling the fog before it can rise to the level of the mattress.

After seeing to his immediate needs, he dons the sumptuous clothing, one item at a time, set out for him by Jurg. He does does not like such frippery, but he will have to accustom himself to it. Appearances are important to the family and the citizens one must eventually rule. As his father has decreed, today Charles must begin assuming his new responsibilities as dauphin.

He wistfully regrets the lost opportunity to run to the glade with his friend Hans for yet one more mock battle. Charles wants to explain his father's wishes to his friend, and he wants to plan for more practice at the glade whenever time allows. He will send Jurg for Hans, as it would not do to parade through the city in these accoutrements himself.

With that, Charles sighs as he finishes dressing, then smiles as the light of day reaches his face, adding to the warmth in the room. He brushes out his tangled hair with a bit of oil to complete the look, then awaits Jurg for the agenda of the day.

As if on cue, the valet enters the room, looking somewhat glum until he notes the effect of the daylight upon his charge.

"You look splendid, sire! No princess will be able to resist you. Let me fasten the tunic, then I will apprise you of your father's plans as you finish making yourself presentable. Then we must to breakfast, as I feel particularly hungry this fine morning."

Jurg's need to assist his brother has not completely vacated his mind, but he manages a smile nevertheless.

Charles notices the concern upon Jurg's face, thinks for a moment, then tells him, "You are troubled, sir. I am sure you have just returned from the dungeon, if I am not mistaken. I am truly sorry for you. You must understand, however, that my sympathies cannot fully extend to your brother. I am aware of how you yourself came to be in our service. And I know it is fate, and not our governorship, that has dealt so poorly with Peter."

Jurg gives a slight nod, thinking indeed of how fate led Peter to this current situation.

"Yet I am not a believer in punishment that will only reinforce the need for the behavior," Charles continues. "At any rate, it is His Majesty who decides and enforces judgment, not I. But I will set my mind to an appropriate solution that will allow your brother to serve us more usefully but not without punishment—else others be encouraged to attack our citizens and trade caravans."

"You are too kind, sire," Jurg says, allowing the concern to show fully upon his face. "But I will put such thoughts aside for the moment."

Charles smiles. As a distraction, he laughs a bit. "Come, sir, and tell me the origin of this finery—silk, embroidery, pointed footware, felt hat. I feel like a strutting peacock! This is not my wont. But it allows me to conjecture the plans of His Majesty. There will be court today, will there not? And will I not attend upon a meeting with him first, for chastisement and instruction?"

"Indeed, sire. He will want to put your wisdom and studies to the test."

"Thank you for your honesty, Jurg. I believe I can trust you to serve my needs, should they not conflict with His Majesty's. For now, a boon: if you would be so kind as to apprehend my friend Hans Handler and summon him to meet me in the bailey before I am called to my father, I would appreciate it greatly."

"Your wish is my command, sire." With that, Jurg bows and takes his leave.

~ Chapter 22 ~

As it turns out, the merchant's son already awaits in the courtyard with news of his own. He is not dressed for training in the glade, but rather he sports the attire of a young burgher. Clearly unused to the fresh, clean fabrics, he is unable to hide his fidgeting.

Smiling at Hans's distress, Jurg calls out, "Young man! If you would please approach, I would be most grateful to lead you to His Young Highness. Or you may tarry here for his arrival, as he has commanded me."

"I should stay here, sir, as I am not sure how His Highness would take to an unbidden entrance," Hans replies. "Please inform him I am here by leave of my father, who wishes my return anon, but allows me to explain myself to the dauphin." Hans continues fidgeting, apparently somewhat nervous, not wanting to disappoint his friend.

He does not have long to wait. The dauphin sweeps into the courtyard, avoiding the appearance of strutting.

Hans's eyes go wide. "Sire! You are a sight! Peacocks would display for you! Stand here, out of the light, that I might conserve my eyes from blindness, if you please, sire."

Charles laughs. "Hans, you are ever my friend and not one to withhold your opinions. In truth, I am of the same judgment! But as you can see, today ends our youthful adventures, I am afraid. Moreover, I can surmise by your arrival here unsummoned—and your own attire—that your father is of the same intention. Our companionship shall not suffer, though. I will instruct my valet, Jurg, to schedule some training and other time together, as His Highness will allow, and then I will dispatch the information for your father's approval."

"Thank you, sire. I do look forward to our time together." Hans sighs. "But for the moment, I must be off. With your leave . . ."

"Of course." Charles turns to his valet. "Jurg, you will please accompany me to my father, as I would not keep him waiting longer."

The dauphin heads back into the castle, and Hans suppresses a laugh as he hears the tinkle of the bells on his upturned shoes.

◆ ◆ ◆

"Welcome, my son, and let me have a look at you!" the prince exclaims with a gesture toward the tapestries lining the public chamber of the castle. This area is used for inquiries and festivities and is illuminated by clerestory leaded-glass windows. In his current splendor, Charles could be the subject of a number of the depicted scenes. Henrik's eyes twinkle as he laughingly suggests, "Why, you are the picture of royalty! Do a turn for me."

"As you wish, sire," replies the dauphin with a bow and a turn. "But I warrant the next time you see me in such overreaching attire, it will at least be without these infernal bells. I feel like the cat whose presence is ever announced to the household mice! This frumpery suits me not, if you know my preferences, sire." His face, somewhat reddened, confirms the truth.

Henrik frowns. "So now tell me exactly why you must present yourself so."

Charles looks up, meeting his father's eyes, and sighs. So, the testing begins! "I know well, sire, that a ruler's appearance must create in the citizens the impression of trust and awe—the more to prevent the use of the guard to enforce laws and judgments. I rather feel like a jewel dangling from the throne, but such decisions are not yet mine to make. I will always acquiesce to your orders, Father, and will present myself in such manner that will do you only the highest honor and obeisance. From which, I surmise an audience is planned for the nonce."

"I do not misplace my pride in you, my son." Henrik's eyes shine. "We shall indeed have an audience today. I wish for you to watch and listen closely and offer me your advice and confidences. To that end, I would spend this time forenoon in some review and questioning." He clears his throat. "To begin, what do you surmise of the state of the realm at this date?"

The dauphin's eyes widen. He was not expecting an open-ended question requiring reflection.

~ Chapter 22 ~

He thinks for a moment, then replies, "I think, sire, we are in very good shape at the moment. The city is clean, and our citizenry is safe and well fed. We have had the good fortune to escape the ravages of the plague of the century past, thanks to our forebears' judgment of the need for cleanliness—surmised as the reason the Jews were not afflicted in other cities.

"Moreover, we are in good position to use the wars between England and France to our advantage, as we have some of the best military trainers and smiths in the world. Therefore, we are in far better shape than our neighbors in the Gallic countries. And finally, the strength in our soldiery acts as a bulwark against any nobility with overreaching ambition."

"Excellent," Henrik says, straightening his posture in pride with a smile. "I see you have put some thought into your studies, son. But you must always continue to exercise the power to analyze. The positions of our neighbors, near and far, are ever shifting, and a prince must know how to turn all such to his advantage. Therefore, what do you consider our most important item of trade—our weaponry, our soldiery, our fortunately abundant food?"

Charles shakes his head. "No, sire. I beg your indulgence to allow me to differ." He draws a breath, strokes his chin. "Our most important item in trade is information, followed only by absolute neutrality. In conflicts, one side or the other always wins and writes history in its own image. But if one's ambition is confined to the welfare of a manageable number of subjects, then it is possible to shift all such conflicts outside to some advantage—if one is careful to do naught to stir the ire of a more powerful enemy."

"Precisely!" Henrik claps his hands. "You have discovered the secret to our survival as a principality. Larger kingdoms are won and lost repeatedly. So now you understand well my timing in asking you to join in the council."

Charles allows his shoulders to relax as he exhales in relief. "Yes, sire. Today you will hold audience and you will accept gifts for the treasury. But the greatest gift will be given freely, and I must be there to accept it. That gift is the news these travelers will bring!"

♦ ♦ ♦

As the day wears on, Charles is busy acquainting himself on a new level with the castle workers. Now they have a genuine hero in their midst. One who is showing himself this day in a regal manner, yet one who is modest and caring enough to inquire of their needs and avoid any recount of his own exploitations. This is a future prince indeed, one who can be counted upon to show concern for their welfare above his own—a rare trait amongst nobility.

Charles admits his father was correct in having him dress the part this day, although he already misses the near invisibility and freedom of a childhood suddenly left behind. It suddenly occurs to him: if he is to be treated as a responsible adult, then there will be some urgency to find a suitable wife.

He turns to his valet, who accompanies him on his rounds. "Jurg, the royal visit of the duke was no coincidence. Do you think he is in need of some service we can provide? Or perhaps," he adds, "as his realm exceeds that of France and includes rich lands, do you think his ambition extends even further?"

"I cannot fathom the thoughts and ambitions of nobility beyond the walls of this city, sire. Yet I trust in the wisdom of His Highness, that we shall all remain safe here. I do not think this duke would wish to try the defenses of the best-trained soldiery in Europe."

Charles purses his lips in thought. "Yet he must have had a purpose in visiting here, I think. Actually, Hans and I have speculated upon it. First, he must know the strength and intentions of his neighbors in order to ensure the peace and safety of his own realm. Thus, I am convinced my father would not hesitate to show our capacity to defend ourselves while reassuring him we have no army formed with thoughts of expansion. But I think there is more. The face of Europe changes, and the duke is strong but aging. Prosperity demands trade; peace demands alliances."

Charles smiles, then waits to see if Jurg understands his drift.

At this point, the two are heading into the castle in anticipation of dinner and preparations for the audience.

Jurg looks thoughtful for a moment, then smiles himself. "You are wondering, sire, if the duke has a daughter. I know for a fact he does, and I am told she is most beautiful to behold. He refers to her as La Claire, which must have some relevant origin."

"In truth, I too know of this daughter's existence, but of her person I know nothing," the dauphin admits. He glances about him, lowering his voice conspiratorially. "I would inquire of this La Claire, Jurg, but with some discretion."

Jurg blushes. "Sire, I am ever at your service. I will serve you ever as well as I have your father, if not better! I ask only that should a conflict arise, you might defend my case to His Majesty."

Charles nods. "I like that well and will accept, sir. Moreover, if I should ever be in need of service that would place you in conflict with His Majesty, or even your own family, I shall offer you the opportunity to decline and will respect it. I have already personally observed your honesty and integrity, and I know you are a man of your word!"

Jurg cannot help but laugh. "I should have known you would be smart enough to ascertain the histories and needs of your household's servants, sire. It will indeed be a pleasure and an education to serve you!"

Jurg gives a polite bow and ushers his charge into the castle.

~ Chapter 23 ~

The castle is already beginning to fill with members of the local citizenry taking their places along the tapestries according to their station in life, with the lesser nobility, officers, and wealthiest merchant families closest to the dais set at one end.

Gossip is readily exchanged, not the least of which is the observation of not the usual two but three thrones. This can, of course, mean only one thing—the dauphin will now join his parents as an adult and not merely stand behind his father. Some of the town wives and young maidens have already glimpsed him in his new finery and run to tell their friends and neighbors, suppressing giggles and blushes of anticipation. The fact that Princess Amalia herself is of bourgeois origin instills hope and speculation among the merchants' daughters that they may be considered as prospects for a title. And such a handsome prince!

The ladies in the observing audience are impressed at the sight as the prince emerges, leading his son. One leans to her children, exclaiming, "Now, daughters, you must do all you can to catch the dauphin's eye. More—you must catch the eye of His Majesty himself!"

Amalia enters the room from the side, carefully surveying the population in attendance. She smiles as she sees the primping and posturing, like a show of puppetry amongst painted faces. She knows, of course, of the negotiations of her husband with the Duke of Burgundy, and she approves. Yet she wishes she knew more of this daughter, whose beauty is of great renown. Would it be wrong to allow the aspirations of the citizenry to last a little longer? She is not schooled in the art of deception. She notes to herself that she must discuss this with her husband, upon whose wisdom she has come to rely wholly. With that she sighs, smiles for the public, and upon the entry of her husband and son, curtsies to them and seats herself upon her throne.

"All rise for His Majesty, the prince!" announces the bailiff, who will also record the proceedings on parchment for approval and seal of His Majesty.

"You may all be at ease, and welcome," the prince says.

There is seating only around the walls of the chamber, in front of the tapestries and windows. The prince has insisted these wooden benches must be reserved for those who are infirm and elderly. Even nobility in attendance must stand. This allows those present to focus their attention upon the nobility and guests on the raised dais, which serves the prince's purpose well.

"Today we shall confine ourselves to those requesting audience," he begins. "There will be no judgments. We are aware that many of you are concerned about our two guests in the dungeon and the actions that led them there. We will state now only that they are properly fed but confined and will have an opportunity to state their case in open council shortly."

Henrik smiles with a look of pride, gesturing to the young man beside him as he addresses the assembly. "We welcome the presence of our son, Prince Charles, to whom all deference must henceforth be paid."

Here, the young dauphin bows to the prince.

"Bailiff," he continues, "you will announce the order of presentation."

"Your Majesties, ladies and gentlemen—may I present to you Grizelda, daughter of the butcher Helmut, who requests audience for his daughter that she might be recognized as of age."

A young maiden dressed in a fine new blue surcotte and pointed hat steps forward shyly. She bows before the seated nobility but says nothing. Amalia rises from her throne, steps down, and gently places her hand beneath the young girl's chin, raising her face for closer examination.

"This must be a bit unnerving for you, my dear. But you should not fear to hold your head high. I see you are without blemish and not caked with powder. Would you submit to a few questions of my son?"

Grizelda is in no position to refuse any request from her lady, which carries the force of a command. She curtsies but still says nothing.

Charles takes on a stern look and straightens his posture, lending the moment an appearance of real importance. He touches his finger to his chin, considers for a moment, then asks, "Have you been educated in the art of running a household, and do you read, fräulein?"

She blushes but now speaks for the first time, her voice a bit higher than natural. "Yes, Your Highness. I can read in good Deutsch and Latin both. My mama has me accompany her to market and allows me to determine the most efficient tasks for the servants on occasion."

"Then you should have little trouble finding a good husband," Charles replies. "If it pleases you to learn the finer etiquette, perhaps to dance, you will certainly be welcome at functions of court. I congratulate you, fräulein, and wish you success and happiness."

Grizelda understands that her public ordeal, such as it is, is now concluded, and she curtsies yet again. She reenters the attendant citizenry and takes the side of her mother, who nods proudly as a statement that she has done well. Of course, the other maidens are busy whispering to each other, finding or creating flaws. This one now has the eye of the prince, and there is no shortage of jealousy in the chamber. What can this maiden or that maiden do to catch similar attention?

There is but one additional announcement of the bailiff. "At the summons of Your Majesty, may I present the merchant Serge Kaufmann, born of this principality and now returned."

Serge steps forward, motioning his servants behind him to place before the dais three trunks of polished black lacquer and intricate carving. He bows deeply to the prince and waits to be addressed.

- Chapter 23 -

Murmurs spread through the room like a wave across the sea. The attendees have been awaiting this man's arrival since his wife began setting up their family's household. And most have heard of the inauspicious arrival of the caravan as well as the heroic exploit of the young dauphin and his companion. Now they have their first real opportunity to see the merchant himself. Perhaps they will hear why he has settled here—the subject of much gossip.

He does not disappoint them; there is the additional sensation of his attire. Blanche did not presume to guess his measurements and therefore did not have an appropriate ensemble prepared for him. In fact, he rather likes to showcase fashion from the rest of Europe. In particular, he chose from Florence a blousing shirt, leather-skirted doublet, and knee-length tunic embroidered with gold thread and lace ties.

If he creates enough of a sensation, the tailors of the principality will be at his doorstep. Indeed, he has created a stir. The ladies, almost in unison, think: *See how he is dressed! Should I be adjusting my own fashion? I must be the first to befriend his wife!*

Even the princess raises an interested eyebrow but holds her tongue. She will have ample opportunity to learn more later. She makes a mental note to invite this family to the castle at a near date.

"Welcome, Herr Kaufmann, to our humble principality and the place of your roots," offers the prince.

"I thank you, Your Majesty," Serge replies. "I do confess to a certain nostalgia—as well as to a curiosity regarding the motives of your invitation. But I feel I have much to offer to the principality, and in turn it offers me the ability to develop trade plans of my own."

Now the citizens are abuzz. *Invitation*? Did the prince invite the merchant to settle in Quellestadt? Why? Between his sensational fashion and the mystery of this invitation, the citizens cannot help but see this as an opportunity to share in the exotic—even as bystander to a folktale or choristers in a mummer's play. But it is important to maintain decorum, so the noise dies down as people step back.

Amalia is amused. She can imagine the tales that will be told in the city. The merchant's arrival is not quite the stuff of legend, but it does not hurt to enliven the population now and then. Besides, she is as curious as they are. The difference is that she is in a position to satisfy that curiosity.

"And yet, Herr Kaufmann," the prince continues, "I would have thought your family would accompany you for this presentation, as was requested."

"My deepest apologies, sire," Serge replies. "It was necessary for my wife and daughter to arrange the presentation of the shop this evening. My daughter, Ebouisante, serves me better than any son in the position of bookkeeper. Also, I thought it fit to introduce Your Majesties to Ebouisante in a less public manner, as she does not yet feel prepared to be named as an adult available for courtship. She is making her way at this very moment to the palace, though, and I shall be deeply honored to present her to Your Majesties privately. It is perhaps a liberty I should not have taken with your kind invitation, but it is an acquiescence of a doting father to the wishes of his most beloved offspring." Serge bows deeply.

Henrik smiles. "We look forward to her arrival, then, sir. And it is our wish that you will remain after the audience, as we would like to inquire further as to the details of your caravan arrival and the actions of our son. We fervently hope you were not too much discomfited, and we assure you that appropriate action will soon be taken."

"There is always a certain danger in the undertaking of any caravan." Serge bows to the dauphin. "Though I am grateful that his young majesty could come to our aid. I would be honored to remain afterward to discuss the matter further."

The princess leans over to the prince and whispers, "Sire, I would most greatly appreciate an invitation to your discussion with this gentleman after the audience."

The prince has a small smile for his wife. "I am sure you would, my dear," he whispers back. "However, I shall instead promise to consult with you immediately thereafter. You know I value your judgment, and I will have much to discuss at that time. Your curiosity will be satisfied."

"Then I am content. For now, I am most curious as to the contents of those chests. I have never seen their like!"

As if on cue, Serge announces, "Your Highness, please allow me to present you with a few tokens of my regard."

Indeed, no one in Quellestadt has seen anything resembling the intricate workmanship of these wonders. The carvings cannot be truly appreciated at a small distance. Yet even from the vantage of the assembly, the artistry seems to be that of a god of woodwork or at least a grand master. The local artists have all they can do to restrain themselves from approaching more closely.

Amalia smiles. She, at least, will have the time for closer inspection. These chests must be preserved and protected. But then Serge gestures to his servants with a flourish, and even she is astonished by the contents revealed.

The chest is lined with lead and filled with richly painted porcelain urns. Serge motions to the princess to approach for closer inspection. Amalia gently lifts a vase as if she were afraid to break the fragile object. The exterior scenes are floral or pastoral. The princess—as well as the gathered citizens—marvel at the quality of the painted china, the gold leaf. Most of all, the appearance of the painted figures captures her imagination.

She turns to Serge with a smile. "Tell me, sir, who is capable of such workmanship? The shapes of these vessels are perfect, the surfaces without blemish! But why represent the characters with such upturned eyes and such rich dress?"

"They are Chinese, madame. The appearance is not stylized. But rather, this is the true countenance of the populace. Their empire is vast, their engineering advanced, their artisanry beyond most of our own. At this moment, I have secured a large supply of such porcelain and a new route for acquisition. You are aware of the trade road to the Orient, sire," continues Serge, addressing the prince. "I fear it is about to close, due to the political exigencies. However, trade will always find its way, with a little hard work and ingenuity. These are the finest examples of the craft, and so I have naturally reserved them as a gift to the Crown."

"But what is the content?" the princess asks, noting some of the urns are not empty. "I see some are filled with a fine black powder. Surely this is not meant to be cosmetic!"

"No, madame," the merchant says, shaking his head. Then he turns and smiles at the prince. "I am sure His Highness is familiar with the latest in weaponry—that is, artillery! Projectiles are thrown not by mechanical means but by alchemical. The French are even now acquiring the equipment needed to throw missiles long distances without a trebuchet. These are called cannons and guns. The necessary element is this gunpowder, and I present it to you for study and practice. Unfortunately, I am unable to provide the weaponry itself, but I will be delighted to provide your generals with the names and connections to the Frenchmen who can. For now, I would suggest removal of the powder and more aesthetic use of the vessels."

"We thank you, sir," offers the princess. "Surely this is the most wonderful gift. We will treasure it. But what is contained in the other chests?"

"The Chinese, madame, are a wondrous people. They are capable of the highest artistry and high invention. Each of these chests contains fabrics of the finest silk for your tailors, imprinted and embroidered with scenes and patterns comparable to the vessels you have just seen. But more," he adds, then takes a dramatic pause, "each chest also contains a most complex mechanical device, the which I beg your favor to demonstrate. These are more than mere toys. I would have your own craftsmen examine them, if they would do so without harm, as such devices could create yet a whole new industry for the coffers of the principality."

Serge gestures again to his servants to open the two remaining chests and bring out the two devices.

~ Chapter 23 ~

The audience gasps. They have never seen the like. Instant desire and envy registers on the faces of all the bourgeoisie present. Serge is reminded of hunting dogs held at bay after cornering a fox. He smiles. This is precisely the reaction he seeks. *Yes, my wife will be very busy, as will I, in short order,* he thinks.

The first device is an exquisite representation of a goose with springs and a windup key. The workmanship is exquisite—the feathers painted onto fine white porcelain, yet they look quite real. The colors are vivid. Before the captivated crowd, Serge winds the springs. When they release, the neck is shown to be of several overlapping plates, as are the wings. The head straightens and rises, the wings extend, a hidden bell sounds, and the goose releases—lo! It releases an egg covered in gold leaf!

The gathered citizenry is completely flabbergasted! Can such devices be recreated? Each person feels he or she must have one—no, the *first* one! Does the merchant have more? How soon can one get to his shop without looking overly eager? Too soon, and it will present a poor bargaining position for price. Too late, and there will be nothing to purchase!

The second device is equally wondrous. A carved maiden, heavily lacquered with a visage of enamel, anchors an instrument. The face is beautiful yet humble as the slanted eyes face downward, rather than directly at the viewer. Serge winds and releases the spring, causing the miniature harp to sing in wondrous, bell-like tones. And the strings are of gold!

The prince rises and gestures to his own servants to take the chests to the treasury in the dungeon tower, just a level below the prisoners.

He faces Serge with a smile. "We thank you, sir, for these most impressive gifts. We are sure our expectations in the extension of our invitation to you will be more than met. Please remain behind"—he turns to the citizenry with a flourish, exclaiming a bit louder—"as this assembly is now concluded. You may all return to your homes and business."

Serge remains behind, as demanded. He knows he has failed to present his family as requested by the prince, but by now his daughter should be on her way to the castle. Still, he has certainly succeeded in making exactly the impression he intended upon both royalty and citizenry. Yet what more does His Highness plan to demand of him? Will he be reprimanded for failing the summons of his entire family? He frowns, then shrugs. He waits for direction as the crowd departs.

~ Chapter 24 ~

Ebouisante enters the assembly room, head high but biting her lip in some trepidation, as she knows she is late for a command appearance. She is quickly announced by the guard. Suddenly she blushes as her presence stops the exodus of the attendees in their tracks. They are shocked by her astonishing beauty, even without formal makeup. It is not unusual, as a maiden not formally presented to court is still a child, in no need of the burden of heavy powders, hairpieces, or a formal gown. Yet it is readily apparent to them all that she radiates charisma even without such aids and is unapproachable competition for any of their daughters.

Ebouisante takes a quick look about her. These are the citizens she must impress. Her own first impression is of a great puppet show—everyone in heavy powder and ostentatious finery, rendering looks of approval or disapproval with no knowledge of the real Ebouisante at all. On the other hand, this clearly tells her the best approach to these people, especially to enhance her father's business as well as her own unexpressed intentions. They would hardly expect a young maiden would dare to judge *them*! She would sooner be the puppeteer than the doll.

Recognizing the strident gleam in the maiden's eyes, Princess Amalia smiles broadly and extends her arm. "You must approach, my child, and let us examine you. You are the picture of health and exuberance. It will please us most dearly to have you in attendance. Of course, you have already made the acquaintance of our son, Prince Charles."

Ebouisante curtsies deeply, then rises and faces the young dauphin squarely, without flinching.

He exclaims, "It is a sincere pleasure to meet you more formally." He bows.

"Come, let us retire to the meeting chamber," the prince addresses his son and the merchant. "Ebouisante, I shall leave you in the capable hands of my wife, who shall inform you of the customs of the realm."

The princess invites Ebouisante aside as her father joins the prince and his son in the chamber behind the thrones.

Ebouisante curtsies again, then chooses her words carefully. "Your pardon, Your Highness, if I seemed too presumptuous or if I offended you or any of the present company upon my arrival. I am but a country maiden in grateful service to my father and therefore to the principality."

The princess smiles, then gives a knowing wink. "You must know, my dear, that I am not raised of the nobility, nor do its formal rules of behavior come easily to me. But it also means there is no need for false modesty when we are alone. I do not discount your beauty, but I rather admire your intelligence and education and the services you provide to your father. I am well aware he has no son and no apprentice, and therefore I should think you are invaluable. And as he has clearly done very well as a merchant, the more praise to you!"

"Thank you, madame!" Ebouisante does nothing to hide her enthusiasm. Herein lies opportunity, indeed! "Though it is true I must serve the difficult role of both daughter and journeyman to my father, he has seen fit to allow me a liberal education. I have had access to the greatest of teachers and libraries in our travels. I surmise you care to hear the state of the continent, both in politics and business. I will not dissemble that I have little or no experience in observation or practice, but I beg that you consider the perspective of a young maiden. That accepted, I should delight in bending your ear, asking only in return similar education of this very principality and the ambitions of all of Your Highnesses."

Ebouisante blushes. Has she asked too much? No, she does not miscalculate this princess. Ebouisante knows Amalia seeks information she can use to influence her husband, and it is appropriate for Ebouisante to barter to her own family's advantage.

◆ ◆ ◆

The prince and his small entourage make themselves comfortable in the counseling room. Serge is impressed, even as His Highness motions him to a seat. Once he is addressed, he is quick to express praise for his surroundings. A large hearth adds warmth to the room, furnished with a heavy oak table polished to perfection, as well as large, richly upholstered chairs.

The merchant takes a breath and states, "Thank you, Your Highness. If I may be so bold, this chamber is well appointed and comfortable enough to set one at ease, an atmosphere conducive to clarification of one's thoughts."

Henrik, for his part, waives off the comments dismissively. "You may allow yourself the courtesy of relative informality when we meet privately, sir. It is my intention to avail myself of your knowledge and experience of the world in your travels. First, however, I must compliment you upon the beauty and unique nature of your gifts. They have certainly piqued the interest of my good wife. And I have no doubt the bourgeoisie are now trampling all over themselves in an effort to be the first to your door in order to acquire some exotic item of potential prestige among their peers and neighbors."

"My intentions precisely, sire," Serge replies. "To be quite honest with you, there is no better forum than an audience with the prince to display the best of one's wares," the merchant says with a laugh. Now he leans forward, brow furrowed, stroking his chin. "As I stated during the audience, I admit I am curious as to why you kindly extended me this invitation to return to the city of my birth and childhood. I always had the intention to pay a return visit, so it must be more than a coincidence of fate that I received your invitation at just the precise time when the Medicis of Florence told me trade with northern Europe would be a good way to secure a fortune."

Henrik raised his eyebrows. He is a bit surprised Italian

magnates would give thought to the fortunes of the north, drawing the same conclusion he did.

"Just so, sir," says the prince, recovering his composure. "I think you understand the reason for my invitation to you."

"Yes, sire. It is a great opportunity—"

Serge would say more, but Henrik waves him to silence, then addresses his son. "Charles, what do you think?"

Charles furrows his brow a second, then smiles with realization. "I surmise that if trade in furs and salt with our neighbors to the north and east becomes more difficult, then establishment of new ties to the south and west would serve us well—especially as the Ottomans lay siege to Constantinople and close the trade road to the Orient."

"Excellent!" Henrik says. "Keep that thought, son, as we continue this discussion privately, later." This is not the time to expand upon a lesson in front of a subject of the crown.

◆ ◆ ◆

Ebouisante and the princess have now had the opportunity to form high opinions of each other, allowing mutual admiration to blossom into instant friendship.

Amalia thinks a moment, then says, "It is important to maintain trade, Ebouisante, do you not agree? The fur and salt trade of the Hanse is in some jeopardy, and I am sure His Highness is exploring new avenues of commerce."

"Of course, Your Highness!" exclaims Ebouisante with a smile. "I think we both understand this is the reason for His Highness's invitation to my father to return to the city of his birth."

"And we are not disappointed. For example, the gifts your father presented us are incomparable," Amalia remarks. "Has your father established a permanent trade route or association to keep you supplied with such items of beauty?"

"Perhaps, but it is difficult, madame," Ebouisante answers. "The Ottomans have surrounded Constantinople, and the long overland road to the Orient will be closed. This will create the necessity to establish routes at sea. It would behoove those of us in the west to establish sea routes with new and sturdy vessels to visit the cities that have other access—and even to the islands of spice. My father has liaisons with the Portuguese and the Moors and Aragonese, who would likely be the next great traders. And Cosimo di' Medici has an idea to establish a chain of banks to finance merchandising as far as this principality throughout Europe."

This revelation leaves Amalia aghast. Eyes wide, she exclaims, "Would you submit to usury? That is to be left to the Jews!"

Ebouisante shakes her head vigorously. She answers, "Nothing unacceptable to the Church, which is inclined to allow a small profit—if a larger one accrues to the Vatican itself."

"I understand, my dear. I must contemplate the consequences and discuss them with His Highness."

Ebouisante is pleased with her exchange with the princess, particularly happy to provide Amalia with information of use to the royals, especially establishing influence that would benefit her own family's trade.

A smile reappears on Amalia's face. "And I would feign pay a visit privately to your home to view some of these wonders in person. I deign to think," she allows, "that most of the wealthier wives of burghers will want items of a like kind to your gifts merely to impress their friends and neighbors, never even giving a thought to the difficult artisanry on display before them. But such would be enough to enrich your father's coffers," she adds with another wink. "And so, we must meet again soon, and I would be introduced to your mother."

The princess rises, which is the signal for Ebouisante to withdraw. She curtsies politely and backs out of the chamber, eager to rush home, assist her mother, and tell her what success she had with the princess.

~ Chapter 25 ~

Henrik smiles as Serge leaves the chamber. Trade with southern Europe will certainly help ensure the wealth of his realm, and he has plans to consolidate things further, which he will take up with Serge and Artur soon. For now, there is other important business.

The prince beckons to his son to follow him out of the chamber by an entrance previously unknown to the young man. This is a small door in the guise of a stone wall, easily pushed aside, carefully hidden behind a large tapestry of the last battle for Valhalla. The irony does not go unnoticed by Charles, who maintains his silence until the portal is shut behind them.

"Are we escaping the Götterdämmerung, sire? I hardly think we are in such dire straits." He manages a smile, but his father is not amused.

"I would not be so smug, son. No fortress is impregnable, as the tapestry reminds me always, and it is always wise to plan an escape from any damaging situation. But such passages should never go to waste entirely, even in peaceful times. Follow, and you shall see."

Charles is not surprised to see the revealed corridor in ill repair. The castle staff would hardly be privileged to the knowledge of its existence. Although it is certainly not his place, he makes a mental note to attempt to sweep it out himself—and to unleash a mouser cat.

He follows his father silently, noting the passage forks. One short corridor clearly leads outside the castle on the opposite side to that of the city itself, and the other toward the interior of the building. Charles makes a mental note to explore this later, as potential secret interior connections could have many uses. The two men take the short path heading outside, then circle around the outer wall toward the woods.

There, to the young man's bemusement, they are met by two men of a stature that can only be described as stunted. They are bearded and disheveled, dressed in deerskins rather than wool or finer cloth. Clearly they are rugged creatures, muscular for all their height. They bear no sign of fear for their ruler, yet they are quick to bow out of respect. Charles thinks for a moment, then offers a bow in return.

One states, "Ye're like your father in many respects, Your Highness. Handsome, thoughtful, careful t' evaluate your situation before actin', ye are, and yet respectful of the odd stranger. Ye must have surmised we're no threat t' ye, though ye must wonder why such a secretive assignation."

"I am not of a mind to contradict you, sir," the dauphin replies with a laugh, "and your flattery is very kind. I will certainly admit to curiosity to the reason for this meeting, and I am sure you have surmised that His Highness is of a mind to turn me into his apprentice. It is a role I actually relish. Also, I am curious about the fact that I have not been formally introduced to you, yet you know who I am."

"Though ye may not be cognizant of us, sire, it's certainly in our interest t' be cognizant of ye. We're a poor group of men. I am called Erich, also known as the Grump, due to an admittedly overinterpretation of my attitude." He snickers. "Our appearance'd raise nothin' but derision amongst the city folk, it would, so we're content t' keep t' ourselves. Yet the occasion arises t' have need of more than the sustenance available in the woods. This in turn requires some form of trade. We prefer t' work directly with the prince, who has the kindness t' treat us as equal t' all of his subjects and sees value in our labors."

At that, Henrik speaks up. "That I do, gentlemen. And I see from the heavy sack you bear that you have had some success. Do be so kind as to allow me to assess your bounty."

The little men smile, spread a blanket, and empty the contents of a bearskin. The setting sun glints brilliantly off the surfaces of an array of polished gems and rocks. There are garnets, amber, even the rare ruby, lapis, and others. So they are miners!

"I thought the gems of the Jews were purchased from certain caravans. I had no inclination that we might have our own local supply!" the dauphin allows with a bit of a laugh.

"We're not likely t' share our source, but ye're correct that these're mined within your own realm," Grump says. "Your Highnesses're free as always t' remove your tithe, and we'll return at our usual time t' recover the payment, we will. It's well heard that ye're a hard bargainer, ye are, and quite honest with us. Thus, it's always an honor t' work through ye, as it's unpleasant for us t' be seen in the city ourselves. We're e'er in your debt, we are, and always appreciate your protection, we do."

Charles is impressed with the hard work of the little men; he certainly understands their reluctance to subject themselves to the ridicule of callous citizens. Yet they are certainly valuable to Quellestadt and deserving of respect.

"Soon," Grump says, "we'll be 'specting our friend, a great hunter, who accepts minor recompense in 'xchange for services in fillin' our larder. We'll therefore take our leave, we will, and allow these mere baubles t' remain with ye."

The dwarves bow deeply and begin to withdraw.

Henrik watches them move out of sight, then clasps his son's shoulder. "So you see, son, there is more to our business than fine soldiery. Of course, it is unnecessary for me to admonish you to treat all our subjects with respect and deal naught but honestly with all of them. In tolerance there is great gain—as well as peace."

Charles bows his head. "You need not fear, sire, as the branch does not fall far from the tree. I am ever in your debt and of your service, and I intend to attend well by your side."

"I expect nothing less, son, and I will endeavor to teach you well," the prince responds with evident pride. "Yet I think your own insights and instinct will serve you well. Let us gather this bounty and return by the route we have just traveled. The sun sets soon, and the corridor is not well lit. Your mother will expect us soon, and I would not disappoint her."

The two gather the gems and rocks, which the younger expects will be stored under guard in the treasury until they serve as barter with the Jews in town.

As the sun sets, it casts a fine glow about the men, almost a halo, which the retreating dwarves note, even if the two royals remain oblivious to it.

"If the son is like the father, we'll have a long run of good life, we will," muses one dwarf.

"Ye speak truth, ye do," Grump replies, "but your comment minds me of the needs of me empty stomach. Let's hasten home."

~ Chapter 26 ~

"Mademoiselle! A word, if you please." As usual, La Claire is at her perch at the top of the tower—a white dove inspecting the atmosphere, soaking in the sunshine as she prepares to take flight, oblivious to danger. This is the appearance she presents to Gaillard the huntsman as he approaches her. As he ascends, he shakes his head, thinking she does not know if he is her protector or the cat ready to pounce. She is nothing if not trusting. She would be a meal to anyone lacking empathy.

Gaillard knows that Her Grace, the duchess, has certainly decided La Claire is more of a liability than an asset. Her attentions to the maiden have only drawn her subjects' admiration away from herself, where she feels they belong. But how does she plan to rectify that situation? Merely marrying La Claire off seems insufficient, and every glance into the dark obsidian looking glass deepens the duchess's anguish. Gaillard reads her mood with trepidation, knowing her deepest desire and the lengths she will go to achieve them. He shudders at the thought.

The duke, in contrast, dotes on La Claire but sees her—and his wife—through a veil. So the role of protector must fall to Gaillard. How is he to maintain his position with Her Grace yet live with his own conscience? *This is perhaps why I am not fit to rule but only to serve*, he thinks to himself.

Conscience is a stone tied to the leg as one is thrown into the raging river. To survive, one must be relieved of it, yet one is rarely able to untie the rope alone. The huntsman must love this woman, even as she casts him into that river. And here rests the stone, oblivious to the world around it, content to remain part of its beauty, soaking up the sun as it may choose to strike it, without motive or ability to move on its own.

So, she is the bird *and* the stone—sculpted to be the most radiant of them, a sculpted statue of a bird in a rare, brilliant geode that hides a gemstone inside.

Thus, he thinks, ultimately deciding, he must take on two tasks. He must crack the rock to reveal the gem inside and provide a protective cave until it matures with self-knowledge. Then he must deceive to his lady love, else sacrifice his conscience to rise to the raging water. So to the task at hand.

La Claire turns toward him, not oblivious to his presence. "What brings you to my aerie on such a brilliant day, sir? Is it to scout the woods below for the best hunting trail for the day? Should I think of you as a hawk circling the sky, seeking prey? Were I a small forest creature, I would feel the need to hide, yet that is not so, as I am always glad of your company."

The huntsman is taken aback, as he thinks this is not too poor an analogy. But she cannot be that perceptive, can she? How shall he answer her?

He responds, "My lady, you are ravishing today. But then, you are ravishing always, and I find it difficult to distinguish you from the bright sunlight itself. You are correct, of course. I do seek the most auspicious trail, as I intend to venture forth this very day."

"Perhaps you also bear news from Her Grace?" she asks.

He nods. "Yes, Her Grace seeks your company below. I hope you will attend to her request with alacrity."

"Of course, sir. One does not seek to cross the command of Maman, does one?" She smiles and gives the huntsman a slight curtsy and a touch below the beard as she makes to depart.

He raises his hand to stop her a moment, suddenly feeling the need to warn La Claire of the danger her stepmother poses to her, now that the true gem within the geode has been exposed. He draws a long breath and cautions, "A moment, my lady." He pauses only a second. "Be aware of my true loyalty to Her Grace as well as to his grace, and therefore to you. I am not a fop nor am I anyone's pet, but I give of my services with careful aforethought." He draws an even deeper breath. "I would advise you to think carefully, if you will, of any commands you may receive and always put them in perspective of what is best for yourself and the people you may serve. Power corrupts, but that is reversible. Poor thought and planning often is not."

La Claire's eyebrows rise precipitously. "Such a serious charge, sir! I wonder what you know of the motives and plans of Her Grace. Perhaps I should not be so anxious to obey her call, though I would rather not face her wrath without cause."

She thinks a moment, then smiles at the huntsman, laying her hand upon his arm. "Rest easy. It is not for me to judge your motives, and I do trust you to look after my interests, as well as that of my parents. Yet it is not for a young maiden, even of the highest nobility, to arrange plans for her future, as her ultimate fate is in the hands of her father. The duke is truly a nobleman and certainly has my best interests at heart. I shall therefore arrange my life accordingly. Think not, though, that I have been entirely idle, as Maman would have everyone believe."

Gaillard makes a dismissive gesture, which La Claire interrupts. "No, sir, I am not deaf to the gossip of the court, which does not spare me the opinions of my stepmother. But I will show you my trust by granting you this revelation: I do study all that Maman wishes me to learn, though I do not give the appearance of having absorbed any of it. I also attend Papa's public court and discuss with him the merit of his decisions and relevant history. I have even prevailed upon the court servants to help me develop some proficiency with everyday chores considered beneath my position. I am a capable cook and seamstress, among other avocations. I know not whether such knowledge and skills will be of use to me, but I do know it is best to be prepared for anything." An idea occurs to her. "In fact, what would you say if I were to request the chance to accompany you to learn the skills of the hunt?"

The huntsman carries a look of astonishment. "A thousand pardons, my lady! I am impressed, and I do believe Her Highness underestimates you entirely! But survival in the forests is no simple matter and not quickly learned—nor do I think your father would grant you such an opportunity."

"It may surprise you to know, sir, that I have already packed a trunk for travel, but not in planning for a pleasure expedition. My father, God bless him, is advancing in age and has many enemies, even as he has a large number of allies. I wish always to be prepared, if his defenses should fail him."

"Amazing, my lady! You are smarter than I would have imagined. I shall certainly consider approaching His Highness with the request to bring you along on one or two short expeditions—with the appropriate protections, of course. But I would ask that you approach him first."

"Thank you, sir. I will now take leave to attend upon Maman. Scout on!"

With that, she gives a deeper curtsy and flies down the stairs as if not to touch the ground even once.

That is quite the act the lady has performed so well these past years, Gaillard notes. This one does have the wisdom of her father, even without the major flaw of her stepmother. Any harm to this one would not be treated lightly by the duke, yet Gaillard would much rather serve and protect the daughter than the stepmother.

Even so, he cannot ignore the duchess, the source of his sustenance. Nor would he ever want to ignore her. She is still a great beauty, though she fears its loss. How ill conceived to present her with a looking glass! He sighs. What is done is done. He shall have to plan accordingly.

Yes, perhaps some dissemblance is required here.

♦ ♦ ♦

La Claire is a bit taken aback by the appearance of her stepmother, who waits at the base of the stairwell. She stands in shadow, casting a dark aura, if such is possible, around her. She is dressed entirely in black, wrapped in a long silk cape with a mink collar. Her raven hair is carefully arranged, and she has applied an entirely too thick coating of white powder to her face. Painted lips of crimson red give the appearance of fresh bleeding. She has even lined her eyelids with black charcoal, accentuating the piercing gaze of dark irises.

It occurs to La Claire that the duchess is attempting to radiate an overly accentuated outward beauty while she attempts to mask disturbance within. La Claire, in fact, suddenly realizes this is the consequence of the duchess's newfound ability to evaluate her reflection in the obsidian mirror. She shivers. Such a change cannot bode well for anyone. La Claire must be careful what she says, as the duchess would not abide any false flattery. Oh, La Claire wonders what plans are hatching in her mind!

"Good morning, Your Grace!" La Claire offers a short curtsy, smiling outwardly in deception of her inner state of fear and disarray. "Your tunic makes you look exceptionally beautiful today. I understand my study schedule for the day and plan to follow it in the utmost detail. You sent Gaillard to ask me to attend upon you. How may I be of service?"

Enchanteresse frowns deeply, then stomps her foot. "Don't attempt to find my better side with such flattery! I am only too aware that the bloom of youth has completely fallen from me so I must choose accoutrements to emphasize my best features—something you would do well to learn yourself! Look at you, dressed almost like a peasant girl and totally without makeup. I would have you learn to be more refined, as I am, so that you may take your place at the court of any suitor your father would arrange. I despair of you entirely."

Enchanteresse pulls her tunic more tightly about her, grinning sardonically, as might a hyena assessing its prey. Really, it reminds La Claire of a vulture.

The duchess continues abruptly, "And do not deny that you cavort with the common servants of the court! I am well informed, my dear, of the great admiration you have attained amongst them, merely by feigning interest in their meager, mundane lives. I am told you have even learned to cook and sew. Perhaps I should just give you over to them and be done with your training in reading, dance and court etiquette!"

La Claire, momentarily startled by the vehemence of her stepmother's comments, lowers her gaze. "Oh, Maman, I do wish you would not disturb your thoughts with such great concern for me." Here she feels she can turn the revelation to her advantage, stating timidly, "If I presented myself more to your aspirations, perhaps you would grant me the boon of travel outside the court—with protection, of course—that I might learn the ways and practices of other nobility."

La Claire truly desires to visit the great courts of Europe to learn more of the courtesies of the day. She would also like very much to enjoy the beauty of the countryside, to meet and greet the peasants, and to inquire of the political allegiances currently in force. At some point, she intends to advise a noble husband, not merely run a household. Such knowledge is something the duchess cannot impart at all, as she shows little interest in it. Indeed, her radius of interest falls little distance from her own person.'

Enchanteresse is taken aback by La Claire's offer. She can hardly believe what she hears. The wench presents the very excuse the duchess means to prevail upon his grace to carry out her plan. *I must be rid of her,* the duchess thinks. *The court must pay attention to me first and foremost. Am I not the duchess? Is she not a mere child? Not only that, but a stupid child.*

She smiles conspiratorially, feigning surprise. "My dear, this is a request I have not anticipated! However, I am pleased you have set yourself a goal and have presented me with a choice of reward, should you attain it. In fact, I may even be inclined to allow you the opportunity very soon."

La Claire realizes this is too easy. The duchess *is* plotting something, and La Claire will have to be on guard. Yet it is difficult not to take advantage of an opportunity when her own aims coincide with the duchess's. When the wind blows in the right direction, the bird is wisest to take wing.

Enchanteresse sighs and shrugs her shoulders. "I may chide you frequently, but I have only done so for your own good. In reality, you have already learned the graces of the court, and I should be delighted to present you to the courts of Europe. However, it would be best at this point first to consider a visit to some of the smaller principalities of our neighbors—to allow you to familiarize yourself to the differences in customs. Your instructors, moreover, have informed me your ability to speak German is somewhat better than your mastery of Latin."

"Why, Maman"—La Claire blushes—"I am humbled and honored to receive such a compliment from you."

The duchess grimaces with a wave. "Nonsense, my dear. You have earned it. I shall undertake to talk with your father this very day. Then, we shall see."

"But, Maman, you summoned me to you, and I should like to know how I may serve you."

"You are correct. I have devised a simple test for you. Come here, my dear. Let me look at you."

Enchanteresse toys with her stepdaughter, speaking the antithesis of her thoughts.

"You are the picture of youth and beauty."

Disgusting.

"You will—you do—make your father proud. If you represent yourself well at other courts, your father will have to fight the suitors off!"

They will beg not to be in consideration, I am sure. "If you would be so kind as to prepare yourself, I shall personally present you at court this day. The nobility and the bourgeoisie will see you and judge, and I shall listen."

She will fail miserably, but what can I do? She is of age for presentation.

"Now go and see to your attire. I shall see you next at the grand dinner."

- Chapter 26 -

I must open her father's eyes to this miserable failure of a daughter. Then I can request exactly as she desires as a means of improvement and consummate my plan.

The duchess turns with a flourish, throwing her tunic about her—as a hawk takes cover under its wing in an effort to blend with its dark environment, that its prey may not see its expression of delight at the upcoming hunt. La Claire is accustomed to this gesture. She shivers a bit, then shrugs and takes her leave.

This conversation has not gone unwitnessed. The huntsman has slowly descended the stairs, staying carefully out of view.

He contemplates his dilemma. The stone is about to be thrown into the river! He must resolve to speak with His Grace before taking leave of the castle. Yet somehow the duke must not suspect Gaillard's true relationship with the duchess—although it is an open secret, if there is such a thing.

◆ ◆ ◆

Gossip of La Claire's presentation has spread throughout the court all day, and now it is time for the feast. La Claire is seen for the first time in sumptuous finery. A blouse of blue-and-white-striped silk seems to flow into her young, pale arms. A vest of deeper blue velvet and a long skirt of the same fabric adorn her frame. A hint of white silk stockings rarely makes its appearance. About her waist is a wide silk ribbon brocaded in gold and tied into a large bow in back. She wears a single strand of pearls around her neck, emphasizing her demure nature. Just a hint of red to the lips is her only facial enhancement—no powder is necessary to improve the appearance of her perfectly symmetrical countenance. In short, all the men in the reception room are instantly in love. Could there be a more perfect maiden?

The duke and duchess make their grand entrance to the fanfare of two long horns, the signal for all present to bow and curtsy. Philip gestures for them to sit. There are benches along two tables set in a

U shape. A third table is at the far end of the room, in front of the hearth, which is ablaze with a crackling fire.

La Claire seats herself next to her father, whose eyebrows do not fail to rise as he catches sight of her. He is suddenly very proud.

The duchess frowns, and her face darkens, despite its heavy burden of powder, rouge, and berry lipstick. She is adorned in a long tunic of the same deep blue velvet as the skirt of her stepdaughter; it is lined in gold thread. She wears a crown of jewel-bedecked gold, which nevertheless appears tarnished upon her head. Her contrast to La Claire is as night to day, a common thought among those present at the repast.

His grace turns to his wife. "My dear, it is so good to be back amongst the loves of my life. You are exceptionally beautiful today, and I can read the jealousy of every lady at court. How lucky I am to have you greet me at home after a long, arduous journey. And, madame, I must especially tender my gratitude for your care and training of my daughter. She is a sight, is she not? I think the young men will swoon, and I shall have my pick of all the European nobility for her."

Enchanteresse's lips tighten, and she cringes slightly. "Nonsense, my dear. I have done but little of what you compliment me. I have prayed that the tutors would teach our daughter well, but I often despair of the results. Her head is ever in the clouds, I fear, but she will have to do, such as she is, for presentation to the court. I do not fear you will exercise excellent judgment in selecting her suitors, and they will fawn all over her in anticipation of such a grand political connection, not to mention a considerable dowry."

The duke laughs. "As always, my dear, you tend to great modesty. You have raised her well, even if you do not wish to accept the credit. I am both grateful and proud."

The duchess smiles wanly, unwilling to challenge her husband further. But in her heart, she believes she has spoken the truth.

"A toast to his grace, the duke of all Burgundy, greater in its range than France itself!" calls the general of the guard, as is customary upon Philip's return to his court.

All present raise cups and bow their heads as they are now

seated around the great tables. They are indeed happy for the occasion. Murmurs flow throughout the assembly about La Claire, whose beauty seems to radiate outward, touching all present.

"I thank you all," the duke says, "and look forward to meeting with you personally, as is our custom. I am eager for news of the court as well as any you may have of our good neighbors, most especially France. And I bring you the bounty of the forests of the Rhine, soon to be supplemented by our good huntsman, Gaillard, and his retinue. I offer him a toast to good health and good hunting, along with the gratitude of my good wife, the duchess, and my daughter." He raises his cup and drinks.

"And now, I should like to present to you my most radiant daughter, Giselle, who has now come of age, even in my absence. May she live long and bear many children. She will certainly grace any court our good fortune allows us to ally."

La Claire rises and curtsies to her father, her stepmother, then to the seated nobility and bourgeoisie, blushing a bit. She whispers, "Thank you, Papa," so only he can hear, then takes her seat as the feast now begins in earnest.

The assemblage is aflutter, giving La Claire the impression of a gaggle of geese scrapping over the fattest insects in their small territory. Those with sons of age are suddenly plotting strategies, as if they have not had years of opportunity, while those whose sons have been recently promised or betrothed are bemoaning their ill fortune not to have waited for such a prize.

The duke takes this all in and laughs. What would they say if they knew he has already concluded an arrangement? This is all grand theater, but he must admit it is fun to watch. He will wait a few days to reveal his plans to his wife and daughter. Let them enjoy all the attention.

For her part, the duchess is unimpressed. Now she shall have to put up with all sorts of plotting and tomfoolery from the citizens. Perhaps there will be much less if she convinces Philip to grant La Claire her desire to visit other courts. Enchanteresse smiles inwardly.

"Your Grace," she says with false lightness, "a thought: Our daughter has a request, especially if she is now to become available for courtship. She would like to travel—under the protection of some of your guard and my huntsman—to gain knowledge and practice of customs, language, and niceties of other reigns than Burgundy. I personally feel there is a touch of foolishness and the wanderlust of youth involved. But as I ponder upon it, I believe the idea has some merit. Perhaps a short journey, then a return home with news and a discussion of potential suitors she has met along the way. What do you think, sire?"

Philip looks sternly at his wife. "I am not entirely sure I am willing to chance the fate of my precious daughter to the roads. There are bandits everywhere."

La Claire, who has been listening quietly, now chimes in. "Papa! You are certainly safe here at court, so you can send your most accomplished and trusted guard with me. I would so like this opportunity! Moreover, I can meet with the women of many a realm. And who better to query the state of politics? I would so desire to be of some use to you." She smiles radiantly at her father, a gesture which has never failed to win his heart.

Philip drops his shoulders, softening his countenance. "Your desires have merit, my dear. Perhaps I shall overcome my overprotective emotions and grant you this indulgence—if you do not go too far. I shall personally direct the guard and the huntsman where you may travel, and I will limit your own entourage to keep you all the less conspicuous. You may have to do some travel off the roads, but I shall trust to my finest guard. And I shall expect reports at regular intervals. You are to return to me in the early spring, and we shall then talk of suitors."

Enchanteresse nods and smiles. Her plan will work! For her part too, Giselle is delighted.

Philip calls, "Guard! Send for Gaillard. I would have a word with him!"

The huntsman arrives with alacrity, a bit flustered, as he has not yet decided how to approach the duke with his dilemma. He is even more surprised when the duke beckons him into a private chamber.

Pulling himself up to his full commanding height, Philip states, "I have been presumed upon, perhaps against my better nature, to require you to postpone your journey a day, that I may allow for new preparations," Philip says.

"Your Grace?"

Here the duke places his hand on Gaillard's shoulder, a sign of trust and confidence. "My daughter, Giselle, will accompany you on this foray, sir. I shall afford you the company and protection of my best guardsmen, that no ill may befall her. She is very dear to me. I would have you introduce her to several principalities, most particularly one I shall appoint to you. Make this a rather short tour, if you will. I shall certainly be anxious for her safety, as I am always for yours, sir. This year there is ample game surrounding our immediate court to allow for winter provisions, but you know I rely upon you to gather more than just food for our larders. Upon your return, both you and she will report to me directly."

Gaillard is nonplussed. He flushes, then bows deeply. "Sire, I had thought to broach this very subject with you, as I have been approached by both the duchess and the exquisite La Claire herself. I myself feared rejection out of hand, but I see their powers of persuasion have already been exercised." He bows his head. "I shall certainly protect her as best as I can and will introduce her widely. She learns far better than her stepmother would think"—here he raises his eyes a bit—"and I do believe this journey would do her well. I dare say it will afford you with an overabundance of suitors most noble."

"Off with you then, sir, and to your preparations!" The duke dismisses him, then returns to the feast.

Gaillard must still share with the duke his concern about the duchess's plot against her stepdaughter. But suddenly he realizes the maiden will be safer with him than she would in the duchess's presence. He will send word back to Philip after he and Giselle depart, to be sure Enchanteresse does not catch wind of it and as a means to assure the duke he truly does intend to protect the maiden.

~ Chapter 27 ~

The morning sun brings no warmth to the prisoners as they contemplate their upcoming judgment. Peter turns himself to face the wall and coils into a fetal position, the better to make himself seem to disappear. Jacques just laughs, and Peter tries to make himself even smaller.

He has reached a low point, and what shall he do? Jurg and Fee are right to bemoan such a brother. And now, he must endure the company of this grotesque simpleton, who displays no modesty, no respect, and no care even for his own fate—not even willing to exert himself to support his poor mother.

Jacques taunts him, as if reading his thoughts. "So, my friend, think ye better than the likes of meself? Ye need t' rely upon your brother t' save ye, while I'll work with the jailer's wife, I will, t' arrange me own fate!"

Almost on cue, the lady rattles the key in the heavy door, then enters with the breakfast tray.

"I can't say I heard everythin' ye said, but I heard enough. I'd be happy t' be of service t' ye both. Ye need fear nothin' from me, ye won't. As I told ye, I'm in need t' leave this place. I've access t' keys and can see t' your escape. And if ye'd see your way t' helpin' provide for me away from this castle, I could be of e'en more service, I could."

Peter shakes his head. "I would not abuse you, nor would I impede you, but I will be happy to remain in custody and accept the judgment of His Highness, whatever that may be. I could not well provide for you, at any rate, and I would suspect my acquaintance here could do no better. Please leave me to my own misery."

"But sir," she replies, "I do have more t' offer, and with that, ye'd have but little t' do t' provide for me, as ye can see I cannot do me own marketing, I can't."

"I would say I were intrigued, madame, but I must chance the mercy of His Highness, that I need no longer remain an outlaw," says Peter.

"But I care not!" interrupts Jacques indignantly. "Speak on, me lady, speak on!"

The lady sighs, then winks conspiratorially. "Ye know, the treasury is but a short distance down these stairs, it is."

"Oho!" Jacques exclaims. "Ye certainly do have access t' keys. But do ye not fear the pursuit of His Majesty? I fancy ye have definite interest in maintainin' the attachment of your head t' your neck, ye do!"

"And do you not fear the wrath of that giant of a husband of yours, madame?" chides Peter.

"Indeed, sirs! But I'd be content t' be far from here, where I could care not for me husband or His Highness, who need not know where I travel. And I would remove very little of value from the treasury, would I, so that it might go unnoticed for a long enough time."

Jacques, suddenly animated with the thought of escape, laughs. "Ye've a deal, madame! But it requires your assistance this very day, it does, as I presume the trial's nigh."

Peter is astonished. He looks from Jacques to the jailer's wife, shaking his head. "I am tired of the outlaw life, madame. But . . ."

"I will not harm ye if ye choose t' stay behind," she says, seeing the fear in his countenance. "I do not want a 'sassination on me head, especially one with a court connection, which would bring out all of His Majesty's guard t' search us out. I leave ye t' your own fate, sir."

Peter is hardly relieved by this excuse to leave him in peace for her own purposes. He covers his cheeks with his hands but says nothing to provoke her.

"And now I must leave ye, as I have other duties for the mornin', I do. I'll return with the noon meal, and then it'll be time for action.

Farewell." With that, she bounds down the stairs, after remembering to lock the door behind her.

Peter looks wistfully out the slit in the dungeon wall. The fog does not seem to be lifting this day; it rolls below the level of the window. Peter imagines himself drifting upon the clouds below, carried far from his no doubt terrible fate. It is a fantasy, a reverie broken finally by the thought of Jacques and the jailer's wife riding the same cloud. He is brought back to his reality by the smell of breakfast—fruit and bread this time, instead of the previous offering of stale bread alone.

"This fruit's not a good omen, it's not," Jacques says with a nonchalant air. "It could just be a favor from the wife, but I suspect it's more of a last supper before a judgment, it is. Indeed, the trial is nigh."

Peter turns to face Jacques, suddenly developing a droop in his carriage. "And we shall have to endure it. But it is nothing we have not earned by our own actions."

Jacques frowns and shakes a finger at his companion. "Sir, ye may be miserable and repentant on your own, ye may. We both do what we must t' survive, and I make no apologies, I don't. I intend t' be out of this cold, wet place—in fact, out of this principality—afore the day's out. Ye may certainly come along, but ye'll need t' do your share of the price, ye will!"

"May God forgive you and save your soul," Peter says somewhat indignantly, waving at him as if in dismissal. Then, with resolve, he adds, "But I shall face my punishment, sir, and attempt to amend my life out of duty and courtesy—nay, out of love, of my brother and sisters. I was too much swayed by the loss of one brother and the depravities it caused. I will not accompany you, but I will do nothing to hinder you, little though I might be capable to do. Nor will I talk to Jurg of your plans, and for that, you might consider what you owe me later, should the opportunity arise. Now, leave me to my misery and the mercy of God, His Highness, and my family"

Jacques shrugs. "Well, I've neither a god nor much family—only me poor mother, who's incapable of sustainin' us both. I've no trade and no prospect of apprenticeship, I don't. So I'll take me fortune where it lies, e'en from the treasury below." He reaches for the fruit, grimaces as with an inner secret, then offers, "I shall bother ye no more. Eat heartily!"

~ Chapter 28 ~

Dien awakens before the sun, rolls on the palette of soft straw, and gazes at Fee. He thinks she's more beauty than she will allow. Oh, perhaps not on the outside, no, but certainly on the inside. Her entire body consists of love—concern for her family and for Dien. And she sacrifices herself totally for the sake of the young maiden. How can Dien not count himself blessed?

At that point, an idea occurs to him. He gently strokes Fee's hair, just enough to awaken her. She blinks, stretches, then smiles as she sees the face of her lover gazing down upon her.

"Well, my love, what a handsome sight to awaken to. I thank you for awakening me just with the sun, as I must return to the care of my mistress before the arousal of the household." She sighs. Lines of darkness begin to etch her features, as the cares of the world return to her thoughts.

Dien kisses her softly. "I'd have ye stay with me fore'er, love. Then the pressures of that be-damned household'd not so visibly age ye. Ye're meant t' work lightly and be coddled, ye are, and ye've certainly earned it, ye have. Ye know I've acquired the permission of Master Artur t' have ye join the service of the Handler family, and I intend t' request that the family adopt the care of your young charge, I do. That way, ye can continue t' oversee her trainin'. I know the mistress here'd delight in havin' another daughter t' raise, she would. Come t' think on it, Fräulein Greta'd be 'specially pleased t' have a sister t' share adventures and secrets, she would. Then we can repost the banns."

"Imposs—"

- Chapter 28 -

Dien puts his hand over Fee's mouth, whispering softly, "Hush, m' dear. I'm at least as stubborn as ye, I am, and I intend t' pursue this. Nothin' will stand in the way of our love. At least, I'll ask the mistress t' approach your lady for permission t' engage your help with her planned autumn soiree. She's attemptin' a Michaelmas feast, complete with mummers, like the English, ye know. T' celebrate the harvest, it is. And ye know we'll need additional assistance and organization. I'd acquaint her with your ability t' work hard and supervise servants."

To Dien, there is no reason for Fee to refuse the offer. He takes a deep breath and throws his arm around Fee's shoulders protectively. "Now, we must both be up and about, we must, and attend t' our duties. But first, I'll accompany ye home, I will. Say nothin' but 'yes, m' love.'"

Fee is too emotionally worn to argue at this time. She knows she will only delay her day if she puts up a protest. Yet she knows Dien's offer is too simple a solution and offers no real protection from Dunkel, who would be enraged and seek any opportunity to assert his "rights."

Outwardly, she smiles wanly. "Yes, my love."

"There. That's not so hard, is it? Now, think on our lives t'gether, rather than that odious master and worthless mistress of yours." Dien sighs and frowns. "Yet I know you'll not, as the lines on your face are still givin' ye away."

The pair dress quickly beneath the blanket, then arise with a sigh emitted from each. Dien hugs Fee and kisses her gently, then they exit into the streets, still enshrouded with the autumn morning fog. Fee actually relishes the invisibility, always preferring to keep her emotions and her problems to herself, but her lover gestures to cut through the moisture as if with a sword, unsuccessfully attempting to open a path for sunlight. She knows he wishes to brighten her life, but the forces of God and nature do not grant him the power.

At the main street, they part. Fee hurries to the city wall to check on her charge and put the Hammer household into motion.

◆ ◆ ◆

As she arrives, she sees little activity within, although the various aromas of the marketplace behind her belie the lateness of her arrival. She sighs again and enters.

Fee suddenly hears a muffled scream and sobbing. This is ignored by the arousing servants, each self-absorbed with the tasks of the day, each grateful he or she is not the subject of the actions or wrath of the master—nor of Fee, for that matter.

She bounds up the spiral stairs, greeting each servant with a deep frown, a gesture of warning, and a quick, "Get to your duties. I will instruct you later."

She arrives to see the master strike his daughter across the face to stop her shrieking and pounding at his chest. Then he climbs on top of her. She just cries, not wanting to be struck again if she screams.

Fee pushes her way into the room and dares to strike the man across the back. He ignores her and continues to assault the maiden. Fee beats him again and again across the back, then looks around and takes an iron from the hearth. As she makes to strike him with it, his powerful arm comes up, and he grabs the rod.

But now he is sated and rolls off the maiden. Besse hastily arranges her skirt and surcotte and crawls away, sobbing, then rolls into a fetal position.

Dunkel laughs, then bellows at Fee, "Take care, woman, that I d' not dismiss ye from the household. Ye're lucky that the mistress'd have the service of no other, and ye run the servants well, ye do. But ye'll not interfere in any of *me* business, ye won't."

Fee forgets herself, shouting, "Mistress? Which is your mistress? For it seems you have too many."

Dunkel gives an angry stare as he occupies himself with arranging his clothing. Then he laughs. "Ye're a strong woman, Fee, ye are, who'd dare t' engage me in such manner. I like that, I do. It's not a trait of the gentler sex, is it? But ye'll ne'er be strong enough t' counter me, so I'll be on me way."

~ Chapter 28 ~

Enraged and frightened at once, it takes all of her internal strength to calm herself. Fee shakes her head. There is little she can do now, but she firms her resolve. She must find safe haven for Besse soon. Somehow, she will!

"I dismiss ye t' your duties," adds Dunkel with a laugh and a smug appearance of self-satisfaction. "Me wife'll need your attention, as does the rest of the household. Be about your work, and mind your own business. I've enough of me own t' attend, I do, as I no longer have a journeyman. So, I'm off, and so're ye." He harrumphs twice on his way out the door.

Fee runs to Besse, enfolding her in her arms. "My poor dear, my poor child. I cannot leave this house again while he lives, can I? It is not for me to pursue my own comfort, not in this world. But I certainly promise to attend to yours, until I can get you safely away."

She lets Besse cry for a time, then realizes the master is right: she must perform her own duties. Then with a start, she realizes she must also attend her brother's trial this very day.

She helps Besse to her feet with soothing sounds, a soft lullaby. She helps her set her clothing. "I must take you out again to the market today, child. We will make our purchases, and I will leave you with my sister, Flor. Perhaps the flowers and spices will soothe your spirit. Then you will be on your own for a time, while I attend to my brother."

Fee runs out the door, fumbles for her own key to the anteroom of Beata's chamber, takes a deep breath, and lets herself in. She busies herself with her work, refreshing the hearth, tossing the contents of the chamber bucket out the tower window into the forest below. She sighs, thinking it would serve the young journeyman right if he were below at this moment.

Did Fee not hear the master mention that he has dismissed the young man? What will he do for sustenance now? She must warn the lady; this would be a good opportunity to advise her to rid herself of Rudi. Of course, love has no sense and no decency. Beata will not forsake her young lover. No doubt, there will now be some plot hatched, and Fee will either be sworn to secrecy or made a guilty party to it. That could cost her dearly with the master, and she must continue to protect Besse.

Here her thoughts pause a moment. Tears well up her eyes. *Besse, Besse. What shall I do? Can you forgive that I took the night to indulge my own fantasies? What fool, I.* Fee resolves not to leave Besse to the machinations of that evil man again. If the mistress will not make Besse her charge, choosing instead to protect herself well by allowing the maiden's interests to fail, then it is up to Fee.

At this point, the lady awakens and calls for Fee. "Fee, come help me bathe and dress. I would be particularly alluring today. Did you not hear of the events at the forge? Rudi is free! He will return today, and we will plan. I shall be in great need of your assistance."

"Yes, my lady."

Fee is too tired and distraught to argue yet not too fatigued to realize that if the journeyman steals the lady, then Fee's own service to the household may become unnecessary. For a moment, she dreams—she would be free to join her Dien.

Then she hardens her countenance. She still would not leave the side of the master's daughter. Besse would have to accompany Fee, at any rate, into the Handlers' household. And who would that put in danger?

Well, no time to deal with that now. Fee will attend to the mistress here, leave brief instructions for the servants, then take Besse to the market. Fee must be at court today.

Now her thoughts turn to the plight of her brother, yet another burden she refuses to see as such. What shall she do? What shall she say to His Majesty that could spare her poor Peter? She must think.

~ Chapter 29 ~

A large but inscrutable figure makes her way through the mists surrounding the outside wall of the dungeon tower. The woman approaches her destination with some trepidation but determination. At last she will escape from the attentions of her husband, and she will keep the young ne'er-do-well firmly under her control.

The trees here have been allowed to grow too close to the castle walls since the great plague of the last century. She drops a bundle under the fir outside the dungeon window. In it, she has placed an ax, some provisions, and a small quantity of coin. The coin is courtesy of the treasury. No one saw her enter it the prior evening.

No one has seen her here either. No one ventures outside the walls on the near-cliffside at this time of year. Some peasants come here in the spring to plant pole beans, using the tree trunks for support. Few forest animals venture this close to the precipice, so the beans are safer here. The woman can see them climbing the trunks.

She sighs with resignation, then follows the wall back to her exit point from the castle. It will be up to the boy to reach the tree from the dungeon slit opening, then use the ax to eliminate the opportunity for anyone to follow by the same route.

Looking back, she is momentarily dizzied by the image of the tower in the clouds.

◆ ◆ ◆

Peter and Jacques have been dozing as the sun fails to dispel the cloud of fog surrounding the city and castle. They are awakened by the rattle of a key in the lock to their prison door.

Jacques stretches, then remembers himself, taking in his surroundings. "The fog—it's a good omen, don't ye think, sir? The lady and I'll be able t' shrink away unnoticed. And I do think this's herself at the door."

Katrina pushes the door open and smiles crookedly at the prisoners.

She moves to Jacques, strokes his chin, then produces a key from a pouch around her waist. She removes his shackle, then unlocks the opposite end of the chain from its attachment to a ring embedded in the floor.

"Now we must move quickly. This chain'll help ye reach a tree outside. Ye must make your own escape. Under the nearest tree, I've laid an ax, a staff, and a sack with bread and fruits as well as a hooded long cape. Me, I'll meet ye outside the gate t' the city, I will. We'll head into the woods and make good our departure.

"Moreover, I've scouted a refuge in the woods for us, in an untraveled place. It's a hovel left by its former owners, who were lost t' the great plague, and it's ne'er been reoccupied. I've provisioned it well. For a time, we'll abide there, we will, while the soldiers perform a fruitless search. When they cease, it'll be easier for us t' escape the principality entirely."

"Perhaps I should carry the bag with the gold and purloined marvels," Jacques offers with a smile. "The better t' make your way unencumbered."

Katrina shakes her head and laughs. "Don't take me for a complete fool, sir. They'll remain with me, t' ensure that ye'll follow our plan precisely. I'll always hold the purse strings, I will—the better t' bind ye t' me."

The old woman makes her way to the chamber door. "I'll now take me leave, love, and await our next meetin' in better circumstances. Good luck t' ye, and may fortune carry us t' our desired destinations!" She turns to Peter. "As for you, young man, I'll make one last offer t' join us. Ye know the price of me assistance. It's up t' ye, it is."

Peter sighs, remains silent for a brief moment, then shakes his head and frowns. "No thank you, madame. I would rather take my chances with His Highness. I feel I have shamed my family, and I am prepared to face whatever punishment is meted. I would rather not be a fugitive and shame my family even more. God be with you."

The jailer's wife shrugs, then departs.

As the door closes, Jacques laughs. "Ha! I'm free! I'll ne'er allow meself t' be caught in such a demeanin' manner again, I won't. I do pity ye, sir, as I doubt ye'll have such an opportunity as I."

Peter is angry. "Be off with you! Do you think I am fool enough to believe you will not contrive to relieve that woman of what possessions she may have and leave Quellestadt for good?"

"Ye think ye know me well, do ye?" Jacques asks. "Well, if ye must know, I'll see t' the welfare of me mama, I will. While we're hidin' in that hovel, she can take care of our marketing and needs in the city, 'cause neither the lady nor I can reappear inside the walls, can we?"

Jacques sighs, and Peter can almost see concern on his face. "Mama's all I have, and I've always tried to protect her, I have." In a blink, the expression is gone, replaced by his usual unnerving smile. "As for my plans with the old lady, what I do is no longer any business of yours!"

Jacques turns, hiding a sinister grimace. He hefts the chain, takes the few steps over to the wall opening, and calculates a swing at the nearby fir.

True to his word, Peter now turns his back so he may not witness the escape. "I know that once you replenish your pitiful body, she will be no physical match for you," he says, angrily staring at the wall ahead of him.

"Neither she nor ye!" Jacques hisses. In one swift move, he encircles Peter's neck with the chain and pulls tight.

Peter grabs at the chain, then at the arm of his attacker, then elbows him as hard as he can in the groin. Jacques gasps and loosens his grip momentarily.

As the two boys struggle for control, Jacques laughs. "Did ye think I'd trust ye? All ye need do is tell your brother, and the guards'll be upon us afore we can blink!"

Peter backs up to the wall for support, then slowly pulls his adversary closer. Jacques takes the opportunity to kick out, attempting to return the injury he has just suffered himself. Peter darts to the side, but the kick connects with the side of his thigh, just startling him enough to loosen his grip.

Jacques pulls the chain free and grins again. Peter crouches, prepared to spring outward against his foe.

At that moment, the door flies open. It is the jailer, who takes a second to survey the scene in front of him. He quickly realizes that only his wife could have liberated the young prisoner from his shackle. This notion startles him so greatly, he hesitates a moment before charging at Jacques in rage.

"Ye'll not escape me, ye won't!" he bellows.

But he is too late. The young thief throws the chain out the opening and connects with a branch of the tree. The end wraps itself around the sturdy bough three times. Jacques quickly scrambles up and pulls himself with the chain, wrapping his arms around the tree. He scampers down as quickly as he can.

Peter slumps to the floor, clutching at his deeply bruised neck, his breath raspy and heavy.

"I'll deal with ye later!" the jailer shouts at Peter just before he climbs to the window and leaps to the tree.

Malnourished as he is, Jacques is still more agile than the near-giant of a man pursuing him. He quickly disappears into the mist enveloping the tree and the castle itself, then he reaches the ground below. He can barely see the jailer struggling to keep a purchase upon the trunk of the great fir, but he can certainly hear his bellowing threats.

As quietly as possible, he searches the forest floor, quickly finding the sack Katrina left for him. Next he searches it, finding the ax. He swings against the base of the bean-vine-wrapped fir, again and again, felling it just before the pursuer sees what he is doing. The tree crashes to the ground, throwing the big man off, then landing on top of him.

Jacques does not hesitate. He raises the ax and lands one gruesome blow, severing the jailer's neck.

Without another thought of the giant man nor a look behind him, Jacques grabs the sack and runs to the wall of the castle, following it around to the gate. There, Katrina awaits him, having kept her word. She asks him nothing but gestures for him to follow into the woods.

Jacques immediately notices the jailer's wife does not have her pouch of gold with her. "The gold—have ye secreted it away, madame?" he whispers, trying to hide his frustration.

"Me young helper, I'll not tell ye of the whereabouts of me gold, nor me other treasures. For now, I'll lead ye t' our new abode."

In fact, Katrina pilfered the gold-leaf goose and harp as well as some gold. She found them beautiful, in contrast to her negative self-image—ugly, worthy only of abuse. Therefore, they were irresistible. She has already hidden them away.

Jacques's curiosity is piqued. He smirks at the notion of *other treasures*. He must learn more!

Eventually they arrive at an old hovel overgrown with vines, with no defined path leading to it.

"Ye'll clean the place, then bring up the provisions I've left in the cellar," Katrina tells Jacques. "Mind ye, leave the outside looking like no one lives here. We don't want t' attract the attention of any passersby, we don't. I only plan a short stay here, until the guard gives up the search. Then we can leave the principality unnoticed, we can."

Jacques will do as he is told—at least until he can make yet another escape. He is annoyed that the jailer's wife has stashed the treasures. Not that he would expect her to trust him, but he has plans for a new life for himself and his mother that will require their procurement and sale. He will contrive to follow the lady to discover her hidden cache—though he will have to be crafty enough to stay out of the regard and capture of the guard.

He must bide his time and wait for opportunity.

◆ ◆ ◆

Peter knows it is foolish, but he has given his word, so he does not call out for the guards. In truth, he does not have the strength of voice after his near choking. Nor would anyone be likely near enough to hear.

Before long, though, a guard appears at the open door of the dungeon chamber. He finds Peter rubbing his neck, nearly sobbing, and sitting with his back to the wall.

"'Xplain yeself, young man! Why's this door ajar, and where's your erstwhile companion? Has he managed t' escape down the stairwell without bein' noticed? I must find the jailer immediately!"

Peter darts his eyes to the window but does not say a word.

The guard follows his glance, if only out of curiosity. He looks out the window but sees only the mist, still not dispelled by the sun.

"Is this a trick? I have very little patience t' be tried! There's a fugitive t' catch. Ye'll pay dearly if ye lie t' shield your compatriot, ye will. But I'll go and investigate down below."

"A boon, sir . . . chamber pot."

The guard laughs. He kicks the pot within Peter's reach. Then he turns and rushes out of the chamber, calling for his colleagues as he bounds down the stairs.

Peter sighs and resigns himself to a longer wait. In time, a familiar face appears in the door.

"Peter! Are you all right?" Jurg rushes to Peter's side. "There is quite the commotion, Peter. The body of the jailer has been found at the base of this tower, crushed by a tree. I rushed here to see if you were—" He winces and hesitates a second. "Oh! You *are* hurt! Your neck!" Sensitive to this injury, Jurg makes a quick decision not to mention the ax blow to the jailer.

Peter looks down. "Sworn to silence. Will not break . . . word. Sorry."

Jurg eyes his brother intently. "I can only surmise that you yourself had no part in any plot, as you are still shackled here. So, I will respect your silence."

Peter exhales in relief.

Jurg points to Peter's neck. "I am sorry you are hurt. I believe their intention was to not leave a witness, but the jailer must have prevented that—only to be felled by Jacques." Jurg pauses for a moment. "You need merely nod if I have said anything you believe to be untrue."

Peter remains still, staring back at his brother.

"And with that, I shall be off to inform His Highness. Your trial will have to be delayed a day or two. If I tell him of your willingness to remain here and face judgment when given an opportunity to escape, your trial may go considerably easier for you."

"Jurg . . . grateful," rasps Peter.

"You are welcome, my brother. I must go now, but I will send some salve for your neck and some fruit and bread." Jurg hesitates at the door. "Oh, my brother. Perhaps you will see some leniency due to today's events. And perhaps Fee and I can help mitigate the judgment. But I still do fear there will be more tribulation for you yet.

"Thank . . . you."

Peter attempts a smile. At that point, the sunlight finally breaks through the mist, enters the window slit, and falls upon his face. He has kept his word.

But as Jurg leaves the chamber, he sees anguish through his brother's smile.

~ Chapter 30 ~

Fee finishes her work in the tower chamber of her mistress. She appears a bit fidgety, certainly not as composed as usual.

With a shake of her head, Beata says, "You are not yourself today, Fee. You have placed my brushes and cosmetics in odd positions, and you nearly forgot to stoke the fire. You must tell me what is agitating you. I do not wish to have my mood disturbed today, despite this interminable fog, which might hamper the approach"—she catches herself—"that is, the view outside. So, speak to me."

"I am sorry, madame, if I seem a bit perturbed this morning. I must attend to my duties with some efficiency today, as I would very much like to attend the trial this afternoon. Peter is my brother, madame, and I simply must be there."

"I understand," Beata says dismissively. "But I think there is little you can do to help him, though I know your kind heart would demand that you at least try. I am not so ungenerous as to prevent you from going, provided your duties here are met. But I strongly suspect there is more than your brother on your mind."

Fee frowns and hesitates a moment, somewhat afraid to make a request that likely would be refused. She lowers her eyes as she states, "That is true, madame. I am concerned about Besse. I think she would be well protected if you would take her here into your own locked chamber."

Beata grimaces thinking about how such an arrangement would interrupt her trysts with Rudi. "You must know I will never allow that, Fee. I could not have her here when . . . when I need my privacy. I must trust in your ability to protect the girl."

"Yes, madame," responds Fee.

She knows Beata has other rationale as well: The master could, at any time, break the mistress's chamber lock, especially now that he is aware of the affair with his erstwhile journeyman. But if Beata allows access to Besse, it will keep the master's attentions away from his wife.

Fee stares out into the fog, her thoughts somewhat muddled. She decides to curtsy, then turns and leaves the room to collect her young charge.

Besse is sitting on the floor of her room, completely disheveled, staring blankly at nothing in particular. Fee is momentarily shocked to see her. She runs to her side, kneels, and takes her up into her arms. Rocking her gently and speaking softly, she tries to comfort her.

Tears fill the servant's eyes, and she nearly blubbers, "My liebchen, my liebchen. I will not leave you again. I will take care of you. I will take care of you . . ." she repeats over and over, more to comfort herself than the young maiden.

After what seems an interminable time, she helps Besse to her feet and then to the washbasin, where she carefully washes the child's face. With lips tightly shut, Fee helps Besse out of her bed clothes and into a blouse, coat, and surcotte.

Still the girl stares blankly, but she allows herself to be led out of the chamber, down the stairs, and out the door. Fee hugs her shoulders, leading her gently to the market and the tent of her sister, Flor.

Flor takes one look at the pair, stops arranging her flowers, and runs to Fee's side. "What is it, Fee? What has happened to this poor young thing?"

Fee gives a warning look, causing Flor to raise her eyebrows.

"Oh!" she says. She turns to Besse. "My dear, you must have some chamomile infusion immediately!"

Flor goes into the back of the tent, rummages among her exotic herbs, and produces a small pouch, which she immerses into the hot water suspended over a fire outside the tent. She breaks off a hunk of bread, offering it to Besse.

"You must eat, liebchen, for strength. Eat, eat."

Besse looks up at Flor, a deep darkness in her eyes, but she is young and will not fight her hunger. She takes the bread and chews slowly. She ultimately accepts the tea, sipping at it, then taking deeper swallows. It does seem to calm her.

Fee sighs. "Thank you, Flor. You are a comfort to a damsel in distress, not to mention an old maid of a guardian. And I must beg a favor. I would like to leave Besse here in your charge while I am at the council."

Flor takes a deep breath. "Fee, my dearest sister, I truly cry for Peter, but you know he must be punished for what he did. Though I do not blame him entirely, as he was certainly led astray by our no-good—" She hesitates, not wanting to think about their departed brother, Dolph, nor wanting to depress Fee further. "Well, I have complete faith in you, sister, who has raised and watched over us all out of love and the kindness of your heart. I know you will do your best to prevail upon His Majesty to be lenient. But I will not allow you to blame yourself—and you cannot deny that you do—for Peter's predicament. It is entirely his own fault."

Flor notes the sag in her sister's shoulders, deepening as she speaks, and decides not to pursue the subject further.

"I am sorry to have disturbed you so, sister," she demurs. "But I am delighted to watch over this poor, miserable maiden while you are gone," Flor says, "so long as you return here immediately after the council with news of the prince's decision. I find the anticipation and the wait unbearable, as I have lost no love for our brother."

Fee's features darken, and she looks as if she will cry. But she catches herself, and soon a look of determination replaces the frown. Flor has seen this before. Fee must definitely have a plan. But the florist will not ask, almost afraid to place a hex upon the idea if Fee mentions it aloud. It is difficult, but she will wait patiently; a few more hours will make little difference.

Meanwhile, Besse has noticed the arrangements of flowers in the tent, with fragrances she has rarely, if ever, experienced. Fee is happy to see Besse distracted. It means Fee will have fewer qualms about leaving the girl for a few hours. Fee sighs and offers Besse a wan smile. She hugs Flor, then turns to head toward the castle.

It does not occur to Fee that such distraction only abets repression of Besse's shattering, humiliating experience. It has ever been the practice of youth to suppress the memory of the worst events while cultivating better ones, however fleeting. Nevertheless, the scars of one's childhood will inevitably influence the actions of adulthood.

"Frau Flor, what is this flower here?" Besse asks, almost accomplishing a smile but not quite capable of it. "It has such an agreeable odor. Do you think I could have one?"

"To give to your mother? That would be a wonderful gesture, child, and I could likely see my way to oblige."

"Oh, no, madame. It would be for your sister!"

"In that case, you may certainly take one, as she clearly deserves and would appreciate the gesture. But wait until she returns—the more fresh it will remain." Flor smiles at the maiden. "I will familiarize you with the different blooms, herbs, and their uses. They are all quite remarkable."

The florist looks up, noting the approach of some citizens. "Meanwhile, I see some customers, on whom I shall attend. You may wander the tent, but do not go behind the back curtain. If you are good, though, I may perhaps show you what is behind that."

"Oh, a mystery!" Besse says, managing a wan smile. "I should love that!"

As Flor assists the customers, Besse moves from bucket to bucket, carefully examining the flowers. Soon she is addressed by Ebouisante, who is drawn to the bright colors and perfumed scents as she makes her own way through the market.

"Could you assist me, mademoiselle?" Ebouisante asks. "I seek a spray of flowers to brighten our shop."

Besse frowns, momentarily taken by surprise, then smiles in realization, saying, "Oh, I am sorry! I am not yet the apprentice here, but I can direct you to the proprietress herself."

"I thank you. I am Ebouisante, newly arrived in this realm with my family from the south of Europe, though my father originates here. And you are . . .?"

"I am Besse, daughter of the armorer to Prince Henrik." She curtsies slightly.

"I am pleased to meet you."

"The same, fräulein," answers Besse.

She suddenly realizes this maiden, the daughter of an important merchant, may be of assistance in planning an escape from her home situation. She smiles with a pretense of friendly nonchalance.

"Perhaps we can alight here a brief time," Besse suggests. "I would appreciate the chance to acquaint myself with someone younger than my servant, Fee, or her sister, Flor."

"I should enjoy the opportunity to make a new friend, as I know no one in this city. It would be a pleasure to acquaint myself with you," responds Ebouisante, pleased with the opportunity to influence another young maiden.

The girls remove some potted plants and arrange themselves on an ornate wood bench in front of the tent.

"You must have had some adventures," offers Besse, "traveling from afar to this city."

"Oh, yes, and I am sure you have heard of one that happened just outside these very walls."

"I have not heard—do tell me!" Besse says.

"My papa and I were rescued from bandits as we approached the city," Ebouisante says. Her eyes are wide in surprise. "Seriously? You have not heard the tale?"

"I am rarely out of the house and hear nothing of events." Besse lowers her eyes. "Would you share your experiences with a poor maiden? I am afraid my life is far less attractive than yours."

From Besse's expression, Ebouisante discerns a darker secret and unease that she dare not discuss. She determines to know this maiden better, to see if she can better her circumstances. A puzzle and a project! How can she resist?

"Would you like to meet here this day each week? We can share our experiences and perhaps even read together!" she says enthusiastically.

"Oh!" says Besse excitedly. "Would you? But I cannot read!"

Before Ebouisante can respond, she is interrupted by the approach of Hans. She blushes and rises to curtsy to her erstwhile savior.

On impulse, Hans purchases a lily and hands it to Ebouisante with a bow. "It is an honor to make your acquaintance again, mademoiselle!" he offers with a smile.

Ebouisante blushes, unfamiliar with such attention. In truth, such a formal statement would make her laugh, but she stifles the impulse.

"I accept your offer, sir, if you accept that I am not to be confused with Enide, who would sacrifice all for love in disobedience. Though I must serve the difficult role of both the daughter and the journeyman to my father, he has seen fit to allow me a liberal education, and I have had access to the greatest of teachers and libraries in our travels. Yet here in this city we settle, to make our fortune, and I am not ready to be bartered or displayed, as is the wont. Oh!" she gestures to her new friend. "May I present Besse, daughter of the armorer."

Hans bows again, then turns to Ebouisante with a smile. "I should delight in learning from you, mademoiselle, if only to acquaint myself with the advances and politics of the world, to which I am not privy. Perhaps we shall have the opportunity to meet again, with more time to discuss your travels. My best regards to your parents," he says as he departs.

Besse sees a bond between these two and surmises that this handsome boy must be the hero of the attack on Ebouisante's arrival in the city. Besse resolves to explore this relationship further, to see if she can turn it to her own advantage.

♦ ♦ ♦

As Fee makes her way to the castle, she almost fails to notice the approach of her brother Jurg. He startles her when he rushes up to her, but she softens immediately upon recognizing him.

"Have you come to accompany me to the castle, Jurg?" she asks. "I am determined to attend. I shall not leave Peter to the mercy of the prince alone. I must do what I can to—"

Jurg raises his finger to his lips while shaking his head. "Hush, sister. I know you well enough not to thwart your intentions—the mother hen must protect her chicks. You shall have your opportunity, but just not this day."

Fee steps aside and quickens her stride, with Jurg following closely behind. "You cannot stop me, brother. I am determined, and I will continue on my way, accompanied by you or not."

"Hear me, Fee." Jurg raises his voice as he places a restraining hand on her shoulder. "The trial will not take place this day. There has been an escape from the dungeon. And the jailer, I am afraid, is no longer able to recapture—"

"An escape! What has Peter done now?" she blurts. "I do not know what more I can do!"

Fee feels as if she were a pot about to boil over on the hearth. Her face takes on a frown that would evoke pity from the most degenerate of men. She covers her eyes with her hand, willing herself not to cry.

Jurg is taken aback. He folds his sister into his arms and rocks her gently.

"No, Fee. It was not Peter but Jacques who has escaped. And yet, there is more . . ."

"More, Jurg?" His statement has served only to increase Fee's agitation. "You have said naught of our brother. What of Peter? Did he not try to escape as well? Have they captured him too?" Fee casts a forlorn look toward the castle. "I must hurry hence. The guards will try to do him harm, but I will stand in their way."

"That you need not do, sister, though I will take you to him. Peter did not try to escape and is in no danger from the guards. He decided to stay and accept his fate. I think he truly wants to turn his life around." Jurg pauses a moment. "But you must steel yourself. I must prepare you if you are to see our brother."

"Oh, Jurg! I can read your face well. You cannot hide from me. Peter is hurt, is he not? *Is he not*?"

Now Fee can no longer contain herself. She starts to sob, burying her face in her brother's tunic. Jurg lets her relieve herself of her emotion. He sighs, says nothing more, then accompanies her to the castle, as one would serve as a crutch to an old lady crippled with arthritis, for Fee can hardly support herself.

The townspeople can only stare as the pair pass by, knowing them well and wondering what terrible fate must have befallen the young man in the dungeon. They know Fee is stalwart, and something terrible about her brother must be afoot to have her in such a crestfallen state. For her part, she is too deep within her own thoughts to acknowledge any of them. But she allows her brother to steer her onward, each step heavier than the last, like a pack animal overburdened with an oversized load.

When at last she has dragged herself up the spiral stairway to the dungeon, she sees Peter through the open doorway. He is huddled in a fetal position in the shadow of the window. Peter rises slowly, not unlike a phoenix from the ashes, and stretches. Fee immediately sees the mark upon his neck and gathers the last of her strength to run to him. They hug for what seems just short of eternity, and both allow tears to flow freely. Jurg decides to leave them alone for the moment, gesturing to the guards outside the entry to accompany him.

Finally, Fee releases Peter, then holds him at arm's length to reassure herself that he is still whole. Peter casts his gaze downward and unsuccessfully attempts to cover his neck with his hand, but his sister pulls it away so she can evaluate the extent of the damage.

"Speak to me, brother, that I may know that you still have a voice."

"Have little enough of that . . . and naught much else." His voice is still hoarse, though finding a bit more strength. "No modesty, no sanity, no freedom . . . no right to be loved by you. What I have is shame

. . . shared liberally with you and Jurg. Even . . . Flor. My life is useless."

"Now hush, brother. You have said too much." She puts her hand gently over Peter's mouth.

He sees only an angel before him and sighs with surrender.

"I can see you have decided to accept your fate," Fee says through her tears. "This says more of you than you would admit, and it gives me just the right opportunity to speak on your behalf at the trial. You must trust in me. But you also must promise me that, given the chance, you will devote your life to the betterment of your position, that you will apply what you have learned to the improvement of the lives of those around you."

"Willingly, sister . . . I will make amends. I am unworthy of . . . love, kindness, but I will try to . . . earn it."

"I believe you, Peter, as you have already done so by foregoing the opportunity to escape. May the Lord bless us both and turn your life to a higher purpose."

Peter smiles. "Should I become . . . a priest?"

At this point, a ray of sunshine pierces the window and alights upon Peter's face. The fog is finally lifting. Fee sees a fallen angel wracked with remorse and not a little worse for wear. She smiles weakly.

"Not that, brother. I would not have you living off the generosity of others, while preaching what their behavior should be, then selling indulgences to the wealthy, as if they could cast off their sins by purchase. No, I have something more worthy in mind." She turns to the door. "Jurg! Let us leave now. I must see to Besse, and I must think."

◆ ◆ ◆

Upon returning to Flor's tent at the market, Fee finds her young charge behind the back curtain with her sister, who is pointing out medicinal uses of the plants and herbs on the tables.

Flor smiles at Fee as she says, "You see, sister, Besse is a fast learner. I was just explaining to her that she must not touch this table, here. There is hemlock—which in small doses can induce a slow death—among other plants not too healthful."

~ Chapter 30 ~

"Flor!" an astonished Fee stomps her foot indignantly. "You must not show her such things! She is young and very impressionable!"

"Perhaps, but I have a proposition for you, my dear," says Flor, having considered how she can be of assistance to the young maiden and her sister in their plight. "I have no children, nor do I have anyone of interest to apprentice. Since Besse is in your care, I would be honored to train her in the trade of flowers, which has been good to me. I would show her how to acquire and process the wilder flowers as well as how to cultivate the ones that sell. She could serve as apprentice and eventually acquire the trade. What say you to that? Of course, should she meet an appropriate mate, I would demur."

Fee furrows her brow. "I think that would be a kind service, Flor—once I have trained her in the necessary chores of household care. And I think I would like her to learn to read as well."

"That is particularly ambitious. I applaud your desire to provide the girl with the best possible opportunity in life." But now Flor speaks softly, hoping the maiden might not hear the discourse. "Lord knows her father will arrange nothing for her and will have not a care for her ultimate welfare. And I have no regard whatsoever for Beata. Word is, her affections lie entirely elsewhere, and it does not go unnoticed that the management of the household falls upon your shoulders alone. I am surprised you do not already exhibit a major stoop, carrying a weight not unlike Atlas's himself upon your back." Flor shakes her head. "I confess I do not understand why or how you do it. Others would gladly arrange for you to become part of their household, and your burden would be considerably lighter."

Fee is alarmed at this thought and speaks more adamantly in an agitated whisper. "Think no such thought, Flor! Even with Besse with me at another household, she would not be safe from her father. And Beata would be entirely lost without me, not to mention every servant of the household. I cannot leave them, even for . . ." This is not the time to tell her sister about Dien. "Well, I simply cannot."

Fee clears her throat and speaks more loudly now so the maiden will hear her. "Now, Besse," she continues, "leave the goods in the back of the tent to Frau Flor, and come along with me. We have food and other items to acquire, and we must be home in good time."

"Fee, dear, wait! And what of Peter?" Flor asks sheepishly. "How fares he?"

"Oh, he is whole, if not entirely well, and he is entirely repentant," Fee replies. "I have a plan for some redemption. Pray for him—for us."

"That I will, sister. That I will. You must tell me more later."

For her part, Besse wishes to stay with the flowers and herbs. This would be a good potential future for her, and she is surprised to find herself thinking of it. Yes, Fee has indeed been kind to her—certainly kinder than her mother, who barely puts up with her and looks at her with disgust. But Fee cannot remove her from the household. Flor can perhaps . . . Here Besse has the image of a dungeon with a dragon preventing her escape. But how absurd, to think of Flor as the dragon slayer, come to rescue her. Maybe Hans? He seems to have no fear, if he can accost bandits! And so handsome.

Or perhaps if Besse can learn more of the herbs and concoctions in the back of the tent, she may be able to take her fate into her own hands. She could thereby perform a service to Fee, who would likely be equally glad to be rid of her unwanted charge. Besse smiles, although it is a sardonic grin, if anyone should see it.

"Coming, Fee," she says warily.

Accompanying the servant means returning to her dungeon once again, and it is now clear that Fee cannot always forbear the dragon. But then, Fee wants her to learn to read. Besse cannot imagine how that could be accomplished, as Fee is illiterate herself. Perhaps she can take advantage of the compassion and interest of her new friend, Ebouisante. Yes, Besse realizes with a start, she can take advantage of circumstance to plan her own life—if only she can be clever enough.

For once, Besse may have something to look forward to, and that is truly a new experience for her. She thinks to herself, *We shall see, shall we not? And I must be more active about it, must I not?*

~ Chapter 31 ~

Bo, the young bandit, paces back and forth outside the wall of the city, under the tower he is sure houses the armorer. His brow is furrowed in concentration and consternation. The armorer killed his brother and companion in crime and in life, and he must compensate. There is no thought in the boy's mind that the manslaughter was a result of an attempted robbery gone awry, only that he has been unable to work alone and is now near starvation.

Bo notes that the man's wife always seems present in the tower. There must be a way to get to her. Kidnapping is a desperate maneuver, but these are hard times.

A guard walks the high wall, and the boy ducks into the shadows. He does not go entirely unnoticed, however.

At that moment, Rudi is approaching the wall, his face betraying his excitement at the possibility of a new life. He expects he will convince the love of his life to accompany him. She can hardly choose Dunkel Hammer over him. He will win her over. The thought of burying his face in her perfumed, luxurious long blonde hair is almost a distraction and is interrupted only by the sight of a shadow moving before him.

He nears the wall cautiously, observing the somewhat clumsy movement of a young boy. He grabs the boy by the scruff of his ragged tunic, pulling him into the light. A look of surprise crosses Rudi's face for the span of just a second as he recognizes the boy.

"You seem to find yourself in the wrong place at the wrong time repeatedly! Have you been spying upon the lady of the tower, perhaps with nefarious intent? Know she is under my protection more than her drunken husband's. But either of us is more than a match for you." Rudi shakes his head, tightening his grip in rising anger. "I have already told you all that I would offer you, but now you have forfeited even that small chance at a better life. I will alert the guard to be on the watch for you at this very spot. Be gone, and do not let me see your pathetic visage again!"

Bo is nonplussed and pulls away from Rudi with a grunt. "Ye're not the master of me, sir, ye're not! I'll not be a bother t' ye or the lady, but I'll come and go as I please, I will."

He brushes himself off, head held high. But then he slinks away within the shadow of the wall.

Rudi chuckles, allowing his anger to subside. No, the boy is no threat to any of them. He will leave Bo some dignity and just let him depart. Rudi would rather concentrate upon his love.

Beata, for her part, has heard the commotion below her chamber. Guessing full well that at least one of the voices must belong to her beloved, she leans cautiously out the window to apprise herself of the activity below. She is a little angry, which causes her to flush, making her appearance even more attractive to Rudi. She has already admonished him to stay away, for fear of the wrath of her husband. She does not want the added danger of an encounter between Rudi and Dunkel to spoil her future. Yet perhaps if Rudi's insistence on meeting is more than just an affirmation of his love, she can turn it to her advantage. Her frown turns into a smile.

Rudi has rehearsed a speech. "Is it the pale, beautiful moon or the bright sun which appears before my eyes? The one is far and unattainable but certainly desirable, while the other cannot be viewed directly, or it shall bring tears and force one to look away. Yet I am transfixed, for I have neither the heart nor the ability to turn my head from that which has already turned my head irreparably. You cannot send me away—even a day without you is an eternity, not to be tolerated. Let down your hair that I may climb to the heights of heaven, which is wherever I may find you."

Touched, Beata cannot help but laugh. "Prettily spoken. I find myself unable to resist such poetry nor you yourself, my love. Fortune has it that the master of the house is about his business outside the city. I shall help you up if for only a brief moment, as I would discuss an idea with you." Her tone darkens. "Yet you know he will return early, as he has word that you plan to present to the guild this very day in petition of becoming a master yourself. I am sure he plans to oppose you vigorously. So, I shall offer my solace in person even before you make the attempt."

She passes down her makeshift rope of knotted linens, while allowing her hair to cascade down the outside wall.

Rudi climbs, reaches the threshold, and deftly throws himself over the ledge and into Beata's chamber. She pulls her long tresses in, quietly walks to her vanity, seats herself gracefully, and proceeds to brush any potential tangles out of her locks, her back to her lover in unspoken rebuke to his audacity.

Rudi stops for a moment, turning to face his love. "I would needs catch my breath after such a climb, but, as always, it is your beauty that leaves me entirely breathless. Come sit by me and let us entertain ourselves, as I have plans for the day, as you have said, and must soon be off. But I cannot leave without seeing to your safety. I did, in fact, encounter one outside the wall who could mean you ill."

"I have no enemies—but one too many lovers, I think, my dear." She laughs. "Why should I harbor any concern? I am safe enough here, which is all the more reason for me to remain."

Beata throws herself onto the bed beside her young lover, instantly transporting the pair into an imaginary, fragrant paradise.

Rudi smiles briefly, then shakes off the mood with great reluctance. "You should not be so flippant with such concerns, liebchen. I can guard you only from the outside to a certain extent. And though you have made no enemies, you should know that the *master* has made many. You may be a means to their ends. I shall install shutters in the window opening, and you must keep them locked to all but myself."

Beata sighs. She loves Rudi's devotion but will not be stifled by either him or her husband.

"I am prisoner enough without at least the friendship of the zephyrs and the stars as companions. And I fear nothing with you willing to avenge any wrong that may reach me. *You* should have no fear, my love. But those who would wish either of us any harm definitely *should* have fear."

She smiles at him to end that line of conversation. "Now let us put our lips to better use than argument. I had asked you to stay away because I would die if any ill befell you. But now that you are here, let us take advantage. Kiss me!"

Rudi complies, temporarily giving up trying to convince Beata to abscond with him. The tower may indeed be safer for her than a house in the woods, but he will continue to risk visiting her here.

The two embrace longingly, ultimately pushing themselves under the cover of the bed and enjoying each other more intimately.

Afterward, Beata nestles her head in the crook of Rudi's arm. Rudi bends his head to reach her lips, but she puts her hand over his mouth and whispers to him instead. He is astonished to hear her propose a scheme!

He says, "*You want me to attack the man?* Even besotted, he is a formidable foe, and worse so in anger! You must know, if he continues to drink, he will not live long. Yet I am as impatient as you, my love. Come with me now—we need not wait. I have prepared a cottage for us. You deserve the open air, and I have disguised it so the master will not find you. We can live free!"

Beata reaches out to hug Rudi. "I will not, my love," she almost whispers. "It is not safe to go. It would guarantee Dunkel would seek me out, and I would be more accessible to any others who would seek me out to ill effect, as you have mentioned. They need only follow you to me!"

Rudi sighs in resignation, dresses himself hurriedly, blows Beata one last kiss, and leaps to the window.

"You shall not keep me away," he says, "and I shall watch over you until you come to your senses and it is safer to join me. I have created an abode just for us, and I will spare nothing for your comfort.

Wish me luck with the guild masters—I go to make my presentation."

Beata laughs, holding the coverlet close to her bosom. "You are more dramatic than romantic, love, but I shall pray for you. I know your work surpasses that of my erstwhile husband, and I cannot imagine your not capturing the reward you seek. Just avoid Dunkel at all costs, and I will rest more easily. And remember my whisperings, that we may be together all the sooner!"

"I shall avoid the master. And I shall think long and deeply upon your whisperings, liebchen."

And with that, he takes hold of the makeshift rope and vaults himself out of the window and down the linen rope.

Beata shakes her head, internally laughing at this display of exaggerated male exhibitionism. But secretly, her heart skips a beat. She decides it would be prudent to leave the comfort of the bed and pull in the knotted bedsheets before redressing.

◆ ◆ ◆

Her prudence turns out to be well founded. Below, the young thief has returned and sees Rudi coming down the linens. Once Rudi departs, Bo believes he has an opportunity—only to be foiled once again as the mistress pulls in the bedsheets.

Bo sighs and decides to follow the journeyman, more cautiously this time, keeping himself generally concealed. He hopes to learn some advantage over this potential adversary. He will not give up on his plans, which are, after all, born of desperation.

Rudi does not notice the boy, his mind focused both on the liaison and the task at hand. He follows a carefully preselected path, however, designed to throw off any pursuit. He does not want anyone to discover the hidden location of his long, hard masterwork.

It is now time to retrieve it, as the guild is to meet this day. He will demand attention regardless of his former master's objection. Of course, he will have some obstacles to surmount, but he is confident he can do so.

As always, the meeting will be held at the home of the

consensus grand master—who unfortunately is Dunkel Hammer at the moment. It rankles Rudi that much of the fine work attributed to the man has been his own, but a master always gets the credit for the work of those in his employ. Of course, Rudi's own work is based upon techniques imparted to him by the master, but this does not occur to Rudi.

Ultimately, he reaches the entrance to a small cave in the hills. Shortly thereafter, he emerges with a look of determination and a stand covered in linens. He heads straight back to the city, unaware he has been observed.

The pursuer silently congratulates himself. Perhaps he does not need to kidnap Beata after all.

~ Chapter 32 ~

Besse returns home with Fee, and notes the particularly savory atmosphere. The long table is set with extra bread bowls. She notes choicer cuts of pork and actual squab, a treat she has not enjoyed for over a year. The master's house will serve as a meeting place for the armorers' guild this day, and the master expects mead rather than ale and fine foods—but not too fine.

Besse's head swims with the anticipation of a good meal but more so with the revelation that her father will be otherwise occupied. She can retreat to her room unbothered and unencumbered.

She is also thinking about the prospect of apprenticeship to Flor. Would it be possible to move in with her, as is the custom for the other trades? Is this Besse's chance to escape this prison and its abusive jailer?'

As if reading her mind, Fee sighs. "Do not get your hopes up too high, liebchen. Flor does not have room to house an apprentice and will be content to leave you in my care for the nonce." The servant knits her brows, deciding to mitigate Besse's fear and disappointment. "However, tonight I think you shall be safe enough once I deliver these treats to the kitchen staff, then I mean to depart briefly on an errand. The dinner will be served by the by, and you will be expected to attend. Ask the lady of the house to come for you in your chamber, that you may enter together."

With that, Fee delivers her goods, then leaves the house, shaking her head. The poor girl considers it a treat to be fed a normal meal and to remain unmolested by her father. Even the poorest child is entitled to love. Sometimes the children of the well-to-do are poorer than those of the peasant class, who do well when surrounded by adults who care for them.

Fee is bound for the home of the new merchant family. She noticed Besse conversing with Ebouisante and discreetly ascertained that the bright, fresh young maiden serves the business of her father—which means, importantly, she can read. She has taken an interest in Besse and in general wants to see to the improvement of the situation of all women. This seems to be an unattainable goal, though Fee is not of a mind to disabuse the notion from Ebouisante. She pities the man Ebouisante marries, however.

Fee has too much responsibility on her shoulders to take on the potential problems of yet another youngster. But she sees some opportunity to alleviate one of her own.

She arrives at the shop almost unaware, having been carried by her musings and innate sense of direction. This realization startles her a bit, then she smiles. Her instincts have served her well so far, and she is inclined to trust them.

"Good day, Madame," she says with a slight curtsy as she encounters the merchant's wife.

Blanche smiles in response, always glad to see a potential customer. "Are you here to make a purchase for your lady, or perhaps your master?" she asks, beckoning Fee inside.

The thought almost makes Fee laugh. "My master is Dunkel Hammer, madame. His wife cloisters herself in her chamber and is not likely to desire such fine luxuries. But I would thank you deeply if I might have a word with your daughter, if you please."

"Ebouisante? What business would such as you have with her?" Blanche is both a bit startled and disappointed. Then she muses to herself, *here is an unusual liaison.*

She shrugs, then calls out, "Ebouisante, dearest, there is someone here who would greet you and perhaps make you an offer of business. Do come to the storefront."

Ebouisante is now curious and obediently shows herself with a small curtsy. "To what, madame, do I owe the pleasure and courtesy of your visit? Oh! You are the servant and companion of that poor young maiden I greeted at the florist's tent. I hope I have done nothing to offend you or her or her father."

"Oh no, fräulein! I have merely noted your kind offer of companionship to Besse, and I come to thank you—and to ask a boon. Would you be able to see it in your heart to teach Besse to read? You have seen the girl. I fear for my ability to ever arrange a match for her, and her father has no such interest. The more skill she acquires, the better her chances." Fee lowers her eyes, and Ebouisante can see the pleading in them. "Please do not outrightly refuse me, but consider the proposal. I would find some way, in service if not in coin, to compensate your time. I think having a teacher and role model such as yourself as would do the maiden a world of good."

"You do read me well. I love a challenge, and any maiden who seeks my help need hardly ask. I shall be delighted to be at your service, if only you will not object to any ideas I might inadvertently impart to Besse." Ebouisante turns to her mother. "What do you think, Maman? Do I have your permission to pursue this quest?"

Blanche flushes a bit as she realizes her daughter's "quest" is not merely the education of one poor, unfortunate maiden but rather a lifelong goal.

"I will not dissuade you, my dear, nor could I once you have set your mind. I wish you success. Truly."

Ebouisante understands her mother's blessing well and is grateful to have the support of her mother in her pursuits.

Turning to Fee, "I shall clear my evenings, and I will appear at your door, if that suits, madame."

"Actually, I was hoping you would be free sometime before the master returns from his forge each day."

"That would be more of an irregular interval," Ebouisante replies, "as I have my own duties here and to my father's business. However, shall we instead agree to meet at the tent of the florist as I finish my daily shopping round?"

"Done," Fee says, "and with my deepest gratitude, fräulein." She turns to leave with a curtsy to Blanche and to Ebouisante.

♦ ♦ ♦

Fee breathes deeply with a mixture of hopeful anticipation and concern as she returns quickly to her duties at home. She does not want to leave Besse alone too long with the master returning this early from work.

As she returns, the fowl and the meat are cooking. The table is set. Fresh straw has been laid on the floor. The home has almost a party atmosphere with extra torches providing ample light. An aroma of a feast, almost bacchanalian, pervades the room as the first guests arrive.

The masters first greet each other, then nod their heads in approval to Fee. Some have brought their wives or consorts. The women gather in a corner by the hearth and comment on the latest news or fashion as it fancies them.

Ultimately, Dunkel and his apprentice enter the chamber, and Fee sees to it immediately that he is not without a stein of ale in hand. It draws a smile from the armorer.

"I see that ye desire t' serve me well, Fee. No doubt any of the gentlemen at hand'd be content t' steal ye from this household. But I'll always see t' it that ye remain in my service—or none at all!"

Fee frowns deeply. While the guests have heard what they consider to be a great compliment to her, she does not miss the implied threat. She scurries off, tending to the order of the meal and the servants involved in providing it.

Next, she climbs the stairs and knocks on the chamber doors of her charges. She calls through that dinner is served and that the presence of the ladies of the house is both required and appreciated.

Beata steps out of her chamber. She is radiant—her long blond hair drawn up and tied into an elaborate coif. Just the right amount of powder and berry rouge are applied to her long features, and she bears a long silk tunic with lace fringe, all of a deep red color.

~ Chapter 32 ~

"You look amazing, madame." *The princess has been released from her tower prison,* Fee surmises, *if only for a moment.* "You will certainly be the envy of all the women below."

"Let us fetch Besse and descend to our guests."

Besse has changed into her favorite gray clothing, including the one tunic of plain wool, the only one she possesses not in tatters or torn. The contrast to Beata cannot be more clear—the swan and the awkward goose, the light and the shadow.

"But you have not combed your hair, dear," Beata says to the girl disgustedly. "Fee, you must see to her appearance quickly, and I will see you in the great chamber below."

She turns her attention to the guests as she descends. "Ah, my dear Hildegard. You look positively ravishing. You must refer me to your tailor. And where did you acquire such exquisite cloth?"

Fee is grateful that Besse seems somewhat distracted. She brushes out her hair at the vanity in Beata's chamber and adds a touch of oil for a slight gloss. She then gives the maiden a light hug, whispering in her ear, "Your new friend, Ebouisante, has agreed to spend time with you at Flor's tent. She really likes you and wants to teach you to read. I hope you will accept the offer. Reading is a skill I lack but which could serve you well in the future. Now, liebchen, let's join the feast."

Besse frowns, but she is actually happy. Anything that serves to remove her from her current miserable existence is welcome.

"Thank you, Fee. You are kind to think of me."

Inwardly, she admits to herself, *she offers me the opportunity to run my own life. But she is only a servant, and she should not boss me, just because Mama ignores me. I must develop my plan to be free of the beast, then perhaps I can maneuver some assistance from that arrogant, self-absorbed, self-styled beauty and rid myself of this one too.*

As she joins the crowd below, Besse nods absently and curtsies to the guests. The meal proceeds apace, and she hardly notices the best meal of her life as she eats. Too soon, she excuses herself to return to the confines of her own chamber.

While this room used to feel like a sanctuary, shutting her off from the dangers and vagaries of the outside world, it now feels more like the torture chamber of the dungeon. And she feels like the chicken trapped in the coop, while the fox can enter or leave at leisure, with only the feeble old farmer's wife to protect her. But today, she can at least hide in a dark corner alone with her thoughts, able to plot and plan.

◆ ◆ ◆

The ladies downstairs excuse themselves upon Beata's offer to visit the shops of the city, intrigued by the mention of the newly arrived merchant family offering exotic wares. Perhaps one can find a trinket or a prize unique enough to become the center of conversation of their own guests. Beata merely savors the opportunity to leave her own confinement safely in the company of others.

The servants clear the table, and the men settle to business over steins of mead. They extend their praise and appreciation of the meal to Beata before she departs, oblivious to the fact that the lady of the house would never have anything to do with such menial chores as planning or organizing a meal.

"So, Master Dunkel, it would seem we have very little business to conduct this day," one of the masters says. "What would you have us discuss?"

Dunkel states, "I've concern, gentlemen, that the wars in Europe are drawing t' a close, they are, and there may be less call for our artisanship. I'd like t' propose that we sponsor a roundabout of royal tournaments that might stimulate some attention among the knighthood, it could. Your lovely wife, Heinrich, is always the center of fashion and could take the helm of the ship of feasts and markets. What say ye?"

"She would certainly enjoy that!" Heinrich agrees. "But there are ample conflicts that I think would sustain our craft. Think only of the Teutonic Knights and the Poles, or the Poles and the Lithuanians. Nevertheless, your idea has merit. I would ask for contributions from all those present if we are to host arrangements."

"A vote, gentlemen, then a toast t' Heinrich and his beautiful bride!" Dunkel says.

The men lift their steins, and Dunkel calls for refills.

At this moment, there is a slight commotion at the door.

"Ye can't enter here, sir, ye can't," calls out an angry servant with some annoyance. "Ye've been banished from this household. We'd be punished if we let ye advance. Please, ye must leave!"

"What is it, servant?" bellows Dunkel. He does not even deign to know the names of his own servants—with the exception of Fee, of course. "Who's there?"

"It is I, sir!" calls Rudi, brushing aside the poor servant with no apology, as if she were an entrapping curtain. "I have a presentation to make, and I demand consideration!"

Dunkel's face reddens with outrage. He bellows, "That ye'll ne'er have, boy, ye won't! Ye've been dismissed, ye have, and ye'll never be under consideration for the privilege of becomin' a master in this profession! Begone!"

But Rudi is determined. He places his burden squarely in the center of the room and unveils his work.

"There, gentlemen. Decide for yourselves. I submit to you my masterwork for your judgment!"

There is a collective gasp. The masters did not know of the journeyman's dismissal and were therefore not informed of his submission for consideration of awarding a master's status. Dunkel, of course, had not said anything of these matters.

But now there is fire in his eyes. "A piece of trash! Ye'll not be judged here, ye won't. Take your work and leave now!" he shouts. Then he looks to the men around the table. "Sirs, I must tell ye that I've dismissed this—this upstart. He's no longer welcome at me hearth nor me forge, and I'll not certify him for advancement. Therefore, he can't become a master in this guild, he can't. Ye must send him away!"

The masters do not wish to anger their host, though they know that much of his work is really that of this talented young man. It is, in fact, readily apparent in the quality of the suit of arms in front of them, from the polished sallet to the sabatons. The breastplate is fluted, in the local style, and cinched just so at the waist of the placard. The cuisses and greaves are shaped to a man of some muscle, and the poleyns over the knees have been etched delicately. In all, this is not just a masterwork but a work of art.

"And, gentlemen, I have created a new process," continues Rudi, ignoring the ire of his former master. "This armor can withstand the attack of a somewhat-distant English longbow. Moreover, I would be willing to share the precise coating process or coal mixture to accomplish it, once I become a master in my own right. Will you consider me?"

It is Heinrich who responds, having considered the most diplomatic way to approach this dilemma.

"Journeyman, this is excellent work. But the rules are clear: your master must sponsor you, unless for some reason he is not capable. We are truly sorry, but you must leave. Before you do, son," he adds, "would you honor us with the name of your model? He must truly be a fabled knight!"

Nonplussed, Rudi hesitates a moment, then lowers his voice. "I do have someone to wear this armor, sir. I am sorry you would not consider me at this time, but I shall return, and frequently, until you do." Then to Dunkel, he squares his shoulders and states, "I am not sorry, sir, that I have offended you. You shall hear from me again. Remember how I assisted you at the inn, sir, and know there is more I can do to persuade you to sponsor me."

"That ye *shall* not, young man!" responds Dunkel, still flushed with anger. "Any events ye would reveal about me were also shared by ye personally, and no one'll tell us apart. Be off with ye and this piece o' trash."

Oh, but there is one, thinks Rudi as he holds Dunkel's glare. Rudi knows there is a witness he might persuade. And if not, there is always another way. Dunkel's drunken ways will surely have their effect soon enough. Rudi sighs, gathers his work, and leaves.

- Chapter 32 -

"Now," Dunkel says, turning to his guests with satisfaction and a smile, "let's repair t' the inn outside the gate for a few more libations and t' give the ladies an opportunity t' enjoy the city." He is sure he has nothing to fear from his journeyman and is determined to forget about him and enjoy the occasion.

No one has any objection, so they all rise, thanking him for his hospitality. Of course, they all know Rudi is worthy of admission to the guild as a master. But they also know Dunkel's days are numbered if he thinks he can continue to produce at such a high level of craftsmanship when most of his work has actually been that of his erstwhile journeyman. Plus, he is hardly ever sober. He has a worthy apprentice, but the boy is not ready to replace the journeyman. The other masters hope Rudi will have but a little patience.

And of course, they know nothing of Rudi's cryptic remarks about the inn nor of Dunkel's retort. It is perhaps better to put it out of mind than to question either man on the subject.

But at least two or more of the guests do have a mind to offer a position to Rudi until he can stop worrying about interference from Dunkel and become a master himself. What an opportunity to learn the secrets of the greatest armorer of the continent!

~ Chapter 33 ~

Although the woods are ablaze in autumn color, they can offer places of gloom, especially when the morning fog permeates them and beasts of prey are prowling afoot. Giselle shivers, pulling her scarf more tightly about her as they ride through the forest. She wonders if, after all, it has not been the wisest of decisions to accompany the huntsman.

But she trusts him. And her father has certainly sent two of his best guardsmen to watch over her. Moreover, no young life is complete without some adventure, and she means to learn something of the lifestyle and opinions of the northern European principalities—away from the crushing influence of her stepmother.

She has spent many an hour querying the huntsman, Gaillard, about his life and the people he has met, and he has not disappointed her curiosity. She also admires his ability to hunt and provide the group with ample food, not just in the form of game. He also knows which berries and even leaves are the best tasting and most edible. Indeed, the meat seems to taste even better when cooked fresh over an open campfire and infused with the essence of the wood used to provide the flames.

The man is in his element and is clearly happier than when confined to the court. But he does seem clearly troubled about something and unable to discuss it. La Claire shrugs that off, unwilling to press him and cause a resentment or a rift between them.

"You seem worried, mademoiselle," says Gaillard, as if La Claire's concern about him were reflected in her own expression.

She did not even notice his approach. She chides herself that these are locales of some danger. She should be more vigilant of her surroundings, despite the presence of a protective guard.

She takes a deep breath, then raises her eyes to meet his with a slight frown. "I am truly sorry, sir. I was just musing. I am wondering if we will encounter something more worrisome than the occasional deer or fox. Perhaps we may meet some of these small men you have mentioned, who mine in some secret location not far from here. Would they be trustworthy or adversarial? How proficient are they with bows or swords?"

Gaillard laughs, setting her instantly at ease. The effect surprises her, as she now realizes just how much she trusts the man.

"You need not fear, mademoiselle, as those men are my friends. I hunt here frequently, and this is the best time of year to do so. I provide food for the small men, as you call them, and I have taught them the methods of preservation. Occasionally, they provide me with a potential bauble for your stepmother, which she treasures, but I generally ask nothing of them in return for my services. I just enjoy the pleasure of their company, which is honest and requires no diplomacy. One can speak one's mind freely and hear responses and advice in return that will go no farther than this wood."

He lets La Claire absorb this information for a moment, then continues. "We bring provisions to carry them into the winter. And before returning to Brugge, I shall exchange a gem or two for money from the merchants in town, then purchase vegetables, herbs, and other supplies they need or request."

La Claire is perplexed. She holds up a finger to interrupt the huntsman. "But why, sir, do they not make their own exchanges and deal with the local guard to hunt for them?"

He laughs. "These are small men, who, if not reviled, are at least ridiculed. They prefer not to enter the city. You will see for yourself. I tell you this to prepare yourself, for their size does not reflect their intelligence or their ability. These are not children, mademoiselle," he admonishes, "and should be addressed as you would any respected adult."

La Claire bows her head slightly. "I thank you for your advice, sir." Her face brightens. "In fact, I look forward to the opportunity."

At this point, one of the guards approaches Gaillard, leans toward him, and whispers.

Gaillard sighs. "I do not like it, but I understand," he replies softly, leaving La Claire with a puzzled expression. The huntsman ignores her for a moment and continues his reply to the guard. "I am aware you have tried, and perhaps this is the only way."

The guardsmen suddenly disperse into the woods. La Claire raises her eyebrows in surprise

The young maiden and the huntsman ride for a while on their own, but soon there is a rustle in the woods. La Claire blanches and freezes as if she could blend with a stand of white birch. Then she suddenly gasps as she and the huntsman are surrounded by a group of strangers. But these are no mere bandits but rather fairly well-equipped soldiers, some with mail or sturdy armor.

Gaillard draws his sword in alarm, but he is no expert with this weapon. With a sudden thought, he decides it may be best to use it as a salute. He touches it to his forehead. He turns to see that La Claire has raised the hood on her tunic as a form of camouflage, in order to prevent the men from surmising her gender. This is a futile gesture, of course, as she carries no weapon herself—excepting a concealed dagger, which she manipulates to hand, hopefully unseen.

"Good day to you, sirs," offers Gaillard. "I hope we are well met. We are at your service."

The apparent leader of the group laughs gruffly. "Well met, indeed, and well provisioned with meat! I am called Borg, and I am the leader of this motley group. We have of late been soldiers in the war against the English, but now we are reduced to mere soldiers of fortune. We have trained in this principality, but there is little use for us now. Therefore, we fend for ourselves. How convenient of you to dispense with your guard! We shall now avail ourselves of your excellent provisions as well as a horse or two—and one more thing."

Gaillard makes one more attempt at diplomacy. "Would you bargain with us, sir? Perhaps we can exchange some meat, along with lessons in hunting and preservation, for some additional protection in this wood."

Borg smiles and responds without hesitation, "Well said, but not quite what we have in mind. We shall take what we like."

Gaillard shrugs his shoulders, as if ready to comply. He adds, "You mentioned you wanted one more thing. We have nothing more to offer."

The huntsman knows what—or who—Borg wants, but he wants it stated so the nearby guardsmen will hear. He adopts a look of consternation, gesturing silence to the young maiden, then turns back to face Borg.

Borg brandishes his weapon, stating, "You will drop your sword, and we shall also take the maiden. She might fetch a price in town, as she clearly has some value. You cannot fight all four of us, I warrant. We shall leave you with your life, however, if you comply without resistance. We are not murderers—so long as we are not provoked."

Now Gaillard sits tall on his horse, raising his voice. "And you are no gentlemen, sir." Shadows move, and the huntsman is ready. "We shall offer you some provisions, and then you must be off."

Borg is angry. "You are in no position to bargain. If you resist, your life is forfeit, and we shall do as we please with the maiden."

Borg gestures to his companions. But two of them drop silently with arrows through their throats. Borg is surprised and turns to face the duke's guardsmen, advancing with longswords drawn. He and his remaining man draw their own swords and advance to the battle. There is a great clash of metal on metal. La Claire retains enough composure to urge her horse to a position out of view behind the advancing guardsmen.

The huntsman looks on with satisfaction, then draws not his sword but his bow. Taking careful aim, he expertly finishes off the one soldier. Then he faces Borg, who realizes he is completely outmanned. Borg retreats.

The guardsmen make no effort to follow. Instead, they immediately surround La Claire and escort her back to the huntsman's side. They usher the group—people, horses with packed provisions, and all—away from the clearing and back into the woods.

Gaillard dismounts and bows. "I am sorry, mademoiselle. Let me explain: We were aware this ill-mannered band was tracking us the better part of a day. The guards had no safe opportunity to circle around behind them, though. We felt we needed to offer them an opportunity to make their intentions clear, so we had to appear unprotected momentarily. That is why the guards fell back into woods just before Borg and his men appeared."

He shakes his head, then looks into La Claire's eyes. With a sincere look of concern, he continues. "You should not be exposed to the spillage of blood. You must forgive my inability to protect you from such exposure to the base nature of men, who are given to an excess of"—here he hesitates—"physicality. We must hurry on to the abode of the little men, as I would endanger you no more."

She is nonplussed but regains her composure. "Think nothing of it, sir. I am not as fragile as all that, and I have seen the blood of your prey spilled afore this. But I do fear we might encounter yet other such groups. What are these soldiers to do, with the end of the wars? It is a thought worth the consideration of my father and the local princes, I think. Let us continue onward." She is determined not to reveal the degree to which she is inwardly shaken, but she allows herself a little shiver.

"You need not entirely fear that, mademoiselle," offers the huntsman, somewhat relieved to see Giselle so rapidly recover from the attack. "The Teutonics are at odds with the Polish king, and there are always the Latvians to consider. I also think the islanders to the west are soon to be at odds with each other. There will be ample need for soldiery."

Nevertheless, dark thoughts accompany La Claire as the group rides onward to the base of a small mountain, where a fresh river flows and a house can be made out along its banks. It is a bit ramshackle and in need of a few repairs, but the inhabitants are not home. She and the huntsman alight at the entrance, which is a bit low even for her. She smiles, then remembers this is not the home of children but of grown men.

She takes it upon herself to enter and sees a single large room in some disarray. Without a thought, she straightens out the pots of the hearth and the few utensils, then beats out the covers of the seven short beds and runs a hot pan over the bed straw in an effort to rid it of lice and other unwanted inhabitants. The guardsmen barely fit in the room, but they bring wood to stoke the fire in the hearth. La Claire takes some provisions and starts a large pot of venison stew, adding a few vegetables from the larder adjoining the house.

Thus it is as the men in question return from the mine. They are greeted with horses strapped to nearby trees, a savory aroma from their little home, smoke rising from the chimney, and the sound of laughter inside.

Grump smiles and turns to his companions. "We've been invaded, we have, but by a friendly force, methinks, me friends. I recognize this steed as the property of our friend, the huntsman. But in the past, he's ne'er provided us with such a fine meal as I'm smellin' now, so let's see what's afoot."

His companions leave their burdens behind the house, then join him as he pushes open the door.

"And t' whom do we owe the honor of such an invasion?" asks Grump.

But he stops short. The little home has been swept and dusted, the beds refreshed, and bread bowls have been placed along the large table with seven places unoccupied. And is that a maiden stirring the pot on the hearth? A truly beautiful one, at that. And such a powerful and flavorful scent, promising a wonderful stew! Remembering to close his jaw and starting to salivate in anticipation of what would be a feast for these men, Grump turns to Gaillard.

"T' what do we owe such an honor, sir? I, at least, am overwhelmed. It'll be difficult t' reciprocate for such a kindness, it would, e'en if ye did invade our humble abode without warnin'."

The huntsman laughs. "My apologies, sir, for the intrusion. I have some excellent provisions for you, which we have already salted and stored in your larder. Please enjoy the meal prepared by our charge, who is the daughter of Philip le Bon himself! She travels with us to explore a bit of the world before her father determines the best match for her." He turns and offers the maiden a smile. "She is not only beautiful but also amazingly capable of domesticity, a trait not generally cultivated in the nobility. I venture to say, she has taken this training upon herself, as her stepmother would certainly disapprove. Judge for yourself how well she has learned. Please sit and enjoy the meal!"

Grump bows. "As always, sir, ye do us great honor and a great favor, ye do."

The men all seat themselves and enjoy the meal as directed. As they finish, one smiles, pats his full belly, and addresses Gaillard. "Sir, ye're well met, as always. Ye must leave the cleanup t' us, as I'm sure ye're anxious t' be on your way. And the young lady'll not wish t' be kept late, nor should she demean herself further in service t' such humble servants as us."

The huntsman laughs. "You are certainly logical. But it is always a pleasure to see you all and an honor to serve you. I would ask a boon, however."

Grump raises his eyebrows and his voice. "So now we get t' the real meat of it! Anythin' ye like, we're at your service, we are."

Gaillard holds up his hand. "Please hear me out first." He glances briefly at La Claire, lowering his eyes, then faces the dwarf and continues. "It has been our mission to show the maiden the various cities and principalities of this region bordering the realm of her father." He hesitates a moment, then lowers his voice. "I am ashamed to admit, however, that her stepmother has other designs for this journey."

At this, there is a collective gasp—the loudest from Giselle herself, who had not suspected her stepmother to be nefarious to the extent of wishing La Claire harm.

She quickly shakes her head, finding herself reasoning. *Certainly, I am no threat to her, not even for the affections of Papa. Nor does she have children of her own. Can she be that vain, to see me as a rival? I will not believe it!*

The huntsman continues, "I would ask, gentlemen, that you consider keeping her here for a time. She would be safe in your care, and she can certainly care for all of you."

"Do I have anything to say, sir, about that?" asks an indignant La Claire, looking even more beautiful in anger, which adds a blush to her cheeks. "It is impossible that my stepmother would wish me that degree of harm. I do not believe such statements. I will not be left behind. My father provides me with more than adequate protection."

"Mademoiselle," Gaillard replies grimly, "the guards must follow the dictates of both of your parents. I myself am subject to the commands of both of Their Lieges, but believe that I would never allow harm to come to you!" he pleads. "I will need to plan something until I can reach the duke. I beg you will allow me to keep you out of harm's way."

"Mad'moiselle," interrupts Grump, "It'll be our pleasure t' be of assistance. And we've known this man for years, we have. I'd ask that ye trust in his judgment, for he clearly has your best interest in mind above his own, he does. He'll have t' face the duchess himself and then face the duke, he will."

La Claire nods. "That is true, sir. And it is true that I could be of much use to you, as you have seen, but there is no accommodation for me here. No, I will return and face my stepmother on my own. His Liege will not allow harm to come to me."

"No, mademoiselle. You will *not* be safe in Brugge!" exclaims Gaillard. "I will reveal that Her Grace has beseeched me to see you remain *out* of the realm. You must not trust her intentions. I will dispatch one of the guards to the good prince of this land to see to your safety and comfort here. Please grant me the time to accomplish this goal while you accept the hospitality of these gentlemen." He bows to the dwarves, then to Giselle.

"Well, then, I will stay for a time, if you all think it best," sighs

La Claire in resignation. Yet she resolves not to stay long nor allow herself to hide from society in fear.

The huntsman and the guards prepare to take their leave. He lowers his eyes, bows once again to La Claire, and says, "I am deeply sorry for the circumstance, mademoiselle, but I promise to see to your safety. I shall return as soon as feasible."

La Claire returns the bow with a curtsy. "That is quite all right, sir, if not truly satisfactory. I trust these men will be excellent hosts, and I know I can be of great service to them."

This turns out to be the best statement she could have made, as the little men all blush. They are now implanted with the thought that someone has an interest in their welfare, a thought that is new to them. And that someone is of such high stature, not to mention beauty.

It is precisely the effect La Claire hopes to achieve if she must live with these men for a while. She hopes, however, that the duration will be just long enough for her to straighten up and provide for their abode and to impart some manners and kindness. Perhaps this is just another part of an adventure, and she will have some stories to tell her family. Such a thought!

♦ ♦ ♦

Outside, Gaillard nods his approval at the guards who have protected the humble abode while he and La Claire were inside. He takes on a stern countenance as they mount, shakes his head, and addresses them.

"Gentlemen. We have a real quandary. I cannot return the young maiden to the care of her father. No amount of protection there would shield her from her stepmother, especially when His Liege is away from his court. Therefore I ask that one of you stay here with her."

Although he cannot be sure he can trust the loyalty of these men, they did protect the maiden during the attack. He decides he has little choice.

One of the guards steps forward.

"We are within the principality of Prince Henrik," Gaillard addresses the guard. "At first convenience, travel to the castle and report to His Majesty so that he can make appropriate arrangements for the maiden. Hold nothing back; be truthful with him. As for me, I will return to Brugge to deal with her ladyship. I must think of a ruse to satisfy her while still imparting to the duke the true circumstances that befall his daughter." He shakes his head, straightening his back, then adds, "May the Lord watch over us all." But in his mind, he really means several lords—the one above, the one duke, and the one prince!

The arrangements are made, the provisions and horses divided, and the huntsman travels onward. These woods have always been so hospitable to him, but now they seem to offer nothing but shadow and menace. Of course, he realizes this is merely his inner mood. Woods are woods and nothing more. They need to be faced only with vigilance. They offer whatever knowledge is needed to survive them and to take advantage of the bounty, but always with gratitude.

He is satisfied that La Claire will be in good hands—or at least the best he can arrange. The guard is strong and able to watch over her. And once he knows she is here, Prince Henrik will not allow her to be exposed to any danger. He is not likely to make an enemy of the duke. Moreover, he has a kind heart.

He hesitates a moment, then snaps his fingers and speaks to the air. "That is it! A heart! I know what I must do."

Just as this thought occurs to him, he hears a roar followed by a whimper from the nearby glade. It makes him cringe. Then, resolute, he advances toward the sound, entering the glade. It is clearly much used, with trampled ground and parts of broken weapons and shields lying here and there. He realizes this is a training site for the local guard but only dwells upon that thought for an instant.

The site is unoccupied for the moment—with the exception of a large bear towering over a waifish young man who has dropped his sack. In the trees beyond cowers a frail older lady, her eyes wide open in fear, her skin pale as a ghost's. The boy is on his knees, bent over, and covering his head with his hands. He is poorly dressed, with ragged leggings, a threadbare tunic, and no shoes.

Gaillard pulls out his bow and one arrow, nocks it carefully, and draws back. He calls out quickly to the boy, "Do not move. He will not attack if you pretend to be dead!"

Then he lets fly. The arrow hits true, directly into the heart of the beast. One great roar, and the bear falls.

The boy waits until the huntsman approaches him and helps him to his feet.

"Ye must be sent by an angel, sir," cries the old woman, her voice tremorous, as she emerges from her hiding place. "We are eternally in your debt, we are. Thanking ye is not enough show of gratitude for savin' me boy. We're much put upon these days, but if there's any service we can perform for ye, we're more than willin', we are."

Gaillard shakes his head. "You will do no such thing, madame. In fact, it is a mere matter of fate that I am here to be of assistance to you. Let us carve up this beast, and I will afford you some salt and rope to preserve and carry the meat. Do you live hereabouts?"

"In a manner, yes, sir," she responds, having restored some of her wits.

The huntsman sees this is a woman who was once beautiful but now has acquired the lines of much worry and sorrow. He is not so sure of the youth, who has stopped whimpering and offers him a short bow. He has the faraway look of one whose mind is elsewhere, perhaps always thinking—or always plotting.

He teaches the boy the necessary butchery and preserving, but he carefully wraps the heart of the beast and saves it for his own purposes. Then he bows to the couple and continues on his own journey as he shakes his head.

Jacques retrieves his sack filled with some gold coins and the gold-leaf goose and harp. As planned, he had bided his time for days, then followed Katrina to her cache. So these were the treasures she mentioned! This cannot possibly be all the gold, however, as it is too little an amount to have supported them for long. She must have taken more and hidden it elsewhere. But there is no time to seek where she has hidden the rest. It has been nearly a day since he left her back at her hovel and found his mother.

For now, Jacques hefts the new burden of bear meat over his shoulder. He will trust his newfound good fate by heading in the opposite direction, out of Quellestadt. He beckons his mother to follow.

~ Chapter 34 ~

Ebouisante enjoys the protection of the morning fogs of autumn. They afford her the ability to escape the city unnoticed, once the gates are opened for the day, and to indulge in a walk in the woods.

She has discovered an eddy in the river not visible from the road. There the water is warm, even at this late date, as it is heated by the forge output above. Each day, she sheds her clothing, still enveloped by the cloak of fog, and bathes herself. She emerges refreshed. She then dries herself, applies an essence or perfume of crushed flowers, and dresses, prepared for the rigorous labor of the day. All of this she accomplishes before the breakfast meal of fruits and bread.

When Ebouisante returns, her mother always chides her for leaving the city alone. But Blanche knows well the habits of the Poitiers merchant class women, who have a particular penchant for bathing outdoors and a tendency to eschew powders and makeup. She has asked her husband to provide a guard surreptitiously, but Serge is reluctant, as he would not subject his naked daughter to the gaze of men.

Now only a few days after La Claire's arrival in the woods, Ebouisante enters her private pool, cloaked again by fog. She sings some ditty she has heard from a passing minstrel on the road while caravaning with her father. She is only momentarily startled when a fawn and its mother appear at the edge of the pool, languidly observing her as they dip their heads into the water, then withdraw without drinking, perhaps because of the temperature of the water, perhaps because of the taste. Ebouisante finds the entire scene idyllic, and her mind wanders to some chivalric tale of the court of King Arthur. She tries to remember the reference, wondering if she has this book to share with Besse.

Indeed, Besse has proven to be an attentive student, already having learned her alphabet and having acquired the ability to sound out words. But she does not speak French, and Ebouisante's library of Germanic books is quite limited. She must seek out more. The Nordic myths are certainly interesting and might make a good text or two for teaching.

Ebouisante wants to impart more than the ability to read to Besse. She would like very much for her to learn to appreciate the Greek philosophers, the teachings of the church, and, above all, the writings of Christine de Pisan, which she finds liberating. In contrast to Christine, Plato has described a utopian city, but even that is dominated by men and certainly unachievable.

She shrugs, then laughs. "This world would certainly be less contentious if run by women, but it is just as certainly not ready for that," she thinks out loud.

As she muses, there is a rustle in the bushes behind her, but she is oblivious to it. Then suddenly there emerges a large man with a decided limp and an orange complexion that nearly glows despite the fog. His brow is furrowed, and his intent ill. It is Dunkel Hammer, feeling he has encountered incredible good fortune, having come upon such a beautiful and entirely unguarded damsel—almost an offering of the gods.

Now Ebouisante is alarmed, and she fully understands the danger she is in. She thinks furiously.

As she does, Dunkel smiles. "Well, what have we here! A young and, I might say, quite attractive morsel. And I'm just hungry enough t' be of a mind for a bite, am I."

Ebouisante sinks into the river, allowing only her head to remain emerged. She furrows her own brow, indignantly declaring, "Sir, you are no gentleman. If you had a shred of chivalry, you would turn your back and retreat into the wood."

Dunkel laughs. "If ye knew me, ye'd know I've no pretensions of bein' any kind of a gentleman. So, I think I'll just seat meself here on this old log and enjoy the view 'til ye're ready t' come out."

The maiden, still indignant, replies, "In that case, sir, I shall certainly turn into a prune. I will not so accommodate you. And I trust you are not coming in because you cannot swim."

"I'll admit that, I will, certainly," Dunkel says, rubbing his chin. "But, fräulein, I certainly have all day, I do, and I believe the prize is worth the wait, it is."

This is a quandary. At the moment, all Ebouisante can do is hope for some distraction, but how can she produce one? Or perhaps she can draw the ogre into the water... She dives beneath the surface, aiming to follow the current into the main course of the river.

Dunkel smirks, thinking she will soon surface for air. But when he does not see her for almost a minute, he becomes angry. His image of a siren on a rock, glistening naked in the breeze, has been replaced by an image of a mermaid capable of submerging a long time.

He will not let this one get away. He removes his clothing and steps into the water, a bit surprised to find it so warm. He enters only as deeply as he dares.

As he wallows around, reaching under the water to no avail, he does not notice someone removing his clothing from the shore—not a naked young lady but a young man. It is Hans, who has been taking advantage of some free time, wandering different parts of the woods before returning to duties with his family.

Hans did not expect to come upon Ebouisante's bathing site, but after hearing the commotion, he crept up unnoticed behind Dunkel. He surmised Ebouisante's plan as she submerged.

Now he slinks away with Dunkel's clothes, then quickly and quietly finds Ebouisante's. He goes a short distance downstream, burying some of Dunkel's clothing under some leaves. He keeps the tunic, though, as he continues farther downriver. There he hangs Dunkel's tunic as a curtain over a tree branch and places her clothing on a rock on the shore behind it. Then he extends a branch carefully over the water, securing it with the rock as best he can.

- Chapter 34 -

Ebouisante surfaces in the colder water downstream. She gasps, then breathes deeply, as she see a young man busying himself on the shore. She quickly understands his purpose: he is preparing a means of modest escape!

She swims to the branch, noticing how the rescuer grants her privacy and does not attempt to look at her. He hides behind the makeshift curtain as if it were the wall between Pyramus and Thisbe, separated lovers of legend.

"Now, there is chivalry!" she says, just loud enough for him alone to hear.

Then Ebouisante laughs as she recognizes the curtain is the fat man's clothing. Won't he be alarmed when he finds himself in this dilemma!

When Hans hears her voice, he sits up straight behind his makeshift curtain and croons:

A virgin trusting nature's secrecy
Bathes solely in the gaze of God above
And possibly observed by some small dove
Which so admires, yet knows the maiden free

Who would emerge in all innocency
From woods with heart and mind concerned with love
And suddenly, sans warning, would discov'
A maiden whom he should not deign to see?

The very object of his dreams is found
And needs he must now turn his head away
Lest she would think his presence would offend

He sinks behind a tree onto the ground
And with loud voice entertains to bray
Some simple sonnet serving signal sent.

Ebouisante smiles and claps her hands together. “How lovely and sweet! Especially after such a brush with fate worse than death. How come you by, stranger, at such perfect timing?”

Hans is pleased at the reaction. “Not a stranger, and not so strange. Do not think, mademoiselle, that I have stalked you into the forest, as I did not have the least idea that bathing outdoors is your custom. Yet I would thank the happy fate that brings me to your aid.” With an exaggerated sigh, he laughs, adding, “However, I might tire of having to spend my short life saving you repeatedly.”

“Hans!” she calls out in delight. “It does seem I owe my life to you yet again.”

Ebouisante hurries to clothe herself behind the curtain. She is a bit surprised to feel her heart skip a beat. No one would mistake the orange ogre for Cupid, but it nonetheless seems he has thrown her together with Hans in dire circumstances.

She sighs. “It seems you are destined to be with me in my most dire moments, sir. But should I grant you my heart in gratitude?” she says coquettishly.

“If you do not care for me, mademoiselle, at least do the courtesy of confirming it once and for all,” he says indignantly. “Young and naïve that I am, I will not pretend to lavish my heart foolishly upon innocent young maidens merely for favors. I pretend no experience in such matters, but I have seen enough tragedy to avoid being the cause of ill fates.”

“Ha! How poetic!” she shouts. Then she remembers the possible proximity of the armorer and lowers her voice precipitously. “We should talk more on the way to my father’s house, if you would do me the honor of accompanying me. I think we should hurry,” she adds, “before the old man discovers his loss and pursues with rage.”

She steps out from behind Dunkel’s tunic, throwing her hair back and catching it up into a knot.

“And do not jump to conclusions, Hans. I did not say I do not care for you. How can I not, when rescued not once but twice? This is a dangerous principality indeed for foreign maidens. But you know

I dare not throw my heart away foolishly, when our fathers have designs for our futures."

"Just so, and I stand corrected," Hans demurs with a slight laugh.

Her use of his familiar name has not escaped him. He realizes she is a clever one, this Ebouisante. How simply to send a message of her own heart. He must be content with that, for now.

"Who is that ogre, anyway?" she asks as they begin walking.

Hans answers, "The ogre, as you would have him, is one Dunkel Hammer, the armorer to the prince. Very strong, of course, with such a profession. He is one of the finest at his art; otherwise, the prince would have none of him. He is a drunkard and abuses everyone he knows. His wife is a great beauty with long golden hair who keeps herself locked in her chamber to avoid him. And I certainly pity his daughter, who has no ability to escape him. Her servant—or rather her mother's servant, Fee—clearly tries to protect her as best she can."

Ebouisante gasps. "Did you say Fee? I know her, and I know this girl. She is Besse, and I am teaching her to read. We meet at Fee's sister's florist tent. I shall certainly never approach the household now! She has told me . . . unspeakable things about the man." She shudders. "But I see from his appearance he has yellow jaundice and a big paunch, which is a sign of his drinking and a sign he is not long for this world."

At this point, the pair hear Dunkel's grumblings as he finds his tunic by the river. But of course, Hans has buried the rest of his clothing elsewhere. They hope he will search for his clothing rather than hunt for the two of them.

And indeed, that is exactly what he does—to no avail. They hear a great shout, causing them to step carefully in a pattern that would be difficult to track. They giggle a bit, a catharsis from the recent fears. Hans is glad he did not have to confront the man directly, as he would have been a formidable match compared to the poor bandits he chased off from the caravan a few days earlier.

◆ ◆ ◆

Dunkel cannot decide what to do without his clothing. He found his tunic along the river, at least. The rest cannot be far, he hopes. He wraps himself in the tunic as he continues to search.

He bellows, "If I find 'em, I'll kill 'em!"

What a morsel he has missed! The mouse has escaped the trap. Perhaps he can set another one. But there must be two of them, he realizes, to have accomplished this. So perhaps she does have a guard, one who feels Dunkel is too formidable to attack. Therefore he is young and inexperienced, though hardly fearless.

At this point, the armorer is startled by an uncouth young boy running past with what appears to be a greave from a suit of armor. Even a glimpse allows Dunkel to recognize the high level of craftsmanship. He realizes this is the same armor his cursed journeyman presented! He cannot suppress a growl and a deep look of anger.

The young thief, for his part, is astonished to see this old man who conjures thoughts of a giant gourd. He knows him instantly. This man murdered his brother.

The boy turns pale, quickly changing his path with an abrupt right turn. He uses the advantages of youth and speed to disappear among the trees. He plans to deal with Dunkel at a later date, but one-on-one he stands very little chance. What would prevent the armorer from killing again?

Dunkel does not spare the thought to recognize the young scoundrel, deciding instead to continue on his quest for his clothing and the maiden and her protector, whoever he might be.

With his attention to the ground, he collides with someone. These woods are too populated these days!

"Oaf! Watch your path, young fool—" Suddenly he stops in recognition. It is Rudi! "Why, if it isn't me nemesis himself! Lose somethin', Rudi? It appears t' have passed by this way in the company of a young bandit in a big hurry, it has!" Dunkel laughs heartily.

"Sir, out of my way! I will not truck with you!" Rudi says. Then he smiles as he looks the armorer up and down. "Besides, you seem to have lost something yourself! If you will allow me the opportunity to finish my pursuit, I shall return to you here and bring you more suitable wear for the cold forest, although it goes against my better judgment." Rudi adds with a laugh, "Perhaps then you can consider returning the favor by acknowledging my right to become a master!"

"That'll ne'er happen, son. Nor'll I countenance any contact with me wife! Begone and leave me t' me own dilemma. I'll find a remedy soon enough without your *largesse*. As it's clear, I have a pursuit of me own, which'll not allow me t' dally here. Yet I s'pose I should thank ye for your offer, so I'll do nothin' t' obstruct ye in repayment," he harrumphs.

Rudi cannot suppress a giggle. "A kind offer, indeed. I quake in fear of you, sir—as I would of any large gourd. Good day. I am off on my own quest."

"See t' it that your quest doesn't include me wife! Off with ye. Mine is so much the greater wrong here, it is, and don't forget it!"

The two men go their separate ways. In a short time, still looking for the burial site of his clothing, Dunkel hears a distant shriek. Next he hears, "Got you! I shall move my prize far from your ability to find it. Do not ever let me set eyes upon you again, or your body shall be as tattered as the rags you wear!"

This makes Dunkel laugh. He thinks one should not be so careless in the woods. This lesson applies as much to himself as to Rudi. He shrugs, giving up his search, and determines to go home as unnoticeably as possible—though he has never cared a wit for what others think of him.

◆ ◆ ◆

Hans and Ebouisante enter a small clearing. They are discussing literature once again, and Ebouisante is surprised to find that Hans is familiar with *The Book of the City of Ladies*.

"What man reads Christine de Pisan? I suppose you would ridicule her criticism of *The Song of Roland*."

"Ah, yes—Jean de Meun," retorts Hans. "I am supposed to say here that we live in a man's world and that a woman's place is at his side or in his home. In fact, there is some truth to that, as our society now stands. Yet we have seen the capabilities of Eleanor of Aquitaine and more recently of Jeanne d'Arc. Would you think that women should take up the sword equally with men, considering the danger? Or should they remain protected?"

Ebouisante, grateful to converse about something other than being saved, waves him off. "The sword is one thing, sir. The mind is another. As Christine tells us, with equal education should come equal opportunity. My own father has no sons, and I like to believe I serve him well."

Hans agrees. "Granted, mademoiselle—perhaps better than a son could serve, as I can tell you have some abilities gained from study abroad that I envy myself. But this is not a world of equality in commerce nor in the military, and you cannot deny it."

The conversation is interrupted by the appearance of an old hovel just off their path. Although it is somewhat disguised to blend into the woods, it appears to be occupied, with a wisp of smoke emanating from the chimney.

Hans places his hand gently upon Ebouisante's, stopping their progress. "I know this house. It had been unoccupied since the last plague. Now there is a pile of removed rubble to the side. Should we satisfy our curiosity as to its occupants?"

"Curiosity is not always wise, but I shall promise to protect you, should any danger show itself. It is my turn, at any rate," suggests Ebouisante, laughing.

Hans feels his chest quiver a bit. Has he fallen for this damsel? If so, that could be a greater danger than accosting a strange squatter in an old abandoned property. Despite all the talk of the modern roles of men and women, he is still subject to the command and arrangements of his father for his future, including a mate.

Nevertheless, he laughs in reply to Ebouisante. "I might give you the opportunity, then, and the debt shall be repaid. Let us see who dwells here."

He decides he will lead them to the doorway. He rationalizes that bandits would not likely ensconce themselves in such a house, where they could be too easily tracked. As they approach, the two are greeted by heady aroma of a rabbit stew and something else—something sweet. Cookies?

They call out a greeting, and a hideous old lady appears before them, matching their look of surprise with one of her own. Then she shrugs and gestures the two young people into the house. They accept her implicit offer of hospitality.

For her part, Katrina is anxious to hear the news of the city, as she dares not go there herself. Jacques has been gone longer than anticipated. It has been overlong since he left to retrieve his mother so she could join them and do their marketing. The old woman is becoming worried. Has he been captured? Or has he seen some advantage in seeking his fortune on his own? It must be the latter, as no guards have approached her.

The lady gestures to the table and smiles. "Please seat yourselves, sir and fräulein. I'd gladly trade ye a hearty meal for news of the city, I would. Please don't be alarmed by me appearance. It's a curse—and not deliberate, I assure ye. And it belies the nature of the soul within, it does."

"We are Hans Handler and Ebouisante Kaufmann. And you are Frau . . .?"

She interrupts quickly, hoping to protect her identity. "Madame will do, children. Please tell me of the town and what brings ye into the forest. I'm perhaps hungrier for news and companionship than ye're for a meal, yet a meal I'll provide, I will."

With a large ladle, she scoops a portion of the steaming stew into two bread bowls, placing them in front of the now-seated couple. Then she sits down at the table herself and folds her hands in her ample lap.

Hans and Ebouisante look at each other and smile.

"We are but acquaintances, madame, who have met by chance in this wood," Hans begins. "And now we are proceeding to return to the city."

Ebouisante speaks up. "He is very modest, madame. It was more than just a meeting. He has saved my life twice now."

The hostess's eyebrows rise. "Really! Of this I'd hear more, I would."

"I speak the truth," Ebouisante continues. "I was accosted by a large man whose skin has been tainted by the color of a life of too much ale. This young gentleman was kind enough to help me arrange an escape before any compromise could be accomplished."

Hans blushes at this, then hastens to add, "But do not worry, madame. I do not think you would personally face any danger from this man. I know him and his reputation. His interests are well known to lie entirely with the younger generation of maidens."

"What a tale!" Katrina exclaims, brushing her hands on her surcotte. "You must tell me more of your adventures, and more of the city. I am so isolated here." She shakes her head.

"Oh!" responds Hans. "There has been much to tell. A thief has somehow escaped from the dungeon, but no one seems to know just how."

Katrina holds up a hand. She responds anxiously, "Men accostin' maidens in the woods and thieves escapin' from the dungeon! It but fills me with fear. I'm unguarded here. I hold nothin' of value in this dwellin', I don't. But I must live here alone. Moreo'er, I've lost the young man who was plannin' to bring his mama here to do me marketin' in the city. As ye can see, one such as I'd not be well accepted within the walls, no. I'd be grateful if ye'd make inquiry for me, as I'd still prefer t' remain outside the walls and not face ridicule from citizens less considerate than yourselves."

She sighs and furrows her brows, which Ebouisante mistakes as a countenance of despair and resignation.

Ebouisante says, "Oh, Hans! Do you think you could help this poor woman? Surely we cannot leave her to such a fate without assistance."

"Of course!" he replies gallantly. "I shall make a point of watching over you, madame, and I shall do your marketing myself. But I think it may be wise to concoct a story to keep you protected here, as that is a service I cannot promise. Although I have some training, I am a merchant's son, not a mercenary soldier."

He hesitates a moment, then touches a finger to his forehead.

"I have it! We shall tell the populace to avoid the old hovel in the woods, as therein lives a woman who means to lure children with cakes and dried fruits—to unknown purpose."

Katrina can only hope that Hans never learns of her complicity in Jacques's disappearance. Until then, she can certainly use this assistance She smiles weakly, briefly nodding her head.

"Sir, ye're most kind. But ye must let me compensate ye for yer time and efforts. I do have a small amount of coinage remainin' t' me, I do."

Hans waves her off. "No, madame. I will not accept it, and I am in no need of it. Your occasional companionship and an excellent meal such as this would be more than enough recompense. And now, we are grateful for your kind hospitality, but we must depart. If you would entrust me with a list of your needs, I shall return daily."

"For t'day, I'm well provisioned, I am, sir. If ye'd return t'morrow, I'll decide what I need. I thank ye in advance for your kind service, I do."

◆ ◆ ◆

Ebouisante and Hans leave the house, deciding it is now safe enough to head directly to the city gate. The fog has lifted, and the two are cheered by birdsong in the trees and the bright sunlight creating picturesque shadows across their path.

Hans thinks Ebouisante will not be safe from the armorer if he realizes she has a witness to any accusation she may choose to make.

He sighs, and says, "Mademoiselle, I am going to ask a boon: If you would keep today's events to yourself, I would most assuredly appreciate it. I fear the wrath of the armorer, should any of this become public. You and your family would not be safe. Also, I fear it is no longer safe for you to wander these woods alone. If you would trust me to accompany you, I would be most happy to do so. I could serve as lookout, with the same discretion I showed earlier. We can do this as I visit the poor old lady each day, if that suits you."

Ebouisante thinks for a moment and realizes Hans's offer has merit.

"I was not actually attacked, after all," she ponders out loud. "And it would not be good to create enemies just as my father is trying to establish business ties within the city. However . . . the man is a beast, Hans," she says more decidedly. "He abuses his wife and daughter and is now a threat to me as well. I will agree to your request to accompany me. I most especially enjoy your company, and I intend to continue my daily walks and bathing as the weather permits. That man is not long for this world, I think, but one never knows. We must plan something to protect us all. Therefore, I will consider only a short term of silence, after which I will ask *you* the boon of accompanying me to the prince."

Hans thinks this is the best he could achieve, for now. However, he will have to think of something more productive than a simple accusation placed before the judgment of His Highness, who has more weighty problems to attend. Yes, something more must be done . . .

Ebouisante has her own concern as she watches Hans's face cloud in thought. He is young and impulsive. She worries he will likely do something foolish, even though he has shown intelligence today. She must use persuasion to keep him in check. Yet she also longs to assure the safety of Besse and her mother—as well as her own safety. She will have to speak out soon.

The two walk briskly toward the city, hardly noticing that Ebouisante has placed her hand into Hans's. And they do not realize that fate will offer them an opportunity soon enough.

~ Chapter 35 ~

Gaillard the huntsman rides up to the castle, ignoring the thunderstorm surrounding him. To the guards, he gives the appearance of a dark bandit, devil-may-care, bravely riding forward with singularity of purpose. However, they do recognize him and allow him entry unmolested. Their curiosity is piqued by the sack affixed to the side of his saddle.

He strides purposefully into the castle, startling Enchanteresse, who is in the meeting chamber addressing the servant staff. She was not expecting his arrival so abruptly. With a deep breath, she composes herself quickly, then turns to face her erstwhile lover as she dismisses the assembled staff with a wave of her arm.

To the huntsman, she still looks darkly beautiful, her black tresses carefully knotted and arranged under a hennin with a black veil. She is dressed in a long black tunic with a high lace collar. Her nails are also long and painted a dark red. They match her lips, which stand out, surrounded by an excess of white powder.

Gaillard realizes she is trying to look even younger, but she is not succeeding. There is a greater air of arrogance about her, even as she walks with a slight stoop, as if she carries the weight of her evil decisions upon her back. Yet he thinks it seems to make her all the more attractive. He prudently decides to let her address him first.

Enchanteresse makes him wait a long moment, then favors him with a sardonic grin. "I was not informed of your return, huntsman. Is that a gift you bear? Attend me in the adjoining chamber, where we may enjoy a more private audience."

She seems to think for a moment, though she is actually taking a few seconds to still the palpitations of her heart. Not wanting to seem too anxious, she suggests, "But first change to something more appropriate and dry yourself off. I will see to it that a fine stew and some fruit and mead await you." Her smile widens, almost grotesque. "I want to hear news of your journey, and, as I see that you are alone, news of your company and my stepdaughter, whom I presume you have attended well. You *must* tell me of her location and of her health, if she has not returned with you. His Liege will be very concerned." She raises an eyebrow, designed as a warning not to discuss anything here. "Now, off with you, and I will await you with impatience."

Gaillard bows and responds, "May I say you are a sight for my sore eyes, my lady. You look more ravishing than ever. One might even say glowing."

Her appearance darkens, and she raises her voice. "Do not flatter me now, Gaillard! The truth is out. I do not find your words as soothing as I once did—though I certainly confess to missing your presence." She softens, stroking him under the chin. "I look forward to a feast of the fruits of your labor and to seeing you shortly." She straightens. "You are dismissed!"

As she turns, he smiles, then frowns, realizing the force of flattery is not entirely lost upon her. He must be very convincing.

At this point, he notices the large obsidian mirror in a corner of the chamber, covered with a silk cloth. He has no doubt the duchess looks into it frequently, but only when the chamber is empty of other members of the court. He shudders, suddenly shaken. How can such an object cause so much trouble, so much pain? Such surfaces can only reflect the truth. That is why Gaillard forbade them successfully for so long.

The thought almost distracts him from the arrival of a servant, who clears his throat and says, "Sir, you must allow me to direct you to a changing room. My men will provide you with drying cloths and a finer outfit to wear in the presence of her ladyship."

Gaillard recognizes the servant as one of the castle valets, a well-bred young man unfortunate enough to be a younger son of a merchant and therefore without inheritance, much like the huntsman himself. Gaillard accompanies the man, who relates stories of increasingly frequent outbursts of rage from the duchess.

Shaking his head, the servant confesses, "My lord is totally perplexed with her behavior, but it is always worst after she peers into that dark glass. One would think there is a demon in it that grabs hold of her soul and twists, as one would wring out a damp cloth. It is a marvel to see—but very frightening. No one wants to be in her line of sight when she is in that mood, if I may be so bold as to state. But of course, I say too much. I hope you will pardon me, sir, but I am sure you are in need of understanding the way of the court as you return to it."

Gaillard recovers his composure and responds, "I thank you, and I will follow your lead. You are aware that I had previously demanded that no reflective glass be made available to her ladyship. So I am not entirely surprised by the consequences of this gift from the duke."

No further word is said as the huntsman follows the servant, nor as he decides to bathe as the servant lays out dry clothing. He takes his time dressing, in no hurry to confront the duchess.

When he finally makes his way to the designated room, he finds her seated at a richly carved table, nibbling grapes from a bowl of fruit set before her. He smiles, as if delighted to see her, then shrugs and deposits his cargo upon the table.

"Your ladyship," Gaillard says with a bow. "As we speak, my companions are arriving with a bountiful supply of meats for the table as well as some herbs and spices acquired in trade that will make your feasts more savory. I present them to you and His Liege with humility and gratefulness for the kindnesses you have shown me. I must admit I am always dazzled to be in your presence. Thoughts of you have completely occupied my mind during my entire absence. You are even more ravishing than in my dreams." He manages the ghost of a smile.

Here he expects her to offer her hand to kiss, but she surprises him by waving off his compliment.

"Your flattery is all well, huntsman, but I tell you again, it carries little effect on me these days. My ears have been tortured by the constant expression of how everyone misses my stepdaughter and how it has diminished the beauty of the court." She slams the table. "It is infuriating! All the exhortations of my own beauty have been nothing but lies!" she shouts. "And to be replaced by an absent-minded, dim-witted, useless damsel whose only value lies in being the daughter of a duke! So, sir, do not humiliate me further with false protestations and compliments. I would merely oblige you to reveal your gift in that wretched sack you carry."

Gaillard controls his voice carefully, speaking slowly. "Your ladyship, you do me a great wrong if you truly believe I do not think you the most attractive lady in the entire court, if not the entire continent. I am devoted to you always, and I have brought you this token to prove it." He opens the bag and shows its contents to the duchess.

"Why, it is a heart! Would you bring me a new one, as if you have never stolen mine?" She thinks a moment, then her eyes go wide. "Oh, my! It is proof you have carried out my command!" she says excitedly. "Forgive my anger, sir, and attend to me in my chamber later. A better gift you could not offer me, were it gold or silver. But you must hie to my husband, and I shall prepare the court for mourning."

She flushes a bit, suddenly realizing what she has done. But she knows the huntsman will pass it off as an accident and attempt to belay any blame, most especially from her. That would be proof enough of his ultimate loyalty. And he did come to her before confronting the duke.

As Gaillard departs, she gathers herself, then lets out a wail heard throughout the castle.

Her servants come rushing into the room, unbidden, to see what could have upset their lady so. For his part, Gaillard knows the reason for the wail. He wishes to abscond with the sack to bury its contents, but first he is stopped by the duke himself, who is not far behind the servants.

"You must see me immediately after I tend to her ladyship," the duke commands, eyeing Gaillard sternly.

Standing behind the duke is the guard Gaillard designated to bring the truth about Giselle to His Liege. The guard nods, a sign that the message has been delivered.

The huntsman gives out a sigh of relief. He bows quickly to the duke, then hurries to complete his short mission before he returns to face his fate.

Duke Philip rushes to his wife's side as the servants stand back in shock. "My love, my love—you must comfort yourself." He shakes himself, allowing a few tears to flow down. "Yet I am in deep grief too. We all are in deep grief. I shall declare a fortnight of great mourning, and we will console each other. Allow the warmth of my embrace to suffuse your soul."

He tries to hug her, but she pushes him off in disgust.

"I shall not be consoled, My Liege—not even by you. The loss is too great!"

"Leave us alone!" shouts the duke with a wave of his hand. The startled servants bow, curtsy, and withdraw hastily.

Once they depart, Philip closes the heavy oak door behind them, then turns to face his wife.

She is startled as his countenance transforms from grief to anger. She knows he loved his daughter deeply, and she believes he is too aggrieved to display any other emotion—a situation she intends to put to her own advantage. Therefore, she continues to sob, not wanting to miss the opportunity to show herself as the true sufferer.

"Oh, my husband. I must send the huntsman away. I cannot bear to look upon him, as it will always remind me of our beautiful Giselle. Do you know everyone calls her La Claire? Skin as white as the clouds, with naught but the blush of youth to improve her countenance. I must don a black veil immediately. But will you hug me again to help me compose myself?"

"I shall not!" the duke thunders. "Do you think me a fool? Do you not think I have my own guards and messengers? Shortly, I will question this huntsman. I suspect I shall hear quite the story, one which centers upon your own orders and complicity. Know that my daughter is not dead but alive and in safekeeping, no thanks to you!"

The duchess is both startled and flabbergasted as she stares at her husband. "*What is this*? What do you think I—oh! How could you!" she dissembles, hoping to save herself.

Her eyes widen with the realization she has been betrayed. Surely not Gaillard? She vows to investigate and punish—yes, punish severely.

"Now, I command you to have your chamber packed," Philip continues, his eyes flashing. "You shall be banished from my realm! I care not for your future, but I shall allow you to take one servant—that old crone who is still dedicated to you. And you may take some coinage from the treasury and your jewels, as I care not to see such reminders of you again. Now leave me, and leave Brugge within two days!"

Enchanteresse brushes by her husband with contempt as she exits. She ascends to her chamber, stopping only to slap the face of the huntsman, who has returned to meet with the duke.

Gaillard shakes himself, then smiles in realization of what must have occurred.

As he approaches the chamber entrance, Gaillard sees Philip facing away, crying quietly. The huntsman knocks, then bows as he awaits acknowledgment by His Liege.

After a while, the duke composes himself, then turns. "Arise, sir. You have done me a great service, though I grieve at the loss of her ladyship. I have banished her from the entire duchy."

"I am truly sorry, My Liege," offers the huntsman. "But I do know my true loyalty lies with you and, of course, the lady Giselle. With your permission, I shall follow the duchess to help her secure new settlement and to keep her from encountering the lady La Claire, if at all possible. She is certainly likely to ascertain La Claire's whereabouts. To that end, I have already sent one of your guards to contact the prince of the principality where she is secreted, to ensure her safety. Indeed, Prince Henrik is known to be the most benevolent—yet intelligent and strong—ruler of the area. I, for one, certainly trust him." He does not add that he still has enough love for the lady to want to see to her safety.

Philip's eyebrows rise. "Henrik, you say? And is this city north of the Bavarian mountains, in the foothills?"

"Indeed, My Liege—the very same."

Philip continues, "Do you know that I have just returned from the very same principality, having arranged the betrothal of my daughter to His Highness's own son? I do trust this prince. In short order, when my affairs are in order here, I shall return to the principality to complete all the arrangements, with an appropriate dowry for Giselle. In the meantime, I will send an emissary to report back to me on the safety of my daughter."

He puts his hands on the huntsman's shoulders, looking him directly in the eyes. "Pray, keep her ladyship away from that area, if you can. News and rumors travel far. Now, I must inform the court that their beloved La Claire is away in safekeeping and that I have banished her stepmother for her crimes." He looks aggrieved, lowering his eyes. "Leave me to mourn the loss of my love, but be kind enough to send me a bailiff of the court."

The duke does indeed wear the look of a forlorn, lost lover. The huntsman would like to offer him an embrace of consolation, but he knows it would be improper. Instead, he bows and takes his leave, offering a hand over his heart as a gesture Philip fully understands.

As he goes, Gaillard thinks of the many mortal men of mythology who have fallen for the beauty of some goddess, sealing their fates. Then he realizes the analogy could easily apply to himself as well. He will accompany the duchess, attempt to find an appropriate court in which she might settle, then leave for Quellestadt himself to provide services to Prince Henrik.

♦ ♦ ♦

Enchanteressse now realizes she might be in some danger of her life if she remains in Brugge and others find out about her order to the huntsman. She instructs the old nurse and her servant to pack as quickly as possible. She sends one guard to inform the stable boy that she will require three horses for travel and several pack horses. She decides to ride and allow the carriage to follow behind the small entourage. In fact, the court is accustomed to such travel from castle to castle, so she need say nothing more.

She will take the obsidian with her as well. It can take her place in the carriage. She cannot part with the ability to see her own image, much as she is both drawn to and repelled by it. She does not trust the obsequious words of her subjects any longer, as they are all words of deceit and betrayal.

As she prepares to leave, she is met by the huntsman, who bows deeply before her. He says, "I will see you to safety with adequate provisions, my lady, likely in the court of King Charles of France."

"That will not be necessary," she replies indignantly. "I will have my most *loyal* guards with me." If she can trust no one, then she certainly cannot trust the huntsman.

Moreover, Enchanteresse has other plans. She herself will seek out her stepdaughter. That, at least, will offer her some satisfaction.

Ultimately, the huntsman rides out of the city on his own, silently, dealing with his own thoughts.

~ Chapter 36 ~

Rose descends the stairs at the inn, prepared to serve customers. The rooms are full this day, as the Handlers' feast approaches. Merchants from neighboring principalities have been invited along with their wives and children, and this is a very busy time. The innkeeper offers his dining room as something of an indoor market, allowing the visiting merchants to display their wares on the tables—for a small fee, of course. Some merchants, having sent their spouses into the city, take the opportunity for more private entertainment provided by the serving staff upstairs, a boon both to the maidens and the innkeeper himself. At the moment, he is circulating among his guests, flattering one here, commending another there, offering additional services wherever possible.

To her relief, Rose has been unburdened of contact with Dunkel Hammer. She's thankful the innkeeper has shielded her. She partly confided in him, stating only that the armorer has threatened her. The innkeeper was discrete enough not to inquire further. Rose is his most productive employee, and he is content to offer sanctuary.

But she is unable to stray far from the inn for fear of encountering her former patron. She must think of a means of either protection or escape, for she knows Dunkel has killed once. In an uninhibited, drunken state, he might just do so again, especially when a witness to the first killing is so defenselessly available.

She sighs, inwardly cursing herself for the hundredth time for being such a fool as to have approached him. She then pinches her cheeks to redden them a bit, wipes her hands on her surcotte, and descends into the crowd. Perhaps soon she can find someone to attach to for protection or even an opportunity to move to another city.

A quick survey fails to reveal any immediate prospects. Therefore, she mimics the behavior of the innkeeper, though adding in a little flirting with men circulating among the tables or hawking their goods at their own tables but appearing to be alone for the moment.

She asks where each one is from, generally expressing her desire to see such and such a place or a city, which must surely surpass the beauty and attraction of her current location, and wouldn't it be nice to be invited to visit? Certainly she has services to offer to any man who would extend to her the opportunity to see the world. Perhaps a visit to a castle in the high mountains, where the fresh snows would serve as a backdrop to enhance the beauty of a young maiden? She moves from table to table, admiring the goods but expressing her dismay to the proprietors that her meager income and existence prohibit her from enjoying such luxury, especially without a patron.

Suddenly the temperature in the room seems to drop. The roaring fire in the hearth is unable to quell the chill wind that enters the inn as the door opens and the armorer steps in.

"What's this?" bellows Dunkel. "Is there no table for a loyal customer of years? Is this an inn or a market?"

The innkeeper blanches in mortification, rushing to turn the armorer around.

"Sir, allow me t' afford ye a pint of ale on the house, but I must send ye on your way, I must. Ye'll scare me staff, ye will, and I can't afford ye that displeasure."

Of course, the innkeeper has one staff member in mind, and she is too valuable an employee to allow the armorer to do any harm or raise a fight. This is especially true today, with so many guests to be served.

But Dunkel will have none of it. "I thank ye for your hospitality, sir, but I'm in need of some strong libation and some pleasant company, I am."

He spies Rose, who has not had enough time to make any effort at escape.

Dunkel laughs as he points to her. "But not that one." Then he thinks again. "Or maybe, yes, that one." An opportunity alone with Rose would assure her silence on the events of recent memory.

Rose, for her part, can barely suppress the instinct to flee, as a mouse would a cat. Yet she understands she is safest amongst company and in the sight of the innkeeper. She blushes, saying nothing, but turns her back on the armorer, quickly selecting a merchant upon whom she can shower flattery and attention.

As Dunkel begins to approach her, the innkeeper intervenes. "I'm truly sorry, sir, but the inn is closed for general service t'day, it is. Here's a pint," he says, beckoning a servant to bring some ale. "I hope ye'll be kind enough t' enjoy it with me compliments and then depart. All of me staff are busy t'day, they are."

Dunkel grunts, then shrugs. He decides to accept the ale, downs it quickly, and turns to depart. "I'll be back, me Rose, me flower. Don't think ye'll escape me attentions." Frustrated, he frowns and takes his leave.

Rose pretends to ignore him, but she is quite frightened. What can she do to protect herself? There is no potential solace from any of the present company, and she dare not reveal the body of the young bandit while the armorer still has access to her.

~ Chapter 37 ~

For Fee and Besse, dark thoughts occupy their minds as they approach the market and Flor's tent. Today will finally be the judgment of Peter, and Fee must attempt to be present to mitigate any punishment His Highness may mete.

She delivers Besse to her sister. Offering a kindly smile, Fee smooths Besse's surcotte, then straightens and says, "I think you can now do the marketing on your own. Here is a pouch. See how well you can bargain."

Ebouisante is there and says excitedly, "I would so enjoy to accompany you, Besse, if we might read together first." Besse is still working on basic words and grammar and is not truly ready for Chrétien de Troyes or Christine de Pisan.

As they seat themselves, Ebouisante confides, "Men are such beasts at times, do you not agree, *mon amie*?" She lowers her voice—a near whisper. "I have recently come across your father in the most negative fashion, and I fully understand your fear, which is now my own."

As Ebouisante recounts the events in the woods, Besse shows no emotion at all, merely nodding acknowledgment. This causes Ebouisante to fear for Besse's welfare even more. She seems so totally withdrawn from the horrors.

But in actuality, Besse is not entirely apathetic. She just has her own plans. She is not comfortable sharing them with her friend. Besse has only one confidante—Dolly—and she is not prepared to expand that role to another. But she is happy her plans might also benefit Ebouisante.

Ebouisante sighs, shrugs her shoulders, and decides to concentrate on teaching the poor young girl to read, in hopes that it might help get her away from her family and into a new life. Now she fully understands Fee's concern in having recruited her assistance.

◆ ◆ ◆

Fee hurries toward the castle, inwardly rehearsing what she will say to the prince but apprehensive she will not have such an opportunity.

As Fee makes her way, the prince and his son meet in the chamber behind the throne, as is now becoming a daily habit. In fact, there in that very chamber, Henrik is looking sternly at his son.

"What think you of the current trade situation of the Hanse, and how might it affect our realm?" he asks.

Charles takes a deep breath and begins. "Sire, there is much. The Hanse is losing its trade as new consolidated states show hostility. The best goods and craftsmanship now reside in the south. First, we must encourage all our merchants to extend their contacts beyond the old boundaries. It is a wise move to have invited the Kaufmanns, well connected and familiar with these lands. Second, we have a dilemma as the wars between England and France draw to an end. We will be left with a large number of soldiers and knights, many we trained ourselves, with nothing but brigandry to support themselves."

He hesitates in order to think a moment. "Unless we can interest the Poles or Latvians in the soldiers. To date, those realms have relied on Bohemians. This means trouble for our main line of business. However, a possible solution to both presents itself. If we can provide sufficient protection for our merchants, perhaps at shared expense, we can gainfully employ these men. We can offer the same service to merchants and even traveling priests throughout Europe. Our training is the best, as is our accoutrement for knights and guards."

Charles smiles with an additional realization. He states enthusiastically, "As we develop both manufacturing and merchandising, we can become a center for trade, with high potential for tithing. And protection will allow our merchants to explore all of Europe and perhaps beyond, to extend their business."

There—he has now developed a plan of his own. He bows, awaiting judgment.

The prince smiles, takes his son in his arms, breathes deeply, and says, "I am very proud of you, son. You will make a fine ruler. We will continue this discussion in the near future. Now, accompany me as we pass judgment in public audience."

The younger man bows again, relieved but happy, and walks a step behind his father into the main audience chamber. He glimpses the citizenry along the walls of the room, noting there are several faces he does not recognize. These are visiting merchants and their wives, here for the Handlers' feast.

The prince and dauphin seat themselves on the raised platform at one end of the room, soon joined by the princess. The crowd is now murmuring but hushes with the entry of the bailiff.

Fee knows she cannot push her way through to the front, as she would not be considered the equal of the visiting merchants and dignitaries. She frets about looking for a location that will allow her to step out when she must speak. Finally, she settles into a corner spot next to a door. If she cannot be in front of the group, she can at least be on an edge. She shifts from foot to foot nervously. For her part, Fee would have preferred a private judgment, with an opportunity to present her own ideas and pleas.

Henrik claps his hands, loudly announcing, "Let the bailiff call the court to order. We are here to pass judgment upon two citizens: one accused of thievery, the other of attempted robbery. The proceedings shall begin."

In the center of the court chamber, the bailiff bows, first to the royalty on the raised platform, then to the assembled citizenry and visitors on each side. He unravels a scroll of parchment, frowns, and reads, "We are in attendance of His Royal Highness Prince Henrik, on this twenty-fifth day of September, in the year of our Lord one thousand four hundred and fifty, to hear judgment upon the young men Jacques and Peter. Each is charged with a crime worthy of banishment according to the general laws of the realm and in accordance with same laws of all neighboring principalities and with the blessing of the church, represented here by Father Georg."

At this point, the priest steps out of the crowd into the center opening and bows to the prince, indicating he is indeed present and available for counsel. He then steps back into the audience.

Fee's face darkens, especially at the mention of her brother's erstwhile cellmate, who nearly killed him and then escaped. How ironic that Jacques will not truly face judgment, while Peter will certainly suffer further. She *must* have an opportunity to speak.

She mutters a prayer under her breath, begging Jesus to allow her to continue to protect her family and offering to take on the suffering herself, if only she may speak in Peter's defense. The people next to her are a bit perturbed by her mumbling and attempt to hush her, but she will not be distracted. Eventually she finishes her prayer, feeling no better. She quiets down, so as not to call more attention to herself prior to her opportunity to speak.

The bailiff continues, "Although accused of the crime of thievery and very possibly of the murder of our beloved jailer—"

Here and there, slight coughs can be heard in the audience. No one who knew the jailer, including his now-absent wife, would describe him as "beloved." Everyone finds some amusement in the statement.

"We have been unable to capture the boy Jacques, who is at large within or without the principality, and in possession of precious gifts and gold belonging to Your Highness. However, we ask judgment that may be meted out upon his capture at any future date."

Henrik responds, "Is there one who could corroborate the actions of this brigand?"

An old Jew steps cautiously out of the crowd. The crowd murmurs; surely the testimony of a Jew would not be acceptable in court. He hears them but shrugs and decides to proceed.

"If it please Your Highness, I have in my possession one large ruby, at first mine, then taken, then returned to me by the graces of your son, who sits beside you, and the merchant's son, Hans Handler.

The ruby was taken out of the possession of Jacques, who admitted to having stolen it."

Henrik leans toward Charles. "Is that so, son?"

"Indeed, sire. It is the complete truth."

"Is there one here to contest the statement of the dauphin?" challenges the prince.

Jurg steps forward. "If it please Your Highness, there is more. You will shortly have before you my brother, Peter, lately attempting to turn brigand, with poor results. He was imprisoned in your dungeon with Jacques and can testify to being nearly choked by him as the thief consummated his escape. I ask the most severe punishment, even in his absence, for such brazen thievery and attempted murder."

This is a bit brazen, if not entirely out of line, but Jurg is visibly angry about the near fate of his brother at the hands of the thief.

Henrik cuts Jurg off abruptly, warning him, "The attempted murder is hearsay and can be confirmed only by one who is himself about to face this court." The prince decides to demur, though, and test the dauphin. He smiles as he gestures at him. "What say you, son, to the judgment?"

"I certainly believe the testimony of our faithful servant, sire. There is no need to question the boy Peter now, as we shall do just that in other matters. This Jacques appears to have already banished himself. I would be content to make formal that banishment and to direct a detail of our guard to search him out. I think we should utilize the good graces of our many visitors here in this chamber to spread the word. Perhaps we could offer a small reward for the return of the brigand."

Charles gives the audience a stern look but glances toward his father, who offers him a small grin of approval.

"Bailiff, see to it that this judgment is recorded and consummated, as I do sustain it. And now bring out the boy Peter." Henrik is clearly pleased.

Peter is brought into the chamber, his arms alone in chains. He keeps his head bowed as he approaches the dais. He kneels on one knee in supplication but says nothing before being granted permission. He is clearly weakened and has a completely defeated look upon him.

Fee gives a short cry, which she muffles with her hand. The moment is nigh.

"Stand up, boy, and let me look upon you," says the princess, startling the entire assembly by interjecting herself directly into the inquiry, always the exclusive province of the prince.

With some pity, she believes this boy is a victim of circumstance. She has seen his injury but wants to assure herself and her husband of it, so that the prince might exercise some compassion in his judgment.

Peter obliges, and the imprint of the chain upon his neck is now apparent.

"See, sire," she says to her husband. "The mark upon the boy certainly reveals a greater punishment than you would normally mete yourself. It also confirms the accusations of his brother, Jurg. I would beg your indulgence to ask how came this boy to such a situation in life, as his brother and sisters are certainly law-abiding, useful citizens of the realm. Speak, Peter, and we shall listen."

Peter rises slowly and catches a view of Fee starting to emerge from the crowd. He gestures to her to retreat, lest she cause injury to herself in the proceedings. He bows to the royalty, takes a deep breath, and proceeds hoarsely.

"I am but a member of a family of farmer peasants completely loyal and up-to-date in tithing—that is, until the death of my oldest brother. We lost the land to that same brother's weakness for gambling, and I lost an idol. My other brother and sisters have been able to find gainful employ, while I, without land to farm, have found no skills and no apprenticeship for support. I was driven to brigandry only out of desperation, Your Highnesses. And as you can see, it is a skill which eludes me completely. I am truly sorry. Yet I do not know what to do if I am banished from the presence of Jurg, Flor, and Fee—most especially Fee. My family has always tried to comfort and assist me, though I deserve it not a whit. So I shall leave with a heavy heart and endeavor to improve my life to erase the shame I have brought upon them and upon your generosity. I beg for some mercy, though I am undeserving, sires."

"A pretty speech for one so uneducated," retorts the princess.

"Oh, no, madame. I have learned proper manners from Jurg and Fee and proper speech from Mama, herself the daughter of a merchant, though I admit I cannot read."

The prince takes this opportunity to intercede. "As I hear no objection from your siblings, young man, we will consider your account of your life accurate. And do not think us without pity. Yet we have a duty to all our subjects, yourself included. You cannot commit a crime without some consequence. Is the merchant Serge in the audience?"

A well-dressed gentleman steps forward, bowing deeply to the prince. He wears both a fine wool tunic and a silk cape, a new fashion to the citizenry. It raises murmurs in the audience. He smiles, having worn the cape especially to encourage a new style and new business. Then he straightens himself and addresses the prince.

"I am here, sire, and at your service. What would you have of me?"

"Not your attire, sir, which is clearly grander than my own!"

This elicits a laugh from the crowd.

Henrik pauses, then continues with seriousness. "I would have you confirm that this is the young man who led an attack upon your caravan as you entered the city."

Blushing with some embarrassment, Serge bows again and clears his throat. "Yes, sire, it is. But no harm was actually done, thanks to the dauphin and his friend and your excellent guard. My daughter and I would agree with mercy tempered with justice, if that be your inclination. We are not vengeful people, and I know he will ultimately be judged even more harshly before God."

"You show great compassion, sir, and we like the granting of forgiveness, which we will take into consideration." The prince turns to his valet. "Jurg, would you speak on your brother's behalf?"

~ Chapter 37 ~

At this point, Fee enters the central court unbidden. Fully knowing she might face some ill fate for it, she blurts out, "If it please Your Majesties, I would speak on my brother's behalf!"

The crowd gasps at such a show of insolence. What will the prince do?

Yet the prince's visage softens, and a glance shows that the princess too only smiles upon the poor, desperate woman.

Henrik says, "Fear not, Fee, is it? We understand your devotion to your family; your brother, Jurg, has spoken of it repeatedly. You may surely speak on Peter's behalf, but be careful what you say, as our judgment is clear and straightforward in these matters."

"Please, Your Highnesses . . ." Fee's words begin a bit squeamishly, then gather determination. "This is a poor boy with no choices or opportunities in life. Please note that he had opportunity to escape along with this accursed Jacques, but Jurg will confirm that Peter chose rather to face his judgment in full attrition. For this, he nearly paid with his life."

"What would you have him do in atonement, Fee?" the prince asks.

Fee blanches and begins to stutter a bit. "Th-thank you, sire, for the qu-question. All Peter knows is farming, and he is a fine farmer. If you would but g-grant him land, he could make it produce well, and he could pay g-good tithing upon it, even if he may not possess the land itself." Almost choking on her statement, she finishes in a rush of words. "He would do well as a useful and loyal citizen, whereas he would do poorly if merely cast out of the realm entirely. I beg for your mercy, sire."

At that, Fee is completely exhausted. She almost faints but is promptly caught by the nearest men in the audience. They move her to a bench along the wall tapestries, placed carefully beneath an exquisite weaving of Madonna and Child.

The metaphor is not lost upon Henrik, who strokes his chin a moment and waits for her to recover a bit as the crowd continues to create some noise. Then he responds in a kinder tone, "What you say has some merit. Let us consider it a moment."

Emboldened by his father's prior approval, the dauphin looks up to this father and smiles. "Perhaps, sire, we can show both mercy and intelligence. We can grant this poor servant her wish and restore the lad to his original farm. We can require he pay double tithing and allow him the opportunity to reclaim the land if he produces well for ten years. What say you, sire?"

Henrik nods. "We like this well, and it shall be written and carried out as you say. Bailiff, you will see to it. Remove the boy and place him in custody of his brother, Jurg, until he is ready to prepare the land." The prince now turns to Peter. "Know, young Peter, that you have been spared sterner judgment in our hope that you will become a more productive citizen."

With that, the royalty rises and dismisses the audience. But as they turn to leave the platform, a guard approaches and bows.

"With permission, Your Highnesses," he says.

He leans to whisper into Prince Henrik's ear. Henrik's eyebrows rise, and he beckons the dauphin close.

"Son," Henrik says softly. "It would appear our new jailer has discovered a theft of the treasury—some gold as well as the goose and harp recently gifted to us."

Charles knits his brow. "Sire, Father—this means the jailer's wife, Frau Katrina, was complicit." He nods. "But of course she was! This explains everything. She had access to the keys. She must have entered the treasury and also unshackled Jacques. But we do not know her whereabouts nor those of the thief."

"No, son, we do not. But we shall not pass judgment upon Katrina."

Charles in turn raises his eyebrows, momentarily speechless.

"I would not have it known how easily our treasury can be pilfered," Henrik explains. He turns to the guard. "You will say nothing of this to anyone, and neither shall the new jailer."

As the guard exits, Henrik turns back to his son, whose face is still marked with confusion. "Charles, there is another reason why we shall not pass judgement on Frau Katrina. That woman had need to quit her husband. I trust she did not anticipate his death. She has certainly been punished in many ways."

"Yes, sire," Charles says with a slight bow, aware of the woman's maladies and her husband's tendencies. He is sure he has much to learn from his father if he is to balance authority with compassion and maintain integrity.

◆ ◆ ◆

Fee hurries to her brothers and offers them a tearful embrace. Jurg takes Peter in hand, taking him out of the castle, where the lad delights in the fresh air for the first time in weeks.

He decides to buy him a meal at the inn outside the walls, and Peter is both thrilled and grateful.

"Come, Peter. We shall retire outside the walls, and I shall acquire us some sustenance away from those who might look upon us with some disapproval," Jurg says as he places his arm around his brother's waist in support.

As they depart, they note the arrival of a well-appointed coach with four fine horses. A footman places a footstool and opens the door. A fine lady dressed entirely in black with a high collar in the French style descends. She carries an air of arrogance more than of elegance, but she is clearly quite beautiful, in a dark manner. She frowns at Peter and Jurg, thinking them of little consequence, and enters the castle.

Jurg suddenly realizes this is the Duchess of Burgundy, of legendary beauty but also of legendary tyranny. He shudders, ushering his younger brother onward.

~ Chapter 38 ~

The duchess's arrival is announced to the prince. He, the princess, and the dauphin walk briskly into the hall, prepared to greet the lady appropriately. They are of course aware of the potential danger to her stepdaughter, kept safely for the moment with the dwarves and intended for their son. This raises instant suspicion as to the nature of her visit.

The duchess's presence seems to startle the prince and dauphin, not to mention the citizenry who have not yet left the chamber, into silence.

Charles looks into Enchanteresse's eyes for the briefest moment and is taken aback. He sees hatred and determination. The duchess can disguise the rest of her demeanor, but the eyes tell the truth. He suddenly fears for the fate of the duke's daughter, now within reach of this lady. He determines to use the secret passageway to the royal guest suite as discreetly as he can.

He bows to his parents, then to the duchess. "Please excuse me, Your Grace, as I have duties to attend." He turns, gives a look to the prince and princess to beg their acquiescence, takes a deep breath, and departs.

The princess nods her acceptance, deciding to inquire later of her son's motives. She steps forward and breaks the silence. "My lady, you are most welcome to our humble principality. We have of late been graced with a visit from your husband, the duke, and we are most pleased to offer you fine accommodation and repast. This is especially so as we are now completing our harvest."

The princess advances, hugs Enchanteresse, and offers a brief buss to both cheeks, as is more the French custom.

"I will excuse myself and allow my husband to entertain you," the princess says, "so that I may see to our finest chamber and to a fine dinner. You must stay with us, as the available accommodations in the city are all in use, and none would adequately meet your needs and tastes. We are honored to be graced with your visit."

She does not add aloud, *And it is best you stay here, where we can keep you under observation!*

"I thank you, Your Highness, and I will accept your kind offer of hospitality." Enchanteresse pitches her voice high to give it a tone of gratitude she does not truly feel. "You are both looking quite fit and beautiful, if I might say so. But I am grateful for a word with His Highness."

The princess turns and leaves the chamber, first raising an eyebrow for only her husband to see. It is a warning he fully understands. With her back to the duchess, she can allow her smile to turn into a frown as she contemplates the purpose of this visit. It cannot be good for Giselle, the duchess's stepdaughter. Presumably, Enchanteresse does not know of La Claire's betrothal to Charles—but then, neither does Charles!

Henrik offers, "Would you care for an opportunity to rest, perhaps to bathe and dine, before we talk, your ladyship? I am at your service, of course."

Enchanteresse almost turns her smile into a grimace, but she catches herself, offering a speech she has practiced repeatedly before her arrival.

"How kind, Your Majesty, but I am here on an urgent matter. I seem to have lost my stepdaughter, and I have been informed by my guardsman, lately companion to my huntsman, that she is under your protection. I wish to see to her state of health and her needs, you must understand, as she has been my charge these many years. And I do miss her companionship. Can you help me or at least enlighten me?"

Of course, she must proceed with caution. If her plan has been revealed in full to the duke, perhaps it has been revealed to Prince Henrik as well. Has her husband told this prince why he must protect

Giselle? She must pretend he knows nothing. His offer of hospitality must mean he is either ignorant of her intentions or is willing to play the innocent himself, at least publicly.

It is ironic, she notes, that that obsidian glass, which she cannot bear to leave behind, originates in Quellestadt. It alone shows her the truth no one else will admit, and it drives her to ill deeds. Yet she will not be deterred.

The prince hesitates, knowing. If she is here alone, without his grace, then Philip must know the true story and she has been expelled. She can only want revenge. He will not lie to her, nor will he reveal too much.

He nods his head and replies, "Your stepdaughter is indeed under my protection, under instruction of your husband, madame. Yet she is not on the castle grounds. I would be happy to inform her of your presence. I am sure she will be delighted to see you. I will send my guard to fetch her here, if that would please you."

Enchanteresse controls her voice carefully, not wanting to sound anxious. "That would not be necessary, Your Highness. I would prefer to surprise her—like a birthday gift, as it were. Can you tell me where to find her?"

Henrik controls his voice carefully as well. "Please make yourself at home, madame, and I will send my guard for her. You have traveled far, and the meeting will be most pleasant for you both if you are adequately rested and fed." He turns. "Guard! I would speak to you quickly." To the duchess, "Please, madame. Follow this servant, and he will show you to an appropriate chamber. A short time longer will not dull the anticipation of your reunion."

Enchanteresse must acquiesce. She cannot afford to offend the regent of this principality, especially as she is aware of the intended betrothal. Ultimately she curtsies and shrugs, following the designated servant deeper into the castle.

Enchanteresse realizes the prince might now have the maiden removed from his jurisdiction. To this end, she has already put into place a plan. She has instructed her own guard to follow any soldiers leaving the grounds. And she has an errand for her aging personal servant.

When the duchess departs, Henrik turns to the guard. "Ride quickly to the house of the dwarves, and warn them to keep the young maiden safe and hidden until I can dismiss Her Grace. Her presence does not bode well. Instruct the young maiden to answer the call of no one but me and to admit no strangers. When it is safe, I will send my son for her directly, and he will know her by name."

"Yes, sire," says the guard, a bit perplexed. He bows and leaves, quickly mounting a horse and riding out of the city. He pays no attention to the rider following behind.

Enchanteresse settles into the designated chamber. She notices none of the rich accoutrements as she seats herself at an intricately carved table, drumming her carefully painted and sharpened fingernails against the wood. She must calm her impatience. If she has waited this long to fulfill her quest, a few hours more will not matter.

Her trusted servant enters the chamber, anxious to see to her mistress's comfort. The duchess beckons her closer.

"How may I serve you, my lady?" she whimpers.

"I have an errand for you. You must hie to the tent of the herbalist we passed as we ascended to the castle. You must acquire a particular herb—and an apple, I think. I will prepare the apple, then you will take it to the maiden. We will soon know her whereabouts. You will offer it as I shall instruct." The duchess frowns, then raises her voice. "Now go!"

At this, she feels a slight breeze on her neck. Was that a movement of one of the wall tapestries? She dismisses it with the thought that this chamber is inadequate for one of her stature.

Yet there was indeed a movement in the tapestry. Charles has found the entrance to one of the secret passageways. It is serving his purpose, as he has heard the duchess's exchange with the servant. He must discuss this with the prince and plan better protection for the maiden.

~ Chapter 39 ~

Fee returns to Flor's tent, visibly relieved. "It went well, Flor. He will recover the farm and pay double tithing, but I think he has learned his lesson."

"He is not to be banished, then?" Flor smiles widely and lets out a sigh of relief. "Once again, we all are indebted to you, sister. I think you could charm the wings off a crow!"

Flor begins to cry, but these are happy tears. The sun breaks through the clouds and brightens her face further. The sisters hug, then Fee remembers she must pick up her young charge. She turns to see Besse emerging from the back of the tent.

"Flor! I have asked that you not allow Besse access to your medicinals," she scolds.

"Fee," retorts Besse, "if I am to apprentice myself to your sister, I must learn it all. And I am reading whole sentences now, thanks to Ebouisante. She is promising to teach me numbers as well. I will get the marketing and be out in a moment."

Fee sighs.

An older woman in a plain tunic of brown wool approaches the tent before Besse exits. Neither of the sisters recognizes her. She has a very long and crooked nose. Along with that prominent feature, the wrinkling of her skin gives her the appearance of an old tree. She walks with a makeshift cane, shuffling slowly along as she approaches Flor.

"Madame, are you the proprietor of this establishment?" she wheezes.

"Why, yes, madame. How may I help you?"

"I have traveled far these many days, and my mistress charges me to obtain some very specific herbs, for which, if you have them available, I will recompense you well." She points at the tent and smiles crookedly.

Flor understands immediately. Discretely avoiding the obvious question of who the mistress is, she ushers the old woman into the back of the tent as Besse emerges, sack in hand. Fee shrugs and accompanies Besse away from the tent.

◆ ◆ ◆

Jurg and Peter arrive at the inn. They enter into the chaos of merchants from surrounding principalities. The proprietor immediately approaches, welcomes them warmly, and gestures to Rose to find the gentlemen a table.

She recognizes the valet but not his companion. Could this be someone important to the prince? He is young and handsome enough, but he looks a bit shaken. Regardless, this is another opportunity for protection.

She offers them a savory stew and bread along with mead or ale. Jurg orders the stew for both of them and asks for a light ale.

Peter is astonished by the general commotion and the variety of goods on display around him. He is even more surprised by his lack of desire to pilfer any of it unnoticed. This makes him smile, which Jurg mistakes for an appreciation of the serving maidens—and most particularly of Rose.

"There will be plenty of time for attention to the ladies, Peter. Let us concentrate on feeding you for now, then on reestablishing the farm. You know you will have hard times ahead, especially with double tithing and without your brothers and sisters to help clear and plant. There is also the winter to consider, as you will not be able to plant any crop until spring. Fee and I will see to it that you are fed until you can be on your own. Neither of us will allow you to fall back to your old ways." Realizing his misdirection, he follows Peter's gaze toward the tables filled with goods. "Perhaps it was a mistake to bring you to a place that surrounds you with such temptation."

"Oddly enough, Jurg, I am not tempted at all by this bounty."

Peter makes a wide, encompassing gesture. "And I do not want to rely on your and Fee's generosity. I am willing to do anything I can for the prince, if it will help provide sustenance until I can make the farm produce. Would it be too much of a burden for you to ask him?"

"I will certainly try, but I am afraid you may have to accept some of our largesse this year. If it makes you feel better, you can repay us with some of your good harvests in the future. Ah, here is the food now," he says as Rose returns. "I want you to indulge yourself. Put some meat on those bones for the hard work ahead."

"Thank you, brother. I am eternally indebted to you and, as always, to Fee."

He smiles at Rose as she serves, which she takes as an invitation. She sets the scooped-out bread bowls before the men and ladles in a hearty stew, whose aroma is pure ambrosia to Peter.

As she pours into Peter's bowl, she leans over suggestively and whispers in his ear, "A word with ye, sir, if ye're free t' give it."

Eyes wide in surprise and curiosity, Peter replies, "Please, fräulein, I cannot afford any additional services—although there is none other I would seek for them. Your beauty speaks for itself."

"Nonetheless, I'd have a word with ye, I would."

Jurg arches his eyebrows and offers Peter a piercing look of warning but then decides he must let his brother fend for himself when possible. He waves his brother off.

Peter follows Rose to a corner of the room, where she begins to allow tears to blur her eyes.

"Sir, I must confess t' ye that while I'm very happy here, I'm in need t' leave. I surmise from your conversation with your companion that ye've a farm outside the walls of the city. Am I correct?"

Peter frowns at the misunderstanding, answering sheepishly, "I do not own the farm yet, fräulein. But the land is ancestral to my family, and I will be reclaiming it."

"E'en so," Rose says hopefully. "There is one in the city who'd mean me much harm. I can prove it to ye." She takes a deep breath. "If ye'd do me the favor of hiding me from him, I'd work for ye, if ye'd have me. A home—and 'specially a farm home—needs the domestic touch of a woman, it does. I can be of great help t' ye. And it'd be of great help t' me t' be out of reach of one who'd possibly e'en kill me." The tears now flow freely.

Peter can hardly believe his ears. What can he do? Surely she does not know his own plight. How can he help this maiden, especially now? He is hardly a knight in shining armor. He sighs deeply. Although . . . wouldn't it be a small attempt at redemption to help someone in need?

With shoulders squared, he states, not entirely with confidence, "I will help you, fräulein. I will return here this evening, after dark, and you may show me what you will. But we will not sleep together. If I find I can be of assistance, I will."

Rose curtsies. "Thank you, sir. I'll be e'er grateful, I will."

On second thought, she gives Peter a quick buss on the cheek and turns, flouncing her surcotte. He cannot see her smile.

- Chapter 40 -

The morning fog is of shorter duration as the days begin to chill and dryer air reaches Quellestadt. Soon Bo, the young bandit, will have little to no cover in which to enter the city unnoticed. Still, he has been making arrangements for his survival. He seems to be attractive enough to the young servants in the merchants' households, and rotating liaisons afford him some nourishment and temporary shelter.

Today is a very special day. He will take one last advantage of the fog as he approaches the armorer's tower home, then he will connect with a particular maidservant, Liesel. He has carefully thought through his plans but still feels some trepidation about confronting Dunkel in his own home—within which he has carefully secured and hidden a particularly sharp stone and a sling. The man must either pay—or pay the consequences.

I must have resolve and courage, mustn't I, if my brother'll be avenged, he thinks over and over again to instill just those attributes as he approaches the door with practiced stealth.

He makes a scratching sound in a prearranged pattern on the door. A rather buxom young maiden opens it, smiling.

"Devious one!" Liesel says. "Shall I endanger meself for ye yet again? Ye're here enough t' bore a young maiden with familiarity, ye are. What'll ye say t' convince me t' let ye inside?"

"A pretty predicament from a prettier young thin'!" He presents her with a rose taken from wild bushes growing outside the walls. "Perhaps a gift! Admittedly a poor one, it is, from a poor man, but one palin' in beauty compared t' ye. If ye've but a small portion of stew for a starvin' boy, the beggar can favor one so attractive with a little more personal attention, he can."

"G'wan!" she replies. But she blushes.

The bandit does not really think her so beautiful, but that matters not a wit. She believes him. No one else treats her with such attentions, and she must admit she enjoys his company and its perks.

"I shouldn't ne'er let ye in, or Fräulein Fee'll tan me hide, methinks. But ye're a charmer, ye're."

Liesel places her finger on her chin and sways a bit side to side demurely, thinking it makes her more attractive. Then she steps aside, and he brushes her cheek with a light kiss as he enters, causing her to blush again.

Their exchange keeps them from noticing a hand reaching out to catch the door before it can close shut behind Bo. The hand then places a small rock between the door and its frame.

Both unaware, Liesel feeds Bo a bit of stew from the large pot hanging over the hearth, and he warms his hands over the fire.

Their appetites sated, the couple next go upstairs to the servants' quarters to share a dalliance punctuated by deceivingly untrue words of love. After, Liesel smooths her surcotte, offers the bandit a short kiss on the cheek, then returns to her duties, expecting him to show himself out, as has been his habit.

But today is different. Unwitnessed, he retrieves his slingshot, smiles to himself, and secures a hiding place beneath the spiral stairs.

Yet Bo is not the only one in hiding. Now that he has propped open the door, Jacques has discovered the shadows between the tower and the wall. He is acutely aware of the risk to his very life, having returned to the city. He takes a deep breath and withdraws further into the darkness, reviewing his plan repeatedly in his mind.

◆ ◆ ◆

Rudi has spent a few days repairing the damage to his masterpiece. He realizes he has been so preoccupied that he has done nothing to contact his love. Granted, she asked him to stay away for safety. But he feels emboldened and not a little lovesick, so he decides to visit yet again.

First he checks to be sure Dunkel is busy at his forge. Rudi carefully conceals himself as he observes. It is clear the old master is incapable of any work of quality at this point. It gives Rudi a great sense of self-satisfaction, but he fears a bit for the apprentice, who is not ready to do for Dunkel what Rudi had been doing for years.

This gives Rudi the idea that it is time to extract Beata from her self-created prison, force the issue of his own mastership, and invite the apprentice to work for him. He is resolved; Beata will not deter him any longer.

He follows the shadows of the forest trees to the city wall. At the base of the tower, he sings like a bird seeking a mate. A curious guard on the parapet walls leans over halfheartedly but sees nothing.

Beata, however, listens for a moment, sighs, and decides to send over the makeshift linen rope. She wants to scold him, but she has truly missed him.

"No poetry today? I am heartsick," she exaggerates, the back of her hand over her brow, mocking him as he enters.

Rudi does not feel the least bit chastised. He laughs. "Ah, my Beata. So beautiful, so desirous, yet I can never hope to live up to your expectations. I am a mere blacksmith and little more. I can create a suit of armor to protect you, yet you would not don it. Better to lock yourself in a dark chamber and tease the only lover who would dare the rage of your husband to care for you." He sighs and dons a stern demeanor. "I bring you not poetry, my love, but escape! It has been long enough, and I have prepared a cottage for you, full of light and the best of everything. It is well into the woods, and I will protect you. Come with me, and be my love."

Now it is Beata's turn to laugh. "There, my Rudi, you can wax poetic. But I agree—I tire of this situation, and it is time to act. Stay with me today, and we will make further plans."

- Chapter 40 -

She runs her hand through her long blonde hair, which seems to shine even in the absence of bright sunlight. Rudi moves toward her, takes her with no resistance, and kisses her deeply. He lifts her gently and carries her to the bed, where she carefully arranges her hair, reaches up to him, and smiles. A cloud passes over the sun, slowing the lifting of the morning fog. The lovers are left to woo and plot in near darkness. Both are relieved to have committed themselves to action. They agree to do so this very night, before their resolve weakens.

- Chapter 41 -

At the market, Fee and Besse are having trouble finding the items needed for the day's meals. The stalls are nearly sold out.

"Of course!" Fee exclaims, suddenly remembering. "Tonight is feast night at the home of the Handlers. There will be as many as fifty guests. Dien says His Highness himself will be in attendance and has offered some of his own servants for the occasion. Dien will need help in the household."

Her mood sobers, and she frowns. "He invited me to assist with the preparations. But I turned him down, Besse. I will not leave you alone in the house this evening. Your father is in a particularly sour mood. I have never heard him rant so! And such language!" She shakes her head. "It must be true what they say, that his best work of late has not been his at all, but of that philandering journeyman of his. I knew his intemperance and his ill behavior would all come to no good."

Besse pulls on the servant's arm. "Please, Fee, stop worrying. Let us find what we will. Your sister is sure to need my assistance today, what with all the merchants' wives in the city. And I am eager to spend some time with Ebouisante at Flor's tent. Ebouisante has promised that I will get to read an actual book with her today, for the first time! Isn't that exciting?"

Fee pats the hand on her arm and smiles. "Oh, my child. How foolish of me, to think of myself when there are your needs to attend to. You are right, my liebchen. We will make do with carrots and cabbages and a bit lower quality of meat. Or perhaps we will spend a bit more than usual and afford ourselves a bit of venison. Here, you go on to meet Ebouisante, and I will finish the marketing."

- Chapter 41 -

In truth, Fee would rather be alone with her own thoughts. Dien has been pressing for a wedding, and he does not seem to understand that she cannot leave Besse while Dunkel can reach her.

And now Jurg has told Fee of this Rose character who has attached herself to Peter. It seems he gets out of the pot and into the fire. This woman will not do him well. How can Fee convince him? And if she can, how can she then help him reestablish the farmstead? It will take more than Peter alone to meet the prince's demands. Jurg and Flor are of no benefit in this regard. They have their own duties. So much, so much!

Better to focus on each day as it comes. First take care of Besse, then Peter, then herself.

Fee finishes her marketing and sighs, stooping like an old woman barely able to move under the burden of her responsibilities.

Fee and Besse each arrive at the floral tent a short time apart. They inhale the aromas of flowers and herbs, an antidote to the heavy odors of slaughter and tanning in the meat market.

Ebouisante has been displaying her parents' wares to the newly arrived merchants' wives. They especially show interest in the smaller mechanical items and jewelry. Her mother did not think it appropriate to show merchandise outside the store, but Serge realized the potential immediately. Ebouisante has not proven herself wrong, as a group of ladies head directly toward the store to purchase the items.

She smiles inwardly, then outwardly as she spies first Besse and then Fee. Fee notes that the merchant's daughter seems to be emitting a radiance that brightens the entire market. *How beautiful she is*, thinks Fee, wishing she could do something to improve the appearance and attraction of her own young charge.

Then she frowns, casting a shadow on Ebouisante's brilliance. Making Besse more attractive would only worsen her current situation with her father. Even beauty has its ill effects. Wit and wisdom are better attributes for survival—though Fee senses a distinct lack of both in Besse. She hopes that contact with Ebouisante will afford Besse an opportunity to develop those traits.

Ebouisante is ebullient. She speaks rapidly. "Good day, fräuleins! So good to see you. Are you not excited about the feast this evening at harvest, after the English fashion? Gute Handler herself extended the invitation to my family. I have never had the opportunity to enjoy such an occasion!" She tones down her excitement. "Will you be there? Hans—I mean, the young Herr Handler—has told me that you, Fee, were asked to help Dien with the service and that the Hammers are invited."

Fee flushes. Neither Dunkel nor Beata will attend.

Sensing the awkwardness, Ebouisante deftly maneuvers the conversation. "Oh, and I have something for you, Besse. Come see this book. It is my very first reader, but I have carefully written out a translation from the Latin for you. We shall read together today!"

Fee surrenders Besse to the care of Ebouisante with a slight curtsy.

"Sister, a word!" Flor says, getting Fee's attention. "I have been thinking: I would like to keep Besse with me for a few days in the spring, during the planting season. Can you arrange it?"

Fee is sure Dunkel would not allow it, and Beata would certainly not allow it, as it would leave Dunkel free to seek her "companionship," which she is not prepared to offer.

"We will have to see, Flor," replies Fee. "I cannot say it will happen without the permission of the master or mistress, and that will be very difficult to acquire."

Fee hopes to cut the conversation short, but she is not entirely successful.

Undeterred, Flor replies, "Please try, dear sister. I regret that I cannot offer quarters to the girl as an apprentice. But planting and caring of the flowers and herbs, and the ability to forage for them in the woods, are all important to learn."

"I know, Flor. I know," Fee says resignedly. She hugs her, then offers, "You are very kind to do what you do for her. It seems that your indulgence and training, along with Ebouisante's attentions, are all I can do for her as well. She is certainly not of fair enough appearance to attract a mate on her own, nor is she so inclined. And Dunkel has reason to keep her at home forever, so he will not see to her future in that regard. Nevertheless, I shall try to find a way to convince him."

Fee means to sound hopeful, but in fact, her thoughts are more along the lines of despair.

◆ ◆ ◆

"*Der Herr und die Dame setzen sich, und sprechen zusammen*," reads Besse—slowly and with some correction from Ebouisante. "I am reading! I cannot believe it!" she exclaims. "Thank you, Ebouisante, so much. I have never had a friend like you. Fee cannot read. Won't she be proud of me?"

"Very good, Besse," Ebouisante says. "You are a fast learner, and there is so much I want to share with you. I must have you reading Plato and Aristophanes—and, ooh, Christine de Pisan. Wait and see. There is a whole world outside these walls, and books are the gates."

Besse is excited. She speaks so fast she almost slurs her words. "Do you have any reading I can take home with me, Ebouisante? I do like stories. Fee tells me stories. Me, I will tell you a secret. Sometimes when I need to be alone and hide, I tell stories to my dolly, which Fee made for me. Then I can pretend to have a friend, even though I am old enough to know she is not a real friend." Suddenly she stops. "Oh, I have said too much!" She blushes, then blanches, but she does not cry.

Ebouisante is now certain that Dunkel is abusing his daughter. Her eyes widen, her demeanor becomes more serious. She instinctively puts her arm around Besse's shoulders. Then she makes a decision: she cannot leave this poor maiden to such a miserable fate.

"Besse, you have a friend in me. Please excuse me while I talk to Fee."

She turns to enter the tent. She marches straight to Fee.

"Forgive me, Fräulein Fee, but I fear greatly for Besse."

Fee's eyes go wide as she realizes the merchant's daughter has likely surmised the truth. She decides to be forthright with this maiden who is clearly wise beyond her years.

"That is very kind, Ebouisante, but I do my best to protect her. If I could find a mate for her, though she is so young . . . or if I could perhaps sequester her outside the city—"

Ebouisante suddenly smiles and interrupts, "I know a place! There is a lady in the woods who would welcome one to assist with chores and provide companionship."

"Is it possible?" asks Fee. "Would Dunkel not find her there?"

"The house is hidden, without a path. Herr Handler and I run chores she cannot do for herself." She has a sudden thought. "The entire city will be distracted tonight with the feast!" she exclaims. "Would you allow Hans and me to assist by accompanying her this very evening? I know this is very short notice, but I feel we must act. Time is not on Besse's side, Fee." She takes a deep breath and holds it a long time in anticipation of Fee's response.

Fee suddenly feels a twinge of excitement. Dare she hope?

"In a sense," she says, "it allows her the best opportunity. But you and Herr Handler are both a bit . . . inexperienced to take on such responsibility. And will you not be missed from the feast?"

Yet Fee may not ever have a better solution. She suppresses her excitement and answers quickly, "I understand I may not accompany you to this refuge. I will need to satisfy myself that she is well. I wish to have her continue to work with and learn from my sister, and I can see her when she is here. Though Flor will have to keep her out of sight of the armorer . . ."

She sighs. "I will think upon it, and perhaps I will approve of your offer." She pretends to hesitate a second. "In fact, I do. But we will have to work quickly. You must speak with Herr Handler, then make the arrangement and come for Besse tonight."

Fee places her hand over her heart. "Thank you. You are a good person, mademoiselle, and it cannot be mere fate that has sent you to us. I only wish I had means of showing you my deep gratitude," responds Fee sincerely.

To herself, she thinks, *there is no Eden on earth, but this will at least be a respite for the maiden.* She knows the master will eventually seek out and find the house in the woods. He need merely pay someone to follow these young ones discretely. Or he can make inquiries and find her here at Flor's tent. A better plan is needed.

"You are most welcome, Fräulein Fee, and you must think no further upon the matter. Leave it in my hands."

Suddenly, Ebouisante's altruistic impulse gives way to a fearful thought of what a dilemma she has presented herself—and not herself alone. *What am I doing?* She must speak with Hans. She and Besse both need to be protected, and she cannot abandon her parents. This Herr Hammer will be angry and even more dangerous!

It will be necessary to do something more.

~ Chapter 42 ~

Rose has spent a few days with Peter at the farmstead. All the while, she has become more anxious. She does not want to tell Peter she has served the armorer well. She should not have anything to fear from Dunkel. But it is only a matter of time until he sobers up enough to realize *she* is a danger to *him*, and then he will almost certainly come after her. And she has a growing realization that Peter is no match for the angry strength of the armorer.

Now she urges Peter onward, into the city. He carries gifts for his sisters and others to deliver to the Handlers for the feast. Rose knows this is the ideal opportunity to force Peter to act on her behalf.

"I cannot very well *attack* the man, Rose!" Peter pleads, shaking his head. "What would you have me do?"

Rose harrumphs in frustration. "You *promised* me, Peter! I *told* you I witnessed Dunkel put that body behind the inn, and I *told* you he knows I saw him. Just gain us entrance to the Hammer household, and do as I tell you."

Peter is indignant. This is his sister's household!

"I will not endanger anyone else," he says. "What would you have me do? Rob the place? How would that help you?"

"Don' be stupid, Peter!" she shouts, now angry and frustrated.

She realizes why Peter never made much of a bandit. He lacks the skills and the courage to face real danger. She believes he is very lucky to have the love and cleverness of his sister, not to mention a brother who is a valet to His Majesty himself. But Peter's relationship with Fee is her means to gain entry to the household. Moreover, if Rose can get him to act, he will be tied to her forever, and she will be safely out of that inn.

Rose grunts in frustration. "There's nothin' of true value in that house, no," she continues. "But there're weapons that can be put t' use with the proper element of surprise, there are." She flushes, not bothering to hide her anger. "I mean t' have my freedom from that curse of a man!" Her voice rises in volume.

This is the night of the Handler feast, which will be great cover for action. All interest of the citizens will be distracted. She must get Peter to act *now.*

Peter, of course, is brooding in the fog. He has promised to help this maiden, but he questions in his mind whether she really deserves it. Regardless, he cannot leave her in danger from the man. Perhaps he should have thought more about this plan of helping a maiden in distress as an act of redemption for his banditry . . . But he has committed himself. He will care for her.

◆ ◆ ◆

The two stop briefly at the market. Flor sees them coming up the street, wipes her hands on her apron, and steps up to greet them. She gives Peter a big bear hug. She has not seen him personally since his release from the castle dungeon. Tears flow freely.

Eventually Rose clears her throat.

Flor turns to her. "You must be Rose. It is a name unworthy of the beauty you display." She frowns. "I am not sure what you see in this good-for-nothing lad, but if he loves you, then you are always welcome in my tent."

Peter flinches. He does not love this woman. Then he shrugs and hands Flor a carved gourd. It has the image of a bouquet of flowers, specially designed to please his sister. The beauty of the carving is to be enhanced by placing a lit candle within.

"Why, Peter, it is lovely!" she says as she places it prominently upon a table at the tent entrance. "Did you carve this yourself?"

He nods. "I mean to keep my promise to His Majesty and make the farm come back to life. At the present, I can only collect a few wild gourds and make them something of a gift. I have more in my sack. I intend one for Fee and the rest for the feast at the Handlers tonight."

Rose suddenly has an idea. "May I enter the tent, fräulein? I might wish t' make a small purchase from ye. Peter, would ye wait for me here, please?"

She follows the herbalist into the tent. After a moment, Peter can hear a short argument. When the ladies emerge, Rose carries a small vial, which she tucks into her surcotte.

Flor snorts, looking at Peter with disapproval. "I do not know whom this is for, brother, but I caution you to watch yourself. Revenge does not suit you—either of you!" she adds, nodding toward Rose. "Do not do anything that would land you in the dungeon again. It would kill your sister Fee as well as me to see you there again—"

Rose interrupts quickly. "I told your dear sister the danger you were in from those rival thieves, Peter, because I knew you would not do so yourself." She furrows her brow, silently warning him not to expose her prevarication. "Now I will be able to help you in return for the kindness you have shown me."

Peter grunts in acquiescence as they depart. Flor glances out of the tent at Rose with a look of deep scorn, which Rose proceeds to ignore entirely.

◆ ◆ ◆

Next Rose accompanies Peter to the Handler home. It is clearly the largest in the village, so heavy that the roof leans over the street, as if anyone passing beneath is to be judged by the house itself. But it is neither brooding nor foreboding. Bright flowers fill boxes hanging from the windows, which are so old that the glass is almost opaque. There is even a servants' entrance on one corner. There is a plethora of activity on this special day: servants coming and going with deliveries from the market or gifts from guests who will arrive later in their most splendid attire.

Rose sighs. Someday she would love to attend such a function, but such would only be a dream, unless she could goad Peter into becoming the wealthiest farmer outside the walls—he with double tithing to pay. Does she fancy herself a farmer's mate? Perhaps not. But beauty does not last forever. She plans to supplement their income as long as she can with her own old profession—and he will have little to say about it. She will keep a clean and bountiful household, eventually with servants of her own. He will find her irreplaceable. And that is that. Then no one will dare disapprove of her!

Peter, oblivious to her machinations and contrite from his past life, lends no thought to a future with this woman. He focuses instead on the present. He approaches the servants' door and knocks heartily.

Dien himself answers and recognizes Fee's brother. He grimaces. "And t' what do I owe this honor? Ye've shamed your family, ye have, and I hope ye'll spend many years in amends."

Peter bows his head. "I am indeed ashamed, sir. But I promise you will have naught but good to say of me in the future. Rose here has helped clear the old farmhouse, and I shall be able to concentrate upon redeveloping the farm. You will see. I will be a model citizen with a productive farm—God willing. And Rose will help."

Dien opens his mouth to speak, but Peter continues quickly.

"Please, sir, say nothing more for now. I have brought a gift for the feast. Please accept it with all humility. It is but little that I can do."

He reaches into the sack, removes one gourd, and hands the remaining gourds in the sack to Dien. Then he bows and gestures to Rose for them to leave.

She turns with a flourish to catch Dien's eye. In this she succeeds—but with disapproval and a frown. She resolves to be more careful in her selection of future clientele. This man is clearly devoted to Peter's sister, and it is a mistake to attempt to flirt with him. She will need to catch Fee's grace, not her enmity. She mouths a quick "sorry" to Dien.

♦ ♦ ♦

Peter next leads Rose to the Hammer household. She is not surprised to find it in a tower of the city wall itself. Dunkel would certainly want to be on the periphery of the citizenry. He is not one to participate in the social activity of the town, but his wife would expect to live within the confines, as is due to her station. How she can possibly live with that man is a mystery to Rose.

Rose hands Peter the vial, then Peter knocks at the door. A servant recognizes him and bids the duo enter. The two take a deep breath, ready to act. Rose converses with the servants, pretending interest in their work, exercising her skills of false flattery to draw the attention of this one and then that one away from Peter.

Peter takes this opportunity to talk to his sister, who has returned from her marketing and is now supervising the dinner preparation. "I have brought you a gift in gratitude, Fee. It is but little yet from the heart. See, I have carved a rose, and you can place a candle inside to make it glow. In the future, I will supply you with the best produce, and you shall not have to pay."

"Hush, my brother. I know you have suffered much. I need no gifts from you. But I shall accept the gourd. Know that whenever it glows, I will think of you." Fee lowers her voice. "But I would caution you to keep a close eye on that woman. I cannot believe she means well, having so attached herself to you. There is a plan in that mind, and I would have none of it. You have had enough trouble already."

Fee looks directly at Rose, frowning, as if to say, *I know what you are doing, and I do not approve.*

To Peter, she says, "She is buxom and beautiful—I will give you that. But hers is a darker beauty. It speaks of plots and deceptions. Beware, my brother."

"You must trust me, dear sister. She can keep a house like few others—a skill I have not. And I will be careful. She is a desperate maiden, Fee. She has been threatened, and I must protect her. But I will speak of that no more here." He puts on a smile. "What is that savory aroma? Perhaps a rabbit stew? Would you allow your poor brother a taste?"

Fee nods as he reaches for the one wood bowl amid bread bowls. "Yes, but do not use that bowl, Peter. It is the master's."

- Chapter 42 -

As Fee turns to address the other servants, Peter now smiles to himself. *The master's bowl. Serendipity. Maybe the fates favor us,* he thinks. He dare not hesitate, though his heart beats heavily against his chest. He glances at Rose, who is watching him carefully, even as she distracts the servants.

He takes a wooden ladle and leans over the pot on the hearth. He takes a small taste, all the while careful not to be seen emptying the small vial into the wood bowl. But now they must stay to see that only Dunkel uses the bowl.

"Rose," he says, calling her over, "perhaps you would like to assist the servants with the meal preparations?"

Rose would rather depart the household as soon as possible, and Fee has no desire to work with this woman. She frowns at her brother.

"Please allow us to stay until the supper is served, then we shall take our leave," Peter pleads. He looks to Rose expectantly, hoping she now understands. "You shall see how useful Rose is. And I would like to be in your company this afternoon, sister, as I have had so little of it this last year."

Fee is not sure she should allow it, but she has missed her brother. She agrees.

After a while, she sees the servants are actually more productive—they happily work while being entertained by Peter's stories of banditry and the foolishness of travelers. His tales are obviously aggrandized and totally exaggerated, if not completely fabricated. Fee herself must admit she likes a good story, and it takes her mind off what she herself must do this evening.

So the day wears on, until she hears the master throw open the door. He is clearly besotted, as usual, and he stumbles up the stairs to Besse's chamber.

Immediately Fee leaves her brother's side. She races up the stairs after Dunkel.

"You shall not touch her, master! Leave her be!"

"I've told ye, *servant,* not t' inter—not t' interfere! Now step aside!"

He pushes Fee out of the way, almost tumbling her down the stairwell. He then stomps into Besse's room. As she tries to recapture her breath, Fee hears a muffled cry. For a second, she sees Besse cower and hide her Dolly. But then Dunkel throws the door closed and blocks it with a heavy chest of drawers.

Fee sinks outside the door and sobs, feeling no more useful than a sack of garden vegetables.

Then she fills with resolve. *Enough! No more!*

She must act. She will get the girl out of the house this very night—and then do what she must. Damn the consequences.

Of course, Fee has little idea of the potential consequences of this very day upon the future of many people important to her. Nor does she know that Bo, Jacques, Rudi, Beata, Peter, and Rose are all steeling their nerves for action in her very household. The weather, like their intentions, may be clear—the fog lifting for one of the last times of the season. But not all storms are the work of nature.

- Chapter 43 -

In the forest, shadows replace the gloom of the fog. A heady scent of pine and spruce is in the air. The small men have departed for the mine, and La Claire busies herself with tidying the hovel they call home. She is not truly unhappy, but this is certainly not the life she envisioned for herself.

Earlier, she had applied only a touch of powder to her face after washing. She dressed herself in plain linens and a surcotte, obtained for her from the city. She does not know the prince himself actually provided it, but she does know he is aware of her predicament.

She lets her mind wander to better days at her father's castles. She misses him with all her heart. Will she ever see him again? She finds that she holds no enmity toward her stepmother, who, after all, has seen to her education and welfare until this point. Rather, she pities her stepmother for her vanity.

The fire in the hearth crackles and illuminates her small world. It reveals frown lines, yet reflects her beauty and makes her almost seem to shine.

La Claire's reverie is interrupted by a knock at the door. It is an old lady, but not one she recognizes instantly. The woman is very wizened and hides her face inside the hood of a somewhat-soiled wool riding cloak. She carries a small sack that seems to be a burden for her.

In fact, the old servant is here to carry out her orders. After a fruitless search for La Claire inside the city, Enchanteresse's guards determined that the maiden must be sequestered outside the walls. While searching the nearby woods the previous night, the old woman secretly espied the dwarves and followed them home. She immediately knew the little men could not have cared for the cottage so well on their own—what men would perform "women's work"? So, she peered into a makeshift window and discovered the hiding place of her mistress's stepdaughter. With the little men away at their work, she has returned, availing herself of the opportunity to approach the maiden while she is alone, without protection.

"Please, mademoiselle, help an old lady. Would ye perhaps purchase some apples for the masters? See how fine they are! So red, so sweet! Here, I'll share one with ye."

She carefully selects a fruit from her sack. She has coated one side of this apple with an infusion prepared per Flor's instructions. She takes a bite from the other side, then offers the apple to La Claire.

The maiden remembers the directive to not interact with strangers. But how dangerous can such an old woman be?

She accepts the apple gracefully and bites generously into it. It is indeed sweet. She smiles.

"How wonderful, madame! I have never tasted better. The miners must have such a treat." Her smile fades a bit into a pout. "But I fear I have no marks for the purchase. What can I offer you? Perhaps some freshly baked bread? I do wish I had a meal prepared for you in return for such generosity."

"A pity, mademoiselle," the old woman squeaks. "I cannot merely hand ye me goods. Your offer of bread is tempting, it is, but of no use t' my master. Perhaps I might return when the gen'lemen are home." She shrugs. "But please feel free t' finish this one morsel as me gift t' ye."

"Thank you, madame," La Claire says. "You are welcome to return later, and I shall have a hearty meal for you." Giselle yawns. "Oh! Pardon me! But I am sure the men of the house will delight in your offerings."

"Think nothing of it, me dear," the old woman replies, patting Giselle on the hand. "I'll take me leave, for now."

Yet she lingers until La Claire yawns again, then starts to sway. Now she turns and departs, hiding a smirk beneath her hood, satisfied that the potion is working.

~ Chapter 43 ~

Closing the door, La Claire finishes the offering. She decides to tidy up the hovel, and she reaches for a broom, but she is suddenly overwhelmed with fatigue. She shakes her head, determined to continue her task.

She is not one to nap when there is work to be done, but she cannot seem to find the energy or the will to work. Perhaps a short break. *I can allow these tasks to wait a bit,* she thinks. In truth, they *must* wait—her eyes are quickly closing on their own accord.

She turns to lie down upon the bed her protectors created for her, but she cannot make it to the soft, straw-filled mattress. Instead, she faints gently upon the long table. The apple falls out of her hands onto the floor.

◆ ◆ ◆

It is there the dwarves find her when they return. Alarm etches all their faces at once.

"Is she dead?" asks one.

Grump pushes his way through his colleagues as they crowd around the table. He leans over the maiden in closer observation, then grunts and waves the group back.

"She's barely breathin', but not yet dead." Suddenly he notices the dropped fruit. "And look! Here on the floor. She's bitten into a bad apple, she has. We must send for the prince at once!" he says excitedly.

Says another, "I'll go—directly through the city, I will."

Shortly thereafter, he hurries through the city gate, out of breath and ignoring the taunts of the guard. He runs directly to the castle entry, where he is stopped by a guard. The little man recognizes the guard, as he was one of La Claire's protectors who gathered at the cottage with Gaillard.

With some trepidation, the soldier exclaims, "Slow down, sir! I know you would not enter the city and present yourself without summons! The prince and his family are preparing to leave for the feast at the Handlers'. They will be cross to be disturbed, but the more so if I prevent your entrance if, as I suspect, you carry dire news.

Nearly out of breath, the dwarf pleads, "Please, sir, ye must tell His Majesty that the young maiden he's protectin' has been poisoned, she has! He must send his physicians at once!"

The little man is animated and flushed, and the guard can see this is no ruse. Moreover, he is one of only a few guards who know the identity of the maiden in question.

"Wait here, sir," the guard replies. "I will tell Their Majesties immediately and directly."

"Thank ye, sir! And please hurry!"

Just then, Flor is approaching the castle, having just closed business at her tent. The entire day, she brooded over her suspicions about the old woman and Rose. Now she is intent upon informing the prince. *I would not have His Highness blaming* me *if these purchases are set to ill uses!* she thinks with trepidation.

As fate would have it, she overhears the dwarf's outburst. Her worst fears are confirmed. She stops in her tracks and gasps, bringing the back of her hand to her mouth.

She blurts out, "Sir guard! You must take me with you to see His Majesty. I have news that helps explain the situation, and I also have something to save the fräulein, whoever she is."

The guard turns. It is clear the herbalist is involved somehow in this poisoning. Just how or why can be reckoned later. For now, she clearly must be brought to the prince immediately. He beckons both her and the little man to follow.

Inside, the guard's request is quickly passed to the prince and princess, who hurry down the stairs, followed closely by the dauphin. They direct the guard to admit the dwarf.

The small man is so agitated that he forgets to bow to the royalty. "It's the young fräulein, Your Highnesses—she's barely breathing and cannot be aroused! And there, by her side, an apple! It must have been poisoned!"

He covers his mouth as he realizes his faux pas, having omitted his show of obeisance. He bows deeply now, after the fact.

The prince does not even notice the lapse in etiquette. His eyes widen in shock and anger, and his body shakes.

He bellows, "How could she have come by such a poison? I specifically sent word to her to accept no gifts nor talk to any strangers!"

Flor curtsies, tears in her eyes. "Your Majesties, I beg your forgiveness for speaking before being addressed"—she is also clearly agitated and speaks rapidly—"but I can definitely help here. Yesterday an old lady approached me with a request for a potentially lethal potion. She did not reveal her intended purpose for the potion. However, I could not risk the consequences—not to mention your sanction of my business—if her intentions were nefarious. So instead I pretended to meet her request, providing an herb that would only put her quarry to sleep."

Charles has kept his silence, but now he will not contain his own anger and fear. He interrupts the herbalist. "Why would you even provide that? Are you sure of its harmless nature? Explain yourself!"

Flor turns and curtsies respectfully to the dauphin. "Yes, Your Highness, I considered the option of refusing or providing something entirely harmless. But this old woman might stay with her victim long enough to see evidence that the potion 'succeeded.'"

She reaches into a pocket in her tunic and produces a small sack. "And here, sires—here is an antidote. The aromatics in this vial will revive the maiden rapidly, if you can get it to her before eventide. Otherwise, she might sleep for days, or her breathing might slow and affect her ability to awaken at all."

The prince sighs. "Fear not . . . Flor, is it? You did well to come to me with this information, and you were smart to anticipate that it would be best not to comply with the old woman."

Flor sighs in relief. She has cleared herself. Given the heightened urgency of the maiden's situation, Flor decides to withhold mention of Rose at this time. She resolves to inform the prince later, once the maiden is safe.

The prince turns to his son. "Here, Charles. You must take this to the maiden immediately, then bring her back here. In fact, we shall be at the feast, and you must oblige us by bringing her directly there, if she is sufficiently recovered."

"Yes, sire. But why would you not just send a guard?"

"You shall see, son. You shall see. Just follow my command."

"With alacrity and humility, sire."

The dauphin, somewhat perplexed, takes the small sack with the aromatics from the florist. With a beckon to the little man and the guard, he departs.

◆ ◆ ◆

The dauphin, guard, and dwarf ride into the woods toward the base of the foothill. The ride is uneventful, then they are greeted at a clearing by one of the miners, hopping from leg to leg in agitation. The cottage is visible a short distance ahead, and Charles is a bit surprised at how tidy the house and garden look.

Grump's face registers his surprise at seeing the dauphin himself.

"Ye must come quickly, young sire! I fear we may have lost the young maiden. So beautiful, she is! She carries no fear of the world, and I worry that such a weakness may've been fatal for her." He pauses as emotion overcomes him. "Oh! We promised the prince t' keep her safe, we did. We should be punished for leavin' her alone. Yes, we should. A million pardons, Your Highness. This way."

Charles frowns at the little man. His is a sin of omission, realized only too late, and Charles would not dream of inflicting punishment for it.

He places his hand on Grump's shoulder, then says, "Fear not, my friend. I carry the antidote in a small pouch. The maiden is not entirely in jeopardy of her life." He removes his hand and gestures the man onward. "Lead on, sir! I assure you, we have arrived in time. Do not flagellate yourself. She has merely suffered the effects of a strong sleeping concoction. Their majesties and I have had the good fortune to be informed of this fact by the very provider of the potion that beset this maiden. I will revive the young fräulein, then escort her to my parents."

"Oh, thank ye, sire!" Grump responds with great relief. "It's a miracle!"

Charles gestures toward the home as they near the door. "I see she has been of great value during her stay, as this place clearly shows a woman's touch."

"It's as ye say and as ye see. The maiden has been invaluable." Grump hesitates a second, grimaces, then adds, "But it's clear we can't provide adequately for her safety, nor is her presence a secret any more. We'll be very sad t' see her go but much happier in the heart t' see her directly under the supervision and care of Your Majesties."

Grump directs the dauphin to a table upon which the young maiden has been set carefully. The other miners step back, looking to Charles with expectation.

"Here she is. You say she's merely sleepin' and you can revive her . . . well, it still seems a miracle t' me, it does. And we all owe you deep gratitude, we do."

They all bow to the dauphin, who nods his head in response before approaching the maiden.

Charles sees a vision. She is surrounded with flowers from the garden, and a small white cluster of edelweiss rests in her carefully folded hands. He bends over, drinking in the fragrance of the flowers. On a whim, he gives her a light kiss on the lips before placing the open vial beneath her nostrils.

And lo! She stirs. She shakes her head, turning side to side to escape the odor. As he pulls the vial away, she stretches her arms and begins opening her eyes.

"It is I who am grateful, sirs," Charles replies. "This maiden of great beauty—so white of skin that it could be the very source of sunlight—is somehow of great importance to my father. Now," he says, turning to her with a smile, "I see he has the finest of judgment."

Giselle yawns and stretches again—a striking vision to Charles.

"It seems I owe you a debt of gratitude myself, sir," La Claire says, calling Charles's attention directly to herself. She speaks with slight slur, as she has not yet fully recovered. "And to whom do I owe the honor of calling my savior?"

"Milady," interrupts Grump, "ye must address this man as 'sire.' He's Prince Charles, he is—son of Prince Henrik, who rules this principality."

La Claire lowers her eyes. "A thousand pardons, sire. I thought you to be an angel of God, for you are most handsome and most gracious. It seems I owe you my life, and I hope not to appear too ungrateful. A million thanks to you and to your father, who has provided me with shelter—and to these men around you for the same and for their boundless hospitality."

Charles laughs. "Think nothing of it, mademoiselle. It is I who am faced with a vision. Though you have busied your hands with the needs of these ruffians"—here there is a chorus of snickers among the men—"you have managed to refine their appearance and their behavior without diminishing an ounce of your own beauty. I would guess you are of noble descent, even if you demean yourself with the activities of a mere housewife."

Now Giselle laughs. "Perhaps you mistake me, sire. I consider it nothing less than a privilege to serve the needs of these men, who have treated me with great kindness and respect. Therefore, I feel you owe some apology—if not to me, then to them for considering them ruffians, as you call it."

The little men gasp at their charge's forwardness.

"Ye must pardon her, milord. I fear the effects of the poison haven't entirely dissipated, they've not," says one.

Charles waves his hand in dismissal. "No, she is absolutely correct." He gives the men a formal bow of gratitude, astonishing them. "My father and I are totally indebted to you for the care of this angelic maiden, and I will see to it that you are rewarded appropriately. For now, consider your tithing suspended for three months. Even this is hardly enough compensation for your service."

He nods to the miners, then turns and offers his hand to Giselle. "But come, mademoiselle. I am charged with your safe return to our court. We are expected at the feast of our principal merchant. But first I must ask with whom I have the great honor of conversing."

"Thank you, sire. I am Giselle, the daughter of Philip, the Duke of Burgundy." She manages a slight, if shaky curtsy, with a smile that brings light to the entire cottage.

Charles nods vigorously. "Then I understand much, Mademoiselle Giselle. Your stepmother, the duchess, is currently gracing our court with her presence, and your father himself is due at the very feast to which we must hie ourselves. His majesty, my father, likely has the intent of returning you to his care."

La Claire shakes her head a bit to awaken herself and to clear her mind. "Do you think, sire, that my father is here for that purpose? For if my stepmother has discovered my presence, then he would feel the need to come to provide protection. Our huntsman, Gaillard, placed me here under the warrant of your father—I mean, His Majesty—because he feared my stepmother wants me dead!"

She blushes, appearing on the verge of tears. This only serves to further soften Charles's heart. He appears pensive, with furrowed brow, for a moment.

"Then there is more to this than meets the eye. If Her Grace knows you are here, then *his* grace certainly knows you are here. More to the point, my father would certainly have sent word to your father regarding your safety within this realm and would have allowed you to stay under the protection of these loyal, hardworking men. Therefore—"

"Therefore," continues LaClaire herself, "Gaillard must have informed His Majesty of my entire predicament and left me here in hopes of keeping my location secret from Her Grace." Her eyes go wide and she takes in a sharp breath. "Oh, my! You do not think he will assume one of these kindly men betrayed my hiding place, do you?"

"Mademoiselle, my father and I trust these men completely. I presume you and the huntsman traveled with a contingent of guards—it is far more likely that one of them would hold some fealty to Her Grace," Charles says as he pats Giselle's hand reassuringly.

"Indeed, sire. I think you are correct. But with my location no longer a secret and with your being sent here to rescue me, it is time to return to the protection of my own father." She pouts. "Then why do I feel so torn between his court and the opportunity to remain here?" She sighs.

"Your Grace," interjects Grump, "ye're always welcome here, ye are. And we promise we'll keep the place clean and hospitable in anticipation. But," he adds with a bow, "it's time t' return. Ye could do far worse than accept the offer of accompaniment of His Young Highness, no?" He winks and smiles, giving the look of hidden wisdom and merriment all at once.

La Claire sighs again, then straightens her posture with recuperated composure. "I thank you, sir. I thank you all. I shall miss you terribly, and I hope I may return someday to visit. I have come to love and admire you for your honesty and sacrifices as well as your courage and loyalty. I shall never forget."

She kisses each on the forehead and curtsies, then takes the arm of the dauphin.

"Let us not keep our fathers waiting, sire."

A tear forms at the corner of her eye, but she still maintains the dignified look of regality as she exits the home.

The dauphin is surprised to find he feels both impressed by and comfortable with this young maiden. A lady of nobility and sincerity, she is willing to behave like a common housewife without condescension, yet she is quite at home on his arm.

He then blushes as he thinks, *Perhaps Father had special intentions when he sent me to revive this young lady. Why send me to her rescue and not just a guard?*

Charles smiles inwardly with the revelation, but says nothing to La Claire.

~ Chapter 44 ~

Dien surveys the general chaos in the Handler household, suppressing the image of a general melee, but he's proud he has it all under control. He frowns in annoyance at the memory of Peter's visit but then turns it to a smile when he examines the content of the sack. The carved gourds are actually quite artistic and will make wonderful additions to the entremets at the feast. He resolves to thank the boy personally, shrugging his shoulders with the thought that doing so will make his intended very happy.

He wonders how to convince Fee to leave that godforsaken household. She so deserves a better life. At any rate, he cannot spend time fretting over it now. There is far too much to do. As he must fully concentrate upon his tasks for the Michaelmas feast, he does not notice the disappearance of the slight smile and inner glow that had accompanied his thoughts of Fee.

Dien is a bit exasperated, even as his plans come together well. The mummers have arrived to perform their play. They are rehearsing outside, out of sight of the guests. Dien had been informed well in advance to expect the duke and his retinue, then just today he was told to expect the duchess and *her* retinue. Now the prince has sent word that the dauphin will be accompanying a young maiden—and nobility at that! How shall Dien arrange the messes—generally, in groups of two for nobility, and in groups of four for the others?

Shaking his head, he seeks out the lady of the house, Gute. "Mistress, are there any more available servants t' help? I must send two out for marketing, and there's precious little t' be had!"

Gute smiles gently. "Fear not, Dien. The prince has sent his dispensation for priority at the butcher's and for vegetables from the castle garden. Also, the duke has arrived, and he has offered the assistance of two of his own servants."

Dien breathes a sigh of relief as Gute leaves the kitchen.

He wishes inwardly for the presence and help of his love, but he knows *that* family will not attend, and Fee must not leave Besse alone.

He hears a great fuss in the main hall, and Artur himself enters the kitchen, beckoning to Dien.

"You must know, Dien, that His Highness, the dauphin, has just returned with Mademoiselle Giselle. I trust you have made all the necessary arrangements, yes?"

Dien smiles, nodding the affirmative. "Thank ye, master. The mistress herself has just returned t' the solar, and the mummers've also arrived, sir. I set them t' preparin' themselves, I did, and I fed them well, with but a little ale t' calm their nerves. They're quite ready, they are. And we're ready t' begin the feast."

Of course, this was not all quite true, as the cooks still needed to prepare for the one additional guest, and others were still busily rearranging the tables and seating to accommodate her. But by the time Artur will report to his wife, all should be in order.

Artur nods and takes his leave.

At this point, young Charles appears—at the servant's door! He is clearly not dressed for the feast, but he appears buoyant and excited. On his arm is the mademoiselle Giselle, a bit startled to be presented first to a servant!

"Dien, I must hurriedly present to you the mademoiselle Giselle, daughter of Duke Philip. If you would please afford this young maiden access to the maidservants' chamber, and I to yours, we would be grateful for the opportunity to freshen ourselves to appear at this feast. From the heady aromas, I would say you have outdone yourselves, and we will be well entertained!"

"Your Highness! Ye do us great honor, ye do, and we'll comply immediately! Hilde!" he calls to a servant. "Show the mademoiselle to your chamber, and I'll accompany His Highness meself."

- Chapter 44 -

He grimaces inwardly at this latest development. "What next?" he whispers to Hilde out of earshot of the esteemed guests. "I should always expect the unexpected, I should. But this is just too eventful. Any more surprises, and I suspect the feast itself'll present more entertainment than the mummers." He sighs. "Thank ye for your help with the young maiden. She is nobility, so treat her accordingly!" He shrugs as he heads out with the dauphin.

Upon his return, he finds the cooks and servants milling and busily gossiping among themselves. He claps his hands and takes on the sternest frown he can muster.

"There's no time t' tarry! The guests've arrived!"

The servants break off their conversation, and they scurry to comply. Each is precisely schooled in his or her job. Fine dyed wool cloths are set over the tables intended for the nobility and for the most treasured of friends and merchants. Then freshly baked bread bowls, one for each guest—an extreme luxury—are set out along with carafes of wine and mead at the head tables and ale and water at the lesser tables. Fortunately, Dien has seen to it that extras are prepared, in case of need or demand for extra servings.

When two more servants arrive from the castle to assist and the servants sent to market return, Dien quickly assigns them duties at the tables. Wooden chalices are set at most of the places, as are knives carefully wrapped within wool napkins. At the head table, which is placed on a raised dais, the napkins are of a finer quality of linen, imported from the Bavarian principalities. The knives have carved silver handles, and at each place a new tool, with silver handle and two piercing tines, is set.

This completed, the servants take their places at the sides of the tables, facing the open center of the chamber. Dien gestures to Gute, and she and Artur stand to either side of the chamber entry. Jurg is now in attendance, smiling at the guests outside the door, which he now flings open.

The invitees know their rank in society; they arrange themselves in an appropriate order of entry. As they do so, they give their names to Jurg, who announces them to the host and hostess. The guests receive an embrace, a brief bussing on each cheek, and perhaps a quick comment or two about the great beauty of their garb or an inquiry into the status of a business or the health of a relative. Then a designated servant escorts each guest to a table.

Next come the older children, led in ensemble by Hans and Greta. The siblings bring the young guests to the end tables nearest the door, where they are allowed to choose their own places. For most, this is their first formal feast, and their faces betray their wonderment at the art surrounding them, the finery of clothing and jewelry, and the promise of exquisite dining contained in the aromas surrounding them.

And they know there will be entertainment as well. Those familiar in their schooling with the English custom of the Michaelmas feast wonder if there will be some reference to the story of Saint George and the Dragon. But of course there will! There must! And will there be surprises? The Handlers are famous for their surprises! The anticipation is almost too much, but they must all settle at their places on the benches—without pushing or shoving, as such an event requires the best behavior.

Amused by the attitudes, Hans and Greta make sure all introduce themselves, and they compliment each maiden on some aspect of her appearance. This, of course, raises speculation among the young women and girls as to who might be selected to become betrothed to Hans himself. How handsome, with a tunic of fine linen, with threads of silver carefully placed to sparkle in the light of the torches, and with a belt pouch of red silk! The Handlers are quite wealthy, and he, a hero, would make a fine catch.

It does not take long, however, for them to notice he has eyes only for the new maiden in town, the daughter of Serge Kaufman, who has the audacity to wear no powder or rouge upon her face yet seems to outshine them all.

Finally, Jurg claps to silence the crowd. They resort to whispering, like the babbling of a creek over rocks, until he gives them a stern look. Then he stands tall, and in a deep and imperious voice, he announces, "All rise and pay homage to Their Graces, the Duke and Duchess of Burgundy!"

The duchess raises her flexed hand to the duke. She is dressed in the black of mourning, an exquisite sable collar on her high-necked tunic. The sight of her engenders speculation among the crowd.

The duke himself looks resplendent in a rich silk tunic rimmed in gold thread. But Jurg does not fail to notice the barely veiled look of disgust as the duke lightly touches the hand of his former beloved and escorts her to the head table, where the servant has been carefully instructed to seat the duchess to the left of the mistress and the duke to the right of the master.

Jurg waits for the attendees to quiet themselves, then clears his throat and announces, "All praise to the dauphin and Giselle, daughter of his grace, the Duke of Burgundy."

At these words, the duchess stumbles as she ascends the dais.

"Are you all right, my *dear*?" asks Philip, gloating. His estranged wife is pale, but he does not notice it due to the multiple layers of powder she has applied to her face.

"Oh, quite, my lord. Thank you." She recomposes herself as if nothing unusual has happened.

Her stumble does not go unnoticed by the prince, who knows it confirms his suspicions about the ill event at the cottage in the woods. This will, indeed, be an interesting evening in many ways.

He whispers to his guard, who nods in understanding and leaves to instruct two of his colleagues to stand guard at the entrance to the household.

As they enter, the dauphin turns to La Claire, now accoutered in a fine blue-and-yellow silk tunic with puffed sleeves and a low collar. A deep-green emerald on a gold chain hangs from her slender neck. The duke brought these splendid clothes in anticipation of formally presenting his daughter to the court of Prince Henrik.

Charles whispers to her with a smile, "You bring sunlight into this hall, mademoiselle. With your presence, the torches are superfluous."

She blushes imperceptibly, offering her white-gloved hand to young Charles, who places his hand firmly upon hers. He escorts her to the dais, where they separate so they may be seated next to their respective parents—she next to the duke, and he next to the intended seat of his mother.

Jurg then states, "All bow your heads, and all hail Their Highnesses, Prince Henrik and Princess Amalia!"

Of course, the royal couple is the most radiant of all in their best formal clothing—matching deep-blue velvet tunics with ruby and garnet jewelry for her and gold chains, a jewel-encrusted belt, and an engraved gold scepter for him. Both are adorned by the crowns of state, heavily encrusted with rubies mined by the dwarves. The crowd is thrilled to see these crowns, as they are rarely worn, except for celebrations of state. But no one would dare even whisper a speculation as to why the royals would wear these crowns to a mere feast of a merchant.

The princess hugs Gute, and the prince raises Artur's bowed head and takes his arm, as his wife does of the hostess. They walk together to the dais. At this, the guests applaud. They do indeed love to see their regents show humanity, compassion, humility, and regality—all in one gesture.

The prince is seated to the right of the duke, the princess to his left. Normally, the center seats would be reserved for the master and mistress of the household, but they have demurred to their rulers. This leads the guests to even more speculation as Gute seats herself next to La Claire, and Artur next to Hans. There must be something momentous about this arrangement.

As the guests at the dais seat themselves, all others are seated. And now the crowd whispers incessantly, causing the princess, the duke, and Artur and Gute to smile, which only fuels the conversation.

Jurg claps in a preset signal, and Dien gestures to the servants to roll out the first service. The air crackles with excitement. The guests had expected a mere feast with entertainment, but it seems they are in for an entire pageant!

~ Chapter 45 ~

"Oh, yes, Dolly, he is a mean father," mumbles Besse in a dark corner. "We do not like what he does to us, do we? I must hide you, so that you cannot watch. But you must know, don't you? But I know something, Dolly. Yes, I do. I have learned something that will help us. Yes, I have."

Fee enters the chamber as Besse repeats herself over and over, hugging the poor rag doll tightly, silent witness to evil events in the darkness. Besse hardly notices as Fee bends down, hugging her the way Besse hugs the doll.

Eventually the maiden acknowledges her presence, looking up at her with fierce indignation. "You cannot help me, Fee. I know you want to, but he is very strong, and he is the master of this household. You cannot help me, so I must help myself."

"What do you mean, liebchen?"

Now there is a trace of worry in Fee's voice, a trace even of fear. What can such a defenseless maiden do? Fee's thought is to reassure her another way.

"Liebchen, liebchen! I *have* found a way. I will have you out of here so very, very soon—even tonight, while the town attends the feast at the Handlers'. Yes, my dear, I will. But you must be brave, and you will have to help an old woman. Do not be frightened of her. She will be kind to you."

Actually, Fee has no idea how kind the old woman will be. But Fee knows the woman will appreciate Besse's assistance and will want her to stay. Life will certainly be better for Besse at a cottage in the woods than it is for her here.

And if the girl has something up her sleeve, some plan to help herself, then it is good they are extricating her tonight. It may prevent Besse from doing something that could bring the wrath of the master—or the prince—down upon her.

"Stay here, liebchen. I will return soon with some stew for you, and we will pack your meager belongings. Yes, you will leave, but you will be safely escorted. Have no further fear."

Fee's voice is tearful. She knows she will now see but little of the child she has raised with no help from the mistress. Besse is only beginning to comprehend how to do housework and run a household, and she must continue to learn to read. But the exigencies are what they are.

Fee leaves the room with a heavy heart. At the stairwell, she spies Dunkel starting to ascend toward Besse's chamber yet again. Her face hardens in anger. She has only her whole body and soul to block his advance. She bounds down the stairwell toward the master, wanting desperately to loom over the large man, if only that were possible.

"Stop, you monster!"

He laughs. "I am the master of this house, Fee. I'll have my way with any and all of its inhabitants, I will! Ye'll not stop me. If ye try, ye'll leave my employ once and for all!"

"Ha!" she replies. "As if I have no place to go, sir. If it were not for leaving the girl entirely at your mercy, I would have been gone a long time ago."

"Insolence! Ye *will* leave me. I'm sick of the sight of ye!

Fee does not budge. In frustration, Dunkel grumbles and turns to head back down the stairs again.

"Now, where's my supper and my ale—no, my mead! I'm in a mood to celebrate your departure, I am!"

Hidden under the stairwell, a solitary figure grasps his weapon and rock, yet he sees no opportunity to strike with the servant in the way, practically hanging on the man like that. *Begone, wench!* Bo thinks. *I'll be even your savior! Ye'll surely thank me, ye will, and they'll ne'er catch me!*

He waits impatiently.

◆ ◆ ◆

Dunkel seats himself heavily at the table in the great hall. He shouts, "Bring me mead and a fine stew! Do it quickly! I'll not have any more insolence from my servants!"

From their vantage just behind the entry from the kitchen to the solar, Rose and Peter cringe. The potion is in the bowl. Rose squeezes Peter's hand as they peer out carefully and pray silently for the success of their scheme.

Instantly, a servant brings his stew and a chalice of mead. The wooden chalice is carved with images of Norse gods, most prominently Thor with a giant hammer. This is a luxury Rose would not expect of the pinchpenny.

The master growls, takes the proffered supper, and next calls for a hunk of bread and a spoon. He takes a large drink from the cup. "And more mead!" he shouts as he shovels a mouthful of stew, then another, then another into his mouth.

"This has an extra pleasant taste, it does," he says out loud to himself as he spoons up the stew. "A new spice? That Fee shtill has shome shurprises for me, doeshn't she? Doeshn't she?" Suddenly he is slurring his words, but he finishes the meal plus an additional pint of mead.

Behind the hearth, Rose suppresses a chuckle, pleased with this manifestation of success of her plan. Peter scowls at her. He takes no pride in this action. The pair retreat into the kitchen.

As Dunkel rises from the table, Fee appears and circles the man without a word. At the open hearth, she calls for a bread and spoon. She hollows out the bread and with tears in her eyes scoops a good helping of stew from the pot. She leaves silently and ascends to her young charge.

The mistress has not appeared at Fee's door to demand her own meal—which is a bit surprising—but Fee is grateful for the time to do what she must for Besse. She sighs and enters the door.

Besse will not eat, not even a small handful. She looks up at the servant, her eyes almost pleading. "Did you mean it, Fee, that I might depart this dungeon this very night?"

"Come, liebchen—let us bundle your belongings. But first, give me a hug."

Besse is taken aback a bit to hear such a request from her servant, but she will not refuse a moment of comfort and solace. She wraps her arms around the ample waist of the one person who has really cared for her her entire life.

The action brightens Fee's spirit a bit, and together the two begin the small chore of packing. Now Besse even smiles, which Fee finds a bit alarming. She supposes the maiden realizes she is truly leaving the brute. Fee can only hope for the best. Once again, anger wells within her, and she is resolved to keep the maiden safe. *I must prevent the master from seeking her out, which he surely will. But how?*

◆ ◆ ◆

Now is the time for Jacques to enter the household. The servants are startled by his sudden appearance, and Liesel approaches him, her hand outstretched with intent to push him out.

He laughs. "Ye'll not forestall me, *servant*. Tis me father's house, and I'll see him, I will." Then his eyes widen as he spies Peter and Rose. "So, ye're alive, are ye?" he says to Peter. "I wonder what business ye have in this house. Perhaps the master is really wealthy enough t' rob, he is. But ye'll not have the chance. Stay out of me way."

He brushes them all aside and holds his head high, entering the solar before Peter, Rose, or any of the servants can recover from their shock.

He will confront Dunkel once again. In fact, he is desperate, having lost the purloined items. This man is his father and cannot escape his responsibility!

And there he is, slurring his words and barely holding up his head. He is clearly drunk and would not remember any such encounter. Does Jacques dare take this chance to attack the old brute? He gives a quick glance around the chamber, then realizes there is nothing of value to purloin.

Still hiding in the shadow of the stairs, Bo sees Jacques just as Jacques sees him. For a moment, the thief and bandit eye each other with surprise and suspicion. Then Jacques grins. Bo watches this unknown thief stomp into the hall, but he can think of no reason to stop him. This boy has more courage than Bo can muster. But it is no surprise they share the same intentions toward this man, who does what he pleases with no regard toward who gets hurt, like some arrogant king!

Soon Bo hears a thud, which is followed shortly by Jacques's exit from the solar. He shrugs his shoulders at Bo, then winks and starts to stride out of the house.

Bo decides he does not like this boy, whose arrogance leads him to put himself in danger. This thought surprises him, as he realizes it could apply to himself!

But wait. Now Jacques turns around and pushes Bo out of the way behind the stairs.

"Not ready to leave?" Bo says with a laugh.

"Hush! I'll be taking me leave soon enough."

"Ye just want to see the results of your effort, ye do. Is he . . .?"

"We shall see."

~ Chapter 46 ~

The first course of the Handlers' feast is rolled on elaborate carved wooden carts with wheels into the center of the hall. Heady aromas fill the chamber, and the chatter dies down as guests marvel at the arrangements of fish, fowl, and fruits. On each cart is a carved gourd, lit from inside by a candle—provided by Peter. There are dragons, faces, angels. The guests applaud in approval as the prince rises, and all must quiet down now.

"We have asked our kind host and hostess for permission to speak before grace. We have a few announcements, which we are pleased to make."

The crowd begins to murmur in a frisson of excitement, then quickly hushes—some with an expression of embarrassment. The guests did not anticipate any explanations for their observations about the royals, but it seems at least some will be forthcoming.

"My Liege, My Lady," continues the prince, nodding to the duke and duchess. "*Frauen und Herren*," he says to the crowd, "we welcome you to the household of our esteemed host and hostess, Artur and Gute Handler. We are ever in personal debt, as is our treasury, to your hard work and hospitality." He nods to the host and hostess.

He is interrupted very briefly with polite applause, until he holds up a hand and turns to address the guests.

"For many years, the Handlers have been inviting you to this feast at the time of our harvest, and we are always delighted to be included in the festivities. Yet we have other important matters here. We are especially honored that our lord and lady, the Duke and Duchess of Burgundy, have deigned to see fit to join us this year. We are proud to announce a substantial contract of soldiery service to His Liege. As we have also just concluded a contract with his lordship, the Duke of York, it is particularly apropos that we celebrate this year with the English theme of Michaelmas. We also thank Burgundy for the provision of excellent wines to accompany our meal."

As he speaks, servants present the guests servings of a delicious soup of wild fowl garnished with herbs and vegetables from the market and the prince's own garden. Then they follow with servings of stew, fish, and fruit in messes of two at the head table and of four to six at the other tables. Expert carvers stand ready to offer their assistance at each table.

Goblets of imported glass from Venice, provided by Serge Kaufmann at the head table, are a marvel to behold. Most of the guests have never seen the like. They are filled with aromatic, beautiful red wine perfected over centuries in the duke's realm—the gift of Bacchus transformed by the finest vintners. This truly promises to be a fine celebration.

As he clears his throat for his next announcements, Henrik approves of the sense of heightened excitement in the room. "Lords and ladies, Frauen und Herren, I have just a few more important announcements. If you all will raise your goblets in a toast to My Liege and lady, Duke Philip and his wife, on the occasion of their consent to the betrothal of their most exquisite daughter, Giselle, to our son, the future ruler of Quellestadt, Prince Charles!"

The guests wildly applaud this announcement, then raise their cups.

Though not informed in advance, the young prince is not surprised, as he certainly surmised this was the reason he was personally sent to retrieve the young maiden. And now having met her, he heartily approves. This is certainly a strategic alliance, avoiding any risk of invasion by Burgundy, whose realm is larger than France and whose conquests, both military and political, are widely celebrated.

For her part, Giselle is taken aback. She had always hoped her father would consult her in such a matter. She blushes freely but keeps her place. Nevertheless, she realizes, she could do worse than be a princess in this realm. And to be married to one so intelligent, so compassionate, and so brave—not to mention so handsome—would be the dream of any maiden. She turns her face toward young Charles, and he nods with a smile. *And I think he likes me!*

Enchanteresse, having failed in her attempt to rid the world of the young maiden—the maiden who even now captures the hearts and minds of yet another populace without lifting a finger—keeps her dark thoughts to herself. She must give the appearance of consent, but she need not look happy about it, so she merely bows her head.

Philip rises to acknowledge the cheers of the guests. He nods to the prince, then to the dauphin, to show his approval. He gives his wife a stern look, a silent order. Her thoughts are roiling, and Philip knows it, watching her face turn redder and redder until he thinks her head might explode.

Suddenly Enchanteresse rises, politely excusing herself to her estranged husband, the prince, and the host and hostess.

"I feel quite ill. I profusely apologize, but I would not encumber your excellent hospitality with my own distress. Please excuse me."

"I am most discomfited, your ladyship," Gute replies. "I would not dream of forcing you to stay, at the risk of increasing your own discomfort. Perhaps if you are well later, I shall bring you a basket, that you may at least enjoy some of the evening's offerings."

Having no intention of being available to accept such a gift, the duchess smiles inwardly, bows to her husband and the prince and princess, then departs.

She must plan further, but perhaps it will be a bit easier now that she knows the whereabouts of her previous ward. After all, accidents do happen. She shall bide her time awhile longer.

She does not notice the duke nod to his guard at the door, who discretely follows her outside and approaches her.

"My lady, forgive me," the guard says, "but I am instructed by His Liege, your husband, to accompany you out of the principality immediately. If you will return to the castle to gather your entourage, I would be most grateful to serve."

"The impudence!" she hisses. "Throw me out, will he? Well, I have no intention of sharing in the celebration of that empty-headed strumpet! Let us proceed."

The guard is grateful not to be the immediate object of the duchess's hatred or punishment, and he sighs in relief. He manages to convey an air of distress at the plight of the duchess, although it is entirely insincere. Yet he will carry out his orders.

The lady herself, of course, busily hatches new plots as she almost absent-mindedly calls for her retinue and they prepare to leave. Her old attendant will accompany her. Despite the woman's failure to ensure the dispatch of the duke's daughter, Enchanteress will forgive that failure in favor of having one trustworthy, loyal servant. *In fact, while I may not return to the duchy myself, that one can. She may yet serve a use, if she does not bungle my orders again.*

The duchess's entourage settles on horseback. As the guard assists in securing her belongings to the pack animals, they are joined by the prince's own guard. Now the soldiers surround the expelled group and escort them to the city gate. There Enchanteresse is suddenly accosted by a most handsome and well-armed man.

She is more indignant than alarmed. "Are you here to do me harm, sir? For you could do no more than has already pierced my heart!"

"Your ladyship," says the man with a bow, "I am known as Borg. I place myself at your service, as you and I have more in common than you would know."

"I am intrigued, sir," she answers, waving off the guard. "What could we ever have in common?"

Borg smiles. He has succeeded in catching her attention. "Why, madame, I am a well-trained soldier once of Quellestadt, one who was hired by His Liege to serve in his guard these past two years. And now I am dismissed from this principality and from his grace's service!"

He clenches his fists in anger. The prince had ensured that Borg was fit for only one career—soldiery. His services were hired out to the Duke of Burgundy. But then those prospects disappeared when the war between England and France ended, allowing the duke to reduce the number of men he needed for defense.

With no opportunity for further employment, Borg and other displaced soldiers were forced to do what they must for sustenance and survival. Soldiers of fortune, some call them. Brigands, others say. And now they have been discarded by the very rulers who have trained them or ensured recompense for their services. To be banished is too much to bear! Something must be done. But the time is inopportune. He must wait.

Borg takes a deep breath, forcing himself to relax. He continues, "I wish to accompany you and serve in your protection. From what I have heard in this principality, His Liege's guards should not be . . . trusted"—whispering the last phrase so as not to offend the guards—"to serve you above other allegiances."

Enchanteresse raises her eyebrows, then smiles a sardonic grin at best. "You are right, sir. I would hear of your travails and plans, and then we shall see. You may accompany us."

She does not know if she can trust this man, but she knows he would not dare attack her in company of the guards. Perhaps he could be of use.

Just as the entourage begins to depart the city gates, they are stopped by two soldiers.

"You may go, madame," says one. "However, we are arresting your servant."

Enchanteresse visibly reddens, even through layers of caked facial powders. "Impudence! She is not your subject, and she is of invaluable aid to me. Moreover, she is old and deserves some respect and good treatment."

The old servant cringes, but allows herself to be taken down gruffly from her horse.

The soldier warns off any additional reaction from the duchess with a stern glance as he accuses, "She has attempted to poison your stepdaughter, and she may not leave."

The duchess's face betrays her lack of surprise at this revelation with rage. "Have you proof? If not, begone!"

"Indeed, madame, we have proof. Once she talks—and she will—I would advise you to move on as quickly as possible," he warns. "Word will spread, and you may find it difficult to acquire sanctuary."

"Audacity!" Enchanteress's eyes go wide. She raises a hand to strike the man, then settles heavily onto her steed in futility. "Very well, take her—but treat her well, or I shall hear of it and act upon it."

She turns to urge her party onward as the guards accompany an astonished old lady back within the gates. The old woman has only been a faithful servant but has now been discarded. Oh, yes, she will talk! If only to beg the mercy of the nobles.

Following her new guard, Borg, Enchanteresse rides out of the city holding her head high, not allowing even a glimmer of her inner conflict to show in her visage or her carriage. Once out of sight of the walls, however, her shoulders noticeably droop.

Where can I go? she despairs. *I do not deserve such treatment. That snippet has no business thinking she is better than I. I raised her, not her own mother. I trained her. I taught her. I gave her sanctuary! And now, she is to become a true princess! It is not fair! How shall I go on?*

She does not go far, however, before a familiar rider approaches the group. His face is full of concern and compassion—two emotions of which the duchess is entirely incapable. She straightens herself astride her mount, lifts her chin: the now emotionally naked Diana confronting the astonished Actaeon.

"Gaillard! What fare you here?" Her face hardens as she recalls the heart in the sack, the heart that was *not* that of her stepdaughter. "You have failed me abominably, deceived me, yet you would still dare to show yourself in my presence! Is that homesickness I see in your face? Well, I would well advise you never to return to Burgundy, for our plot is no longer a secret. You will not be welcome there!"

Then, suddenly, astonishment and realization appear for the briefest moment upon her visage. "You knew!" she exclaims. "You knew she was here! You went directly to Philip!" She shakes with anger. "How dare you! It is you who are the source of my banishment! How could you, if you ever loved me?"

Gaillard spreads his hands, consternation on his face. "Anger has never been becoming to you, my lady. It ages you."

She raises her arm and points at him, fire in her eyes. "How dare you!"

Borg recognizes the huntsman who defeated him in the woods. He reaches carefully for his sword, taking advantage of a chance for revenge under the pretense of protecting the duchess.

Enchanteresse, still breathing heavily in anger, speaks directly to Gaillard. "Why should I not let my guard end your miserable life?"

Gaillard shakes his head and continues, "Can you not see, my lady, that I am still in love with you?" His eyes blur with tears, and he reaches out for his erstwhile lover. "I have cleaned a small home for you—for us—in the woods. I can provide for us, and you shall be waited upon hand and foot. Come follow me, and I am yours."

Enchanteresse straightens her back and replies imperiously, "That may never be, sir, as you are a reminder of my failure. Indeed, you are failure itself, and I will not countenance it. Borg! Let this miserable example of cowardice be. That shall be my payment for services rendered. Huntsman, begone, and leave me to my misery. I shall ride to France, and His Majesty will honor me with a presence at court. He would be most grateful for any intelligence I can provide concerning Burgundy."

Though she feels betrayed, her heart will not allow her to be the cause of the demise of a man who truly professes his love for her.

As Borg hesitates, she becomes adamant. "Borg, sheathe your sword if you wish to serve me!"

The soldier, still angry, takes a second to contemplate his future. He decides service to the duchess is preferable to being hunted as an outlaw. He shrugs and complies.

- Chapter 46 -

That is it, then. She will ride south, avoiding her husband's realm and allies, then cross the Juras into France, where the duke is not the subject of much love.

Gaillard relaxes his shoulders. He bows to the duchess. "Always remember, my lady, that you will be welcome with me. If I have failed you, it is only because I have not failed My Liege, nor have I allowed harm to come to his daughter. I have more loyalties than just to you, madame, but know that I shall always love you."

Enchanteresse looks away from him, unable to meet his eyes. "You have brought me much shame, sir, for your betrayal. I am resolved to France."

"So be it, madame," he says as his brows furrow in concern. He turns his back as the duchess rides away, facing his own future. He can make a future for himself in Quellestad, where his skills and assistance are welcome.

- Chapter 47 -

As the events outside the city gates unfold, the feast continues at the Handler household. The tables are cleared of the first course, and the first entremets are revealed. Servants carry out a large table draped with white linen, upon which sits a huge confection of cakes and spun sugar. The guests are astonished and delighted to behold the handiwork of confectionary artisans of the highest standard.

A giant dragon of purest white, specked with gold leaf, sits threateningly at the center, surrounded by gourds carved to represent a walled city of gold domes. Now the neck fins are manipulated by long, thin poles, becoming bellows that force the fire of a lit candle through the creature's mouth, and a red glow appears in its eyes. Applause soon breaks out among the guests, amazed and highly entertained.

"I think you have outdone yourself, Frau Handler," offers Princess Amalia. "I have never seen the like. You must provide me with the name of the artist, for truly that is what this is—art. I must plan a wedding feast, my dear, but I doubt I can impress to this extent."

"You are too kind, madame," Gute replies, "but I am humbled by your approval. There is, of course, more to come. See there—a table with a spun-sugar horn of plenty, with the best fruits of the harvest at its open end. This is the Michaelmas feast of the harvest, after all. And there—a table of carved gourds of fanciful designs with candles shining through to enhance the images." Gute is clearly proud of her arrangements but not arrogant. "Of course," she continues, "I am not personally responsible. Goodness," she says with a laugh,

"I am certainly no artist or artisan. And I will certainly throw some extra compensation to our Dien, who is amazingly resourceful and has worked very hard—as he does every year—to make our feast a success."

"It is certainly kind of you, madame, to acknowledge your household servants. Your generosity is legend, I must say. The prince and I consider it an honor to call you our friends."

Gute glances over at her husband, who is rising to his feet. "Pardon me, Your Highness, but I think this is a good time for the host to make a statement."

"Certainly—as you will," answers the princess with a nod.

Artur stands and claps his hands loudly, capturing the attention of the assemblage. He waits a moment for the general commotion to drop from a boil to a simmer, then sighs and smiles.

"Your Highnesses, My Liege, Frauen und Herren, Gute and I want to welcome you to our annual harvest feast. As you can see by the magnificent artistry of our confectioners and carvers, our theme this year was inspired by a contract with the good Duke of York from England. Before you lies an exposition of the elements of the story of Saint George and the Dragon, of which you will learn more later.

"We are especially honored to have the presence and beneficence of Their Majesties, the prince and princess, and their son, the dauphin; and of His Liege, the Duke of Burgundy. I must apologize for the abrupt departure of her ladyship, the duchess. Nevertheless, we welcome you all in celebration of a successful year, more especially in celebration of the betrothal of His Highness, Prince Charles, to her ladyship, Giselle, the daughter of His Liege, Duke Philip."

The guests break into applause, and Artur waits for subsidence before continuing, "And yet, we have one more reason for celebration . . ."

Gute beams at this point, and Hans covers a smile with his hand. But how will Ebouisante respond? He throws a covert glance down the table and catches her eye.

At first she blushes to receive his attention, but then her eyes widen as she realizes what Herr Handler is about to announce. She struggles to suppress a touch of anger at not having been consulted. Yet she finds that her heart agrees with this decision, so she quickly lowers her head and smiles, a demure appearance that hardly befits her assertive personality.

Artur takes a deep breath, then says, "Gute and I are proud to announce the betrothal of our beloved son, Hans, apprenticed to our business, to the beautiful daughter of Serge and Blanche Kaufmann, Ebouisante! We welcome her into our family and look forward to a long and wonderful relationship with such an illustrious family."

Again, a round of rigorous applause, even as many of the young, unattached maidens at the more distant tables frown in disappointment. Why weren't their parents more aggressive in pursuing the Handlers on their behalf? The two greatest prizes in the principality have now been awarded, all in one evening. Who will be left for them? A round of collective sighs breezes across their tables.

Prince Henrik rises, raising his hands to silence the crowd. "I propose a toast to the couples. May they have a long life of happiness and success together! Prosit!"

He raises his glass of wine and takes a long draught. There is more applause, then all raise their mugs—some in quiet envy; others more heartily, with sincere good wishes.

Now guests commence whispering to each other. "These are good matches. An alliance with Burgundy can only improve the security and prosperity of the principality and its neighbors. And an alliance of the Handlers and Kaufmanns can bode well for the general trade. I hear Herr Kaufmann has created connections all the way to the Papal States. And it is clear that our northern trade is in some jeopardy."

None of this is heard by the prince or princess, of course, but these assertions are actually quite correct. These alliances are precisely what His Majesty had in mind. It is the precise reason he invited the Kaufmanns to settle in his domain.

After a time, the entremets are removed, and fresh bread bowls, plates, carafes, and pitchers are placed upon the tables. Wine, ale, and mead are refilled. Servants enter the room with large trays of meats, foul, fish, fruits, and vegetables. The carvers and servants again take their places with their respective messes and begin to serve their charges. Everything is exceptionally savory, and no expense has been spared in the salting and seasoning of each venison or pork roast. Delicious scents fill the chamber, and almost all mouths are watering in anticipation. What a celebration! No one will forget this grand evening.

Conversations of planning ensue, particularly among the parents of the boys and maidens at the far tables. This is a grand opportunity for them, after all, not just to conduct business but also to appraise the possible matches for their children.

"I should very much like to speak with you, sir, and with your lovely wife," say some. Others, unimpressed, answer, "Perhaps after the feast."

Some offer flattery: "I am truly impressed by the carriage"—or the poise, the demure nature, the assertiveness, etcetera—"of your young daughter" or "your very handsome son."

The children themselves speculate. "Oh no, Gerta—my father is talking to the father of that lout sitting over there, the one who cannot even use his napkin after each bone he gnaws to pieces!"

Or, "Look, Franz! Your parents are conversing with the parents of that beautiful, buxom maiden over there. This could be very sweet for you!" This is rejoined by an elbow to the midriff. But some boys are too young to be interested in such things.

Weaving in and out of these tables, the servants snicker under their breath, as their own children are not faced with any such anxiety or anticipation.

Ultimately, the conversation winds down as the guests are satiated. The servants begin to clear the tables once again.

At an appropriate point, Artur nods to Jurg, who opens the door to allow the entry of a gentleman in green leggings, tunic, and a hat at least two sizes too big for him with a large feather to its side. This is the second of the entremets. The crowd hushes as he approaches the head table and bows deeply. He has of course been apprised of the guests present, as well as the departure of the duchess.

He clears his throat and begins, "Your Highnesses, My Liege, ladies and gentlemen, we are but a troupe of poor mummers hoping to catch your eyes and ears in entertainment—a favor we beg of you but briefly and with all due gratitude to Herr and Frau Handler, our host and hostess."

Polite applause arises as this point, and guests lean forward, the better to hear above any commotion.

"Tonight we bring you the traditional Michaelmas tale of Saint George and the Dragon, which is as follows:

East of Carthage, lost crusader
Far from England's welcome shore
This Odysseus finds invader
Flaming creature famed of yore

Kingdom cringing, crying, cowering
Libya's daughters gone before
Now one virgin princess flowering
Lone remains of kingdom's store

Must to sacrifice herself, so brave then
Spite king's efforts to implore
First the Dragon, then the maiden
Neither will hear nothing more

Many brave knights try to save her
All surrender 'fore the roar
Burned and poison'd, none do favor
No true hero to the core

Couldst decipher means of conquest
Only pure of heart this chore

Might accomplish, but True God bless'd
Beast's betrayal, none before

Now Sir George sans trepidation
Sees the quest, cannot ignore
Knows he's sent here, revelation
Brings the brave knight to the fore

Promised riches, promised princess
Though this man the beast will gore
Disdains all and only winces
Will do right, wants nothing more

Counter evil, spouting fire
Burned and poison'd to the core
Dove will save him from the mire
Brings him acorn from woods' floor

Once revived, faith never vanquished
Pierces yon famed beast of lore
Quits the kingdom, quest accomplished
And to all, true faith restore

Now to England's waiting shore."

With that, the narrator bows deeply again to the table on the dais, then to tables on each side of the chamber. He backs slowly out of the room.

Enthusiastic applause greets him, and he can catch snippets of speech.

"Remarkable presentation."

"This promises to be a wonderful mummery. Frau Handler has outdone herself."

He smiles and withdraws.

Next, a frowning man in a white tunic and makeshift crown enters, accompanied by a young boy dressed as a maiden. The maiden character is his daughter, the princess.

The man bows to the head table, then speaks, "My daughter, as King of Libya I have reached the end of my travails. I would sooner sacrifice myself than send you to the beast. Yet if I cannot imprison you, then I cannot stop you. Would you save the heart of an old man and allow me to persuade you to remain?"

The princess replies, "To what good, sire—Father? If I do not go, he will set his poisonous fire upon all our kingdom, and none shall remain. I will go, which will give you at least a year. Perhaps I can tell him to move on, that we have no more virgins to offer. You will not stop me, for then your subjects will rebel and take me at any rate."

The king buries his head in his hands, then reaches out and takes the "maiden" by the shoulders. "My better judgment tells me 'tis true, but mine own heart rebels, for I love thee more than mine own life!"

As usual, impromptu conversation amongst the audience interrupts—or perhaps enhances—the presentation.

"She is so scrawny—were I the dragon, I would reject her instantly. See, she has little meat and no breasts!"

Subdued laughter.

"Perhaps she will taste better well done."

More laughter at this reference to the dragon's ability to cook his own meal.

"Is this Libyan kingdom worth saving?" one asks. "What have they to offer to the world?"

An answer from across the room: "Certainly no virgins!"

More laughter.

The princess waits for the commentary to subside, then continues, "Fear not, sire, for I have no fear in mine own bosom. I shall go forward to do what is right, and you shall continue ruling your kingdom with intelligence and mercy."

- Chapter 47 -

The king shakes his head. "We are out of brave knights, my dear, who might save you. Would that I were younger, and could face the beast myself!"

"Brave words, befitting a king, sire!"

A man enters wearing a painted suit of armor and surrounded by a painted horse.

"Who are you, sir?" the king questions. "Do we dare believe you are a knight come to save our precious daughter? For if you should succeed, we shall offer you great riches and her hand in marriage."

Another interruption: "Riches, maybe, but would you marry that?"

"I shall accept neither," the man on the horse answers. "I am but a poor crusader, called Sir George by those who know me. And they know my faith is true, though I have been brought off course for England for reasons unbeknownst to me!"

Another comment from the audience: "His *true faith* has clearly led him astray." It is followed by more subdued laughter.

Yet there are two present with more pressing matters in mind. Ebouisante leans over the table and nods at Hans. It is time. This is his opportunity to come to the aid of young Besse, and the woman in the woods is prepared to receive her.

Hans nods in return, whispers an excuse into his father's ear, then quietly rises. He skirts the outside wall of the chamber, leaving the feast via the kitchen, much to the surprise of the servants and cooks.

Hans's departure goes unnoticed as the performance continues. All present are well entertained at the appearance of the Dragon and the fight and final conquest.

They are more so delighted when the desserts arrive afterward.

"Lebkuchen!" some exclaim. "See, they have castles and dragons burnt into them. And see the table with the spun-sugar north wind and the sugar snow? Our hosts have truly outdone themselves. What a feast! What an entertainment!"

Suddenly, the door is thrown open, and anxious people burst into the chamber. As they see the tables filled with treats, their eyes go wide, as they themselves have never been so privileged to experience the like. Thus, they hesitate, but only for a moment. Then they recapture their excited fear as they yell out, "Sire, sire—there is fire! Fire at the Hammer tower! Fire, fire!"

~ Chapter 48 ~

Fire within the confines of the walls of any city promises to be devastating. Some chaos ensues. Guests jump to their feet in alarm. Couples squeeze hands, kiss, or even hug. Children seek out their parents. The excellence of the celebration is completely forgotten as the level of anxiety rises.

The prince surveys the scene and shakes his head, knowing he must take charge. "Frauen und Herren, if you would please indulge me for a moment."

He rises from his seat on the dais, commanding the attention of the guests before they can start a total panic. Now they must gather their wits, as they do not dare anger him.

"If you will, we must thank our host and hostess, Herr Artur and Frau Gute Handler, for this most incredible feast and entertainment. We are sure, under the circumstances, that they will excuse us all from expressing our appreciation personally."

Artur nods to the prince.

"With your permission, my lord," His Highness says, turning briefly to the duke, who also nods in return, "we will ask that the men leave first, in an orderly manner, to assist in quenching this fire. The abode in question is in a corner tower of the city, and you need merely follow the crowd. It is imperative we put it out before it escapes into the structures of the inner city, or there will be very little left for us to celebrate. Mesdames, if you would collect your children and return to your lodgings. You may pick up some lebkuchen from the table as you leave. Please do not despair. Our guards will see to the safety of all within the city."

The guests allow the royalty and nobility to leave the chamber first. Hands squeeze again, and hugs are shared with whispered words of love or admonishments to be careful. Then the men move quickly toward the door.

An almost palpable smell of fear rises to join the savory aromas of the feast still lingering in the hall. Some men have thoughts concerning the safety of loved ones. Others, with some guilt, have thoughts concerning the safety of goods brought for trade—even the wagons and the horses. What about the horses? The atmosphere visibly darkens even as some of the guests take torches to light their way through the city.

Greta rises and scans the area quickly, noting the absence of her brother. Where is Hans? Is he already out of the chamber? He will certainly go to fight the fire, without a second thought. Then she sees Ebouisante is still seated at the dais table along with her mother, who is leaning over to hug and comfort her. Greta has never seen Ebouisante frightened. She is always the picture of confidence and self-assurance, capable of holding her own and functioning in a world dominated by men. Now she appears whiter than La Claire! Greta hurries to her side.

"Ebouisante—my future sister, my dear—do not fear. The men will control the fire. It is in the tower of the city wall, so it is easier to contain. You will be safe here, if you and you mother would like to stay. I will ask my mama and papa to prepare accommodation."

"Oh, my dear Greta," Ebouisante speaks through deep sobs. "That is so kind, but it is not necessary. It is Hans! We are executing a plan to remove Besse, the daughter of Dunkel Hammer, to safety this very night. He has left the feast to get her."

"Oh!" Greta exclaims. "Then he is in that house, in that tower!"

Ebouisante gathers her wits and stops crying. "I cannot stay here, Greta. I must go to him—to them." She steps off the dais, a new look of determination in her face. No fire will prevent her from carrying out her promise to bring Besse to safe refuge. She is sure in her heart both Hans and Besse are safe.

Greta holds up a hand to stop her. She will assure herself of her brother's safety. "You must remain here. I will go see to Hans. It has always been my responsibility to save him from himself. I shall return promptly."

Greta turns this way and that, waving her hands in the air before her in some agitation. There is no time to plan, and now she must also help see to Besse's safety. She is frightened by the prospect that this may be one heroic action too many for Hans.

Greta looks quickly for her parents, but they have left the chamber. This she must do alone.

She has virtually never left the safety of the walls of the city, but she does not know where her brother's path will lead her. There, on that table, is a bread bowl. She will take that. It will help her find her way in the dark.

With no small amount of trepidation, she grabs the bread and flees the house.

◆ ◆ ◆

A crowd assembles outside the Dunkel tower household. There is great fear; it is almost palpable in the unnaturally warm wind escaping the open door.

The city guards have lost no time arriving, and Captain Erich sees the first servants fleeing the tower. He has the presence of mind to order his men to quickly detain anyone coming out, as the prince will certainly want to question everyone later.

Glancing about, he suddenly recognizes someone ducking beneath his men, clearly not wanting to be captured. It is Jacques! But why would he be in this house?

He points at Jacques and yells to the guard, "Catch that one!"

But he is too late. The boy ducks furiously and manages to elude his potential captors. His speed is helped by the thought that capture within these city walls means death.

The air fills with the odor of burned straw. Peter and Rose run out, coughing from the inhalation of the rapidly increasing smoke. The guards surround and hold them.

"Let us go!" shouts Rose. "We must find water t' help put this out, we must!"

The guard holding Rose is not to be deterred. He looks at her sternly. "There are ample people to help, but you must remain here, by the order of the captain."

Peter puts his arm around Rose's shoulders. "Rose, my dear Rose"—interrupted by a cough—"we must catch our breath. Rest yourself. I know you want to help, but we will be of little use."

Of course, offering assistance is truthfully the farthest thing from the woman's mind. It was merely an excuse to escape—and it failed miserably. Rose sighs and frowns. If Peter has been successful, and the armorer fails to awaken and escape, there will certainly be an inquiry. She will have to ponder how to extricate herself and Peter from this dilemma. It actually surprises her that she cares about Peter enough to think of her life tied to his.

The pair are soon joined by the small number of household servants, in equal need of fresh air. As they were all close to the only entrance to the tower, they are out quickly, none the worse for wear.

Next the apprentice exits, covering his nose and mouth with a cloth, coughing only a bit but clearly frightened. His eyes are wide as he approaches the captain.

"Sir, sir! There are others inside! The master, the mistress! And Fee! She is still in there, making sure everyone gets out. You must help! Oh, oh! And where will I go? What shall I do?"

"Calm down, boy!" Captain Erich states. "We will find accommodation for you. For now, stay here."

As smoke now visibly emanates from the open doorway, the crowd is surprised to see Rudi defiantly exiting with the young bandit, Bo, in hand by the top of his ragged tunic. Rudi sports a bruise above his right eye. He pushes the boy into the hands of a guard, then, to everyone's surprise, races back into the smoke! No one is foolish enough to run into the home after Rudi.

Just then, the dauphin arrives on the scene, surveils it briefly, and calls to the guard captain.

~ Chapter 48 ~

"Captain," Charles shouts over the rising noise of the now-burgeoning crowd. "We must harness the assistance of the populace in order to put this fire out expeditiously. Send everyone back to their homes, and tell them to bring every pot and bucket they can find, filled with water from the wells. Then form them into a line and have them pass the buckets toward the flames."

The captain nods. "Yes, sire. That is a brilliant idea. Let us hope it works." He turns to his guards. "You must act quickly to follow His Highness's command."

"Yes, sir!" answers one.

"Sire," the captain continues, addressing the dauphin, "we have gathered all who have escaped the tower."

Charles responds, "Good thinking, sir. His Highness will certainly want to question all within the household. And did I just see someone run *into* the flames?"

"Yes, sire. I believe it is the former journeyman of the armorer. I can only imagine he has concern for the mistress of the house. *His* mistress, sire, if you understand me." He clears his throat, embarrassed by having stated what is in his mind. Then he shrugs and tries to divert the thought. "Or perhaps he is just a brave one to save as many inside as possible. I do not believe it is safe for anyone with that smoke, but we could not stop him. I have ordered my men not to allow anyone else inside."

Part of the crowd disperses to comply with the order to obtain pots and buckets, while others go to gather their families and servants to flee the city. Seemingly, then, it is madness to see a maiden rushing toward the tower, now with visible flames emanating from the ground floor through the open doorway. Yet there is Greta, fighting back tears as she grabs one arm after another, asking after Hans, who is nowhere to be seen. She pushes her way to the front, where the guards restrain her.

Captain Erich approaches her. "Fräulein, you must leave. This is a dangerous situation, and no place for onlookers."

Greta looks around desperately, consternation on her face, fear in her heart. She spots the dauphin and begs. "Your Highness! Sire! Please help me!"

"Captain, I know this maiden," Charles says as he strides over. "Calm down, Greta. What is it?"

"Please, sire—I must find Hans! I know he is in there!"

His eyes go wide in surprise. "Are you saying Hans is *inside* that tower?"

"Yes, sire," she responds breathlessly, the consternation still clearly etched into her visage. She looks like a concerned mother, with lines of strain wrinkled from too many similar situations. "Ebouisante told me. She sent him to help Besse, the armorer's daughter."

Hans emerges from the smoke, a dazed Besse in his arms, her eyes fixated upon her handsome savior. He gently puts her down, then takes her hand to lead her away from the crowd.

Suddenly Greta spots them both. "Oh! There they are!" she cries with relief.

Charles has no time to digest the thought of why Hans would do such a thing. He shouts out, "Hans! Hans! You must stop!"

Friend or not, even Hans will not disobey the dauphin. He stops, pushing Besse a bit behind his back and whispering a word of comfort.

Besse has rescued Dolly, and she hugs the ragged doll close to her. She says nothing, but her thoughts are roiling with the mixed sensations of freedom, admiration for her rescuer—so handsome!—and the pain of recovering her breath from the exposure to the smoke. Yet oddly, she cannot find gratitude among her feelings. And where is her father? While he lives, she can never feel saved.

After coughing deeply, Hans gives a slight bow, then begs, "Your Highness, please excuse me. I am on an errand of mercy, which I cannot explain here. I beg your indulgence to leave. I promise to return soon, and I shall answer all questions then."

Charles knits his brow, perplexed, then nods his head. "As a token of our friendship, I shall trust your word, Hans. Return to me here with alacrity. Captain, make way for Herr Handler and the girl."

- Chapter 48 -

As Hans turns to go, he spies Greta for the first time. "Gretl! This is no place for you! Have you been following me again?" he says with some agitation.

"As always, I must chase after you to save you from your own foolishness," she chides. "Let me come with you—I can help you."

He shakes his head. "No. This errand I must run on my own. Please go home. You must help Mama and Papa preserve the household and all the merchandise!"

Without another word, Hans clutches Besse's hand and heads for the city gate.

Greta curtsies to the dauphin, then turns toward her home. She waits a brief moment until all eyes are off her, then she veers off toward the gate to follow her brother, ever suspicious of his motives and safety. She has been his voice of reason in the past, and she cannot leave him to his immodest sense of bravura. She can always trust him to get himself in trouble, though she must admit, it always seems to be in the service of someone in need. Nevertheless, she must follow. She shakes her head and breaks small pieces of bread to create a trail past the gate.

The dauphin shakes his own head but has little time to ponder Hans's action. Citizens are now arriving with water. They form a bucket brigade, with the guardsmen themselves taking empty pots and buckets to the city wells to refill them.

As the brigade is at work, one last person emerges from the door and collapses, dropping a torch, her tunic on fire. It is Fee.

Dien spots her immediately. He quickly removes his own tunic and throws it over her to smother the flames. Then he takes her into his arms as she alternately coughs and whimpers.

She is aware enough to see not just her lover but a true angel. She thinks, *Besse is safe. My work is done.* With that, she slips out of consciousness.

♦ ♦ ♦

The fire finally quenched, the dauphin addresses the tired yet still excited citizens and visitors: "We are most grateful for your brave assistance. You may now return to your homes with the knowledge that you have served Quellestadt well."

As Erich ushers the people away, Charles next turns to the detaineees who have exited the tower. "As we will need to make inquiry, those of you who were in the household will be offered the hospitality of our castle for the nonce. You will accompany the guards now, and your immediate needs will be addressed."

Then finally, he puts out a hand to stop Dien from attempting to awaken Fee in an effort to bring her to the castle as well. "Dien, for now you may carry this brave servant to the Handler household and attend to her there. We will send our physician to assist. But you must keep her available to His Highness for questioning."

Dien nods his head in lieu of a bow. "I thank ye, sire! I shall make haste t' comply!"

As he bends to lift his love, he notes the group leaving with the guard includes servants of the Hammer household, a ragged waif he does not recognize holding a slingshot (*How odd!*), Peter and Rose (*Fee will not like this. What is Rose doing here?*). But where are Rudi and the mistress, or the master for that matter? Are they still in the tower? And wasn't that the young thief and murderer, Jacques, who barely escaped the guard?

~ Chapter 49 ~

As surreptitiously as she can manage, Greta follows her brother out the gate of the city, into the darkness, with only the stars shining through the trees to light her way. Hans has quenched his torch, making the quest all the more difficult. She huddles into her tunic with hopes the trail of bread will not fail her, should she lose track of her quarry and need to return on her own.

Darkness in shadows, shadows in darkness—is that even possible? Greta cringes but follows determinedly.

What Greta finds frightening, Besse finds comforting, as always. With Hans at her side, she has no fear of bandits or animals. She actually embraces the dark, which has always been a comfort to her. She actually finds the presence of mind to note the path they take, as she knows she will have to retrace it repeatedly for marketing. Besse remembers the old woman will depend upon her.

That thought actually surprises her. She has never had to think about taking responsibility for herself, no less for someone else. In fact, she has never had to feel grateful or obligated to anyone.

For the first time, it occurs to her that she has never thanked Fee even once for all she has done. After all, Fee is but a servant. But she has been more like a mother to her, certainly far more than her own mother.

The thought is fleeting, however. She visibly hunches over, hugging Dolly even closer, as she trudges onward beside Hans.

Her thoughts turn inward once again as she realizes she has no real control over what the future holds for her. At least, not yet. She resolves to correct that problem. She will never allow herself to be abused again!

Now she notices the handsome young man at her side with even more admiring and calculating eyes. This would be a catch indeed!

Hans meets her glance. She retreats into a cough, averting his view.

"Fear not, fräulien," Hans reassures her, miscalculating the intention of her gaze. "We shall be in the woods but a brief time, on a path well known to me, even in the dark. I will deliver you to safety. There is, as you know, a kindly lady awaiting our arrival. She has provisioned her cottage with all you will need for sustenance."

Hans realizes he must prepare the maiden for her first encounter with the old woman. "Do not be taken aback by her appearance. She unfortunately suffers a very visible malady that cannot be transmitted to you. But her heart is of a greater size, and you shall, for once, be treated with kindness." He smiles. "Moreover, Ebouisante will continue to be your friend, and she and I will visit with some frequency. She reminds me to tell you that she intends to continue working with you on your reading. I hope you will do well with it, but not adopt all her fanciful ideas! She seems to foresee the advancement of women—which is not so bad on the face of it, but this is still a man's world."

He glances at his charge and thinks better of saying anything more. She is certainly withdrawn and not paying attention. This is no surprise. She has just faced two major traumas this very night.

In short order, the pair arrive at Katrina's cottage. Hans strikes the torch, revealing a swept entry.

Besse begins steeling herself for the sight of the old woman. But it is the home itself which takes Besse aback. The cottage has been decorated to look like a giant gingerbread house.

Besse has never been afforded the luxury of cookies or cakes. Fee has always walked her quickly past the bakeries with incredibly enticing scents wafting out of the open stalls and doors. But Besse has heard children speak of these treats with wistful longing in the marketplace.

Is this where Besse will spend her years? It is a pure fantasy. She feels it is perhaps compensation for her lifetime of suffering.

- Chapter 49 -

Yet there is too much light emanating from the windows, and she instinctively shrinks back and shivers.

Hans notes her reaction and deigns to offer her a hug. "You must not fear, Besse. I have told you the lady is kind and supportive. No one will accost you here. Ebouisante and I have begun to spread a message within the city, warning others not to venture this way, for fear of encountering an enchanted cottage inhabited by a witch who attracts and eats children. Of course, this tale is the opposite of truth. But as you can see, we have assisted the lady in giving this home an enchanted appearance, in case anyone does wander this way."

Hans ushers Besse inside, where she is indeed shocked by the appearance of her new guardian, despite Hans's attempts to prepare her. The old woman is covered with bulbous growths. If wandering townspeople were to meet this woman, they would certainly believe she was an old witch who eats children.

But Besse overcomes her reaction quickly as the lady offers her a small cake for the first time in her life. There is one for Hans as well, who eagerly accepts it with a word of gratitude.

Besse takes a tentative bite. How delicious! She smiles, perhaps for the first time in weeks. Can such food exist? Is she to eat like this for the rest of her life? But at what price? This thought causes her to push the small cake away.

"Please, *gütige Frau*—I have done nothing to deserve such a treat."

Katrina's eyebrows rise. "But why, liebchen, must you do anything? All children must taste of the delights in life—as well as the difficulties. It's me prayer that ye'll overcome any revulsion of my appearance, for ye can be of great assistance t' me here, ye can. Ye can help with the marketin' and maintenance, and I can teach you t' cook, t' weave, t' live!"

The old woman settles into a rocking chair near the hearth. "Helpin' this poor young maiden has given me an idea, it has. Though ye may not know it, I've done me share of ills and sins. I've no children of me own. I'd ask that ye allow me t' repay my debts by bringing me the orphans of the city—that I may raise and teach 'em, so that they're not forced t' become beggar waifs."

"You are indeed kind, my lady," Hans replies. "Ebouisante and I will discuss this and see if we can assist you in this regard. It would be a boon to Besse as well, to have other children present."

Besse is overwhelmed by this show of altruism, so foreign to her—with the exception of Fee, of course, to whom she has never given a second thought. She does not care to share her life with these children; Besse equates comfort with solitude in the dark.

Suddenly there is a knock at the door. Hans involuntarily jumps, and Besse instinctively crouches and squeezes Dolly, afraid Dunkel has already discovered her.

"Who is this?" asks Katrina. "Who can find this out-of-the-way hovel at such a late hour?"

Hans takes a steadying breath and opens the door slowly. Through the crack, there appears an apparition of familiar shape. He sighs.

"Fear not, for this is my sister, Greta. She is ever at my heels, out of nothing but the most kindly concern." He turns to her. "Gretl, my dearest sister, you must not have come here. I told you—I do not need your help."

"Yes, you do, Hansl!" she retorts. "You are ever putting yourself into the most dire situations. I must return you safely to our parents and—oh!" Greta exclaims as her gaze falls upon the misshapen features of the lady of the house. "Oh! Forgive my stare, *meine Frau*!"

The lady sighs, then laughs. "Fear not. Do sit yourself by the fire and warm yourself. Enjoy the cake with your brother. I apologize for not having baked another. You are welcome here this evening," the woman continues, "but I hope you will forgive me if I ask that you not return. As you can see, I prefer to guard my privacy."

Before Greta can reply, Hans speaks. "I can assure my sister's acquiescence, my lady, as she would do nothing to bring you grief or harm."

He stares at his sister, and she bows her head with a blush of her cheeks, embarrassed to have exposed any revulsion at the lady's appearance.

She says, "I am sorry to have intruded upon you, *gütige Frau*. Thank you for your hospitality, but I will now take my leave. Come, Hans. We must return to our parents and Ebouisante, your betrothed."

"Betrothed!" exclaims Besse. "I did not know!"

Her thoughts race. She realizes she has been unconsciously making plans concerning Hans, plans she has no right to make. At the same time, she decides she will not dispense entirely with her plans. Scheming is not beyond her.

But first she must arrange her life here, then worry about all else later. The lady is old and will not live forever. Eventually, Besse will need to do something to advance her life. These are dark thoughts, so they comfort her. Perhaps she can take charge of her life, after all. One need only wait and learn.

"Congratulations, me young hero," Katrina says with joy. "I wish ye the best, I do, and I'll delight in having both of ye visit. I'm sure Besse is also grateful and will look forward to seeing ye."

"Yes, yes—do come often," Besse answers. "I want to see you often!"

With that, the brother and sister take their leave. After taking a few steps from the hovel, Hans lights his torch and notes the trail of crumbs.

"Are you trying to attract birds, dear sister?" He pretends offense when she elbows him, then he laughs. "It is a meager attempt to create a trail back. But then, you have never been outside the walls, have you? Ebouisante and I must show you more of the delights of the woods."

Greta is grateful her brother cannot see her flush in the light of his torch. "The woods, dear brother, are *for* the birds. Take me home." She laughs, dispelling any remaining internal trepidation. Then she takes Hans's arm, and the two walk briskly toward the city.

~ Chapter 50 ~

In short time, Hans and Greta approach the tower. At this point, the fire is largely out, except for a few flames escaping the highest tower windows.

Hans spots the young prince surveying the charred scene. He turns to his sister. "You *must* go home now, Gretl. I must speak to the prince. And this is no place for a maiden."

She looks toward the tower. "It is no place for anyone, right now, Hansl. I shall leave you to your promise to His Highness. But first I will admonish you to return to your family and your betrothed as soon as he allows. People are worried about you and your heroic antics."

Thus, she gets in the last word. She gives Hans's arm a squeeze as she inwardly smiles.

Hans hurries toward the dauphin at first, then, remembering himself, he approaches with more respect.

Charles frowns, folds his arms, and taps his foot. "Hans, you have much explaining to do, but I shall allow it to wait until my father's inquiry. For now, I would ask you to accompany me, along with the guard captain, to inspect the interior. I must investigate this scene myself and report to His Highness. I am not sure all who were inside are now safe. The whereabouts of the armorer and his wife are still unknown. And one man, perhaps the journeyman, was seen running *into* the home, despite the smoke and flames."

As they walk toward the still-smoking remains of the tower, Charles frowns. "I think, in fact, we must consider a better way to prepare for such disasters. We are very lucky the fire encompassed only this corner of our wall and did not escape into the city—where there is so much construction of old timber, so much fuel. And we must have better access to water in the future. I will suggest at least one additional aqueduct, to begin."

The two young men stand side by side, each lost in his own thoughts, while they watch the men inside extinguish the last of the flames. Then suddenly, men carrying buckets run out of the home, eyes wide with surprise.

Captain Erich motions the men over and speaks with them quietly. After a moment, he approaches the dauphin and Hans.

"Perhaps, Your Highness," he says with a small bow, "it would be best if you allowed me to continue this investigation myself. I shall report directly to His Majesty." His face is grim, communicating more than his words.

"Thank you, Captain. However, you need not spare me nor my friend. We can learn but little of the world if spared of its evils as well as its celebrations. We are trained to protect ourselves and others, and we cannot do so without the sight of the gruesome. Lead on, sir. We shall follow."

The captain nods and leads the party into the home, where the damage is immediately apparent. Puddles of water remain on the floor, with pieces of burned chaff floating in them. Everywhere is the destruction of fire. To Hans, it is as if someone has tried to put out the fires of hell. *I was just here,* he says to himself. *Besse was just here. Others were just here!*

Sensing the discomfort, Charles puts his hand on the young merchant's shoulder. "I am sorry, my friend. This must be difficult. Yet you were here before this disaster; I need your insight to recreate the event. When you and the maiden emerged, the conflagration already raged behind you. I need you to recall what was occurring while you were—"

The dauphin is interrupted by a shocking discovery. Before them lie the burned remains of the armorer.

Hans involuntarily covers his mouth with his hand and averts his gaze. *What would we have suffered had we not escaped? Is this what would have been left of* us?

The prince realizes what he has exposed his friend to. "Oh, Hans! I am so sorry. You must go home now, and my father will hold his inquiry as quickly as is feasible."

Hans closes his eyes a moment, then shakes his head. "You must pardon me, Charles—my prince. I will collect myself. I am at your service." He bows slightly.

He squeezes his eyes shut again, an aid to remembrance, in order to sort his thoughts of the order of events he witnessed in the tower. "I remember the journeyman running past me into the house and up the spiral stairway. I presume he ran to the aid of the mistress of the house, who was sequestered in her chamber on the second floor. I will not leave until we ascertain their fate. I pray they fared better than the armorer."

"I understand, Hans. We will ascend to her chamber, investigate quickly, then you will leave."

"Yes, sire."

The young prince hesitates a moment and looks around. Carefully eyeing the body, he notes a dent in the back of the head.

Next he scans the entire solar. Immediately he notes that sconces of exquisite manufacture stand in stark contrast to the sparse frugality of the rest of the chamber. The sconces still hold enough oil to burn. But one sconce is missing, until Charles spies it in the hearth, having spilled its contents.

The young dauphin closely studies the area around the hearth. He knows fires often begin when straw rushes are placed too close to a hearth—a foolish and dangerous predicament, as the straw can catch an ember. Yet there is no straw at the foot of the hearth—nothing burned.

Charles moves on, and the two reach the charred chamber door of Beata. Surprisingly, perhaps because of the door's thickness, the chamber interior is relatively intact. Even the bed linens suffer no more than some smoke damage.

The pair see no trace of Beata or Rudi. But as they near the window, the answer to the mystery presents itself. A rope of tied linens is visible on the ground below, catching the reflection of the moon.

"So," says Hans, "it is a relief to know they have escaped. But where have they gone?"

"I shall place a guard on the house, ostensibly to protect the contents but mainly to watch for the return of the journeyman and mistress. They must be summoned to the inquiry, along with the other survivors."

Charles turns to his friend, his hand on his shoulder. "And now you may take your leave. Please return to your family and your betrothed."

◆ ◆ ◆

Hans does so. He embraces his family, then buries his head in the bosom of his love, where he can finally allow himself the catharsis of a good cry. Ebouisante caresses him gently and softly calls him a true hero, having saved Besse.

At the tower, Charles takes one last look around him and reflects briefly on how many lives have changed as a consequence of the fire.

Yes, he thinks, nodding his head. *There must be an inquiry, for all here is not as it seems.*

~ Chapter 51 ~

A larger crowd than usual has gathered for the prince's public counsel. No one wants to miss the inquiry to establish the cause of the fire at the Hammer household! The townspeople and visiting merchant families may be fatigued from the activities of the night past, but they murmur to each other with some excitement.

The occupants of the tower huddle together in the center of the hall, awaiting inquiry. They have not fully recovered from the shock, to the extent that none of them has even had time to feel a sense of gratitude for having escaped alive. The group stands close together in false hope of some collective comfort, yet each is focused on his or her own thoughts.

The servants cluster together in trepidation, afraid of being blamed.

Fee will not release Dien from a bear hug and cannot stop sobbing.

Bo looks furtively about him for any possible means of escape, though he finds none.

Rudi and Beata, who came directly to the castle on their own accord, are aware that they cannot show any love for each other publicly. Still, they steadfastly hold their chins high—even if Beata's chin quivers a bit.

Peter takes Rose's hand and squeezes it in reassurance. Rose lets out a deep breath of relief—his gesture means she will not have to worry about his testimony.

There also for the inquiry, only Hans stands aside, in no need of reassurance from anyone.

- Chapter 51 -

The townspeople chatter as they eye the motley group in the center of the room. Listening in, Princess Amalia notes that even in a time of plentiful harvest, there is an insatiable appetite for gossip. She hears many a contradictory version of the fire and death of Dunkel Hammer in the murmurings of the crowd:

"Do you think someone set it on purpose?" asks one of the merchants.

"This is a peaceful city, it is. You cannot believe it was more than an accident!" a fellow merchant answers.

"Well, that man certainly was not loved," another counters. "Who knows what enemies he made? Then again," he reconsiders, "there were many more people in danger than just the armorer. In fact, the whole city!"

Yet another citizen: "Hush! His Highness'll figure it out."

"Everyone hated Dunkel," a trader says. "But some hate the bourgeoisie even more. I say the fire was intended to destroy us all, along with many prominent merchants from the surrounding principalities."

"Yes, certainly," someone agrees. "I hear other merchants outside this realm are going bankrupt from the lack of trade in the Hanse. The Swedes particularly hate us, and we are not so welcome by the Angles and Saxons on their isle."

"But then, my dear Annalise," comes the retort, "why not set the fire at the Handlers' home during the feast?"

"Too suspicious and too easy to stop the villain."

This explanation is well received. "Oh, yes. Of course!" several mutter.

The princess is amused by such nonsense. She duly relates it to her husband, but Henrik does not share her delight.

"This must stop," he declares. "We must ascertain the truth. That is why I have retained all from that household for this inquiry. Charles and I will question them one by one. I will tell you, though, even our son feels there is some suspicion of this fire."

The prince rises, and all those present bow or curtsy before him. On the platform are the prince, the princess, and the dauphin, and his betrothed, La Claire. All eyes go to La Claire, now elegantly dressed with a bejeweled tunic over a red silk surcotte. Around her neck she demurely displays her betrothal gift. It is an emerald provided by the very Jew the dauphin and Hans previously assisted.

Henrik stands. He claps his hands to silence the crowd and clears his throat.

"We have several matters before us today. We will take up the matter of the servant of the Duchess of Burgundy"—here he nods to La Claire before continuing—"as well as matters concerning our soldiers. But first, we shall hold inquiry into the events of last even; in particular, into the matter of the fire in the tower residence of our armorer, Dunkel Hammer." He pauses a moment, then adds, "We have decided, however, that the inquiry itself will not be open to the public. All those not bound by this inquiry must leave."

A wave of disappointment courses through the assemblage. The prince stands his ground, looking sternly out at the group. Then he softens his gaze with a slight smile.

"Fear not. We shall issue a proclamation once the matters are completely resolved—which should assuage your deep appetites for gossip. Now go!"

He looks toward his wife, who nods her approval. He waits for the chamber to clear before taking his place upon the throne.

There is a slight commotion as the populace slowly exits. Rudi briefly leaves Beata's side, seizing it as an opportunity to approach a select few he must address before the inquiry. He pulls Bo, Rose and Peter, and the apprentice aside. In hushed tones, he begins with the young bandit.

"Watch what you say, boy. Only the truth is wanted here. Prince Henrik"—a slight hesitation—"actually, both princes will recognize immediately any dissemblance. They are very discerning. So I will advise you to answer only what you are asked. It would not be wise to raise the issue of avenging your brother here, as it would likely land you in great trouble. I will vouch for the fact that you were not in the house to pilfer, though, should it come to that."

"What'll I tell His Highness, then?" Bo asks sheepishly, eyes downcast.

Rudi thinks for a moment. "Who let you into the house?" he asks in return.

"Why, a young wench, sir."

"Watch your language, boy." He gestures toward Beata. "The lady of the house will not brook her servants described in such fashion. However, that shall be your story, and it rings true. You were there to see the young maiden, and I interrupted you. At which point, I attempted to relieve you of your weapon, a row ensued, and I sustained this injury." He touches his bruised eye. "Then we were driven out by the fire."

Bo gives Rudi a look of suspicion. "Why should ye be so helpful t' me, sir? I've been nought but trouble t' ye, I have."

Rudi shakes his head dismissively. "I would not expect you to understand. Just know it is best for the lady that we keep the family secrets within the family. In exchange, I will keep you out of more trouble and allow you to go on your merry way. Expect nothing more, and be thankful."

Rudi moves on to Rose and Peter with a frown. "Now, you two are a quandary. The lady would prefer that you also say nothing of any argument you may have had with her husband. It can cause nought but trouble for you."

"Fear not, sir," answers Peter. "We know exactly what to say, and it will be the truth." He casts a stern glance at Rose. "Rose, if you want a future with me, you shall speak only if spoken to. And mind you answer only what is asked of you."

She nods, blushing visibly and bowing her head. On the outside, she appears the poor, abused, demure one. But inside, Rose fumes. It is a man's world, but she will not allow even this one to rule over her! Still, she does note that Peter is right about her not speaking too much to His Highness. If he knew what Rose knew about

Dunkel, the prince might suspect Rose too much.

Rudi now moves to the side of the young apprentice. His tone softens, but he does not smile as he places his hand on the young boy's shoulder. "You were quick to get out when Fee came upstairs and alerted you of the fire. What did you see as you made your escape?"

"Only the stairs and the door, and you exiting the lady's chamber. I shall tell only what I saw, but I shall be truthful." The boy looks directly into Rudi's eyes, silently defying him to demand otherwise.

"See that you do, and you shall become my own apprentice."

The apprentice smiles. "I should be honored, sir."

Fully admonished, this group rejoins the others, forming an even tighter circle as the inquiry is about to begin. For now, Rudi is comfortable and ready to confront the princes. He returns to Beata's side and says nothing. Now, all are prepared.

~ Chapter 52 ~

The prince now addresses the remaining citizens. He states emphatically, "You will each be called to my chamber behind the thrones for questioning. When you have been dismissed, you will exit the hall without further discussion. We hope we make ourselves clear."

The first to be called into the back chamber are the servants, one by one.

"What did you see? Did you see anyone setting fire to the home?" Prince Henrik asks each in turn.

"Yer Highnesses, I saw nothin'," says each in turn. "Me job is t' cook, t' clean, t' stay behind the hearth, in the kitchen, it is."

"Did you hear any arguments, see any fights?"

"No, Yer Majesties," says one, timidly. "It's not me place t' pay any attention t' the activities of the family, no. When Fee called out that there was a fire, 'twas all I could do t' run out and save me own hide!"

"So it would be. But there were so many people with no real reason to be in that tower. Why were Peter and Rose there, for instance?" interjects Charles.

In response, the servants each speculated that Peter wanted Rose to meet Fee. The princes are satisfied with this, recalling that Peter is indeed keeping to his word to work the old farmstead. And he did provide those beautiful, artistically executed gourds that same night. Plus, he likely would not have had any contact with Dunkel.

The dauphin asks each servant, "And how does Bo, a bandit—if we are to believe the journeyman's characterization of the young man—come to be inside the household?"

He believes the answers will be of great importance. He is, however, a bit disappointed to hear the young bandit is but a beau of the servant Liesel, who herself confirms this information.

She states, "The master wouldn't have brooked having Bo in the house, Yer Highnesses. No, he wouldn't 've. So Bo hid, he did, waitin' for me—for later, ye know." She blushes. "But I think he ran into the journeyman, he did, who would've wanted t' put him out. And just then there was the fire, and it was all of us for himself. Except for Fee, I mean. She wouldn't leave till she made sure of us all, she wouldn't. She gives orders and expects them done right, but we do for her gladly. She's ne'er been a taskmaster, that one. Always thinkin' of everyone else first, she does. Would sooner die than hurt a fly. So we all got out safe. Well, almost everyone," she adds.

"Liesel," asks Charles, "no one seems to be terribly upset at the loss of the master. Are you not worried about where you will work?"

"No, Yer Highness. Anythin' would be better than workin' for *him*! I mean, the lady'll still need her staff, she will. And workin' for Fee is a pleasure."

"Did the master ever abuse any of the servants?"

Charles can see he may have gone too far with this question. The answer is in her posture as she looks down and in the embarrassment on her face.

He quickly interrupts himself. "You need not answer that, fräulein. But I have a different question: Was the master besotted when he arrived home?"

"It would've been his usual, sire, but funny ye should ask. That night he started out angry but not off his head. He ran right up the stairs t' do his dirty business, he did. But after supper, he started t' slur his speech more than usual and act all tipsy, which was more like him, it was. Maybe he'd a stock upstairs, if ye know what I mean. But I thought he kept it all behind the hearth, with us. Course, *we* would ne'er touch it, no. Wouldn't want t' face the wrath."

The dauphin's brow furrows. He asks, "Just one more thing:

Why was the other young man in the house—Jacques? Why would he risk death to return to Quellestadt and enter that home?"

She thinks a moment, then shrugs. "We didn't know, sire, but he said somethin' about being the master's son. Maybe by a different lady, if ye get the gist. He didn't say much afore he ran around the hearth. He was clearly up t' no good—had a gleam in his eye, he did. Do ye think he did the master some harm or started the fire?" At that she blanches. "Oh, pardon me, sire. I'm sorry—I didn't mean t' ask *ye* a question, I didn't!"

Charles laughs and offers a wave. "Think nothing of it."

He thanks the maiden and dismisses her, sending the guard first for Peter and then for Rose. The guard has been instructed to allow only one in at a time.

As the guard approaches, the young farmer sighs, gives Rose a warning glance, lowers his head in the manner of a supplicant, and enters the chamber. He bows before the royalty.

"You may rise, Peter," Prince Charles says. The familiarity is carefully calculated to put the young man at ease. "These are very different circumstances from those you faced here of late. We want you to know we are impressed with your diligence in pursuing your reconciliation. We have been told that you were in the house to see your sister, and we know you were delivering the most exquisite artistry to the Handlers' feast. Yet you always seem to be in the wrong place at the wrong time. What say you?"

"Your Majesties, I pray you will forgive me. I merely meant to introduce Fee to my Rose. I did not expect such events to unfold while we were there."

"This Rose," adds the princess, speaking for the first time, "she is certainly a comely one. I am sure her services were in no small demand at the inn."

"Your Highness," Peter says as his face reddens, "the thought of her profession never occurred to me. She is a damsel in distress, of sorts. And she sought me out."

"My pardon, Peter. We should not have implied any impropriety," she responds with a slight smile, suppressing the urge to wink. "We shall maintain our silence."

The elder prince frowns deeply, but the princess does not seem to notice the unspoken rebuke. La Claire blushes, a bit embarrassed by the exchange between Amalia and Peter.

"Rose felt threatened by the master, whom she left for me," Peter continues in explanation. "She pleaded with me for a better life than the one she led at the inn. I wanted to protect her to be sure there would be no trouble with the armorer." He looks to the royals. "When you were so kind to offer me a second chance, how could I not return the favor to another in need?"

"Peter," says Charles, "did you hear any argument before you left?"

"Yes, sire. I heard the journeyman fight with the boy who was hiding in the home. I saw him wrestle a slingshot away from him, and blows were exchanged. Then we saw the fire right as Fee came running over to us and the servants. We all left as fast as we could."

Charles continues, "Just one more question: What was your sister doing before the fire started?"

Peter's eyes widen at the thought of any suspicion of his sister. "She was directing the servants, then she took some stew up to the young fräulein."

"Thank you, Peter. That will be all," Charles concludes.

After Peter is dismissed, Giselle turns to her betrothed. "Why did you ask that question?"

"Perhaps I wished to put Peter a bit off his guard, to see what else he might have to say."

"You suspect Peter is hiding something?" she asks.

Charles smiles and holds up a finger. "Yes, my dear, but I shall tell you later."

"That is too bad," Amalia interjects. "I was beginning to have hope that the young man was turning his life around." She halts her speculation as Rose enters the room.

~ Chapter 52 ~

Rose seems ill at ease, but she takes a deep breath, overcoming the sensation of walls closing in upon her. She reminds herself of Peter's advice and approaches the royals tentatively, finally offering a deep curtsy. Yet she does not look downward once she rises, but rather looks directly into the eyes of her inquisitors. She will not be intimidated.

Giselle has the distinct impression this woman has encountered nobles before. Giselle then realizes that may very well be the truth, considering Rose's erstwhile profession and the number of nobles visiting the principality. (What would she think if she knew one of those nobles was her father?)

Charles thinks for a moment, then decides to smile, knowing Rose will misinterpret this gesture and perhaps be put off guard. He will not ask her to corroborate Peter's testimony; the servants have already done so. Instead, he goes right to the heart of the matter.

"We understand that you and Peter were at the home of Dunkel Hammer to introduce you to his sister, the servant Fee. You might know that of late, she intervened to plead his case and was instrumental in our decision to allow him to reclaim the farm. He will have to pay double tithing, as you must know. So why would you choose him for a mate?"

Completely taken aback—especially because the question seems totally unrelated to the death of the master—Rose takes a few seconds to think. Then she smiles and looks directly at the prince.

"He's a handsome one, isn't he? I know he has a past—that was clear when he first walked into the inn. But I could see immediately he had poss'bilities. And I really wanted t' get out of that inn. A maiden has few chances, 'specially in me line of work, sire. I have t' take what I find, I do, and I'm not gettin' any younger, no."

"That is quite honest. Did you know the master?"

"Yes, sire." She does not hesitate. "He was a frequent visitor t' the inn, he was."

Rose knows that if the royals were to question others at the inn, they would quickly find out she was a favorite of Dunkel, and even that she had been avoiding him of late. That information would then lead to questions about why she would allow Peter to take her to the master's very house.

But she says nothing more. Fortunately, the dauphin is not inclined to ask why she would feel threatened by Dunkel, whose possessiveness and fierce anger were well known.

"You may go, Rose. We wish you and Peter success."

Rose leaves, and the prince calls for his friend Hans, who enters with a smile and a deep bow. Charles knows Hans was at the feast, of course, until he left to see to Besse's exit. It is clear the young man has no secrets to hide from the royals.

"You promised you would share your reason for escorting the young maiden, Hans. This is the time to do it. So I shall not direct you with questions but rather allow you to talk."

"Thank you, Char—sire," he quickly corrects. He gathers his breath. "I left the feast at Ebouisante's behest to assist Besse. We have secured a safe haven for the maiden. She is under Ebouisante's tutelage, sire. She is teaching Besse to read, even as the servant Fee teaches her marketing and how to run a household. Although, I must admit, her father would not have cared to arrange a betrothal for her, nor would any eligible man take an interest. She is reclusive, for good reason, and not particularly attractive, if you will forgive my saying so. Yet no maiden deserves to be treated as she has been, and so it was my privilege to come to her aid. One has little chance to express chivalry as the mere son of a merchant."

Charles laughs, then interrupts, "Hans, you have had more than your share of opportunity for chivalry! I hope the rest of your life is more mundane. We are friends, and I want that friendship to last many years."

Hans smiles sheepishly. "Thank you, sire. And most especially, thank you for not asking me to recount the reason Besse needs our assistance. As you know, she is not here this day, Your Highnesses. If you must interrogate her, I would only ask that once I retrieve her, you please allow Fee and Ebouisante to accompany her."

~ Chapter 52 ~

"Please continue, Hans, at the point when you arrived at the tower," instructs Charles.

Hans nods, taking another deep breath. "I arrived at the door, expecting Fee to have Besse ready to depart with me. I was prepared to confront the armorer if need be, but I admit I was happy not to have the opportunity. Yet as I waited, I began to smell smoke, so I ran into the home."

"What did you see?"

"I had little time to notice much, sire, as the servants were in a tizzy. I did see the master out of consciousness on the floor. The apprentice ran by me as I ran to assist the master, but Fee appeared with Besse in tow, pushed her into my arms, and told me to leave quickly. She then ran to try to rouse the armorer, whom I presume was drunk. But as we know, she was not successful and was almost overcome herself."

The dauphin's eyebrows knit for a brief moment, then he nods.

"We are very impressed with Fee, Hans," interjects the princess. "She has stood in support of her young brother, and now we are hearing of great sacrifice for the members and servants of the household she serves."

"Yes, madame, it would appear so," Hans replies. "It was she who convinced Ebouisante to teach and assist Besse. I have great respect for her."

"Hans, we have no further questions for you," Charles states. "You may go," he says with a nod.

Hans bows and backs out of the chamber.

Next the guard ushers Rudi into the room. He bows deeply, then rises without looking directly at any of the royals.

Charles looks to his father, who nods for him to continue the questioning. Then he looks sternly at the journeyman. "You are the armorer's journeyman, with little love for the master. We are aware that he has obstructed your advancement in the guild and banished you from the home." It was a statement, not a question.

Rudi flushes. "Yes, Your Highness. I will not deny it."

"From the manner of your departure during the fire, we also surmise that you have reason to protect the mistress Beata." Charles decides not to embarrass Rudi by questioning him further about Beata. "Yet you are injured. How did that occur?"

Somewhat relieved by the shift in subject, Rudi sighs and continues, "Your pardon, Your Highnesses, but I had the misfortune of apprehending Bo, the young ruffian I turned over to the guard. I discovered him attempting to hide when I came downstairs. He carried a slingshot, which I wrestled from his grip, just not too efficiently. The result is the small bruise you see here. Please mind that he was not necessarily planning to do any damage with it. It was merely the means of protection he carries. But I felt it best to confiscate it." Rudy cannot help but wince as he says this. He quickly touches his bruise, hoping to convince the royals that the wince is a reflection of his injury rather than a reflection of his honesty.

Amalia is not so willing to spare Rudi the discomfort of addressing his relationship with Beata. "The demands of love are great—even at times irrational, sir," she says. "We have no doubt of your great love for the master's wife."

Rudi covers his face. "You speak truly, Your Majesty," he responds with a slight bow. "I came back that night to convince the lady to leave the house and join me in the nearby wood, where I have furnished a comfortable home for us until such time as it would be seemly to return to the city."

"You mean, sir, until the passing of the master," says Prince Henrik, now acutely interested in the journeyman's responses.

"Yes, Your Highness. The master has always been too fond of his ale and was clearly near the end, with a rotund belly and a very yellow skin. These are the signs of near-imminent demise."

"I am puzzled by one thing," the princess interjects. "You said you went downstairs. Why not keep yourself sequestered with the lady in her tower chamber, to avoid possible contact with the master, who has thrown you out of his household?"

Rudi is more confident now that there is no need to protect his secret. "I had no particular fear of the master. Nor did I wish to live in secrecy or in hiding. I had the intent to confront him directly."

"Indeed!" says Henrik, raising his eyebrows. "And did you confront him?"

"No, sire, I did not. I instead encountered the young ruffian and disarmed him, then noticed the smoke and the commotion as the servant Fee was alerting the others. The master was on the floor, and I made to assist Fee to help pull him to the door. But just then the ruffian took advantage of the situation to attempt to flee. Fee assured me she could assist the master. So I grabbed the bandit's collar, delivered him to the guard, then raced back inside to assist Fee and the lady. However, the smoke was so bad by then, it was all I could do to run up the stairs. The lady and I were forced to find an alternative mode of departure."

Charles smiles, resuming his questioning with the acquiescence of the elder prince. "So it would seem. We discovered the linens at the foot of the window outside the wall. Please tell the lady her chamber possessions are largely intact, with but a little smoke damage, if she wishes to recover them. I assume you will plan to provide her shelter for the nonce."

"Yes, sire, I have offered it."

"Very well, then send the lady in, and you may depart."

With a bow, Rudi backs out of the chamber, smiling surreptitiously at Beata as they pass.

Beata enters, a bit flushed, and curtsies. The royals look pensively at her, and she lowers her gaze. Suddenly the chamber feels hotter than her own house on fire. She wishes this to end quickly so she might recover what few possessions remain in her chamber, then direct the cleaning and refurbishing of the house.

It is the princess who leads the questioning, placing Beata at some ease. "My dear, we grieve at your loss. You must be devastated. And now you shall have to take the six-month claim to your husband's place in the guild, all without the skills of a blacksmith. Perchance you will want to hire the journeyman?"

Beata visibly relaxes her posture, relieved to have nothing more to hide. "Thank you, Your Highness, for the suggestion. It is precisely what I must do. In fact, Rudi is a superb craftsman. He has actually created most of the armor attributed to my husband for at least a year. He must be accepted by the guild as a master in his own right soon."

"Are you planning to accept his offer of shelter for the nonce?" Amalia asks.

"Why, no, Your Majesty!" she blushes yet again. "That would be unseemly. I will not pretend to Your Highnesses that I have no relationship with Rudi—with the journeyman, that is," she corrects. "We had intended to let nature take its course with Dunkel, then wait the appropriate time to be together. That is still my intent."

Amalia leans forward and smiles. "We know you were in your chamber until Rudi came for you."

"Yes, Your Majesty. My servant Fee came to my chamber to alert me of the fire, but I did not feel it safe to exit downstairs. Rather, I quickly arranged a makeshift linen ladder for escape out the window if necessary."

"We assume this is the same means used by the journeyman to access your chamber, yes?"

Reddening even more deeply, Beata replies, "Yes, madame."

La Claire, who has never been exposed to such behavior, shivers and places her hand on Charles's. The dauphin can only squeeze it and shake his head.

Amalia smiles more broadly. "Thank you for your forthright honesty, my dear."

She turns to look at the prince, who nods his head. Then Amalia addresses Beata again. "We shall offer you sanctuary here in the castle for as long as necessary until the refurbishment of your tower. Then you may return to your home."

Henrik resumes control of the conversation, wishing no further embarrassment of the lady. "Frau Hammer, please have the guard bring in Bo, the young man who did not belong in your household."

Beata curtsies, then turns to leave the chamber. She whispers the prince's instructions to the guard. As she enters the large hall, Rudi comes to his love and squeezes her hand. She smiles at him weakly, then releases his hand before anyone else can notice. She must now work even harder to keep up appearances, as she will be seen more in public.

Bo is brought into the chamber. The young man bows awkwardly and seems clearly out of place.

Charles resumes the role of inquisitor. "What shall we do with you, young man? The servant Liesel has admitted to her liaison with you, so we understand why you were in the household. But why would you tussle with the journeyman?"

"He didn't approve of me in the house, he didn't. But he's not the boss of me, no! We tussled, as ye say, a bit. Truthfully, I wanted to escape the place," Bo says as he lowers his eyes, "but he grabbed me slingshot. Then there was fire and smoke, and ev'ryone was in a panic, so I tried to run. But he's very strong, he is. He grabbed me and handed me t' the guard."

Charles hesitates a moment, internally matching Bo's tale to Rudi's, then proceeds with a new question. "Did you know the master?"

Bo must pause. This is more difficult. Rudi had warned him to be truthful but to say little. "Everyone knew him, they did," he finally says. "I might've encountered him in the woods, on his way t' the forge, or elsewhere."

"That is evasive, my young man," said Charles more loudly, with some anger, noting Bo's hesitancy. "I suspect a less auspicious encounter. Perhaps another reason to be in the household."

The bandit twitches, feeling like a rabbit in a trap. He decides to tell the truth. "Forgive me, sires. I did know the master—he killed me brother outside the inn, he did!"

"Truthfully!" says Charles as his eyebrows rise. "Did anyone actually witness this horror?"

Bo lets out a long sigh, then admits, "Rudi was there, sire—the journeyman. But I've no truck with him, no! He pulled me aside that night and saved me from the master."

Charles considers this revelation briefly, then shakes a finger at the young thief. "It is clear Liesel was not your only reason to be in that house—certainly not at an hour the master would be home, and especially when you had good reason to avoid him. Perhaps you did not want to avoid him at all. Yet it would seem you had no opportunity to confront the master."

Bo says nothing, but looks downward, confirming the dauphin's statement.

"Just one more question," Charles adds. "Did you talk with Jacques?"

"Ye mean the other boy who didn't belong there? I did, sire. I overheard him say the master was his father! I think he meant t' get somethin' from him. So he went right into the solar, he did. Then I heard a thud, and out he came. He made t' leave, I think, then he turned and pushed me aside behind the stairs . . ."

Charles considers this a moment, then waves dismissal at the miscreant. "You may go."

"Thank ye, sire!" Bo says with visible relief. "Thank ye!"

"Wait just one moment," Charles interrupts. "If you wish to remain in our realm, you will not be a bandit. We have instructed the guard to place you at work in the underground canals."

Bo flinches. "You mean the sewers, sire? That's no work for any man, it's not!"

"Nevertheless, it is necessary work for *some* men. And shall be for you."

Bo thinks better of saying any more. With a mumbled "As ye will, sire," he forgets himself and turns his back to depart.

The royals laugh a bit and ignore the faux pas. The bandit cannot be expected to know appropriate etiquette.

There is another bow, another awkward stance, and the apprentice is ready for questioning.

"Tell us about the events in the household last night. Were you in your chamber upstairs?" asks the young prince.

"Why, yes, Your Highness. Then suddenly Fee, the mistress's

servant, knocked on my door and told me to get out, which I did—without my supper. She said there was a fire. I went downstairs and saw the master on the floor and the floor ablaze all around him. I wanted to help him, but Fee told me to just go, that she would take care of him. So I left quickly. I owe my life to Fee. We all do."

Charles smiles, impressed by the respect and affection the household members have been expressing for Fee. But he has no further questions for the apprentice. "That is all. You may go. Guard—send in Fee!"

The apprentice bows and departs quickly as Fee enters. Her shoulders are down, and she is clearly weary, looking considerably older than her years. She curtsies.

The princess has immediate sympathy. "You are the servant to the mistress of the house, are you not?" she asks.

Fee nods in response.

"You are also the sister of the erstwhile miscreant, Peter, and of our valet, Jurg—and if I do not miss my guess, of the vendor Flor."

This is a statement, requiring no answer. Fee tries to allow her thoughts to turn inward and her body to shrink, but to no success. The fox has been removed from the chicken coop, and she can only stand in judgment.

"My dear, take some comfort," Amalia says. "All those we have spoken to today have had nothing but praise for you. You are the rock of your family and of the Hammer family as well. We commend you. Not many think of those they love, of those they *serve*, before themselves."

"Thank you, madame." This is said by the dauphin, not Fee. Charles continues, "We are all pleased and proud to have you as a citizen of our city. But I must ask a few questions. What was the armorer's demeanor last night?"

Fee hunches her shoulders, wishing she could escape notice, but that is impossible. She answers meekly, "Your Highnesses, he was gruff, as was his wont, and demanding. I admit I confronted him, sires, about his mistreatment of his daughter, then he went to the solar for his supper. As he ate and drank, I noticed his speech became more slurred. I poured some stew for Besse, then left to attend to her needs—"

Charles holds up a hand to interrupt. "You must have heard the commotion when Jacques confronted the master."

"No, sire. I was attending to Besse in her room upstairs."

"But then you returned to the solar?"

"Yes, Your Highness. But there was a fire. The master was down, and I could not arouse him, so I—"

"Yes," interrupts Henrik. "We have heard. You ran back upstairs to bring Besse down and tell the apprentice and the mistress to leave quickly. Then you alerted your brother and Rose and the servants in the kitchen, if any remained. Finally, you tried to arouse and remove the master from danger."

"But I failed, sire! I failed!" Fee bursts out in great sobs, unable to contain herself.

"Fee, Fee," says young Charles with a kindly sigh. "You did not fail at all. We are so impressed with you. Take comfort—all of the principality shall know you as a hero. Godmother to so many, loving of all. Did you know that is the meaning of your very name—'godmother'?" Charles shakes his head, then offers a smile. "What will you do now?"

"I must still serve the mistress, sire," she answers through sniffles. Then she composes herself a bit more and lifts her chin. "But I would ask your leave to marry the servant Dien, of the Handlers' household. The banns are posted. At first I refused him because of the needs of the Hammer household, but I think now—"

Charles quickly interrupts, "With our blessing, fräulein! It is time you receive your own reward." After exchanging nods with his parents, he turns back to Fee. "You may go."

Fee returns to the group in the great hall, who have not yet departed despite the prince's order. They have a greater need to huddle for mutual comfort. They all hug Fee in turn, then release a collective sigh.

~ Chapter 52 ~

All share the mixed emotions of newfound freedom and trepidation for an unknown future. Will the royals decide the fire was an accident? Will the mistress keep all her servants? Where is Besse? Did Hans take her out of the home?

There are few answers for now. Best to leave and relieve their exhaustion for now. They all turn to depart.

♦ ♦ ♦

As the witnesses depart the castle, the royals retreat to the rear chamber. Charles looks to his father expectantly for a sign he has done well.

Henrik obliges him with a smile and a pat on the shoulder. "I cannot find fault in any of the testimony, son. It would appear several people were wronged by my erstwhile armorer and wished him ill. Yet there is no proof of conspiracy, and none had reason to endanger anyone else by starting a fire."

"That is so, sire," Charles responds.

"So we shall prepare the proclamation. Have you more to say?"

"No, sire." Charles half smiles, then shakes his head a bit too vigorously.

His father eyes him carefully. "You shook your head with that one, son. I know you. You examined the scene. You know something. Do you want to share it?"

"Trust me, sire—it is best if I do not. The populace is waiting to reenter the hall. May we return to the remainder of our business?"

~ Chapter 53 ~

The Hammer household members reach the doorway just as the guards open it to let the townspeople back inside for the remainder of the counsel. The small group is suddenly surrounded by the whispers and murmurs of the larger crowd. Under the gaze of a hundred eyes full of suspicion, they shrink away, heads held low, as if they carry some form of contamination. They are free to leave, yet they linger near the portal, fearfully awaiting the prince's judgment.

After a short time, the royals reenter the hall and seat themselves on the dais. They survey the scene, then the Prince Henrik claps his hands. The guards bring in the old servant of the duchess. A general cacophony rises, then falls to silence as the prince rises. All bow or curtsy.

"There will be no inquiry for this woman," Henrik begins. "We shall issue one summary judgment."

The old woman cringes, hiding her face behind the crook of her arm, unwilling to look directly at the royals and most especially La Claire. The duke's daughter glares down upon her, the dagger of her gaze penetrating to the old woman's sight.

Henrik also peers down at her. "You will be escorted to the boundary of our realm, where you will be released. You are banished, under penalty of death upon return. Let all who are here and all guards of the realm look well upon you, that you may be easily recognized."

The guard takes the women gruffly by the arm and escorts her out of the castle.

Henrik watches her go, then claps his hands again. "For the next order of business: let it be known that soldiers trained here are welcome to return. We shall help settle them with other realms in need of their services. But soldiers may *not* return as brigands and bandits, or their lives shall be forfeit. We have dealt enough with soldiers using our excellent training for nefarious purposes. It has already forced us to banish the soldier Borg." Henrik pauses for effect. "This we proclaim, and it shall be written, signed, and sealed." And here he stops, letting the silence add emphasis to the proclamation.

"Now, as to the inquiry into the death of Dunkel Hammer, late our personal armorer . . ."

The crowd leans in, waiting for this moment as if they were about to be treated to a most delicious sweet. Just outside the doorway, Fee gasps, then lets out a deep breath, hand over mouth. The others in the Hammer household group shiver and gather closer.

Henrik looks out over the crowd, then states, "We can draw no conclusion as to the cause of the fire, but it is clear the armorer could not survive it."

There is a collective sigh—almost a groan—from the audience. Now there will certainly be more speculation and more suspicion of those in the tower at the time of the fire. Whisperings begin already.

The prince raises his hand to still the crowd and continues, "We are grateful to our subjects and visitors who had the kindness to help limit the damage of the fire. Further, the mistress of the house shall carry the mastership of her lost husband, as is the guild rule, for six months. She has our leave to clean and restore her home in the tower of the wall with the intent to return to it. During the restoration, she is a welcome guest in this castle and shall be allowed to mourn in peace. It is done."

With that, the royals rise and the guards usher everyone out to their daily business.

The household group turns as one to depart before the townspeople can confront them. They are visibly relieved by the proclamation, but they know they will still face suspicion and speculation.

Only Fee remains behind, until she sees her lover emerge. She runs to Dien and embraces him tightly, whispering the news of the prince's blessing upon their marriage into his ear. Then she collapses in his arms as he gently leads her away.

♦ ♦ ♦

As the royals enter the chamber behind the throne, Henrik places a hand on his son's shoulder and gently pulls him aside.

"I know you have surmised more than you have said, son. Tell me."

"Yes, sire . . . Father." Charles exhales. "The armorer was indeed murdered, and I know who is responsible."

Henrik's eyes go wide. "Why did you not say so earlier?"

"Because I shall need to talk to one more person—someone not at the scene—to be absolutely sure. Then I shall answer any questions you have."

Henrik ponders this a moment, then nods. "I know you had the opportunity to examine the house after the fire," he says. "What did you see that convinced you?"

Charles smiles. "It is not what I saw, but what I did *not* see."

"Then one of our witnesses was not telling the truth."

"Oh no, sire. They were entirely truthful in all they said—once prodded to it," answers the dauphin.

"Then it must be something they did *not* say, as it is something you did not see at the tower."

Now Charles laughs. "Not at all, sire. Nothing was left out of the testimony."

The prince hesitates a moment, rubbing his beard and knitting his brow. "You present me with a puzzle, son. I hope you will tell me more details of your suspicions once you confirm them with the other individual." Then the prince shakes his head. "No. On second thought, I will not inquire of your conclusions. I would prefer to think more upon the matter myself."

"As you wish, sire," Charles says, his grin spreading.

"Nevertheless," the elder prince adds sternly, "if I do not discern it myself, you shall tell me. I do not countenance the shielding of a murderer. This crime cannot go unpunished."

Charles bows his head respectfully. "Certainly, sire. I understand. But please note this is no simple robbery gone awry. Many people had motive to kill Dunkel. Their entire lives have been a punishment. Now they all—including the responsible party—have an opportunity to serve themselves, their families, and the principality to better purposes." He pauses as he raises his chin. "I would ask we allow some time for these people to redeem themselves. That is the best form of justice, is it not?"

Henrik again pats Charles on the shoulder. "Six months, then. Careful consideration before a judgment is the mark of a good ruler. You will make an excellent prince, son."

~ Chapter 54 ~

As might be expected, the excitement of the fire and the armorer's death winds down over a few weeks. City gossip tends to the more mundane once again. Yet the citizens still anticipate two weddings in the spring—that of the dauphin and the duke's daughter, and that of the rich merchant's son and the even richer merchant's daughter. Word of the noble maiden's emerald betrothal gift still circulates, and Ebouisante noticeably sports a finely inscribed gold band on her left ring finger, said to contain the vein directly to the heart.

What goes unnoticed is a simpler band of rushes, changed daily, on the hand of the servant to the armorer's widow. Fee continues to serve the lady in her temporary housing at the castle. And under Fee's guidance, the tower house has been cleaned scrupulously. She has busied herself with the purchase of all the necessary replacements for destroyed household goods.

Away from the tower home, Besse is proving to be a better companion than any Katrina has ever had. They fill an emptiness neither of them realized she had. Besse has even developed a nickname for her out of affection. To Besse—and later to Hans, Ebouisante, and others welcome in the hovel—she has become Granny. And now Granny can reach deeply into her soul and express her true motherly nature, previously suppressed by the abuse she suffered at the hands of her husband.

But Besse still retreats into darkness to find solace and allows no torch or fire into her own room, the most sparsely furnished in the cottage. She does the marketing with the greatest frugality. She never indulges the luxury of any particularly sweet or savory goods but is willing to purchase ingredients to create such treats and dishes with her guardian.

On her marketing trips, Besse always stops to visit and occasionally assist Flor, who often rewards the maiden with a quantity of herbs or a flower for their table. Knowing Besse's current living arrangement can survive only as long as Granny herself survives, Flor continues to train Besse as she previously promised Fee. As the training progresses, Flor feels more secure leaving Besse alone to tend the tent when necessary.

Ebouisante continues teaching Besse as well and the two become closer. Today they meet at the florist's tent for another lesson.

"I see you are eating well, Besse," says Ebouisante in greeting. "This is good. Granny must be treating you well. You are already beginning to fill out in the face and belly—and yes, even in the breasts."

Besse reddens a bit. "Only you can mention such things, Ebouisante. I enjoy helping Granny, and she does feed me well. She is a surprisingly good cook, in fact. And these are good times at the market, with the new harvest still available. A huntsman brings us the best parts of his kill as well, and Granny prepares veritable feasts for us together. And we are always grateful when Herr Handler stops by to check in on us."

Besse catches herself as she mentions Ebouisante's intended. But her friend interprets the enthusiasm in her tone as gratefulness, missing the glimmer in Besse's eyes.

Besse cannot help but conjure the handsome image of the merchant's son. Whenever he visits the house in the woods, she finds herself casting wistful glances at him. After all, he is something of a savior to her. And in her youthful dreams, she cannot understand he has nothing more to offer than what he considers his responsibility to a poor maiden he has rescued.

Ebouisante, for her part, clearly does not see—or chooses to ignore—any interaction between her betrothed and the maiden. This is because Hans is hers and no one else can hold any hope of taking him from her, something especially true with the prince himself having brokered the match.

"I fear there is little time to read or study with all the chores around the house," Besse adds quickly to change the subject. "We have no servants, you know, although I think she could afford them. Yet I will say nothing. I am grateful to have a home and her kind attentions and companionship."

Besse casts a downward glance, which Ebouisante interprets as modesty, gratitude, and perhaps a bit of submission. She has no reason to suspect any darker thoughts behind the expression.

"As you should be grateful," replies Ebouisante. "It is a good life for you. I do believe your mother will soon be able to reoccupy her tower, and you may then choose to return. But I would plead with you otherwise. If I may say, she will have little need of you and is of no mind to teach you further. Granny, however, is in as much need of you as you are of her."

"You are certainly right, Ebouisante. After the kindness she has shown me, how could I just abandon her?"

Besse sighs. In fact, she could abandon the old woman with ease, if Ebouisante truly knew it. While she and Granny share a bond of escape from abuse, Besse does not intend to live her life dependent on anyone, no matter how kindly. She has never given up the goal of determining her own future—no less the goal of living more than the wretched life of an abused and disadvantaged child.

Misinterpreting the sigh, Ebouisante responds, "Of course, my dear. Now let us read a bit of Christine de Pisan. I am also of a mind to teach you numbers and some simple bookkeeping, should you decide to work with Flor in the future. What do you think?"

"I would be most grateful."

Besse glances up to see a familiar face. It is Fee, carrying a sack of her own marketing. She excuses herself to go speak with her. She truly misses the servant, her only protector—if a poor one—in the life she has now escaped. *But you can do little more for me now, can you?* Besse muses. *And you were, after all, only my servant.*

~ Chapter 54 ~

Fee smiles, happy to see her former charge. But she furrows her brow, wishing she could erase Besse's dark memories—no, her entire past in the tower.

She recovers quickly, stating brightly, "You look well, Besse. Your new life seems to agree with you. However, I am glad to see you continuing to take instruction from Ebouisante. I do not think you will want to live in the woods forever."

"You are hoping I will find a mate," Besse says.

It is as if the girl can read Fee's mind. Yes, Fee wishes she could bestow upon Besse the future happiness she foresees for herself and Dien. She absentmindedly touches the band of rushes around her finger. Besse notices it and looks at Fee with surprise.

Fee blushes, then hesitates briefly, concern on her face. "You know I have a relationship with Dien, of the Handler household. He posted banns, and I took them down. Then he put them back, and we have received the prince's blessing." She hesitates again. "I will not be staying with Beata, Besse. Once the tower home is reestablished, I will join the Handler household."

So even the ugly servant can find love and happiness in the end, Besse thinks.

"I do wish I could help you find a mate," Fee continues. "You have no father to make such an arrangement."

"As if *he* would ever have permitted it, no less done it."

Fee is taken aback by the abrupt vehemence of this statement. "You have every reason to belittle the man, even though he is now gone. I do not blame you. But the circumstances of life do not change in a man's world."

"No, Fee, they do not," Besse replies, lifting her chin. "But Ebouisante teaches me to have confidence. We read the most important women authors. And I am learning—I *have* learned—to fend for myself."

There. Now she has spoken her innermost thought aloud. *They will all see. I will make my own life. I will.* She smiles, hoping it does not look more like a grimace.

Fee furrows her brow. Certainly Besse can be forgiven some inner malice. But did Fee just see the poor maiden look like a caged animal suddenly released and instinctively looking for prey? Conversely, Fee has the fleeting thought that Besse looks like easy prey for any demon looking for an innocent to possess.

Nonsense. Fee shakes her head. Such thoughts are worrisome and can do no good for anyone.

Fee feels she does not know what effect the monster had on Besse's inner soul. In truth, though, she *does* know it and no longer wants to deal with it. This last thought evokes pangs of guilt and shame. She literally and figuratively shakes them off, as she has throughout her life, whenever she must put aside her own concerns in order to care for the people for whom she feels responsible. Best to deal with the present and the future. Time heals all wounds, it is said, but it only moves in one direction.

"Besse, you have nothing to fear," she finally says. "You will have a good life now."

It is an attempt to convince herself as much as Besse. But even to herself, she does not sound entirely sincere.

She can say no more, so she collects her bundle and departs, rushing past her sister at the tent entrance and barely remembering to give her a hug.

Now Fee's mind is elsewhere. She must meet Dien at the church. There will be no procession, no best clothes, no surcotte with gold threads, no feast. Not for her. Yet servants must consider themselves fortunate ever to marry at all. This thought affords her the opportunity to smile, and she quickens her step. There will be no more guilt in leaving the tower. She will really have a home now.

In her reverie, Fee almost walks straight into the dauphin as he approaches Flor's tent. She stops, a bit breathless. She remembers to curtsy, begs his pardon, then hurries on to her mission when he says nothing more.

For his part, Charles laughs lightly as he watches her go. He has been apprised, of course, of her destination.

~ Chapter 54 ~

Looking thoughtful and well dressed in a velvet tunic, silk leggings, laced chemise, and polished boots, he makes a regal presence as he enters the tent. Even here, his presence evokes immediate respect from Flor, Ebouisante, and Besse as well as from customers entering and leaving the tent.

Charles takes a deep breath, suddenly assailed by the heady scents of dozens of flowers and herbs in a great jumble, a complicated interaction that reminds him of the similarly complicated needs and interrelationships of this family. He decides the overall result is actually pleasant, then realizes that Flor always arranges it that way to entice the unwary potential customer to enter and return frequently. Flor is but another exemplar in an intelligent family that has survived—yes, even surmounted—the greatest difficulties.

The armorer, in contrast, was despised by all. The dauphin realizes that many are happy to see him gone and that many will be able to redesign their lives. He sees the young maiden reading with Ebouisante and offers a gentle smile. She herself has begun a new life in a location Hans has yet to reveal to his good friend.

Besse, for her part, hides behind Ebouisante, attempting to make herself as small as possible. She casts her gaze only upon the ground. Charles decides to address the young maiden first.

"Besse, I understand?" He extends his hand.

She is obliged to take it and curtsy, never raising her eyes to meet his.

"Yes, Your Highness," she says. "I am so sorry to have . . . to have missed your inquiry." She speaks almost too softly to be heard, and tears start to fill her eyes.

The dauphin must be careful. He understands this maiden has been traumatized and is very fragile. He clears his throat, then raises her chin to look directly into her face.

"You have nothing to fear from me," he says with compassion. "I will ask nothing of you—other than that you take comfort and instruction from Flor and Ebouisante and that you seek to be happy."

It briefly occurs to him to ask Artur Handler's assistance in finding a mate for this girl. But the merchant has a daughter of his own with a wedding and a future to arrange. He places the idea aside, takes a deep inhalation of the pleasing air, and turns to Flor.

"I must have a word with you, Flor, in private. If the young ladies will excuse us . . ."

Ebouisante and Besse are more than happy to curtsy yet again, then leave the tent.

"What do you suppose is His Highness's business with Flor?" Besse asks as they move outside.

"I do not know," Ebouisante replies with a shrug of her shoulders. "I surmise he might be acquiring something for his betrothed."

"Yes, that must be the case," Besse states, yet concern remains etched on her face.

Ebouisante is a bit puzzled. "Besse, do you have some concern for Flor? Is there a problem?"

"Oh, no," Besse hurriedly answers. "I am just grateful His Highness has not asked anything more about that horrible night. I do not think I want to remember any more."

Ebouisante sees an expression on her young friend's face that she assumes stems from a very painful memory—one which must be dispelled.

"Besse, let us concentrate on something else. I have a passage of Christine from the *City of Ladies* I would like to share with you. Would you care to read?"

"Oh, yes, Ebouisante. Thank you."

◆ ◆ ◆

Alone inside the tent, Prince Charles addresses the florist. "I have but one question for you, Frau Flor. Have you recently noticed anything amiss—or I should say, anything missing from your tent?" He watches Flor closely for a reaction.

Flor draws in a breath. Does the dauphin suspect she is complicit in the attacks of the armorer?

- Chapter 54 -

"No, I have not personally seen anything missing, Your Highness. And Besse is also here to keep watch, when my own back is turned or I must leave the tent—for the necessaries, as you might understand."

Charles nods knowingly. "Thank you, Flor. I gauge your honesty as one of the best qualities of your entire family. It is the answer I expected. You have been careful to prevent certain people from acquiring certain—shall we say—herbs. I am reminded of how most recently you thwarted the duchess's servant from obtaining an herb that would have surely killed my very own betrothed. For this you are to be commended. We will not tolerate poisonings in our realm any more than we will tolerate deadly violence against any of our subjects."

Flor curtsies. "Yes, Your Highness. I understand my responsibility in this matter, and I take it upon myself to ensure that harmful substances do not fall into nefarious—or misguided—hands."

Charles nods again. He is satisfied, and his theory is now confirmed.

"I shall now take my leave, but I would like to make a small purchase. Perhaps a rose—preferably of pure white or red, if you have one."

Flor is visibly relieved as she selects the best blooms. "Here is a half dozen. Consider it a gift, sire."

"Many thanks, but I wish to leave you a token of my appreciation." He leaves a sum too large for the purchase and prevents her from returning any of it. "My betrothed is worth far more than this paltry sum."

"Of course, Your Majesty." She curtsies again as he departs.

Outside, Charles nods to Besse and Ebouisante and motions for them not to get up. He stops, however, to speak to Ebouisante.

"I think my good friend Hans is very fortunate."

She blushes. "How so, Your Highness?"

"Not only are you beautiful, but also wise and compassionate."

"You flatter me, sire."

"Not at all, Ebouisante. Hans is a very lucky man. And I have faith in you."

"Faith, sire? I am nothing if not constant. And I am the lucky one. Hans is very handsome and very gallant. He will be a superb merchant, and I will help where I am able."

Ebouisante looks a bit indignant, staring straight into the eyes of the young prince. He thinks, *I do believe Hans has met his match!*

Charles considers his words carefully, then laughs, setting Ebouisante at ease. He says, "You must know a boy's fondest dreams are to rescue a damsel in distress, then to win her heart. Hans has accomplished all of that. And now . . . well, now he must become a man and set such dreams aside. So my dear, now it is up to you to save *him.*"

Ebouisante is a bit startled. What does the dauphin mean? Does he know about Hans's continuing visits to the house in the woods to watch over Granny and Besse? He *is* Hans's best friend, after all—not to mention the prince. No, Ebouisante reasons. He refers only to her own caravan rescue and to Besse's escape.

Regardless, she ultimately agrees with the dauphin—Hans does enjoy the role of the knight in shining armor. She shall have to make him comfortable with other sorts of adventures.

At last, she smiles and says, "Yes, Your Highness. I do believe you are quite correct. I must try to save Hans from his very nature. This will be a Herculean task, but I shall do my best!"

With that, Charles offers Ebouisante a kiss upon the hand, bows, and takes his leave.

~ Chapter 55 ~

Fee arrives at the church door, where Dien awaits. There are no crowds of townspeople, but some of the urchins of the city have followed her, as is their wont, hoping she will pull something out of her bundle for them. In fact, on this special occasion, she has bought some small, inexpensive cakes. She retrieves and distributes them.

Dien shakes his head. "Always, me dearest—always the neediest come first with ye, they do. Now give me your hand. Here's the priest. We'll state our vows by the church door, we will."

Fee laughs. She is startled by how good this makes her feel. Suddenly the church door resembles Saint Peter's gate, and she has been granted admission to heaven. The feeling is fleeting, however, as she once again cannot help herself from taking on inner guilt for others who suffer—and for past ill deeds and the ill deeds yet to come. At the moment, however, the autumn air smells crisp and clean, and she will enjoy her love by her side.

Dien knocks at the door. The priest opens it and exits with a smile, his hands outstretched in welcome.

"The sacrament of marriage is not to be taken lightly, my children. It is an unbreakable bond. Yet I can think of no couple more deserving or more committed to each other. Therefore," he takes on a more serious countenance as he continues, "do you, Dien, take this woman to be your wife, to have and to hold, from this day forward, until death does you part?"

Dien beams. "Yes, Father—and beyond."

"And do you, Fee, take this man to be your husband, to love and honor and serve faithfully, until death does you part?"

"Oh, yes, I do," responds Fee, tears welling up in her eyes as she grasps Dien's hand tightly.

"What God has wrought, let no man put asunder. I now pronounce you man and wife."

That is all. The couple enters the church, kneels and prays before the altar, then exits holding hands.

This is their moment, and neither can imagine a happier one. For Dien, this is his one opportunity—no, his *first* opportunity—to make his beloved forget her tribulations, her responsibilities.

Still hand in hand, the two head to the Handler home, where they take the time to repair to the servants' quarters, where they bury themselves hungrily in each other's embraces, but such moments cannot last forever.

In a few days, Fee will move into the Handler household, becoming an integral part of Artur, Gute, Hans, Greta, and now Ebouisante's lives. But for now, the newlyweds must separate to their respective duties.

As always for Fee, life intervenes.

~ Chapter 56 ~

In the spring of 1451, the air over Quellestadt is fresh with the promise of new life. The birds create a near musical cacophony, reflecting the excitement of the populace below. The community is preparing for the combined weddings of the dauphin and the merchant's son that very afternoon. The atmosphere of prosperity is almost palpable.

Bakers are frantically baking breads and pastries. Butchers are butchering an abundance of game brought in by visiting nobility. Even the Jews are selling numbers of gems and luxury items and arranging secured loans to visiting wealthy merchants, princes, counts, and dukes. The inn is doing its briskest business ever. Even Flor has hired some of the village waifs to help comb the fields and glades for flowers to complete the many arrangements the locals and visitors have ordered.

Outside the city stands a profusion of tents with pennants of every shape and color, bearing the heralds of visiting royalty. Children run from camp to camp, making new friends, playing blind man's bluff, tossing leather balls, and pretending to be knights of King Arthur's court. The adults, nobility and merchantry alike, are busily making liaisons or business deals. And there is ample time for gossip.

"See," one lady whispers to another, "the Duke of Burgundy wears a black band. He must believe the duchess is no more."

"It is said," a companion replies, "the lady was not welcome in Paris. So in her travels across the mountains, the sudden appearance of a large beast of prey startled her steed, causing it to gallop off the mountain."

A merchant nods in agreement. "Yes. I heard she was found with multiple cuts. A shard of the blackest obsidian pierced her chest, and only black ooze bled from her penetrated heart."

"Now you are embellishing!" another says with a laugh.

◆ ◆ ◆

Within the city walls, Fee is busy with the specific arrangements for the Handler household. The wedding preparations have caused her to temporarily suspend the hiring of staff to serve the future home of Hans and Ebouisante. Artur has commissioned the new home, located just inside the wall, as a wedding present.

Fee has been instructed to live with them full time for a while. After that period, she will work in the younger Handlers' home by day while Dien continues to oversee the older household. At night, Fee will return to her beloved Dien.

On this busy day, Fee has just enough time for a brief visit to assist Flor. In actuality, she is hoping for a chance to see Besse.

In a recent visit with Ebouisante, Fee has learned the woman they now call Granny suffers exceedingly from her growths and is going blind. Besse seemingly does not want to leave the poor lady. She has not been seen in the city, even to visit Flor's tent, for some time. Two of the orphans from the city have moved in to the house in the woods, and they have taken over the marketing duties.

Fee is glad Besse and Granny have become so close, but she worries the situation is taking too heavy a toil on the girl. Ebouisante has said Besse no longer comes to the door to greet her nor Hans, preferring to remain in the back room. Fee is worried how Besse will handle the loss of the old lady. Has she not faced enough tragedy in her young life?

As fate would have it, on her way to Flor's tent, Fee encounters Beata. The lady looks thoughtful for a moment, then frowns.

"Well met, Fee. I must inform you I intend to move back anon."

Fee is not surprised. She realizes Beata must soon relinquish her position as master armorer, claimed upon Dunkel's death. In the interim, Rudi has reconditioned the Hammer forge and closed his own. Already he has solidified his own reputation as one of the finest smiths in northern Europe. His work is exquisite, and none can reproduce his process of creating the strongest and most lightweight plate armor.

Rudi has done very well on orders from the prince alone. But there are additional orders from other royalty and knights—not the least of which is the Duke of Burgundy, who has a very large realm and much need for soldiery. The guild can certainly no longer deny Rudi the honor of becoming a master. Some suspect it will not take long before he becomes the guild master himself.

"Will the journeyman be joining us?" Fee asks.

Beata is surprised at such an audacious question. She says angrily, "Of course not! How unseemly! Be apprised that I am still in mourning, and he must first become a master in the guild and pursue suit for my hand, if he desires it. However, your services will be required in the tower home upon my return."

Fee must hold back a sigh. "Madame," she says respectfully with a slight curtsy, "I have other obligations and a mate of my own now. You must forgive me if I attend to them."

Beata lays hands on her hips. "It is not so simple, Fee. You have been and will remain my most *trusted* servant. I should not have to remind you of what I can let be known if you choose otherwise."

"You would not!" Fee gasps. "Even so, who would believe you?"

"Anyone with eyes and ears, my dear." Beata's lips pull into a smug smile. "It is a wonder no one has gossiped anything to date!"

Fee stops to think a few seconds, eyes lowered, then she raises them. "Very well. I shall serve you—on condition," she adds with resolve. "On condition that I may return to my Dien at the end of each day, that I may finish my work for the Handler newlyweds . . . and one more thing."

"Brash of you, but go on."

Fee takes a deep breath and speaks quickly. "If I am to live and serve in your household, then Besse must be allowed to return to her chamber in the tower."

Beata opens her mouth to object. As a thought occurs to her, she says instead, "Yes. That would keep up appearances for us all. It is done!"

Fee silently agrees. What would people say if Beata refused refuge to her own daughter?

With that, Fee continues to the market street, frowning as she dodges the children at play. The frown melts, however, as she deeply inhales the fragrant air mixed with the aromas of the market itself. Since the tannery has been banished outside the walls, its foul odor no longer dominates the area. The market is now far more inviting, which should boost business for all.

"How may I be of help today, dearest sister?" Fee asks with a lighter heart as she reaches the tent.

"Fee, you are a wonder. You will work yourself to death, I think. But please, go do what you must and leave me to manage this motley group. Besides, Besse is not here. In fact, she has not been here since late autumn. I grow concerned."

Fee exhales. "You know me well, sister. I did hold some small hope to see Besse. I have had some trepidation upon hearing that Granny is failing. It is possible she is too occupied tending to the poor woman to return to the city. However, once Granny passes"—Fee lowers her eyes, hiding a tear—"once she passes, Beata has consented to her return to the tower. Still, I do not know if that would be best for her. The poor girl has had little experience of kindness before Granny's generous offer, and the tower will engender ill memories."

"You fear she will miss the lady's kind attentions. That may be so," Flor says, "but remember that Besse will have *your* attentions again. For thirteen years, in fact, she has had your ministrations and love."

Fee frowns, still unable to accept any form of praise. She wags her finger. "I was of little use to her, and you know it. If Besse has a future at all, it will be because of you and your training, Granny, and the friendship and teaching of Ebouisante and Hans."

Flor shakes her head. "Once again, you take no credit but all the responsibility. I love you deeply, sister."

Fee considers this a moment and sighs. Besse will be her responsibility once again if she is to return to the tower.

"And look," Flor says, pointing. "I see Hans, our young groom, approaching us even now—and on horseback! What a handsome sight, don't you think?"

Before Fee can answer, Hans arrives at the tent and dismounts. "Fee, Flor—good day! I am just on my way to the woods. I have a sack of items for Besse and Granny."

At first he speaks quietly, glancing around, then he shrugs at himself and laughs.

"In fact, there may be no need for such secrecy. I have just overheard an older child threaten a younger sibling that if he does not behave, he may be eaten by the blind witch with the cookie-and-candy house in the woods! I think our story has taken hold. Perhaps it goes a bit too far," he adds, "if it has turned into a means of discipline. Nevertheless, I am not of a mood to correct it."

"How are they—how are Besse and Granny?" Fee eagerly asks.

"I reassure you, they are both well—though I do not see them come to the door. I think Besse shies away from me, though I know not any reason for it. Of late, she has refused even Ebouisante."

Fee casts a look of deep concern toward Flor, ignored by Hans.

"They have taken in two homeless orphans," Hans continues. "They may even be caring for an infant, based on some of the items they have ordered." He gestures toward the sack tied to his saddle.

Hans starts to remount. "I must go now, as I must deliver this bundle. After, the dauphin has asked me to meet him in the glade to join a hunt. And then I must hie home to prepare for the ceremony later this afternoon. It is a busy day! But first—Flor, would you please deliver a bouquet of wildflowers to my intended, as a token of my love?"

"Certainly," says Flor with a broad smile. She quickly ties together the stems of a dozen flowers in pinks, blues, and whites, with a very pleasant scent. "I shall deliver this in your name in person."

Hans reaches into the purse suspended from his belt, but Flor waves him off.

"Consider this a wedding gift from Fee and me," she says. "And here is a stalk of heather for you to deliver to the lady and Besse, with our compliments." She hands the heather to Hans, who bows before departing.

Flor turns to her sister as the young merchant rides off toward the city gate. "He certainly strikes a handsome figure, even in riding clothes, don't you think?" she offers. "I can definitely understand what Besse sees in him—a mixture of chivalry, charity, and a boy's sense of adventure. And good looks do not subtract from the picture."

"You must stop such dangerous thinking, Flor." Fee strikes an authoritarian pose—hands on hips and feet planted firmly on the ground—while she scowls. "In a matter of hours, Hans will be married—to Besse's dear friend! And truthfully, Besse can ill afford even to dream of such a mate as Hans."

"Yet you know she does. Who is there to disillusion her?"

"Then I must go to the house in the woods and talk to her. I will prevail upon Herr Handler to guide me to her." Fee turns as if to call out to Hans as he rides away. Then she catches herself. "Yet what time do I have today? It shall have to wait until after the wedding. Then I shall be resolute. I might even ask the young master to talk to the soldiers and his friends. Perhaps there is *someone* for her."

"Now you are scheming, dear sister. Some things are even beyond *your* reach. Beware the stewpot you choose to stir, when some of the ingredients are unknown to you."

"How philosophical, Flor. I do know my bounds, and I shall try not to exceed them. But you know I sometimes cannot help myself."

"Then concentrate on your current duties," Flor adds, "which are busy enough."

Fee grimaces. "Of course, my dear. And I love you back for your concern."

Truly, Fee has much to contemplate as she returns to her duties. For now, the wedding requires all her attention. But she will never let Besse's welfare far from her mind.

~ Chapter 57 ~

Hans rides to the house in the woods, dismounts, and retrieves his bundle and the carefully placed stalk of heather. As he turns toward the house, he frowns. Is that a wolf retreating behind a tree? He watches for a brief moment, sees nothing more, then shrugs.

He raps on the door, using his special knock agreed upon for security. The door opens.

To his surprise, a man answers, chicken leg in hand. Hans's eyes go wide, and the man laughs. It is Gaillard, the huntsman.

"You must be the young savior—Hans, is it? Fear not, but enter. I am Gaillard. I am of the woods, and it is my privilege to provide this home with some game in exchange for the best stews and cooking in the principality."

Hans looks around the room and, as usual, does not see Besse. The room has a delicious odor of cooked foods, and the huntsman offers him some sustenance as Granny emerges from the chamber beyond. Her eyesight failing, she must recognize Hans from his outline. She approaches him closely and smiles broadly as she hugs him.

"Good day, *meine frau*," offers Hans, holding out a sack of purchases, from which protrudes the heather. "I bring you your supplies and a gift from fräulein Flor!"

"Hans!" she exclaims. Thank ye, as always. I'm mindful that this is your wedding day. Such a kindness to spend a part of it with a poor ol' lady! Have ye time t' join us?" She motions to Gaillard to ladle out more stew.

Hans bows exaggeratedly, then rises with a laugh. "Unfortunately, *meine frau*, I cannot. I am expected by the dauphin for a hunt before the ceremony. Please give my best to Besse. I hope she is well."

Granny shakes her head. "It's a kindness you should ask, sir. I'm sorry she can't thank ye herself. She's restin', she is. I'm afraid the poor thing works so hard t' look after me! As ye see, I'm able t' do less and less meself these days. Rolf and Gurt do the marketin' and other duties for us. They're off gathering berries, they are."

"Ah yes, the orphans!" Hans replies. "You are so kind to take them in, not to mention Besse. Yet do be careful—I think I saw a wolf just outside. It may not be wise to let the children out on their own."

The huntsman laughs again. "I am sorry, Hans, but wolves are never known to attack men—or women or children, for that matter. There is no need to fear them. Be assured, I keep watch over all members of this household." He claps Hans on the shoulder and smiles, kindness evident in his expression. "I will not allow any harm to befall them."

"I am relieved, sir. And now, I must take my leave." With another bow, Hans turns and leaves the house.

Once again, he thinks he sees, from the corner of his eye, a gray bit of fur in the woods. But once again, he shrugs. He mounts his horse and heads for the glade.

◆ ◆ ◆

Hans would like to take part in the hunt—though he is also surprised he has been invited. He thought it was a scripted hunt, for nobility only. He knows the wedding has brought many nobles to the principality. There is a profusion of tents outside the city, with banners of all shapes and colors. They are here for the dauphin's wedding, of course. But this is an opportunity not to be missed. Hans and his father have been amongst them for days, and the trade has been wonderful. They have sold out their entire stock of furs and salt.

As he reaches the glade—where it seems just yesterday he and Charles were training before the daring rescue of the caravan—Hans sees the dauphin, astride his horse. He rides up to meet him.

"Your Highness," he says as he bows slightly without dismounting.

"Charles, please, when we are alone," he replies with a smile. "We shall always remain friends, and I look forward to more training and good times together. It pleases me especially to share our wedding day with you and Ebouisante. You are a very lucky man, Hans."

"Absolutely, your—Charles. But my Ebouisante is but a thistle to the blushing white rose of your betrothed."

The dauphin holds up a hand to silence his friend and laughs kindly. "Do not flatter me, friend. I am well aware of the great fortune of my own arrangement. I pray only that someday Giselle and I may share a love you and Ebouisante already seem to share."

Hans opens his mouth to protest, but Charles quickly interrupts.

"No. Say nothing," says Charles. "It is true. Yet I am very content with my life."

Hans considers this statement and responds with a smile of his own. "Thank you, Charles. You speak the truth. I am enamored of Ebouisante, and we are quite content."

Charles hesitates a moment. "In your life, Hans, you have had more than your share of opportunities to rescue damsels in distress, have you not? As I have said before, I hope this will not be your lot for the rest of your life. Your wife will require you to develop your trade with minimal, shall we say, adventure . . ."

The dauphin leans across his saddle and looks directly into Hans's eyes. Hans is a bit puzzled. Then a realization dawns on him.

"You did not invite me here to hunt with you."

"That is correct," Charles confirms. "I am sorry, Hans. This is a scripted hunt, and I must return to it anon. But I called you here because I felt the need to share a private moment with you prior to the wedding. To the point," he says, his voice now more authoritative, "I think you are both brave and kind but a little reckless when it comes to opportunities to act like a knight of King Arthur's court.

That makes you a good friend, so long as you do not draw me into your adventures too often!"

Both young men laugh.

"Yet do not think me ignorant of what goes on in my own realm," Charles addsreturning to his authoritative voice. "I am aware you and Ebouisante have continued to assist young Besse even as you have remanded her care to the lady in the woods. And I am aware—though perhaps you are not—she is Katrina, the widow of the jailer, and that she aided Jacques's escape from the dungeon as well as pilfered gold and priceless gifts from our treasury. It is my suspicion that Jacques absconded with the gifts while Katrina kept the gold."

"Charles!" Hans exclaims. He pulls up the reins of his horse, causing it to rear. He has to wait for it to settle, before continuing.

"Then why did you not reprimand me or Ebouisante, and why have you not apprehended Granny—that is, Frau Katrina?"

"Because even if you knew her identity and her crime, she has paid—and is paying—more than the price of the gold she has stolen. I am pleased to see her care for Besse and some of our city orphans."

Hans lowers his eyes, a bit ashamed.

Having caught his friend off guard, Charles decides this is a good time to broach the subject of the death of the armorer. "There is another point I wish to discuss," Charles continues, "regarding the fire at the Hammer household. The sight of the burned body of the armorer bothered you, did it not?"

Now Hans is nervous. He keeps his eyes lowered. "Yes, Charles, it did. I will not deny it."

Charles nods. "Given your nature—always finding people to rescue—one would think you would have saved the armorer when you came upon him incapacitated and surrounded by fire. But rather, you left Fee with the master, whose weight you must have realized she could not manage on her own. That is unlike you."

"Charles—sire!" Hans exclaims again, raising his head to look directly at the dauphin. "As I told you at the inquiry, I *did* try to help Fee with the armorer, but she insisted I leave with Besse. And Besse was my responsibility, above all else."

"You could have rescued them all, though, could you have not?" Charles counters. "You could have sent Fee outside with Besse, pulled the armorer to safety, then departed with Besse as planned."

"If you do not believe my story, why did you not question me further at your inquiry?" The confusion on Hans's face gradually fades into a smile. "Friendship!"

"That is exactly so," answers the dauphin, though he does not smile back. Instead, he holds his friend's eyes in a stern stare. "You did not want to save the man. So you left him there. Am I not correct?"

Hans blanches, then sighs. If punishment were intended or deserved, it would have already been meted out. The dauphin is merely acknowledging his suspicions.

"Yes, sire," Hans says. "In the moment, there was little time to think, but I could have saved the man. I did not."

"Many suffered at the hand of the armorer, not least of all Besse. I understand your desire to protect her. But there is more," Charles says, followed by a short pause. "Was the armorer also a threat to Ebouisante?"

Hans is impressed by the intelligence of his friend. He decides to reveal the truth.

"Yes. Dunkel did indeed threaten Ebouisante. She has a habit of bathing in the woods upriver, and once, while searching for Jacques, I fortuitously came across her there. I found her in a compromised state, bathing in the river under the observation of the brute. He could have had only one intention. I had to think fast and outfox him, while avoiding compromise of her situation. This I managed to accomplish. Afterward, we considered alerting the proper authorities, but we feared for her safety if we—pardon the irony—*exposed* the man. So as I entered the tower amid the smoke and fire that night, I could not dismiss the opportunity to eliminate the risk the armorer posed to both Besse and Ebouisante, especially with little time to think, under the circumstances."

The shadow of a cloud descends upon the young men and

their steeds as Hans looks pleadingly at his friend. At that moment, Charles looks across the glade and sees Henrik gesture to him from a distance to join the hunt.

Charles's face now softens. "I look upon you, friend, and I believe you are telling the truth. Thank you. Please retire to the city to make your preparations for the wedding. I shall follow upon the conclusion of the hunt."

A shrill note pierces the air.

"There is the sound of the horn now. The limers have already set the trail to a handsome buck. Farewell."

Hans bows again, turns his horse, and heads to the city. He is on to the stables, then home to bathe and change.

Hans rides in a fog, his head dizzy. He must put his encounter with the dauphin into some perspective, but he must also make some attempt to concentrate on the wedding event, and the plans for the house his father has gifted to him and his betrothed, and his future as a merchant.

Hans realizes he has indeed been a foolish youth, but what an adventure is life! Still, now he must resign himself to the satisfaction of his new life, one focused on the needs of a wife and the politics of trade.

He is oblivious of the smells of the market, the stares of the populace, and the games of the children in the streets. In but a few hours, the streets will clear as both children and adults join the two wedding processions to the church. He smiles, sighs, and rides on.

◆ ◆ ◆

Rolf and Gurt barely manage to get out of Hans's way as they rush ahead of him to the house intended for him and Ebouisante. They are not in the city for marketing or even to take part in the wedding celebrations. Rather, they have been sent on a mission.

They arrive almost breathlessly at the home, calling out at the door, "Fee! Fee! You must come quickly!"

Inside, Fee is ordering the placement of a magnificent lacquered

Chinese box adorned with a dragon and so polished that seems to breathe real fire. It is a trousseau containing the items of Ebouisante's dowry.

"Handle this with care," Fee directs the servants, "and place it gently at the foot of the bed. The mistress will be wanting immediate access. Be equally careful with the pitcher and wash basin. Have you ever seen the like? Such fine pottery! So white, to match the lady's complexion, and so blue and intricate the design. And what sort of flowers are those, I shall never know."

She is interrupted as another servant ushers the orphans into her presence. She looks at them for but a second before she understands they are the orphans who live with Besse and Granny. Her eyes go wide.

"What is it? Has something happened to the lady or"—here she hesitates with a thought she wishes not to utter aloud but must—"to my Besse?" She stifles a gasp.

"It *is* Besse, Fee," Rolf says. "You must come quickly!"

~ Chapter 58 ~

To Ebouisante, the day could not be more perfect. Last night, it seemed the nightingales sang only for her. Now, all birdsong is directed at her on this most auspicious day.

There is no one more handsome, more . . . well, charming, than my Hans, she thinks. *And a match for my wit, I must say. Or is that too arrogant? I do not think I could ever marry a man whose only interest is the mundane world. What is life without philosophy, without interpretation?*

Ebouisante shakes her head down from the clouds, realizing she must focus on the task at hand: her first look at the dowry contained in the magnificent Chinese lacquered box upstairs waiting at the foot of the bed.

Fortuitously, Blanche arrives at this moment, already dressed in an elegant hat and her own finest silk tunic, a bright blue with fox-fur trim. Ebouisante has never thought her mother more beautiful.

But everything seems more beautiful to her this day. Even the heavens have granted a perfect spring day, filling the air with perfumed fragrances of lavender and other hillside flowers. Flor must be busier than ever, with this double event at hand.

At that, Ebouisante must wonder, *But where is Fee?* Surprisingly, Fee is the one person with whom she most wants to share this day. Fee will be her personal servant and valet in the new household, and already Ebouisante looks upon her as if she were her own godmother. Fee inspires that in all she meets, really.

"Maman, I am so excited," the bride-to-be tells her mother. "Would you show me what you have packed in the trunk? But I wish Fee were here to see it. Where is she?"

~ Chapter 58 ~

"I am sorry, fräulein," answers the servant who brought the orphans to Fee. "She has been called away on a family emergency. She expresses her deepest regret that she must miss this most precious event."

There. The servant has said exactly the words Fee told her to offer Ebouisante. She remembered to call it a "family emergency," as Fee knew that any suspicion of a problem with Besse would spoil the day for Ebouisante. And that must not happen. No further excuse or information is to be given. At any rate, Fee herself did not have much more information when she left with the orphans.

"I am sorry about Fee, my precious one," Blanche says, "but she would not want you to postpone this event. Let us climb to your chamber and have a look at your trousseau."

Blanche looks over the antechamber and room with a nod of satisfaction as they make their way through the home.

"I am very pleased to see the old timbers and floors have all been replaced. The building no longer leans like an old woman with a cane. And you have a new roof protected by clay shingles, using the method I have taken pains to teach the builders."

Upstairs in the chamber, Blanche crosses the room to inspect the hearth. The air is scented with flowers sent by Flor. Blanche also notes ampoules of perfumes, silver boxes of powders, and silver brushes—all provided as wedding gifts from friends and relatives.

"What beautiful gifts! And the room is well lit without a single torch!" Blanche notes excitedly. "Even though the light enters the chamber from this one window, I see it is reflected and multiplied by these polished stones installed on the high walls."

In truth, the arrangement spreads daylight throughout the room, enhanced even more by the radiance of its main occupant.

"Is it not amazing, Maman?" Ebouisante says. "The reflecting stones are polished obsidian—a gift of the prince and princess. Papa says he has heard that this method was used in ancient Egypt, and look how well it works here."

With a smile, Ebouisante takes a small step toward the lacquered box.

"May we look through the trousseau now?"

Blanche smiles ear to ear. "Why, yes! My dearest one, I have dreamed of this day since you were born."

Ebouisante opens the chest, then utters a short "Oh!" as she pulls out a silk gown of the purest white. She has never seen the like—a white wedding gown! Beneath the gown she spies a hennin, a tall hat with the finest lace veil attached to its point, and two exquisite gold-embroidered slippers. The slippers are a startling complement to the simple, unadorned gown.

"What do you think? White gowns are to be the newest custom in France," Blanche says. "White symbolizes your purity and beauty." She leans close to her daughter and whispers, "I predict not all eyes will be on the duke's daughter!"

"It is magnificent, Maman! Nothing less! It is fit for a goddess—far too much for a mere merchant's daughter! I am overwhelmed. And oh!" Ebouisante now sees the other treasures in the trousseau. "The cloth and linens! Thank you, and thank Papa! I am not worthy." She bows her head in supplication, tears filling her eyes. They glisten, improving her beauty all the more.

"You *are* worthy, and then some. You have been invaluable to your papa, and this is the least he can do. Now to your bath, then let us get you dressed and ready. We have little time, and certainly no more time for conversation and daydreaming!" she adds with a wink.

◆ ◆ ◆

Soon it is time. Hans arrives at the threshold, looking more a prince to his betrothed than His Highness himself.

As his eyes behold Ebouisante, they go wide, and he shudders at the radiance of his beloved.

"I am confronted by the epitome of beauty, dressed as I have never seen," he states, his eyes aglow. "I will always love you, truly."

Ebouisante blushes and reaches for his hand.

Hans must pull his eyes from the vision that is Ebouisante, as he sees their families draw near. "Here are our fathers. Let us begin the procession to the church."

Beaming with pride and admiration, the parents fall in behind the couple. The Kaufmanns and Handlers have already bonded as true friends and business associates, and now they have this joyous event to share.

The streets have been cleared of children, but anyone can follow behind the procession, and many do. The merry group will meet the prince and his bride at the church entrance, with the royal procession using a different route from the castle. Giselle herself has insisted they not diminish or overpower the day for Hans and Ebouisante.

The soon-to-be dauphiness is attired in her finest surcotte, fur lined and embroidered with gold thread on velvet of the deepest blue. She rides with the dauphin in a four-in-hand carriage. They are flanked on one side by the duke on a grand destrier, and on the other by the prince on a fine white Arabian steed. The princess rides a few steps behind, sidesaddle on a fine courser.

Children strew the streets with aromatic petals—provided by Flor, of course. Other nobility ride or walk behind, smiling and nodding to the crowd lining the streets. They move slowly, enjoying the moment, letting their minds wander to the feast and the tournament ahead.

To observers leaning out the windows of the surrounding houses, the two wedding processions resemble nothing less than two slow-moving rivers of color—the Tigris and Euphrates finally converging at the center of civilization. The perfect weather is a gift from God and does not go unmentioned among many of them.

Suddenly the assemblage is shocked by a disturbance. A young lady, clad only in a large comforter, bursts out of a house and races through the streets. She is closely followed by a young man in pursuit.

"Rose, stop!" shouts Peter.

Laughter breaks out at the absurdity.

Finally catching up, Peter pulls Rose back through the crowd.

The periphery guard allows them to pass with a few snickers. Though red with embarrassmet, Peter ignores them.

"You cannot give up your old profession, can you?" he hisses under his breath. "I give you shelter and protection, and this is how you repay me?"

Rose, true to her name, is also red, though from anger. "I ne'er promised ye constancy, I didn't! I'll do as I damned well see fit, I will! And ye can't stop me!"

"See if I cannot! You will come home with me now! I shall never let you out alone again!"

As if oblivious to the ridiculous distraction, the merchant couple does not break its step as it proceeds on foot. The populace now turns all attention to them, as no one can take his or her eyes off the bridal vision in white. This has never been seen before. Every young maiden takes mental notes, ready to be part of this new fashion when her own time arrives. The older citizens mutter criticisms aloud, keeping their true admiration secret.

Both parties arrive at the church. The priest bows to the royalty and greets them heartily.

"This is a very special day that shall be long remembered in Quellestadt. In the presence of these most esteemed of witnesses, I call upon Your Young Highness and your ladyship to state your vows, followed by those of the young master and mistress," he says, smiling at Hans and Ebouisante. "After your statements, I shall pronounce you men and wives and bid you enter the church to pray."

"Thank you, Father," says Charles with a slight nod.

He turns to La Claire and takes her hands in his own.

"As your radiance blinds the eye to all that surrounds you, so shall I ever be able to see only you. I pledge myself to you now and forever, and promise to devote my life to your happiness, even as I see to the welfare of our subjects."

La Claire responds, "And I pledge myself to you. I promise to honor and obey. I devote my life to bringing you joy, and to bringing kindness and understanding to your subjects, upon the honor of my lord, the Duke of Burgundy, and myself. May our love only grow with the years."

As the priest pronounces the couple man and wife, a great cheer arises from the assembled crowd and quickly spreads throughout the city. The priest bids them enter the church, which they do, followed by their parents.

Eventually the crowd quiets, anticipating yet another set of vows. They are not disappointed.

Hans clears his throat, blushing as he takes Ebouisante's hands in his. He lifts the veil of the hennin from her face. She smiles. He begins:

Young love is like first flower in the snow
Requiring but the glacial melt to grow
From seed left firmly in the mother earth
It seeks the sun, rejoicing in its birth.

Yet does it let the wind cause it to sway
From bee to bee or flower to flower play
Until it settles constancy with one
Attuned at last and unable to run?

When does the blossom know it has one home
And must not ever be inclined to roam?
Though others may have settled 'pon its fate,
Only two hearts, entwined, can justly mate.

Though earthly bound,
My love is found.

"My dearest Ebouisante," he concludes, "I am yours forever."

The crowd cheers again, then hushes immediately to soft murmurs of admiration. Hans's escapades are well known, but who would have thought him a poet as well?

"Dear husband," Ebouisante responds. "I pledge my life and loyalty to thee, as I stand now in garb of purity. Let us begin a long life together in bonds of love and respect."

Hans winks, acknowledging that his wife is a lady of letters and intelligence at least equal to his. He does not expect her to pledge obedience, but he knows she already honors him.

Again to cheers, the priest pronounces the couple man and wife. Now the entire entourage enters the church—first Hans and Ebouisante, then their families, then the nobles, then the merchants. Finally, the priest enters, leaving the doors open to the public as he gives a homily and blesses the couples.

Now all four newlyweds emerge. Charles bids both ladies to enter the coach together, then he wraps his arm around Hans's shoulders and urges him into the carriage. The footman closes the door behind them all, and they proceed throughout the city, waving to the citizens.

The assemblage retreats to the castle for what promises to be the feast to end all feasts: five courses with entremets of jugglers, singers, poets, and fanciful platters of carved foods, all accompanied by the finest wines of Burgundy.

A very special set of guests joins the assemblage at the castle. They did not attend the ceremony, choosing instead to enter the castle through a hidden entrance. It is the dwarves. They have managed to clean themselves up and acquire rich clothing. A few citizens politely comment on their attendance, for all know their service to La Claire, as well as to the prince and dauphin.

The feast begins with the first of many toasts to the couples and to the rulers of both realms. And there is more celebration to come. Outside the city walls, preparations are nearly complete for the tournament to follow the next day.

◆ ◆ ◆

Inside the cottage in the woods, Fee attends to Besse, who cries quietly in the darkness.

"Oh, Fee, Fee! It is not for me to have the life of Ebouisante!" she sobs.

Fee hugs her and strokes her hair gently. "Hush, liebchen. It is not for us to question the fate the Lord has assigned us. And I know you wish the couple well. They have both done much for you."

Now it is Fee's turn to cry softly, suffering the guilt of herself having achieved the happiness she cannot secure for the maiden.

She hands her Dolly, whom Besse hugs close. As Fee leaves, Besse turns to the doll.

"We shall see, Dolly. We shall see." She then collapses to sleep in exhaustion.

~ Chapter 59 ~

As had been augured, the weather is perfect for the celebrations the day after the weddings. Spring—with its scent of wildflowers in bloom—is in the air. The temperature is neither too hot nor too cold. The sun shines brightly, revealing a rainbow of color as the pennants flap in the breeze.

There is a torrent of activity here and there as the tournament competitions are about to begin. Squires dress their knights for the joust or the rings. The squires are told to hurry. The noble women on the dais are already waving their scarves of linen or silk, waiting for the knights to approach and tip their lances. Each knight wants to be first to offer himself to the most comely among the ladies. Of course, the new dauphiness herself is taken. She will place her kerchief upon the lance of her prince, who is expected to appear last.

La Claire muses upon the wedding and the last evening, which was a promise of wonderful nights to come. Princess Amalia had seen to it that the newlyweds' bed had fresh linens, the floor had fresh flax, and fragrant flowers were everywhere in the chamber. Charles recited poetry to her and proved to be a wonderful, if awkward, lover. Of course, it had been the first time for them both. La Claire lets out a dreamy sigh. The dauphin is so handsome, so gentle, and so intelligent!

As her thoughts wander, the assembled citizenry looks upon her in her reverie. They smile, then blush as they imagine her evening. Their dauphiness seems to shine with brilliance greater than the reflection of the sun on the silk of her kerchief. Murmurs ripple like waves.

"She is so beautiful! We are blessed," one wistful maiden whispers to her brother.

"Yes, but look at the merchant's daughter beside her," the brother replies. "I cannot say which is more attractive."

"A shame both are spoken for. What remains for Papa to find for you?" This comes with a smirk.

"Fear not, sister. If the doves are flown, there remain the nightingales."

"Ha!" The smirk widens. "For you, it will more likely be the grouse."

"And for you, sister, the goshawk!" He gives her a small shove.

"Stop it, you two," the mother now admonishes. "If you behave thus, we will find only the goose and the gander, as they would be the fittest for you!"

Now the armored knights approach the line of ladies on the dais. The princess nods, and lances are tipped to present to the maidens. The ladies pretend to disdain this one, favor that one. They blush and lower their eyes in false or real modesty. Then each maiden ultimately selects a knight to be her personal champion.

There is much gossiping, of course.

"My champion will defeat yours!"

"Certainly not! Sir Rolf is the champion at the ring, and he will prove it this day!"

"Oh no, Eleanor. Sven will outjoust them all!"

This is followed by playful jostling and a round of giggling.

Suddenly, a hush falls over the crowd. Prince Henrik emerges from the royal tent, which, for the purpose, has been covered with a brilliant blue silk. Atop the tent flies the pennant of the royal crest, with golden lions and swords at cross corners on a background of red. La Claire's kerchief is emblazoned with the same emblem, now establishing herself as a member of the household, to the approval of the citizenry.

Next Charles emerges from the tent. The assemblage has never seen the like. He wears armor prepared for him as a wedding gift. It is none other than the masterpiece Rudi has been perfecting for admittance to the guild. It is a perfect fit, in the Italian style, of the finest hardened steel. Yet it is jointed and lightweight enough to allow fleetness of foot as he strides toward his horse, a fine black destrier.

To the crowd, the dauphin seems to walk upon the air. They blush yet again at the thought of the last evening. This time, they are too stunned for even gossip.

Charles rides to the ladies and bows his lance to his dauphiness. She deftly places her kerchief upon its tip. He retrieves the kerchief, holds it to his heart, and tucks it into his armor. The crowd cheers. This is a moment, an event which will be remembered throughout history, in the hearts of all who serve and admire the royalty of the principality.

As he turns, however, Charles eyes something at the periphery of the crowd. One armored knight without a lance and with visor drawn retreats into the group of waiting contestants at the edge of the forest.

And did Charles catch this knight glancing at the dais? Could Charles be certain of such a thing if the knight's visor is down? Why was his visor down? Armor is uncomfortably warm, and one would expect open visors until the contest itself requires closure to protect the face. This is certainly the case for all the other knights.

Charles frowns, but he cannot linger. His presence is required at the ring, a looped rope hanging from a freely swinging bar perched on a post. He will get two passes to try to pierce the loop at a gallop. Henrik deemed it safe for his son to compete in this event but would not allow him to challenge seasoned knights in a true joust.

Charles takes his place at the appropriate distance and furrows his forehead as he focuses upon the rope. La Claire thinks him all the more handsome—a fierce hawk and a fit mate, exhibiting such concentration of purpose.

He accelerates his steed toward the rope, but then narrowly misses his target. The crowd breaks from its hush into a collective sigh of consolation. His Highness has no enemies or rivals in this crowd, so the sympathy is truly felt.

Charles pulls his destrier into a rear, takes his place again, and attempts even greater concentration. The angle of the sun leaves a shadow inside the loop of rope, and Charles imagines a dark enemy. He charges once more. This time the tip of the lance pierces the ring cleanly.

A great cheer bursts from the audience. Charles thinks he hears the shout of his new true love above, or at least separate from, the others. He realizes it is now the only sound for which he has any care.

He retrieves his lance, rides to the dais, and bows before his family. But as he bows, he hears not a cheer, but a cry of surprise.

A longbow arrow has arced out of the forest behind the massing knights and pierced the heart of the elder prince. Charles looks up to see his father collapse into the arms of his mother.

Charles cries out. Then in a flash, he turns his horse toward the forest. He calls back,

"Captain, see to the ladies!" as he races through the dumbfounded assemblage of knights.

Charles sees his quarry ahead. It is the visored "knight" he saw retreating earlier. The figure continues walking rapidly into the woods. Without another thought, Charles lowers his lance and urges on his horse. Hearing the charge, the knight suddenly turns. But it is too late. The lance pierces the weak armor. Even as the destrier advances and the knight is thrown backward, Charles is coated with blood as it gushes from the adversary's chest.

Charles pulls the reins and dismounts, then approaches the man on the forest floor. His eyes go wide as he realizes it is not a man, but a woman! No, not just any woman. The duchess!

Her eyes are wide with pain and surprise. She coughs up blood. Yet she still has enough strength to offer Charles a sardonic grin.

"I am done," she rasps.

"Do not talk, madame! I will send for the physicians," Charles interrupts, too overcome with shock to remember he himself is the cause of her suffering.

"They will not arrive in time, *dauphin*." She spits blood with this word. "She has won, and I have lost. My guard missed his mark."

"You meant the arrow for Giselle!" Charles shouts, anger now flooding his shock. "For this you shall pay dearly!"

But so she already has. She emits a deep, gurgling sigh, and expires.

Something inside Charles suddenly realizes the longbowman may *not* have missed his mark. The duchess may have wanted to kill her stepdaughter, but her guard may have had his own intentions.

And in his chase of this disguised knight, Charles allowed the bowman to escape. He missed the opportunity to apprehend his father's killer. He did not avenge his father. He killed the duchess!

Overwhelmed, he mounts his horse. He gallops away aimlessly, trying to escape himself. He cannot face anyone if he cannot even face himself.

The other knights and the guard will surely be near. Perhaps some have even witnessed the brutal event and its conclusion. They will try to follow him.

But on this destrier at top speed, no one can catch or even follow his course. He is soon alone with his thoughts, his numbness. His mind empties as he rides.

◆ ◆ ◆

Yet there is a figure unseen in the woods. Borg moves with purpose, a smile upon his lips. He is avenged! Using then discarding and banishing soldiers—this prince left Borg no choice in life. He had to pay!

And her ladyship, she should have known better than to trust Borg to do *her* bidding with no offer of suitable reward! The dauphiness is no enemy of his and not deserving of such a fate. Yet once the duchess trusted Borg enough to recruit him to her own nefarious plan, it was easy to convince her that the tournament offered a perfect opportunity.

As he reaches his destination at the edge of the glade, he hears a voice. It is angry.

"I charged you with keeping me informed of her ladyship's whereabouts and intentions."

It is Duke Philip. He glares crossly at Borg.

"My Liege," Borg answers with head bowed but the smirk still on his lips, "I have done your bidding. I have accompanied the duchess for these months and kept you abreast of her dealings. And I assured you I would foil her vengeful plan against your daughter." His smirk widens with a shake of his head. "Why would I kill the dauphiness just to satisfy the duchess?"

"Why, indeed?" the duke says. His eyes flash. "Especially when it would have done little to endear you to your employer. You should shudder to think of the fate I would have let befallen you, had you actually harmed my daughter!"

Borg flinches at the threat.

Philip continues, "And while you did inform me of my wife's intentions to kill my daughter, you did *not* inform me of your own intentions to kill the prince! You managed to take advantage of both her ladyship and me to your own ends! That is unacceptable. You are very fortunate I am still in need of your services. His Highness is—was—the father-in-law of my daughter, whom I cherish above all else. He was an ally! You have caused much grief. I am outraged!"

Borg bows in fearful respect. Only now does he realize he might have allowed his own rage to jeopardize his life.

"I must now attend to the grieving royal family—thanks to you," Philip says. "And you—your service is not complete. You will now recover her ladyship's whereabouts. She cannot have gone far. Or have you hidden her from me?"

Philip looks around him to see if she followed the soldier, then hidden herself at the appearance of her erstwhile husband.

"How do you know she is here in Quellestadt?" Borg asks. "Even I did not know she would come today."

It is Philip's turn to smirk. "Do not take me for a fool, Borg. I knew she would be here. She could not resist a chance to see her plot against my daughter to its fruition. Her rage made her blind to all else, including your betrayal." He bores his eyes even deeper into Borg's. "Now go—find her and report to me. You must convince her you missed your mark, and you will continue to serve her purpose. But you must *never* act to betray *my* interests again. I must attend to the royal family—*my* family. Do you understand?"

Duly chastised, Borg turns to retrace his steps and seek out the erstwhile duchess, Philip's guard arrives and approaches him with a display of great anxiety.

"What is it now?" the duke demands indignantly.

"Your Grace, it's . . . her ladyship, the duchess! She has been killed!" The guard lowers his head and falls to his knee, as if begging mercy.

Borg is astonished, frightened to immobility. He left the duchess alone and vulnerable.

Philip clenches his fists in anger. "Get up!" he says to the guard on his knees. He turns to Borg. "You will answer to this later! But now you must accompany my guard out of the principality, then they must return to me."

Borg barely manages to nod.

"And keep yourself available," Philip adds, his voice filled with ideas and thoughts Borg cannot begin to imagine. "I have much work for you yet. Perhaps you may redeem your failure to protect the lady. I must hie to the castle now, and I shall expect a report in detail from the guard there."

Borg trembles, then sighs. "Yes, My Liege." He answers meekly.

~ Chapter 60 ~

Grief, pain, denial, anger, shame, then all of these emotions at once, drive the dauphin—now the *prince*—onward, oblivious to the hazards of galloping through a dense forest. Charles plans to ride off the end of the earth if he can.

Somehow the destrier reads his mind. Knowing its rider has lost all direction and reason, the horse spontaneously comes to a stop in the cleared courtyard of a small hovel at the base of a cave.

The sudden lack of motion brings the young man to his senses. He shakes his head to clear his mind. Looking up, he recognizes the hovel. It is the home of the dwarves.

The horse neighs and bows its head as it paws the ground. This serves as an alarm. Grump hurriedly exits the abode. His colleagues have gone to observe the tournament and to assure themselves of the happiness of "their" La Claire.

The dwarf is astonished to see Charles, magnificently accoutered, splattered with blood, his head bowed. It occurs to him something terrible has happened at the tournament.

As Charles dismounts upon unsure legs, the dwarf advances, enfolds the new prince without even the courtesy of a bow, and hurries him into the home. He dips a linen cloth in a washbowl and makes short work of cleaning the armor and the young man's face and hands.

Charles makes no effort to resist his attentions. "Thank you," he quietly says.

Overcome again with emotion, Charles lowers his head into his hands and cries softly. He gives no care if he shows his vulnerability to this man. The dauphin knows Grump is seeing him at the lowest point of his life.

"Sire," the dwarf says, "please forgive me if I ask what happened."

Charles raises his head, looks straight into the eyes of the dwarf, and heaves a great sigh. Holding back sobs, he relates his experience of the retreating figure with visor drawn, of the longbow arrow piercing his father, and of what his own lance did to the duchess.

The dwarf listens intently, wide-eyed. He considers for a moment.

"Sire, ye acted out of instinct, ye did . . . though ye allowed your rage t' o'erpower your better judgment—if ye'll pardon me, sire."

"No, please continue," Charles says. Overcome with emotion, he finds it oddly calming to hear rational words of advice.

"Ye must return, sire. Ye've left your mother and wife alone t' deal with the—forgive me—the body of your father, of His Highness. They too 'll be o'ercome with grief, they will. The tournament'll be in a state of chaos, the guests in a state of confusion. We must do what we can t' restore ye t' yourself—t' your family and t' your subjects, those who rely on your strength and judgment. And we must do it quickly. Ye must take charge, yes. Ye must *rule*."

The prince slowly nods, picking up his head a bit more with each movement. "You are right, my friend," he says.

He takes a breath to regain some composure, then rises to his feet.

"I must suppress the grief, the self-punishment. I shall return. I owe you my thanks."

◆ ◆ ◆

Indeed, the tournament is in total disarray. The prince has been hit! He is down! The spectators cannot help but panic at the thought that the entire assemblage may be under attack. Swords are drawn, and knights and soldiers quickly run to secure the protection of their families and lords. Everyone runs in different directions, the entire scene more chaotic than a general melee.

Captain Erich of the prince's guard takes no time to react to the fall of his master. Even as he kneels before the dying prince, his thoughts are quick and clear. Who is attacking the principality? How many are there? Where are they stationed? Where is the dauphin? And where did the duke go?

Erich must leave the prince in the arms of the princess. He quickly mumbles an apology.

Amalia raises her head to him in an expression of grief and fear, but she nods, offering him her full trust in that one gesture.

Rising, he takes charge immediately. He orders two guards to stay with the royalty and others to assist with protection of the visiting royals and merchants. He then directs a party of four soldiers to search for the dauphin, with maximum speed. The rest he stations around the periphery of the assemblage with orders to protect at all costs.

Only after he sees his orders obeyed with speed and efficiency does Erich turn back to the princesses. He uses his own body and those of two guards as shields as he ushers them off the dais and into the carriage that will bear them and the dying prince to the castle. Erich attempts to use the guards to deflect the ladies' view of the soon-dead man, but the princess pushes him away and walks at Henrik's side as he is placed gently onto the carriage floor. These are her last moments with her beloved husband, and she will hold him as long as she can.

She kneels beside him and takes his hand.

"My love . . ." Henrik barely manages to whisper.

"I know, Henrik," Amalia whispers back through tears. "Rest, my *lieber* prince. You have trained Charles well, and he will be surrounded by love and support."

She sobs quietly as the one true love of her life draws his last breath.

~ Chapter 61 ~

Outside the castle, visitors—nobility and burghers alike—gather in some confusion with the citizens of the principality. There is much grief, surprise, consternation, and fear. Soldiers soon form a perimeter around the crowd, which does little to ease the mood. A few guards circulate through the crowd to offer what reassurances they can.

"There is no attack, only a single archer," they explain. "Several of our men have been sent in pursuit. Soon you shall all be able to return to your tents or homes."

At that moment, there comes a shout from the guard. "Make way for the dauphin!"

The crowd parts as Charles hurries to the castle entrance and dismounts. He draws a deep breath, facing the crowd.

"I would ask your indulgence, with apologies to all the nobility assembled here. First, I will apologize for the disruption of our celebration. As you can understand, it will be impossible to continue the tournament. At this moment, I must have time to pay my respects to His Highness and to direct the preparations for . . .."

The sudden thought of a state funeral for his father causes Charles to pause. He is bereft of hope for his father's survival, but it pains him deeply to think of it, no less speak of it.

"For what is to come," he concludes. "Please excuse me," he adds, no longer able to speak as his voice begins to break.

He bows to the crowd, hiding the tears starting to fill his eyes, then turns to enter the castle.

◆ ◆ ◆

~ Chapter 61 ~

Inside, the guards have moved the prince's body to the back chamber. They now discreetly stand watch over the princesses as they hug each other in sorrow and consolation. Erich moves to the entrance to await the return of the new prince.

La Claire unabashedly leans upon her mother-in-law's arm. She is clearly confused, and not only because of the attack on the prince. She does not know what to expect of her new husband. Why would he ride off, leaving the ladies alone, and where could he have gone?

And then they hear him return. La Claire walks shakily to the entrance, with Amalia a step behind. Erich and the guards stand alert.

As soon as he enters, Charles looks first at his wife, then at his mother. He smiles, holding back further tears.

A wave of relaxation passes quickly through the assemblage, as if a storm has broken. But then his mother sees, with some concern, that the smile is forced. She beckons him to her.

Charles hesitates. The light from the clerestory falls upon him, incongruously bright and cheerful, as if it is unaware of the tragedy that interrupted the celebration. Pennants of visiting royalty adorn the walls, a cacophony of color. It suddenly overwhelms the young man, seeming accusatory.

He runs to his mother, and she enfolds him in her arms.

La Claire stands aside, bewildered. What should she think of the man she has just married?

"Oh, Mama!" Charles cries. "What have I done?"

"My son, my son—I forgive you."

Charles looks at his mother in surprise at these words. "Then you know? How could you know?"

"What is there to know? Your father was hit, and you ran to save yourself from an attack. You are still but a child. How can I not forgive you?"

"Oh, Mama! Is that what you think?" He shakes his head at the thought. "I did not run away, Mama."

Now he breaks out into great sobs. The princess allows him this release, patiently awaiting what more he has to reveal.

Ultimately, he continues. "Earlier, I had seen a suspicious knight with his visor down. So then, once Papa was . . . was struck, I ran after the knight. I caught him and without thinking ran my lance into him. But it was not a he, it was a she! And not just any she, Mama, but the duchess in disguise," he blurts out. "She is dead."

The two ladies gasp in unison, but Charles continues hurriedly, knowing they needed to hear more.

"She had directed her guard to kill not Papa, but"—he turns to his wife—"forgive, me, my love, *you*!"

Amalia raises her fist to her mouth, and Giselle pales, if that is even possible for one of such light complexion.

"But Mama, I knew none of that when I pursued him—her," he stumbles, his words coming faster and faster. "I only knew no one else had any suspicion of her, so I had no time to alert the guard. I had to do it myself. Papa's killer would have escaped! But Mama, I was wrong. She was not the killer. It had to be her guard. A longbowman! He abandoned her and escaped. But he missed his mark." Charles takes a gasping inhalation. "Or perhaps he did not! Papa!"

Tears spilled from his eyes. "The real killer escaped because I allowed my blind emotion to guide my actions. It was rash. It is not the action of a true prince." He lowers his head. "That is what I thought you wanted to forgive."

"Then, son, I will try to forgive you, if only you can obtain the release of your wife and His Liege. And you must also forgive *me* for not knowing my own son well enough to trust his motives and actions."

She looks into his eyes for a moment, seeing he is speaking the truth. She curtsies to him.

"You are the prince now, my son, and I am merely your subject."

"That will never be, Mama. I have always been ruled by you as well as by His Highness. You must not curtsy to me."

"Ah, son, but I shall," she replies. "Especially in public. For all must know I have complete faith in you and your ability to rule."

Charles shudders, lowering his voice. "I am not worthy. I am too young and brash. I have acted entirely out of instinct, which is indiscreet and unforgiveable."

"And you recognized it immediately and have already taken steps in your own mind to correct it. That is the mark of a great ruler." She lifts his chin, meeting his eyes. "Do you not know that monarchs are mere men, subject to all the faults of emotion and, yes, sometimes ignorance? The greatest rulers are fully aware of their shortcomings. But they move to control them, to eliminate them."

"Thank you, Mama."

He embraces his mother once again. As he pulls away, he frowns as he thinks of his father, lying in the adjacent chamber. *There is no going back, Papa. I wish I could tell you how much I already miss your kindness, your indulgence, your guiding hand. May you watch over me and help me not make any more grave mistakes.*

He then turns to his wife of one day.

"I am deeply sorry, my dear. How can you ever forgive me? You must think me a great fool and a child."

La Claire bows her head. He walks to her, lifts her chin, and sees she is welling up tears.

"Will you ever forgive me?" he asks.

She smiles and takes his hand. "Forgive you? What sort of fool am I that could not love a man who would pursue a criminal with no regard for himself yet is sensitive enough to allow his regal self to cry in the presence of two ladies? If I were ever unsure I could love you, all such doubts have been dispelled. I am the luckiest princess, the luckiest woman, alive!"

"But the duchess . . . your stepmother . . . I . . ." His words fail him.

Giselle reddens, surprising herself with her vehemence. "That lady, that . . . that *woman* tried thrice to eliminate me! Oh!"

She breaks down with a mix of terrible emotions: sorrow at the loss of her stepmother under such circumstances, yet gratitude that the duchess's death ensures her own safety.

As the tears flow, the young couple hugs.

Charles at last looks around and notices Captain Erich and the guards, who have been present—though with politely turned backs—for these intimate exchanges. He is slightly embarrassed for a moment. Then he shrugs, accepting the loss of freedom that comes with the throne.

He sighs and says to Erich, "If you would be so kind, would you summon the city criers."

Erich motions for one of the guards to follow him outside. The soldier, relieved to have a direct order and reassured by the resumption of appropriate demeanor in his prince, hastens to comply.

Soon Captain Erich reenters, this time accompanying the duke. Charles bows before his father-in-law. La Claire runs to his side, offering him a curtsy, then an embrace.

"Papa! You must forgive him, as I have! Maman, she would have . . . He is so brave, my husband! I do so love him!"

"You are so right, my little one. I must admit to shock to learn of the fate of your stepmother, confirmed by this captain." He turns to the young prince with a bow. "Your Highness, I grieve at the loss of your father, who became more than an ally, but a true friend. As for Enchanteresse, assure yourself that though I once loved that woman, she would have bereft me of the one I do love with all my heart. You did what you must to save and protect your wife. You have excellent instinctive powers of observation. I would humbly request that you seek me out for guidance whenever I can be of assistance."

He hesitates a bit, then nods toward Amalia and La Claire.

"I know this is a difficult time," Philip continues, "but I offer my deepest sympathy for your own loss and any aid I can give in preparation for the funeral. I am placing my own guard contingent at your disposal to assist with the security of your realm during this transition—if you will excuse me long enough to see to the arrangements for Her Ladyship myself."

"Thank you, Your Grace," answers Charles with a slight bow in return. "I hope there shall not be a need for your guard, but your offer is accepted with our gratitude. I would ask a small boon, however.

There must be an inquiry into the deaths of . . . of His Highness as well as Her Grace."

There is only a slight hesitation here. Charles now realizes he must assume the role of leader, which will brook no sign of weakness.

"I would ask if you would direct the inquiry, Your Grace, as I will need to be questioned."

Philip is astonished. "Sire, why would you place yourself in such a position? I myself would certainly never do so. I will cooperate fully but with discretion, Your Highness. In fact, you must also allow me to take charge of the pursuit of the archer, as a gesture of friendship and solidarity."

Charles nods. "This principality may be governed by my law, but it is governed by *law* nonetheless. The citizens must know no one is exempt."

"So be it, then."

The duke bows again, this time offering a somewhat secretive smile to his daughter, who blushes. Giselle is pleased to see the newfound respect in her father's eyes. This will be a great alliance, with much to gain on both sides.

The guard returns with the criers. They gather before the new prince.

"Sirs," Charles begins in an authoritative voice, "you will go throughout Quellestadt and announce the deep grief of the royal family at our loss and the loss of all our subjects. The funeral shall be three days hence, followed by a general inquiry. You shall also announce the loss of Her Grace, with arrangements to be made at the discretion of His Liege. That is all."

The criers bow and back out of the castle entrance.

Charles turns to his mother and wife. "I must now pay my respects. I will leave it to you, my ladies, to arrange for His Highness to lie in state in this chamber for three days. Guard, please send for the monks and inform the priest, that they may be prepared."

◆ ◆ ◆

And so it is done. The new prince and princess sequester themselves as best they can, consoling each other as best they can, in the short time leading to the funeral.

Most of the visiting nobles and burghers remain to pay respect. They join the line encircling the bier laid in state in the council hall. Once the priest anoints Henrik with holy water, the new prince, along with his wife and mother, follows behind the body. Visiting royalty, noblemen, and burghers proceed after them. The citizens of Quellestadt line the streets, heads bowed. After the service, the body is laid to rest on the castle grounds.

The elder princess will wear black for a year, while Charles will wear a black armband. It will become something of a trademark, as he will wear it not for a year but for his lifetime.

The inquiry is entirely perfunctory. No one will doubt that Charles has heard the duchess's confession, and all know her intentions toward her stepdaughter. Though the duke would also make inquiry as to the identity and whereabouts of the longbowman, no one appears with any information—much to his private relief.

Thus, all town gossip is silenced, and the citizens look upon their new ruler with pride and respect.

~ Chapter 62 ~

"We have secrets, Dolly. Oh yes, we do." Besse has retreated into the darkest corner of her chamber and retrieved the one toy with which she will not part.

"But we are not alone! Everyone has secrets, don't they? Granny certainly does. Where did she come from, and where does she get her money for marketing? I have heard her talk of Jacques. She is always telling Rolf and Gurt to grow up and learn a trade, or they will become like Jacques. They do not know who that is, but I remember that was the name of the thief in the dungeon. How can I forget, Dolly? He is the one who accosted me in the Jews' quarter.

"Sometimes Granny cries when she mentions Jacques. So I think I know who she really is—the jailer's wife. That accounts for her money. She must have taken it from the prince's treasury. I also believe her husband attacked her. We have that in common, do we not? It is the reason we both had to escape.

"And why does the huntsman help us? He says he is from Burgundy. Yet he won't return there. So he has secrets too. Why wouldn't he be welcome there?"

Besse grows quiet for a moment. She pulls Dolly closer, whispering to her.

"But we have greater problems, Dolly. Granny's tumors are growing. She is getting weak and cannot live much longer. I do not want to stay and care for the orphans, Dolly. Granny always serves treats, but nothing here is sweet. Who will help us now?"

Suddenly her eyes light up, as she remembers the one soul who has always cared for her.

"Yes, that's it!" she exclaims. "We must rely once again on Fee. We must look our weakest, our neediest. Can I make myself cry? Oh yes, I can. All I need do is think of *him*."

She shudders and squeezes her eyes shut tightly, as if that would expunge every memory of her father.

"We should just forget him. We *need* to forget him—yes, we do. But it is worth thinking of him this one time if it will ensure that Fee helps us."

Besse opens her eyes and sighs at her doll. "We have had a hard life, haven't we, Dolly? You and I are both just rag dolls, to be thrown about and ordered around. We must do something about it. We must take care of ourselves, because Fee—God bless her—cannot always look out for us."

Besse's eyes now narrow with a sudden thought. "And Fee, what about Fee? She must also have some secret, Dolly . . ."

Besse's rumination is interrupted by Granny, who enters the room unannounced, as is her wont. She bears her newest charge, a baby girl wailing at the top of her little lungs.

Besse quickly hides Dolly behind her as Granny hands her the baby, then sighs and backs out of the room.

Besse rocks the baby and thinks of what to say to Fee. She is due for a visit that day. In fact, she can hear Fee entering the cottage now.

The baby is asleep in Besse's lap, so Besse gestures for Fee to be quiet as she lays the baby, completely coddled in a wool blanket, in a bed of straw. Then she ushers Fee back outside, past Granny and the boys, so they can speak privately.

"Fee, I am glad you are here. I have fears, Fee. Granny is dy-dy-dying!" She forces her thoughts to Dunkel and makes herself cry. "What's to become of the boys, the baby, me? I do not think I can care for them all. And Flor needs my help too. It has been far too long since I assisted at her tent. What do I do?"

Completely taken by this display, Fee folds the maiden to her breast, allowing her to sob a moment or two. Then she takes her by the shoulders, gently straightening her. She avoids eye contact as she thinks for a moment.

Finally, she says, "I know Granny will not live long. In truth, she has already asked me to make arrangements for the boys. I have found apprenticeship positions for them. Rudi has been made a master. He is kind enough to take one boy in, and he has prevailed upon another of his guild to take the other." She sighs—a slight hesitation. "But they must return to the city with me today. That means you will have to resume the marketing. And I am sure Flor will welcome your return."

Besse considers this. She would rather work with Flor, if she has to work at all. Then her eyes go wide, no longer teary.

"But Fee!" she almost shouts. "The wolf! I cannot walk through the woods alone. What about the wolf? How—"

"Hush, child," Fee interrupts. "I have already talked with the huntsman. He will watch over you. And I have made you a red cape with a hood. One of the servants from a neighboring principality says all their young maidens wear them. It will keep you visible in the woods, so it will be easy for the huntsman to watch over you."

Besse is relieved. She lets out a sigh, then says, "It has been so many months, Fee, since the royal wedding." She cannot bring herself to mention Hans and Ebouisante. "I cannot live here alone with the baby after, after—"

Fee interrupts the thought quickly, not wanting Besse to suffer any further distress. She frowns but says as kindly as she can, "Do not worry about yourself or the baby. Mistress Beata is moving back into the tower, and you can return to your home."

"Fee, I cannot live there! I will not!"

Besse buries her head in Fee's bosom, unable to force further tears. Fee is moved. She enfolds Besse's head and softens her voice.

"I know, liebchen. I wish I could arrange otherwise." She thinks quickly. "Actually, Master Hans and Ebouisante would certainly take you and the baby in. Ebouisante is expecting and due soon. She will be happy to see you, Besse."

Besse must appear to be happy at the revelation, even though she is taken aback by this news. A baby would only bind Hans closer to Ebouisante.

"Oh, Fee. Such news! I must go to her soon."

Besse speaks the truth, although her intent is not what Fee interprets.

And there is something more Besse must address.

"Granny must have resources to pay for the marketing and upkeep of the cottage. Soon she will be unable to access it herself. Do you know where Granny keeps the gold?" she asks matter-of-factly.

Fee's eyes go wide and her jaw drops. Has Besse surmised Katrina's complicity in the robbery of the prince's treasury? Fee herself has thought of this but could not be sure.

She releases the maiden and looks deeply into her eyes. Frowning, she says, "No, Besse, I do not!"

"But what if she passes and no one knows its whereabouts?" Besse lifts her chin. "I believe she would want the gold to go to me."

"Regardless," Fee states, her hands on her hips, "you will not accept it!"

This time, Besse's mouth drops.

"Do not give me that look of surprise!" Fee chides. "You must know the gold belongs to someone else, and he will have it back."

"But if I am to care for the baby—"

"Besse! Enough! You and the baby will be taken care of. Do not give me more trouble."

"You cannot order me around, Fee!" Besse hisses. "You are a mere *servant*."

Fee raises a hand to slap the maiden, then realizes what she was about to do. She drops her arm, shaking her head.

Besse bites her hand, then relents. "I am sorry, Fee. You have been an amazing help. You have watched over me all my life. And not only me. You watch over Mama, your brothers and sister, and now not just one but two families you serve. I should be grateful. Forgive me."

But these words are far from sincere. Besse realizes she would not do well to aggravate one she needs so much. She must calm down and find a way to turn this to her advantage.

"You have always acted in my best interest," Besse says, head lowered. "I shall do as you have arranged."

"Thank you, Besse."

It is too much to expect real gratitude from Besse, when she has convinced herself that Fee failed to protect her from Dunkel.

Fee takes Besse's arm, and they turn to reenter the cottage. Inside, Granny sits in a rocking chair near the hearth. She has picked up and is cradling the baby. But while the baby remains peacefully asleep, the lady audibly wheezes, even as she attempts to sing to her. The flames cause grotesque reflections off the growing tumors.

Fee is taken aback by the odor of disintegration and the lady's visibly worsened condition. Aromatic herbs from Flor serve to mask the odor, but not entirely. The inhabitants have taken to keeping all windows open, allowing the fresh fragrances of the woods to blow through the chamber.

Upon Fee's arrival, Granny had told the boys to gather their few meager possessions, as they would be leaving to begin apprenticeships. They are visibly excited to have the opportunity for a potential profession and a life of their own. This is, of course, tempered by the concomitant abandonment of the woman who has sustained them with kindness and attention. They stand tall, fighting back tears as they say their final farewells to Granny and Besse. They then await Fee outside, breathing the breeze as if it were their first taste of true freedom, which indeed it is.

Fee approaches Granny with a look of consternation, converting by guilt and shame to one of deep concern. She embraces the woman despite the impulse to abstain. Granny looks up into her eyes. Even with her failing vision, she sees only kindness. She smiles.

"Ye know, my dear, I'm not long for this world, I'm not. I've known ye for only a short time, but I can't thank ye enough for all ye've done for the boys, Besse, the baby, and me. Have ye e'er asked for anythin' in return?"

Granny looks now to Besse. "My dear, take the baby outside and say your farewells t' the boys. I know ye'd prefer t' return t' the city today yourself. I'm sorry t' keep ye here a little longer t' tend t' a dyin' woman's needs. But ye know I can do nothin' for meself, and it'll be but a short time, it will." Here, Besse raises a hand and opens her mouth to speak, but Granny waves her off.

"Don't speak, child. I'll not have any dissemblin' from ye. I know ye too well, I do. Now, go!"

Besse does as she is told.

When she leaves, Granny sighs. "I know ye care for her, Fee. And she's been a great help t' me. But I also know servin' others is not in her heart, as it's in yours. Ne'ertheless, I only wish th' best for her, I do. I'd gladly designate all that remains in the cache of gold t' Besse, for the care of the baby. But I know ye'll provide for them both, and return the bounty t' its rightful owner, ye will."

After a slight hesitation, a cough, and a wheeze, she continues. "I'm afraid I perfume th' cottage, Fee. It's none too welcome a smell."

Fee tries to speak, but Granny once again holds up a hand. "Do not be so kind as t' deny it, my dear. I'll see right through any kind words, I will."

Granny smiles down at the baby in her lap. "Did ye know the baby has a name? We call her Katrina, after meself. Besse didn't seem t' care if I named her. Here as my days come t' an end, I hope some of my spirit'll enter the baby. So be it."

Tears well up in Fee's eyes.

"Now here's where t' find the gold, dear. There's a glade nearby as the sun rises. Don't enter it. Rather, look t' the one old oak tree that comes afore it. What ye seek lies 'neath the tree, it does. I'll not have ye tell Besse, my dear, but I trust ye t' do the right thing."

"I will not fail you in this, Katrina, but the need distresses me greatly."

"Thank ye, Fee. Ye're ever the one to care for the needs of everyone that touches your life."

All Fee can do is offer a weak smile.

~ Chapter 63 ~

And so it goes for a few weeks. Besse comes to the city every day for marketing and to reestablish her apprenticeship with Flor. She visits Ebouisante in her home. When Ebouisante is discomfited by her pregnancy, Besse sits and reads to her.

Ebouisante feels an even stronger bond with the poor, abused maiden, now with the added burden of raising an orphan baby. Of course, as she watches Besse with Katrina, she feels more prepared to care for a baby of her own.

Soon, Fee and Besse assist with the delivery of Ebouisante's own daughter. The birth is uneventful, and Hans is relieved. Ever the proud grandmother, Blanche suggests the name Elsbet, and so the baby is named almost immediately after birth, rather than waiting for some defining characteristic, as is often the custom.

Hans is immediately enamored of his little Ella, planning to offer her the best life has to offer. He pronounces her the second-most-beautiful thing he has ever seen—after Ebouisante, of course. He is quite content and proud.

This bliss lasts a few days, until the couple and, indeed, the entire principality, receives word of La Claire's much more difficult labor.

The princess has a footling presentation, a breech. The whole citizenry holds its collective breath as Fee and Besse, as well as two trained midwives, assist in the delivery. Much blood is spilled.

Charles is kept out of the chamber. While a major storm boils inside him, the prince struggles to present a public appearance of calm and dignity in the presence of friends and councillors—including the duke, who seems to be facing the same struggle himself. Charles cannot contain himself, his face a mask of consternation.

As always, Jurg is at hand to provide the prince with some common sense when Charles's emotions get the better of him.

"I know, sire, it would do no good to ask you to calm yourself. I can do naught but offer you my shoulder on which to lean," whispers Jurg.

Suddenly, a blood-curdling scream of what seems interminable duration pierces the castle. Charles grabs Jurg's arm with a vicelike grip, barely managing to stay erect. Then silence follows. The men gathered outside the chamber stop breathing for another eternity.

This is at last broken by another cry—one a healthy newborn baby.

In short order, Fee comes to the door, opens it, and bows to the royalty.

"It is a boy, sire. Both he and Her Highness are alive. But she will be weak for a long time, Your Majesty. It was a difficult birth, and she has lost much blood. If you please, sire, we shall require poultices of comfrey from my sister, Flor. Then she shall have to replenish her loss with infusions Flor will specify for you, of a cold, wet humor."

"She will receive all that she needs," Charles replies, nodding to a guard, who bows and hastens to the herbalist's tent. "The princess shall have two nurses to care for her and the baby." His pale visage begins to recover its color, and he lets out a long sigh. "Not many survive the breech. "

"Yes, sire, it seems a miracle!" says Jurg.

The assembled men nod agreement.

Charles smiles broadly and squares his shoulders with pride. "Then we shall name him Zaubert, for he is our miracle and he will have a charmed life."

"So be it!" exclaims the proud grandfather, putting his arm around Charles's shoulders.

~ Chapter 64 ~

Once the princess and the new dauphin are well on their way to recovery, the principality regains its sense of normality. This is true for Besse. Each day, Besse begins her day by assisting Ebouisante and Elsbet. The new mother then gladly watches over and even wet-nurses Baby Katrina while Besse assists Flor and completes her marketing. At the end of the day, Besse dons her red wool cloak, retrieves the baby with thanks to Ebouisante, then starts out for the cottage in the woods.

This afternoon, she carries a basket of provisions and fragrant herbs—whose aromas are less and less effective as Granny becomes weaker and weaker. Besse takes comfort in the fact that the huntsman cannot be far from her as she makes her way home.

But Gaillard is not alone. Avoiding detection by the huntsman, another set of eyes follows her without her notice. At first, it would appear to be a wolf.

But this is no mere wolf. It is Jacques, clad in a wolfskin! The disguise has worked to perfection as he has lingered about the cottage for months.

I've been watchin' and waitin', I have, he thinks.

The disguise has served the dual purpose of preventing his recognition and instilling fear into his victims. As a bandit, he uses this latter purpose to his advantage. Many flee at the sight of a wolf, leaving behind some or all of their possessions. The disguise has also allowed him to stalk Granny's cottage. He relishes the fear he instilled in the orphan boys.

He has bided his time, and now he knows the woman is dying. At the window, he can see it personally. She can barely move.

Moreover, the odor emanating from the home makes her fate clear.

She owes me, she does. I must make her tell me where she's hidd'n the gold. Now. Otherwise, it'll be too late.

Jacques realizes this is his best chance. If the huntsman is watching the maiden with the cloak, he cannot be guarding the house. Jacques knows a faster path—he can reach the cottage before the maiden. In his wolfskin, Jacques hurries through the woods.

Still wearing his wolfskin, he carefully opens the door, never locked, and creeps into the cottage. The odors almost overwhelm him.

Katrina calmly continues to rock in her comfortable chair. She allows him to approach closely, as she can do little else. As he nears, she can finally see him in her failing eyesight. She smiles and laughs briefly at the disguise, showing no sign of trepidation.

"Ye can't scare me, Jacques. I've known it's been ye, watchin' the house in disguise. I knew 'twas no wolf." She shakes her head. "There's naught here for ye, and I'm so near death, I've naught t' fear, no. Begone."

Jacques laughs. "Ye'll tell me—where's the gold? I'll have it, as it'll be no use t' ye where ye'll be goin'."

"No! Begone, I say!"

In a flash, Jacques lunges, grabbing the woman by the throat.

"Ye'll tell me, ye will!"

She punches out ineffectively as he continues to apply pressure. Eventually she puts up no struggle. He can only end her long misery.

Then quickly she has a thought. She slumps and feigns death, holding her breath before he can choke it out of her.

Jacques looks down at her and removes his hands.

"No one'll have it, then!" he howls.

Suddenly there are footsteps behind him. Besse enters. She drops her basket and almost drops the baby as she gasps at the scene of Granny slumped in the chair, with a wolf—no, it is Jacques!—hovering over her.

He turns in surprise to see her so soon. Then he offers a menacing smile.

~ Chapter 64 ~

"Ah! I suspect she would have told ye! *Where is it*?"

She screams as he races toward her. Her only thought is to lay the baby on the floor behind her, hoping to keep her from harm.

As she whirls around, Jacques grabs Besse. She beats him on the head, to no avail.

She uses all her strength to pull him around with her to the hearth, where she grabs a poker. Jacques backs off, feinting to the right, then to the left as she takes wide swings, her eyes wide with fear. Then they struggle as he reaches out and attempts to grab it from her.

Jacques howls again, truly now the lupine predator.

"I'm not goin' t' hurt ye, fräulein! Ye're no good t' me dead." He smirks, his eyes menacing under the wolf's head. "I just want t' know where the old lady keeps her cache o' gold, I do!"

Before Besse can even blink, the huntsman appears. In one motion, he charges Jacques and lifts him.

"The bear will crush the wolf!" he says.

He throws the boy aside, sending him crashing into the wall. Jacques crumples into fetal position, dazed and too shocked to move.

Gaillard towers over him. "I should kill you now, you miserable excuse for a man—or for a wolf, for that matter! But I'll spare these ladies the exposure."

He grabs Jacques's collar and drags him outside the cottage, pulling the disguise from him.

"Your freedom—and dare I say your life—is forfeit, *boy*."

He raises his fist and knocks Jacques unconscious.

Besse stands frozen inside the cottage, watching as Gaillard drapes the boy over his horse and secures him so he cannot escape.

"Besse," the huntman calls, using her name to help break her from the shock. "I must deposit this baggage with the prince's guard. Stay inside and lock this door until I return. I cannot be sure this brigand does not have any compatriots skulking around nearby."

Besse shivers, relieved. Then she hears a great gasping intake of air behind her. It is Granny! Besse cries, rushing over to the old woman, who, although weak, is clearly breathing.

Granny opens her clouded eyes and smiles at the young maiden.

"After all this time, he's after that gold, he is. But I wouldn't tell him anythin', me dear. Best t' pretend death, it was. But I'm grateful he didn't harm ye too. And I'm grateful to Gaillard, as always . . . and . . . oh, my!"

Suddenly Granny falls forward, stumbling out of the chair.

Besse shrieks, then enfolds her. "Granny! Granny!"

But the kindly old woman can answer her no more.

Backing off with a heavy heart, Besse picks up the baby, miraculously spared from the fight. She clutches her to her breast. She then retreats to her room, shutting the door behind her, as she is accustomed when she wants to block out the evils of the world outside. There in the dark, she hugs Dolly as well, rocking back and forth.

She is not truly ready to face her future in the city, and she never realized how comfortable she has become under the ministrations of Granny. For the first time, she actually misses someone! This realization leads to great sobs, and she holds the baby even closer.

She does not even know how long it will be before Gaillard returns as promised. Sealed in her room, she is shielded from reality and the passage of time.

Gaillard strides in the front room and quickly takes in the situation. Gently, he knocks on the door to Besse's room.

"Do not fear, fräulein," he calls through the door. "I am to return you to the city. I have already spoken with Fee, and she in turn is speaking with Herr Hans and Frau Ebouisante at this moment. She is confident they will prepare a place for you and the baby at their home—until other arrangements can be made."

He waits for a reply but receives only silence.

"I will handle things here," he continues. "Afterward, I will live in this cottage myself. The prince relishes the bounty I provide for his table, and I am comfortable here in Quellestadt. There is more use for me here than in Burgundy. . ."

His voice betrays sadness and grief.

Slowly, she rises to her feet. She is not anxious to leave the darkness of the chamber. At least she knows she need not return to the tower tonight. She must convince Ebouisante to shelter her and Katrina permanently. She must—no, she *will*—become part of the Handler household.

~ Chapter 65 ~

As spring gives way to summer, life in the city follows a more mundane daily rhythm. Unable to turn Besse away, the Handlers have made her a permanent part of their household. The two women tend to the babies together.

Fee continues to prepare the tower home for Beata's imminent return, but she is relieved Besse will not have to return to that scene of horror. And at least Fee can return to Dien each day at the Artur Handler household for solace of her own.

But there is deep sorrow at the home of Hans and Ebouisante, even as they shelter Besse and Katrina. With a heavy heart, Fee makes her way to Flor's tent. Ebouisante is losing weight and is now so weak as to be confined to bed. Fee believes the young mother suffers from consumption. Flor sends herbal infusions by way of Besse, but they do not appear to be of any benefit. The apothecary wants to bleed her. But Fee has seen what that does. It only makes the individual weaker. And poor Hans! He will not leave his wife's side, except to tend to little Elsbet—his Ella. And that he does only when Besse is there to comfort Ebouisante.

Though her mind is full of worry, Fee is aware of the children running freely about the market, playing blind man's bluff and taunting each other, as children will.

"Peter, Peter, gourd eater, had a wife and couldn't keep her. He put her in a gourd shell, and there he kept her very well!" a young boy cries, pulling a girl's braid.

"Oh, you wicked, wicked boy!" the girl scolds. "Next you'll wander into the woods, you will. You'll think you can take candy off the witch's house, and she'll throw you into the oven and eat you!"

~ Chapter 65 ~

"Ha! There is no witch! No such thing! Aren't you old enough t' know that's just a tale grownups tell t' keep us out of trouble?"

"There is too a witch!" the maiden insists. "And everyone knows there's a murderer walking 'mongst us—me papa says someone killed that ogre of an armorer!"

"*Kinder, kinder*!" interrupts Fee as she steps between them. "None of that is true! Stop arguing and begone with you."

Fee finds these taunts troubling, even though the children cannot know how they pierce the servant's heart. She shakes her head and continues to her sister's tent, almost in tears on arrival. Not even the sweet aroma of herbs and flowers nor the sight of Besse at work creating arrangements for two customers can cheer her. She hugs Flor tighter than usual, tears barely held back. Now even deeper troubles depress her.

"Oh, Flor!" she almost sobs. "The children—they mock us!"

Flor releases her, holding her out at shoulder length. She blinks, mostly to give herself time to think before speaking.

"Fee, Fee, children will be children. Their comments are not directed at you, and you cannot be responsible for everybody!"

Thinking of those for whom she *is* responsible reminds Fee of her current mission and startles her out of her remorse. "Oh, Besse!" she says, suddenly remembering her purpose. "I came here for you!"

Besse looks up as she hands the finished arrangement to the customers.

"Please," Fee continues, "Ebouisante asks for you. You are her best comfort. She does not want you to leave her side. I am sure Flor will spare you for a time." She places a hand on the maiden's shoulder. "I am proud to see how you have matured, liebchen, able to give of yourself for those who need you the most."

"Yes—go," Flor says to Besse. "You are needed elsewhere. I can manage here myself, my dear. Thank you for your help. Please stay with her as long as needed."

Besse wipes her hands on her apron, then removes and folds it carefully. Flor hands her a cloth with some herbs.

"Here, my dear. You must make an infusion of these. They are all I have left to help Ebouisante."

Besse takes the packet and opens it to check its contents. She then shrugs and refolds it before setting a brisk pace as she departs for the younger Handlers' home. A wisp of a smile goes unnoticed as she hurries down the street.

Fee turns to her sister. "You are training her well. It is so kind of you."

"Nonsense, sister. In due time, this will all be hers. Who else would inherit it?" she adds with a frown.

"Oh, Flor! You must not think upon your own lack of children. Besse will do you proud!"

"In truth, Fee," Flor responds with a sigh, "you have raised her. In effect, you have raised us all—Jurg, Peter, myself, Besse, even Beata, and now Elsbet and Katrina. It is a wonder it has not aged you. But I suspect Dien keeps you young."

"He does. I am so comforted when I am with him." Fee smiles, then it fades. "I do not deserve it."

"There you go again! You most certainly do! You never see the good you do for all those you protect and support. But I shall not argue that with you again. It is useless. Plus, I see Beata approaching," she says under her breath.

"A servant serves, sister," Fee whispers between her teeth.

"Good day to you, Fee," says Beata. "I was just taking the air, and I thought I would find some fragrant herbs or flowers for the house. After so many months of vacancy, a certain mustiness has set in, and I mean to alleviate it. Rudi has also remarked upon it. He intends to move in, as you know. In fact," she says, her tone suddenly hardening, "I now expect you to move in as well and assume your prior duties in full."

Fee gasps. "My lady, I am happy to serve at the tower occasionally. But I must also serve the Handlers, and in the evening I must return to my husband. Those were the conditions of our agreement!"

Beata shrugs. "Our agreement requires that you serve the needs of my household, and that will require your presence day and night. Besse may also return, but I suppose she will be happier in the Handler house." She shrugs, indicating what Besse does is of no consequence to her."

"But my lady—"

"You know what I have done for you, Fee. You cannot refuse me. I will say no more!"

Fee stands in silence, tears welling in her eyes.

Beata grins, knowing she has won. "Perhaps you could find a particularly savory roast for this evening," she says, setting her face to a frown. "Then I should prefer you to return promptly, as you have other chores to accomplish and a household ready to supervise."

"Yes, madame." Fee lowers her eyes, performs a slight curtsy, turns, then departs with her head lower than Flor has ever seen.

Beata selects a spray of flowers. Taking a deep whiff, she smiles. But she returns to a scowl as she pays Flor and heads home.

Flor returns the scowl once the lady's back is to her. *She was better alone, locked in her tower chamber, that one,* Flor thinks. *Fee should not have to suffer such treatment any longer!*

A group of children suddenly surround Beata, chasing around just out of reach.

"Beata, Beata, let down your hair!"

"Oh, you . . . you beasts! Begone with you!"

She burns inwardly. To be taunted by those wretched children on the streets! In innocence lies such cruelty. She determines to inform His Highness—no, *Her Highness*. She must put an end to it.

◆ ◆ ◆

As Beata approaches the tower entrance, she looks up to see Rudi awaiting her at the door.

"Ah, my beloved!" he says. "You have no need of such a spray, delightful as it is, to sweeten the home. Your very presence is enough of an inviting perfume."

Beata sighs and smiles despite herself, still prone to the effect of such flattery from her lover.

"Rudi, I would have you live in the tower with me and offer me such flattery forever! We must wed."

Rudi cannot hide his surprise. Did he hear her correctly? Has the moment he has waited and planned for arrived at last?

"Then my dearest, you must allow me to offer you my hand! Which I can now do," he quickly continues, "as I am a master of the guild in my own right and not without a large number of orders for my artistry."

He goes down on one knee and takes Beata's hand in his.

Oh lady fairest in my sight,
tresses light, complexion bright.
With all my love, I beg I might
request your perfect hand tonight.

"Oh yes! Yes, my love!" she responds breathlessly This man's flattery must always touch her heart.

His face bright with excitement, Rudi jumps to his feet to embrace her. Only, she takes a step back and holds him at arm's length.

"Wait until we are inside if you must kiss me." She gives her hair a light toss.

They enter together to the applause of the servant staff that has overheard this exchange at the open door.

"About time," Liesel whispers to another. "And certainly not too melodramatic!"

As the servants disperse to their duties, Fee enters. She has heard the interchange between Rudi, now to be her master, and Beata. She cannot bring herself to be happy for this couple, whose secret she protected for so long, and her only reward the forced sacrifice of her own happiness. She manages to fight back tears, but she cannot quite square her shoulders as she surrenders her market sack to the cook servants and gives out orders in a listless monotone.

~ Chapter 66 ~

Besse reaches her destination. She bids Hans to remain with his wife as she prepares the infusion, then ascends the stairs with a tray of sweets to accompany it.

With Besse now here, Hans is both reluctant to leave and grateful for an opportunity to tend to his business, which is growing rapidly. He plans his first caravan with Serge along the designated route to the south of Europe. At the moment, however, neither man is willing to leave the ailing Ebouisante.

Besse knocks gently at the door to Ebouisante's chamber, then squints as she enters a room full of reflected light. Even the large window bears no curtains, as Ebouisante has ever preferred no separation from nature. Yet the house is within the city walls, and only a lonely, nearly shriveled elm stands within her view. The bed in the center of the chamber is a point of darkness, dissipated by the smile of its occupant as Besse approaches.

"My dearest friend," Besse says, "I have brought you some sustenance and an infusion from the *gute* Flor. Here—I will help prop you up with these pillows, and you can partake."

"Ah, Besse. We have become fast friends, have we not? Think of what we have accomplished together. You are now reading to me, which allows me at least a short moment to transcend this misery."

She coughs heavily. Besse waits to place the tray before her, lest its contents wind up where they were not intended. Finally the spell dissipates, and Besse offers her some lebkuchen, a definite treat and a preference of the ill woman. She washes each bite down with a bit of the infusion, which is not at all ill tasting. Then she lies back and holds Besse's hand as she reads to her from Chrétien de Troyes.

Besse offers, "The women are poorly treated, I think. We should rewrite this from a different vantage, don't you think?"

"Oh, Besse, what a project! I fear I will not last long enough to accomplish even a small part of it, but it is a wonderful idea for you. How incredible it would be for Elsbet to learn to read from *your* literature!"

Besse raises her hands to her cheeks, surprised at this conclusion. "I would have no such ambition without you, Ebouisante. And you would be far more qualified to write than I. It was merely a suggestion . . ."

"To give me reason to live," Ebouisante says, finishing the sentence. She smiles weakly. "I am no fool, my dear. But I shall not live long. Now, do not fret or contradict. In fact, I have something on my mind. Would you fetch Hans, then leave us a moment?"

Besse obliges, fetching Hans from an inventory of the remaining goods in the open room down two flights of stairs, open to the public. There are few shoppers remaining, with the best of the items now gone and very little salt or furs to sell. Hans looks forward to the opportunity to offer more exotic merchandise after he returns with Serge.

But this brings his thoughts back to Ebouisante. Of course she cannot travel with him. Even if she were healthy, there is a daughter to raise and a household to run. But if Hans left now, clearly his wife would not be alive to greet him on his return.

"Hans, she would see you now, if you will," says Besse, interrupting his thoughts.

He frowns. Can this mean the time is near? He says nothing but nods at Besse as he bounds up the stairs. Besse follows more cautiously, though does not enter the chamber.

"My Ebouisante, my love," begins Hans. "You must never leave me. We are pledged to each other forever."

He leans over the bed and kisses her gently on the forehead. She can clearly see tears forming in his eyes beneath a furrowed brow. She finds she is overwhelmed by the scent of him, the sight of him. Yes, she is still deeply in love herself. This makes her hesitate a moment before speaking, but she is resolute.

"If these infusions from Flor were to cause me to sleep for a hundred years, it is your gentle kiss that would awaken me, my love," she answers, then turns away for yet another coughing spell. "Yet our pledge is not just for this life, my darling."

She puts her hand on Hans's lips as he starts to speak.

"No, Hans. You cannot wish me to live forever, as none of us is granted that grace by God." She gently caresses his cheek. "But I would have you promise me two things, aside from keeping my love in your heart forever. I would have you bury me near the glade, that my spirit may be with nature and I may watch over the young men in training. Plant a hazel or willow tree over me, to afford me shade and comfort. Visit me as you will, so that I will know I am still in your heart. And one more thing . . ."

"Yes, anything, my love," he says, now openly crying.

"You must take care of Besse. She has no one else except Fee, who cannot protect everyone forever. I will bid you wait the appropriate time, then marry her. She is a comfort and will treat you well. She tended to Granny, so she will know how to care for you as well. And she will serve you well if you teach her the business bookkeeping as I have shared with you."

Hans puts up his hand and sobs. "I cannot think of such things now, love. There is no room in my heart for aught but one. I cannot love her, so how could I marry her?"

"You can, and you will, as I bid it." She coughs again and looks pained as tears of her own begin to flow. "Now lie with me here a while, then return to your work and send me Besse again. But first, just hold me."

Soon Hans descends, his frown and bloodshot eyes revealing his sadness and consternation.

"She is sleeping peacefully, I think," he tells Besse with a sigh. "I must attend to business while I am able, but I know she would not want to be alone. If you would be so kind as to sit by her side and attend to her needs should she awaken, it would add to my indebtedness to you, Besse."

As she climbs the first step, Hans grabs her by the arm. Tears fill his eyes once again.

"I would have you understand that the lady has entreated me to see to your welfare, and I will honor that charge, as you deserve no less. In due time, we shall marry . . ." His voice falters.

"Say no more, sir," answers Besse, head bowed.

Hans releases her, and she turns, concealing a slight smile as she ascends to her charge.

"Is that you, Besse? Come close, and I will reveal that which I have done for you."

Ebouisante's voice is reduced to a mere whisper, a sign of weakness approaching death. She coughs, and Besse waves off her next statement.

"Do not speak, my friend. I have heard from Hans, and you need not say more. In fact, there is nothing more for you to say at all." She approaches the bedside.

Below, Hans tucks a blanket around Elsbet in a basket and places it carefully on the floor beside him. Suddenly, he hears a screeching, perhaps his name, then ominous silence.

He bounds up the stairs, two at a time, and bursts into his wife's chamber.

"Ebouisante!" he shouts.

But all he sees is Besse, crumpled to the floor, head in hands. She looks up, not quite meeting his eyes.

"She is gone, Hans. I tried . . . I tried to lift her head to help her breathe, but it was for naught. I am so sorry!"

She cannot even cry as Hans rushes to embrace the lifeless body of his wife one last time.

~ Chapter 67 ~

The sun shines incongruously bright upon the family gathering for the funeral of Ebouisante Handler. The monks have arrived to carry the casket, carved with scenes from the *Book of the City of Ladies*, the ideal tribute and surrounding for Ebouisante's final rest.

Hans fights back tears in an effort to appear stoic, while Fee makes no such effort, allowing a cathartic release of a veritable waterfall. Even Dien cannot console her. Besse, for her part, remains silent, seemingly withdrawn into herself, a customary state for her. All of those gathered wear black with the exception of Besse, who has chosen her old, comforting gray surcotte over the objections of Fee.

Now begins the procession to the church. The priest leads the group. The casket is accompanied by two bell ringers, as is the custom, then followed by Hans with Besse on his arm. Fee walks aside of the pair, carrying the infant Katrina, who squirms in her arms until Fee whispers comforting words to her. Next, Blanche leans heavily upon the arm of Serge, both letting their grief show. Blanche carries the infant Elsbet, who nestles in and leans her head against her grandmother's shoulder, as if she comprehends the gravity of the proceedings. The prince and princess, walk with Artur and Gute Handler.

Some townspeople gather, observing the group. Yet others are unaware of the procession. Children can be heard in the distance laughing and playing. One pretends to be the wolf who preys on the cloaked maiden, then they devise a hide-and-seek game based on children lost in the woods and enticed by the candy-and-cookie house inhabited by the blind witch.

The mourners can hear it all. Charles shakes his head. La Claire is aghast. Every time she leaves the castle, she must abide these taunts and games in silence. She cannot—and Charles will not—forbid the city's children to play. But the children do not know, in their presumptive innocence, what harm they bring to the actual participants in the real events on which their rhymes are based. Even the lady Beata has approached the princess about her own embarrassment at being parodied right in the market.

"I know! I know!" one child suddenly says in not quite a whisper. "Let's pretend I'm the armorer, and let's figure out who killed me!"

The mourners wince, even as they pretend not to hear. But La Claire turns to Charles and raises an eyebrow.

He sighs. He too is constantly exposed to the cruelty of the children, but he knows he cannot change the custom, even though he rebukes them repeatedly. Moreover, he overhears the adult citizens gossiping about these same events. Worse, there is still constant speculation regarding the death of the armorer. Too many people have shared their wild speculations since Prince Henrik proclaimed the events surrounding the armorer's death inconclusive.

Charles suddenly recalls that he never had a chance to tell his father his conclusions about Dunkel Hammer and the night of the fire. It seems the mystery is plaguing the entire principality. Only two know what truly happened that night—Charles and the person responsible for Dunkel's death.

In that instant, Charles decides he must call those involved in the incident back to the castle to join him in a special council. They must discuss Dunkel's death—and perhaps it is time other matters come to light as well.

Charles will arrange the council to be held the week next. He must allow at least that much time for the settling of restless souls.

His mind and attention return to the mourners.

♦ ♦ ♦

~ Chapter 67 ~

After the ceremony, Charles pulls Hans aside.

"I share your deep grief, my friend," he says, placing his hand on Hans' shoulder. "What say you of the future of Ebouisante's close friend, Besse, and the orphan Katrina? How will you see to their welfare?"

Hans places his hand upon Charles' on his shoulder and shakes his head. "I have pledged the same to my love upon her deathbed, and I will honor it," he says, his voice and heart heavy. "Besse has been a great source of comfort to Ebouisante. It would be an honor if she would grace my household. Moreover, I shall welcome her assistance with my Ella, who is my dearest gift from my wife. In due time, I shall marry Besse, as I have promised . . . though it will never replace the Lord's great favor of marrying my one true love. In time, it will be my responsibility to arrange a match for Ella, and, I dare say Katrina. But I shall certainly take love into account."

"I understand, Hans. But perhaps you can come to see this arrangement as another chance to save a damsel."

Charles smiles, but Hans can only sigh, remembering Charles's very admonition against just that.

"Charles, Herr Kaufmann and I must make caravan soon. We must consolidate our business. I shall use the journey to prepare my life, then marry Besse I shall upon my return."

"Go in good health and better spirits, my friend. I know I will be able to rely on your fortune to enrich my own and that of this realm. Yet I would have you be careful on your journey," Charles adds. "You will have to deal not only with banditry, but with the forces of the Teutonic knights, who are expanding their territory. I will send two guards with you for protection."

Hans begins to shake his head, but Charles stops him.

"No, do not refuse my offer. We were once protectors of a damsel and her father in distress. Yet you reaped the reward. Allow me the opportunity to reap mine—your continued loyalty and friendship."

Charles smiles a moment—"Not to mention the tithing!"

Hans cannot bring himself to laugh. "Thank you, Charles,

most especially for your attempt to cheer me a bit. I am not yet averse to a bit of adventure, though I fear I may be saving one damsel in distress too many. I promise to bring good trade to Quellestadt and bring better sense to my life. Ella, Katrina, and, yes, Besse, will be depending upon my responsibility."

~ Chapter 68 ~

A group assembles at the castle, at the appointed hour prior to the specified time for the council. They greet each other with some bewilderment. Present are Besse, Fee, Rudi, Beata, Peter, Rose, and Hans. The prince has asked this particular group to convene early, and they share some trepidation. This has to be about the fire last fall at the Hammer residence, as they have little else in common. But hasn't that inquiry been put to rest? And the guards appear to have been dismissed. Why?

The reception chamber has been cleared, and causes the invitees to feel a bit of a chill, despite the fire in the giant hearth on one wall. Light penetrates the room from the clerestory above the hanging tapestries. Besse walks the perimeter, avoiding the light as much as possible, while the others move toward it. The air has the scent of burning oak and cedar, yet chilled more by the swirl of fresh air entering with the guests. They do not know whether it excites them with anticipation or depresses them with foreboding.

Prince Charles enters from the rear chamber with La Claire on his arm. They are followed by Princess Amalia.

"Welcome to you all," Charles states as all bow or curtsy.

"I have asked you here for a reason. Before we begin, our servants will serve you a refreshment."

The guard signals, and servants bring a tray, offering first to Amalia, then to the princess and prince, each of whom remove a goblet of wine. The remaining guests are served ale in glass goblets. They look at each other in puzzlement, but say nothing, feeling rather awkward.

Fee glances about the room and notices the large obsidian glass previously gifted to the duchess Enchanteresse in one corner of the room. It surprises her that an object that invokes such ill memories would remain so prominently displayed. She knows it reflects more than just outward appearances. Suddenly she shakes in fear as she sees Besse approaching it. She rushes to pull the maiden back to the group.

Charles sighs before continuing. "Recent events have made it necessary to resurrect the topic of the death of Dunkel Hammer. It is why we have summoned you all here. We have not spoken of the armorer for months. We shall clear the air, then you will all be ordered to silence. I will make a formal proclamation to the citizens following our discussion."

The prince clears his throat loudly and says, "My father declared that we could draw no conclusions about the armorer's death. Since then, there has been much speculation as to whether he was murdered, and we must put an end to it. We will tell you we know the answer to this mystery."

Suddenly the air is suffused with the pungent tang of fear. The prince's use of the royal *we* clearly means he is passing judgment. Only he purports to know the damning information, and all the attendees have some degree of guilt.

Charles draws a deep breath. "Many motives and plans converged that night at the tower home. Rudi, you admitted at the inquiry that you had intentions of confronting the armorer regarding your relationship with Lady Beata. You did not, however, because you discovered the bandit, Bo—who, I might add, is currently serving the principality by working in the underground canals."

Rudi nods. "That is so, sire." He holds his head high, confident he is once again clear of any fault.

But Charles continues. "The bandit had been remonstrated by the armorer, and he carried a slingshot—David apparently planning to slay the giant Goliath, as it were. At the inquiry, he confessed he was seeking revenge for his brother, whom the armorer beat to death following an attack outside the inn."

Beata gasps as the others' eyes go wide with surprise.

The prince allows the group to settle before adding, "And you, Rudi, were also involved in this incident."

Now Beata turns visibly pale and grabs Rudi's forearm to steady herself.

Rudi's mouth drops open, then he bows his head in some shame. "Yes, sire, I will admit it. The boy and his brother attacked us, and the master could not control his own strength. We had to bury the brother quickly, behind the inn."

The prince eyes Rudi, then turns his attention elsewhere. "And this brings me next to the matter of Peter and Rose."

Their eyebrows rise.

"Your Highness," Rose sputters, "we were in the tower that night, we were, as ye well know, if ye please, so that my husband could introduce me t' his sister." She shudders, a sign betraying her statement as a falsehood.

"Yet there is clearly more," Charles says. "It is, or was, well known that you were a favorite of the armorer in your former profession. Yet you felt the need to leave the inn. Why should you feel threatened by Dunkel? You must have been privy to the attack outside the inn, or you witnessed it or the burial. I assume you tried to use this knowledge to your advantage, but the tables were turned, and the armorer threatened you instead. Am I not correct?"

Rose's eyes widen. "Amazin', Your Majesty. Yes, I feared for me own life, I did. So I'll admit that I begged Peter t' help me, yes. But he wasn't up t' it, was he?"

Peter frowns and moves away from her. This is a half-truth, and he blushes with some shame.

Charles stares and points at Rose. "In fact, you knew Peter would not attack the man, a strong blacksmith, even if Dunkel were drunk. So you tried to prevail upon his sister Flor for another method. But what you did not know is that Flor would not allow the purchase of fatal substances—nor would she allow her brother to damn himself yet again. Rather, she substituted a harmless soporific that accounted for his seemingly drunken behavior." He turns to her counterpart. "So you have done no harm, Peter."

"Thank you, sire," says the farmer, eyes lowered in embarrassment.

"Yet," continues the prince, "just the intent is punishable."

Peter flushes.

"Fear not, Peter, for you have served us well, and still pay double tithe beyond your time of punishment. Also, it has been difficult enough for you trying to inhibit the actions of your mate, nor to mention that from what we hear from the children in the city, you are continually punished." Charles frowns.

"I am sorry, sire. I am not what I once was." Peter is truly contrite.

"We know, sir. We know."

The prince looks sternly at Rudi, Beata, Peter, and Rose, then makes a sweeping gesture to include them all. "It is clear that while you all share ill intentions, none of you is responsible for the death of the armorer."

The prince next turns to his friend.

"Now, Hans, you were kind enough to explain why you were in the house that night, and we have no reason to doubt it. You were there to rescue Besse. You were well aware of the danger the armorer posed to Besse—and others." Here, the prince looks knowingly at Hans. "Whether to help remove Dunkel from the burning solar must have presented a major predicament for you. Yet it is clear you are not involved in the *cause* of the armorer's demise."

The prince frowns and gestures to his friend to say nothing.

As the prince addressed Hans, Besse listened intently and stiffened at his words. Now Charles turns to her.

"Besse, we will not speak of the matters that preceded your escape from the tower that evening. But we do believe you had motive and opportunity, as Flor's apprentice, to take action against your father. It is hard to believe you would have avoided the opportunity to avail yourself of some of the plants in the back of the tent, once you learned their precise effects. Yet we also believe you had little, if any, time to act, thanks to the rescue."

Besse lowers her head and curtsies, then backs away from the group into the shadow of the wall. La Claire considers walking to the maiden to offer her some consolation, considering she has recently lost a close friend and has now been nearly accused of patricide. But as Besse wraps her arms around herself and begins to pace the perimeter again, the princess decides it is best to leave the girl to her own thoughts.

"We must also address the actions of the thief, Jacques," Charles continues. "When I examined the armorer, his condition revealed an attack with a blunt object. We are sure the outlaw administered this blow."

The group gasps collectively at this revelation.

"Bo and others informed us that Jacques believed Dunkel was his father, though he offered the boy no sustenance," Charles says. "We know Jacques is capable of malicious violence." He nods toward Peter. "Jacques would never dare to approach such a strong man. But with the soporific having affected the man, an opportunity clearly presented itself, and he attacked. Was this a fatal blow, however? It did not appear to be deep enough."

Charles turns at last to Fee. "Fee, we are deeply sorry for the consternation you have faced before and after this ordeal. It is clear you have sacrificed much to protect not only your own family but that of the armorer—and not always with much success. But you did not leave the tower until you secured the safety of everyone else. And trying to remove the master while suffering the effects of smoke and fire was too much for you."

Tears well up in Fee's eyes. Now it is Amalia who moves to provide comfort. She enfolds Fee in solace.

La Claire shakes her head incredulously, concluding aloud, "Then no one actually killed the man. He merely died in the fire! Oh! And now the boy, Jacques, is in our dungeon!"

"Yes, my dear," confirms Charles. "And we shall once again hold inquiry, as we know he is guilty of yet another assault, but now we can mete out justice."

"Jacques started the fire, then," his wife surmises.

"No, he did not," Charles politely corrects. "Because if he had, he would have left the home immediately."

"Then how did the fire start?"

Here Charles hesitates a moment. Everyone in attendance senses he has more to say. The silence lingers in the air as the group holds its collective breath.

"The fire started for unknown reasons—as fires sometimes do. And due to several circumstances, the armorer was rendered unconscious and unable to escape. That is how it must rest." Charles sighs, pulls in his chest, and commands, "This will be the last speculation on this matter. We decree any further discussion or accusation in Quellestadt will be punished. So let it be published and cried to the citizens." Charles gestures to the summoned guests. "You may depart now."

"Yes, sire" echoes among the visitors, who make quick to leave the castle and escape the embarrassment. All except Fee, who lingers a moment. She understands that the prince is intelligent enough to have concluded many things, many actions, and now he has hesitated. Suddenly she is seized with fear, and she cowers, unable to move for a moment.

"Fee," Beata suddenly says loudly, turning as she reaches the portal. Everyone, not just Fee, turns at the sound of her voice. "Remember you must return to my service in the tower, as we discussed."

Then Besse takes a step forward, toward the servant. "No," she says stridently. "*I* will require your service, Fee. You already have a place and a husband in the Handler household. Moreover, you have no need to provide further service to Mama—"

Beata, now angry, interrupts. "She will remain with me! Fee, I would remind you why—"

Now it is Charles's turn to interrupt. "Enough! Fee will not be forced to endure such a choice! She has served and protected you both faithfully!"

~ Chapter 68 ~

Besse turns toward the prince, chastised but not finished. Her anger overflows, and she cannot help but blurt out.

"Your Highness, this *woman*"—she spits the word—"has not protected me!" She points a shaking finger at Fee. "It is all *your* fault! You are an *adequate* servant to Mama, even to *Hans and Ebouisante*." She almost spits the names too. "But you were never able to serve *me*!" Her voice rises. "And I know your secrets—yes, I do! Shall I tell Their Highnesses how you knew Granny stole from them, but you said nothing? Worse, that you certainly assisted Mama with her *tryst* with the journeyman, but you helped her stay locked in her chamber while you allowed Papa access to *me*! I demand you serve *me* now!"

This diatribe causes Fee to collapse in tears.

"I said, enough!" the prince bellows, too angry to control his words. Then he remembers himself and says more calmly, "Come, Besse, approach." He points to the obsidian looking glass. "We would have you gaze upon your reflection before you chastise this woman further."

Besse freezes in confusion. "My reflection?" she repeats.

"Your Highness," Fee quickly begs through great sobs, "if you please—"

"We are sorry, Fee, but it is necessary," the prince says with a slight frown.

Besse, breathing hard from the spent energy of her outburst, looks tentatively into the mirror. She has never seen her own reflection, nor would the image of herself allow her such vanity. But now her eyes widen with horror. For there, staring back at her, is almost the exact image of . . . Fee!

"No!" she shrieks. "It is not possible!"

Fee cries out, clenched fist to her mouth. Amalia hugs her tighter as Peter runs to her side. La Claire looks at her husband, eyes wide. Of course she has noticed the resemblance, but she had never made the connection. Rose is startled into opening her mouth, but she quickly recovers and says nothing.

All eyes but Fee's alight upon Besse.

"Yes, Besse," Charles says. "This is the reason Fee has served you so loyally and with such self-sacrifice. She has always protected her family above all."

It takes a moment for Besse to gather her thoughts. She is too flabbergasted to speak, but she must collect herself. "I . . . I . . . *no*!" she shouts. "This cannot be. It *cannot*! I will not accept it."

Fee turns to Besse, pleading. "Please, Besse! You must see how difficult this has been. The master—that monster—made no exception of me when I was younger and seeking employment. I turned to the mistress Beata. I told her she had to help She would not want it to be known her husband was . . . well . . . And she agreed to let me raise you in her home if I protected her from the beast. She agreed to say you were her daughter. It was a chance for a life for you! So many years it went well. No one who knew spoke the truth. Then you grew up, and he . . . he . . ." Fee breaks into great sobs and can speak no further.

Beata lowers her gaze in submission. "It is true, Your Highnesses. But I have come to depend entirely upon the services and kindnesses of Fee, and I cannot release her."

Fee reaches for Besse now, though the girl pulls away. "Every time that monster abused you, I could only think of how he treated me before you were born. Worse, I could do almost nothing about it! I tried, Besse. Oh, how I tried. How could I contain such pain?" Her face contorts in revelation of the truth of that statement, then relaxes as she sighs deeply. "And then what a relief it was, finally, to see you free from him, though it took you from my side. Speak to me, Besse. Do not cut me off."

Besse stands straighter, having allowed her indignance to overcome her shock and alarm.

"There is little to say, except that if you claim to act upon your love for your charges, then you would not neglect my welfare nor that of Katrina. You are a mere servant!" she hisses, clearly disgusted to be identified as her daughter.

Fee nearly collapses, falling to her knees under the crushing realization that she cannot protect everyone she loves. After all the years, after all she has done, the one person she has loved the most, protected the most, still condescends to her. She allows herself to cry inconsolably, wrapping her arms around her own body, finally understanding she needs to protect herself the most.

The princess looks from Fee to Besse, aghast. "You would still demand that your own mother serve you?"

"Actually," Charles interjects, "We assume Fee does wish to serve Besse and see to the welfare of her family—that is, to the welfare of her daughter and granddaughter."

The group is aghast. Could there be an even greater shocking revelation? Heads shake, hands go to mouths. All but the prince and Fee are struck speechless for a moment.

Besse looks about her, desperately seeking a dark corner in which to hide. But there is no such place for her. She is overcome, and she herself collapses in place. Fee runs to her and covers her, as if to shield her once again.

It is Peter who finally asks, "*Granddaughter*?"

Rose cannot withhold a small cry. "Oh, but that explains why Besse wasn't seen in the city for so many months!"

Hans nods, his bewilderment slowly turning into understanding. "And why Fee was called away to tend to Besse on our wedding day! But that means Katrina's father was . . . was . . ."

Charles gives him a stern look. "Yes, Hans, only the armorer had such . . . access to the maiden."

The prince gazes upon Fee, still covering her daughter.

"Now, Fee, you have a choice to make. We will support whatever you decide. Will you serve Beata and Rudi, or Hans and Besse?"

Fee realizes she truly can choose. The veil of her lifelong secret has been lifted. Beata can no longer use it to force Fee's loyalty.

Before Fee can speak, Besse interjects, "Sire, I do not think I can face having this woman in my household. The reminders would be too painful. I relinquish her to the new armorer and Ma—I mean, the lady Beata." There remains an edge of anger to her voice.

Fee frowns. “I cannot bring further pain to you, my daughter.” Yes, now she can say it. *Daughter*. “So I will instead serve the master and lady in the tower, so long as I may return to my beloved Dien each evening.”

Beata nows opens her mouth, but it is Amalia who prevents her from speaking. “Done, then.” She gives Beata a warning glance. “And no one shall object!”

“We agree, Mama,” Charles adds, “but there is one more thing. Besse, you will not deprive Fee access to her granddaughter. She will be a far better influence on Katrina and on Elsbet than you, I warrant! If Fee so wishes to serve your and Hans’s household, you are not to prevent her.”

Fee nods her agreement, but Besse looks away in disgust.

Charles shakes his head and waves a hand at the group. “Now you are all dismissed!”

Hans stands frozen, overcome with the revelations—and behavior—of the woman he has promised to marry. He turns to Besse suddenly.

“You are aware, Besse, that I promised Ebouisante I would marry you and see to your welfare. That I shall do. For now, you must return home and tend to the children and my goods. It is nearly time for caravan, which I shall not postpone.”

Besse glares at him. “You must not leave me now, Hans. It is true what Ebouisante told you—I am in great need of you, especially now!”

“Nevertheless, I am not prepared to be with you now. You must contemplate your relationships and learn gratitude and humility. When I return, I expect to hear how well you treat your mother—your true mother—as well as Ella and Katrina. Now, let us depart!”

He takes Besse gruffly by the hand and pulls her behind him out of the castle. The others follow—all but Fee, who approaches the prince and princesses. She wishes to thank His Majesty, but she also has a greater concern.

~ Chapter 69 ~

Fee stands with drooping shoulders before the royals. She curtsies timidly, then admits, "I would wish you to know, sire, that I have recently returned to your guard a cache of gold I am sure originates from your treasury. Please understand Granny—I mean, Frau Katrina— revealed the location to me shortly before her death. She wished I would apply it to Besse's and the baby's welfare, but she knew I would not do so, as it belonged to the treasury." Fee lowers her chin. "If you must punish me for foreknowledge of her identity, I certainly understand. But we are grateful to her, as she was refuge to Besse."

Charles smiles, gently raises her eyes to his, and answers, "We surely knew Frau Katrina's true identity as well, Fee. But we pardoned her and allowed her the gold to support the orphans—and, yes, your daughter. This kindness more than repaid her crime. And truthfully, we were happy to see Besse out of the clutches of Dunkel."

Fee breathes a sigh of relief. "I should have known you would surmise Besse's plight. I thank you for more kindness than I deserve. You have shown much wisdom, having surmised and revealed so much here today. But I must thank you for keeping one secret safe."

The prince pretends to be puzzled, but Fee can see through the façade.

"Yes, sire. You examined the house after the fire, and you determined much from the inquiry. I am sure you also realized the fire was no accident. You must know I started it."

The prince pauses, then nods. "Yes, Fee, it is true. In our examination of the home, we did determine the cause of the fire based on not what we saw but rather on what we did *not* see—we did not see a natural cause for the fire! There was no evidence that it started by a spark, as there were no burnt rushes in front of the hearth. In fact, the rushes were clear of the hearth for safety."

Fee winces, waiting for more revelation, fearful of the punishment to come. She need not wait more than a second, as Charles quickly continues.

"Moreover, we discovered that one sconce was missing from the wall. As the pieces were of exquisite manufacture, requiring a skilled craftsman, a skilled blacksmith, we knew a missing sconce would not have been tolerated. That meant someone had taken it from the wall, used it, then left with lack of time to replace it—probably in the hearth itself, where we found it when searching for the source of the fire. It is clear to us this was the instrument Jacques used to strike Dunkel. But once down, the sconce could certainly be used to start a fire and then thrown back into the hearth."

The prince acknowledges Fee's fear with a look into her eyes, but then he smiles.

"Fee, though it is clear many in the tower intended harm to Dunkel, it is clear you had no such plan. That night, you merely planned for Besse's escape. But you must have known the armorer would seek her out, and he would certainly conclude you aided her escape. Finding the man unconscious, you could not resist seizing the opportunity. So you did what you had to—for Besse, for yourself."

Fee begins to speak, but Charles holds up a hand to silence her. "Please, there is more. You were careful to see to it that no one else could be hurt by the fire. You risked your own life to assure the safety of all others in the tower, which is the ultimate proof of your sacrifice. Always, the welfare of all others comes before your own, does it not?"

Fee bows her head, then her eyes go wide as she suddenly has a thought. She asks tremulously, "If you have known this since the inquiry, should you not have punished me then? Or should you not punish me now?" she asks, forgetting to whom she speaks.

"No, Fee. Your whole life has been a punishment. You do nothing but serve and protect those you love—and, yes, even many you do not—even at risk to yourself. And we know the chants of the children are embarrassing to you, a fact over which even a prince has no control. But we meant it at the inquiry when we said we are impressed with you and that you have done us all great service. Be at peace. Only we shall ever know the truth, so you need never fear again."

Charles knows he can rely upon his wife and mother to maintain silence. They confirm this expectation by nodding to him and looking at him with pride.

"I am overwhelmed, sire." Fee starts to cry yet again.

The princess rushes to comfort her again.

"There, there, my dear. It is past time someone saw to *your* comfort."

"Yes, my dear," Charles says with a wink and a smile aimed at Fee. "As I told you before, Fee—your name in old German means 'godmother,' and indeed you are!"

~ Chapter 70 ~

Fee takes her customary route to the market. She passes children in the streets. Boys play at killing the giant by cutting down the beanstalk. Others mock each other with threats of the witch in the woods or the evil duchess—now promoted to queen for her vanity. Then there is the vain princess trapped in her tower, allowing her long tresses to be used as a ladder for her lover. There is also a hungry wolf after the child in the red cape. None of this has escaped the notice of the servant. Although she has tried to become inured to it, she cannot deny it still affects her deeply.

She completes her errands, visits with Flor to share an update on the health and activities of her two households, then takes a deep breath and retraces her steps homeward. Her senses fill with the sights, sounds, and aromas of the city, full of life. This city, with its heartbreak and love, its poverty and wealth, its royalty and peasantry, its marriages and murder, is her home. She must focus on the love and attentions of her Dien, not on the taunts of children in the streets. But her responsibilities wear away at the corners of her mind, and reality always intrudes.

Later that night, Fee nestles into the arms of her husband, but she is unable to sleep. Her mind roils with her new status, now a servant in her own daughter's household as well as in Beata and Rudi's—and by her own choice. Besse will not treat her any other way than as a servant. However, Fee fully understands the inner strength Besse needs to overcome the emotional conflicts she must now face.

Dien awakens, misunderstanding her discomfort. "My love, ye must take comfort, ye must. We're together now, and Besse's future's secure."

"Besse will still need my protection, especially while Hans is away. She—we all—still have to face the scorn, the ridicule of the citizens, Dien. They will talk, perhaps not in public, but behind closed doors."

"Hush, hush, my love," he says. "Life must go on, and we must make the best of it. Hans'll marry Besse, and th' children'll be cared for. It's the best we can hope for." He takes on an expression of concern. "If it's any consolation, our lives'll be remembered and told. We may serve as a lesson to their children's children."

Fee looks at her husband, finally coming to the realization of why she loves this man. Only he truly cares for her enough to console her, to care for her happiness. She smiles despite herself.

"Yes, my dearest. If the children will continue to play their games, our stories will live on in the tales they tell. Perhaps in such manner we shall all live—happily—ever after."

~ Epilogue ~

After seeing Katrina and Elsbet to sleep, Besse takes her time ascending the stairs to her chamber, where she carefully closes the door, retrieves her rag doll, and extinguishes the wall sconce.

"Oh, Dolly, I have made a fine mess of it, have I not? Hans is leaving me right when our life together should be beginning. All these years, I have been the subject of pity and shame, and I did not realize why Ebouisante would stoop to befriend me. And Fee, my . . . mother!" Here her voice develops a tremor, a mixture of anger and remorse at once. "My mother could do nothing to console me, and telling me the truth would have been worse."

She raises her eyebrows, then holds the rag doll close, whispering in her imagined ear.

"But everyone still has secrets, Dolly. Oh yes, they do. Now we know Fee's real secret, do we not? But no one but you knows *my* secret. You know that Flor could not stop me from acquiring special herbs from the back of the tent. Not for Papa, no. For someone else. Let them all believe Ebouisante died of consumption, for indeed she did. But it was not the consumption of disease, was it? She had a little push, did she not?"

She grins sardonically. "There, I have said it! And now it shall be forever secret, for you can tell no one, and I certainly will not!"

She rocks the doll held to her breast in the dark, and finally the tears flow freely, witnessed by no one else.

~ Acknowledgments ~

I would like to acknowledge my family for their ideas and encouragement; the Grimm Brothers; multiple historical sources on the Internet; *Life in a Medieval City*, by Joseph and Frances Gies; *The Complete Brothers Grimm Fairy Tales* edited by Lily Owens; and Mr. Wynn Johnson for encouraging publication and introducing me to his publisher. I would also like to express my gratitude to the publisher herself, Judith Palmateer of Amber Skye Publishing, as well as to my editor, Angela Wiechmann, for their hard work and encouragement.

~ About the Author ~

Elliot Francke is a consultant physician in infectious diseases in private practice in Minnesota, where he lives with his understanding wife and best friend of thirty-eight years, Cheryl. His interest in the tales of the Grimm Brothers and others dates from childhood, but his curiosity about the tales' origins was kindled by a visit with his son at the University of Southern California and a discussion about film themes. After historical research, the idea for the plot of *Upon a Time* began to develop. The first-time author is grateful for the encouragement of his wife, three children, friends and readers, and most especially the editor and publisher of this book.